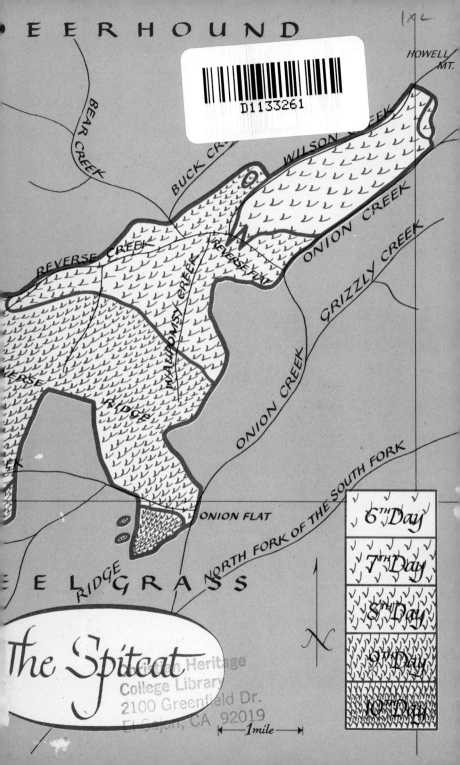

FIRE

A NOVEL BY

GEORGE R. STEWART

RANDOM HOUSE · NEW YORK

FIRE

The characters of this book—including the Spitcat—are imaginary.

CONTENTS . . . . . .

FIRE

SUDDENLY ABLAZE with lightnings, the piled-up thundercloud swept northward across the tops of the mountains. With celestial unconcern the blasting strokes fell here or there— to splinter a snag-top fir on Donner Peak, bring down a telegraph-pole at Blue Canyon, play round a water-tank at Emigrant Gap and send a child into hysterics, flash ineffectively against bare granite on Cisco Butte, split an oak-tree by a nameless meadow and kill the buck standing beneath.

During some minutes, intermittently, the flashes pierced the dimness of the shadowed afternoon, thunder echoed along the canyons, and rain fell spottedly. Then, tensions and stresses eased by the fiery spurting, the cloud took on a milder aspect to the passive earth beneath it. The lightnings died out with a last weak stroke; the drumming showers diminished to scattered drops; the cloud-edge faded from greenish black to gentle gray, and the atmosphere grew lighter. During the outburst the cloud had seemed to rush onward by its own power; now it merely drifted with the breeze. Yet still it moved steadily toward the north—where, half hidden behind

3

the curve of the earth, the blunt crater of Lassen Peak and the two white cones of Mount Shasta broke the far horizon-line.

2

The Lookout turned off the broadcast. All she could get in the afternoon was one Reno station. Its program was not much at best, and during the last few minutes had been interrupted by an amazing variety of squawks and roars and crackles, as if a thunderstorm must be somewhere at work.

Just after she had flipped the switch, the telephone rang. She listened—*long, short, short, short*—her own signal. She answered:

"Cerro Gordo Lookout speaking."

"Hello, Judith," said the telephone, and she recognized the deep, slightly gruff voice of the Ranger.

"Oh, hello, Bart," she said. "Nice of you to call. I'm fine— how are the pups?"

She supposed that he had merely called as he had before, to break the monotony of her life. Being alone for twenty-four hours a day generally, a lookout might be assumed to be lonely.

"Oh, the pups are O. K.," he said, and then went on in a tone which indicated he had not called up to gossip. "Say, there's a lightning-storm working up on us—"

"Oh, I thought—"

"Yes, she's working up along the range from the south— way they generally do. Hit the Sequoia Forest high country two days ago; gave the boys some trouble on the Stanislaus yesterday. From the squawks on the radio, I'd judge she was just cutting loose a little, down over the Tahoe, along U. S. 40. We and the Plumas may be next. Don't sound too bad though. Just the same, I thought maybe a kid like you—"

"Look here now, Bart, you don't need—"

"Sorry! Sure, I beg pardon! I know you're twenty-one, but still that seems kind of young to me. Anyway, even Uncle Amos might get nervous if you perched him in a glass box on top of a sixty-foot steel tower, and a lightning-storm came playing around."

"O. K., if the flashes get within a mile, I pull my switch— it's all printed on this card tacked up here right by the phone. And then I stand on the stool that has glass things on its feet."

"That's fine, honey. What's more, don't forget you're a lookout in the Ponderosa National Forest. If the lightning ain't quite knocking your front teeth in, swing your alidade on every strike you see, and get us a bearing. Write the time down too. That's all, and I've got to call some other lookouts."

The girl hung up with a rising sense of excitement. She had been only two weeks on the job. Although she had seen some smokes, they had been far off, beyond the limits of her responsibility.

She went out through the screen-door to the narrow catwalk which skirted the four sides of the lookout. The storm was coming from the south, but with a child's sense of saving the icing till the last, she looked first toward the west, and next went around the catwalk to the north and east. There was nothing unusual. Then, standing at the southeast corner, looking out level over the gently swaying tops of some pines, she gazed southward.

She was disappointed. Every afternoon she had seen fluffy white clouds build up over the endlessly stretching confusion of long forested ridges and pointed bare peaks which formed the backbone of the northern Sierra Nevada. This afternoon the clouds seemed no different.

She lifted her binoculars. The closer ridges jumped into

sharp detail, but the clouds still looked much the same. She lowered the binoculars, unimpressed.

Relaxing, she raised her right hand, and undid the top button on her dark-green man's shirt. Only afterwards did she realize that she had acted spontaneously because she was too warm. Yes, this was the warmest afternoon yet.

"It's really getting oppressive," she said to herself. And then immediately she *hoped* that she had said it to herself, and not aloud. Even after only two weeks alone on the tower you were not always certain.

But it really was warm! There was no breeze—and at this time of day at least a breath of air should be sliding up from the southwest out of the deep canyon of Potter Creek. There was an oppressive stickiness too.

"Let it come!" she said, and jumped because she *had* spoken out loud. Then, with the lookout's sixth sense which she was rapidly developing, she glanced around automatically to see whether unallowed smoke was rising anywhere. . . .

She walked to the west again. Because of the convex slope of the mountain, she could not see to the bottom of the deep gorge, but she ignored the heavy gray column rising from it. That was merely from Magna lumber-mill, one of her "permanent smokes." She looked farther off through the haze of the afternoon heat which lay upon the baked foothill-country. Miles away through the grayness of the haze, she could barely make out the light-gray smoke-column of a big grass-fire which had sprung up about noon and was running fast. That one also was no problem of hers. It was what she had already learned to call a "state fire," because it lay outside any National Forest and was the business of the fire-crews of the State Division of Forestry.

On the western catwalk she felt hotter than ever, for she took the full beating of the afternoon sun. The air was sultry, and with the still slightly disturbing sense of the sixty-foot drop just beyond the railing, she felt a trifle light-headed. She moved around to the east to get out of the sun. Still conscious of the giddiness, she found that she was again thinking of herself—it had happened before on the tower—in a far-off third-person kind of way: "The girl was uncertain whether anything was brewing or not." She was very careful *not* to speak aloud or even move her lips. "Born and bred within sound [well, *sight,* anyway] of San Francisco Bay she knew more of earthquakes than of thunderstorms."

A sudden puff of cooler air snapped her out of it. She swung around to look south, started, and looked again. Among the clouds that had been so vague, one stood out now —more sharply defined, taller, darker, obviously closer. She made out its bulging at the top.

Going inside, she swung the alidade of her fire-finder, and sighted roughly, more for practice than for use, at the center of the cloud-column. "One-four-let's-see-six" she read aloud from the azimuth-scale. That was somewhere south of southeast. How far away the cloud was, she was not experienced enough to tell—or how fast it was likely to move toward her. But the Ranger's warning was evidence enough that the storm could reach as far as Cerro Gordo before the afternoon was over, and might pass close to the tower.

3

On May 14th the gauges in the Ponderosa National Forest had last recorded rainfall. Headquarters at Suffolk reported point-two-seven, just over a quarter of an inch; Barlow Ranger Station, fifteen miles up the canyon and a thousand feet higher, made it point-three-nine. Since then, thunderstorms had wet down some isolated spots, and fishermen in the high country above six thousand feet had told of a week half-spoiled by drizzles. That was all, and now it was September.

The rainless summer was nothing remarkable—what California should expect in an ordinary year. Nevertheless the situation was not less hazardous for being average.

In May the grass in the meadows had been green; fresh leaves were bursting from the manzanita bushes in the brush-fields; the new tips of pine and fir and cedar were juicy with wet sap. In May, crossing a meadow, you squashed softly and muddied your boots; nights were cold and dews heavy; even in mid-afternoon the air had borne a freshness of spring.

Now in September, the grass was ripe and brown; in the brush-fields the manzanita leaves were half dormant, heavy with stored oil; among the trees a resinous odor hung above the carpet of dead pine-needles, and in the hot summer sunlight the branch-tips looked more gray than green.

The generous wetness of the winter rains and snows had vanished—run away through the dwindling streams, stored up in the new wood and leaves and needles, blown off into the ever-thirsty air above the deserts to the east.

Now in September, as you crossed a meadow, your feet hit hard. Now the afternoons lay so hot and still, so dry, so charged with the emanations of gums and resins, that you might think the air itself would explode at the striking of a match.

4

The thundercloud, again grown more intense, now moved above the Ponderosa Forest, and all five lookouts in the Suffolk and Barlow districts were watching it. From Badger Hill and Hamlin Point, baking in the four-o'clock sun, the cloud was a far-off thing of the higher country; these lookouts observed it from the side, and saw the threatening overhang of its anvil-top. Lovers Leap and Horse Mountain lay right in its path, and their lookouts already had lost all sense of the cloud as a thing apart; they felt merely the chill and the rising wind, and saw above them the threatening darkness of the flying scud. At Cerro Gordo the girl was still in the hot sunshine, but the fast-moving cloud dominated the southeastern sky; she too felt the threat of that green-blackness.

Yet, as a flushed and distorted face is only the outward symbol of an inward anger ready to explode in violence and murder, so the green-blackness was only the symbol of forces and tensions within the cloud. To say that it was seething like a cauldron would be to take refuge in a long out-dated understatement; rather, the cloud was fuming and raging inwardly much like a stupendous steam-engine, coupled with a monstrous dynamo, neither provided with any continuous outlet for the energy which they piled up. Every moment myriads of rain-drops formed and fell through the cloud, only to break into smaller droplets and be whirled upward in swirling vortexes of air. By these internal forces a positive charge of electricity built up in the higher levels of the cloud and a negative charge in the lower levels, particularly at the forward edge.

Meanwhile, as action demands reaction, the negative charge attracted an equal positive charge to the earth beneath the cloud. Like an invisible shadow, this charge drifted along beneath, up and down the canyon-sides, across the ridges.

In the tower on Cerro Gordo the girl stood at her firefinder. The finely molded young face was eager and tense, with the suspense of the unknown. The sun had gone, and the air was chilly. High above, the great mass of the cloud now

billowed between her and the open sky, and that cloud, as
hazardous as a powder-barrel, had not as yet relieved its tensions. She felt a stirring in her hair.

"Electricity!" she thought. "No, maybe just being scared.
Well, why not? Right here on the highest point in ten miles,
on a steel tower sticking up into the air. I hope the lightning-
rods are as good as Bart said they were!"

She thought of standing on the glass-footed stool, and decided not to—at least not until there had been one stroke.

As the cloud moved onward above the forested ridges, the
action within it grew stronger. The tension between it and
the earth piled up to millions of volts. Now, beneath the
cloud, invisible electrical streamers rose here and there from
points of rock or tips of trees, like gestures asking for release
—as if a king rode through the street and poor prisoners
stretched out their hands toward him from their barred
windows.

Suddenly, near the top of Cerro Gordo, the tension grew
climactic, and a mile-long white stroke of lightning crackled
between cloud and earth.

The flash half-blinded the girl; the thunderclap jarred her;
the imminence of death turned her cold. Although the stroke
was past, she was already scrambling to the stool when she
heard the tree go crashing down. "No need to log a bearing
on that one," she thought. "It's right here!"

Half a minute later, however, she was on the job again,
and logged a stroke at 132, miles away toward Lovers Leap.
Twice also she heard thunder without spotting the stroke.

Now, as if relieved by the lightning-strokes, the cloud
looked less threatening. A shower, she saw, was falling far off
to the east. As the minutes passed, she began to think that the

storm would drift on without causing more trouble. She relaxed a little.

At that moment, however, the forward edge of the cloud,
still highly charged, was approaching the ridge north of
Onion Creek on the slope of Howell Mountain. This ridge
was well covered by a fine forest, largely of Jeffrey pine; part-
way up the slope stood a particular tree of that species. Even
an experienced forester would not have noted it especially,
except to say perhaps that it was remarkably vigorous and
healthy. Although the tallest tree in its immediate vicinity, it
was much farther from the cloud than the trees on the ridge-
crest. Nevertheless, as an individual man and woman will
choose each other, and none other, from a whole city of men
and women, so the cloud and the tree drew together from
forces within them.

The charge of electricity following beneath the cloud
dipped into the canyon of Onion Cheek, and then flowed up
the other slope. The vigorously growing tree was of that
nature not by accident but because its roots touched a vein of
underground moisture. This moisture also produced a channel for the electricity, and the charge moved easily through
the sappy trunk clear to the top, where a sharp growing-tip
offered an excellent point for discharge. Within a few seconds
the tree became tense with electrical pressure.

Then suddenly, in a blue-white flash, for a period of some
few millionths of a second, there poured through the tree
between cloud and earth, a force equal to that of many power-
houses.

Fortunately for the tree, the stroke followed the long spiral
of a sap-channel, making three circuits of the trunk but keeping just under the bark. Along this narrow channel, however,
the intense heat vaporized not only the sap but also the wood

itself. The outward pressure was explosive. A long spiral weal rose from tip to root; pieces of bark were blown out and fell through the air. Noises of rending and explosion smote the air, and went rolling off as thunder through the canyon.

While the pieces of bark were still falling, and before the sound of the thunder had reached her, the lookout on Cerro Gordo swung her alidade. She had seen the flash squarely and directly, and its sinuous image still shone clearly on her retina as she blinked her eyes. She sighted through the wires as close to the exact point as she could remember, and read the azimuth as 65.

"About ten miles off, in round numbers; time is four-twelve," she thought, and started to write down the figures, as noise of the thunder enveloped her.

Even in the interval of making the notations the cloud seemed to have grown less threatening. Besides, it had moved farther north. Humbug Point and Sheer Rock, rather than Cerro Gordo and Horse Mountain, were now responsible.

The girl lit a cigarette. Suddenly she realized that for an hour she had been in a state of excitement. Now with the storm over, she felt herself slump suddenly.

"*All passion spent,*" she said aloud. (Quoting a poem, she had decided, was not like talking to yourself.)

She began to think about making a cup of coffee. Before doing anything more, however, she went out to the eastern cat-walk, and looked across toward where she had seen the last lightning-stroke. She would have to keep close watch in that direction.

5

As the quiet of evening fell on the steep slope above Onion Creek, the pine tree was little changed. Its tip had lopped over, like a wilting plant. A faint tar-like odor hung in the still air. There was also a slight charred smell; but, intense as the heat had been, the plentiful sap had oozed in quickly and kept the wood from burning.

Nevertheless, at the base of the tree where the discharge had run along a buttress-root at the surface of the ground, the lightning-stroke had heated a few dry needles to kindling-point.

Lying on the surface they had a good supply of air, and had continued to smoulder. Now, as the evening down-canyon wind began to move gently along the slope, a tiny column of smoke, as from a dying cigarette, curled faintly into the air.

As BY AIR and earth and water, so also man lives by fire. Once savants imagined simple tribespeople in brush-land or jungle who bolted raw meat and huddled at night, fireless, beneath the cold stars. But as explorers pushed farther and farther, there was no such tribe. Then the diggers uncovered, half a million years old, the charcoal left by Peking Man, too primitive a creature even to be called *Homo*. So the proverb might well run, "Where there is man, there is fire!"

Yet the proverb cannot be reversed. Though fire may well rank as the first triumph of domestication, yet it still—like the wild pig and wolf—thrives without man. In English, *wildfire,* first meant what it still implies—a conflagration kindled and burning without the hand of man.

Among such fires, volcanoes were the most spectacular, but were unknown in most countries. A kindling between two branches rubbing in the wind, though a favorite folk-tale, happened too rarely to count; so also, with the spontaneous combustion of gums, and the focusing of the sun's rays through resinous drops, and the flash of electric sparks between dry leaves moved with the breeze. But many hundreds

14

of thunderstorms were always at work somewhere in the atmosphere, and the earth's surface was under the continuous bombardment of a hundred lightning-strokes every second.

Since many of these strokes kindled stumps and dry leaves or grass, man's first problem with fire was not to obtain, but to escape. Later he learned to control; last of all—for convenience, not of necessity—to kindle.

Without the good luck of lightning, man might well have marked time as a ground-ape through a million years before he learned of fire from some rarer source. Many peoples acknowledge the debt in their mythologies, and count fire the gift of the thunder-spirit. Or, less fanciful but clearer-thinking, they say simply, "Lightning kindled a tree, and thus our fathers got fire." They are right not to interpose a fire-bringing demi-god. Lightning is the true Prometheus.

2

In the hot morning sunshine the Supervisor of the Ponderosa National Forest waved good-bye to his wife and two small daughters, and walked along the main street of the little town of Suffolk toward Headquarters. His broad-brimmed hat kept the sun out of his eyes; his green uniform was clean and neat; he was as much at peace with the world as he could be.

Then a pick-up truck with Forest-Service insignia bounced by him.

"Hi, Super!" called the man at the wheel.

"Hi, there!" the Supervisor called back, and suddenly he was not quite so much at peace. First, he had failed to remember the man's name on the spur of the moment. Besides, he had waved his long arm in attempted good-fellowship, and must merely have looked awkward. And also, he had been called "Super" again.

That might really mean that he was making progress. During his whole first year, until a few months ago, they had called him Mr. Jones, or even Sir, particularly the youngsters who had come back from the Services. But why couldn't he be—well, maybe, Slim? He was slim enough all right. The way they said *Super* slid into irony too easily.

He felt an old tinge of resentment at his parents for the name they had given him. He was worse off than a college professor named Dean or a naval officer named Ensign. "Meet Lieutenant Ensign Jones!"—and people stared. "Meet Supervisor Ranger Jones!"—and people stared. Of course his mother's name was Ranger, and you shouldn't name a Jones baby George or John. Still, as Forest-Service people themselves, they should have seen what they were letting him in for, even if at the time it did seem cute to have everyone coming in and shouting "Hi, Ranger!" at him in his cradle.

But by the time he was twelve and went out on his first fire, the name was only an embarrassment. In Forestry School it had been nearly as bad, and in the Service later, particularly when he really had been a Ranger. "They call me Slim!" he used to say when he went to a new post, but it never took, even though he was six-feet-four and a beanpole. No, they called him Jones, not even Jonesy, and from the time he was an Assistant Supervisor at thirty-one, he had begun to be Mr. Jones.

He was within sight of Headquarters now—the low-built tobacco-brown buildings, set against the pine-covered foothills. He felt happier again.

Striding up the walk toward the entrance, he swung off his broad-brimmed hat, and the sunlight picked out a few reddish gleams in his thick wavy brown hair. He stretched his long legs a trifle, and, without thinking about it, let his own momentum take him up the six steps in three effortless strides.

"Good morning, Super," said the switch-board girl, beating him to the salutation.

"Good morning, Jackie," he said, and swung on into his office. There were no telegrams, and the mail not yet in. He tore Monday's page from his desk-calendar, reflecting that September was now far enough along to make a rain possible in a couple of weeks, with luck. The only notation on the new page was: "Call Bart *re* Strawberry."

He reached for the phone, but paused. Through the partition he could faintly hear Jackie's voice: "Hamlin Point . . . Yes . . . Check." The lookouts were reporting in. "Cerro Gordo . . ." he heard. "The Butte . . ." Knowing that he must delay his call a minute, he leaned back and let his eyes fall lovingly upon the newly completed master-map which hung on the opposite wall.

Yes, his Ponderosa Forest actually showed in its outlines little harmony with geography—either physical or political. "Really as artificial," he thought, "as—well—as a juke-box." Established hurriedly in the early years of the century by the stroke of a presidential pen in far-off Washington, it straddled the crest of the Sierra Nevada, and sprawled over parts of three California counties. A wavy boundary along part of its northern edge showed where it followed a watershed, but elsewhere the line—a broad green one on the map—kept to the arbitrary right-angled pattern of township- and section-lines, and where the trend was northeast or northwest the result was a saw-tooth effect.

"Artificial," he thought, "but still a good chunk of real estate!" Officially the figure was 1,091,904 acres, and that worked out as 1706.1 square miles—an area, as he liked to put it to visitors: "somewhat smaller than Delaware, but comfortably larger than Rhode Island."

He turned again to his phone, but as he heard Jackie

answer, he changed his mind, and said, "Get me Arn, please." Waiting, he thought how silly it really was to use the telephone instead of walking fifty feet down the hall—but that was what modern habits got you into. Then he heard his Dispatcher answering.

"Yes, Arn," he said. "What's the sum-up on that lightning storm yesterday?"

"Seven strokes is all we logged. We just got the tag-end of it. They're all in Barlow and Sheba districts. Only one fire—so far! It was a dead tree on the ridge above the Middle Fork. Ben's boys went out from Sheba, and took care of it. Another strike was just below the top of Cerro Gordo—smashed a big tree. The Lookout walked down, and saw it last evening. There wasn't any fire, but it's blocked the road."

"That leaves five. What about those?"

"Four of them hit where some lookout can see right to them. They haven't smoked up yet, and we can rush them fast if they do. The one I don't like is over by Onion Creek somewhere."

"Did you get a cross-shot on it?"

"Yes. . . . Let's see. . . . 4:12 was the time. Cerro Gordo put it down at 65, and Horse Mountain got it at 320."

"They sound like round numbers."

"Yes, but they put the strike on that ridge north of the creek, somewhere along the line of Definite and Deerhound."

The Supervisor thought a moment.

"That's blind country in there, isn't it?" he asked.

"Well, technically, yes. But if the strike was anywhere near the top of the ridge, as it naturally would be, Cerro Gordo can just about see into it."

"You'll scout it by air anyway."

"As soon as I can. The storm hit the Tahoe worse than us, and they're using the plane today."

"What's the forecast?"

"Not worse than usual. No thunderstorms. Light south wind. No change in temperature and humidity."

"Thanks," said the Supervisor and hung up. He was faintly irritated, although not with the Dispatcher or with the Tahoe Forest. "Here I am," he thought, "managing an estate for Uncle nearly as big as—well, bigger than Rhode Island anyway—with a hundred ideas of things to do to make it a better estate. Yet for four months a year I, and everybody else, drop silviculture, grazing improvement, erosion control, roads, recreation projects, fish and game, and everything else, just because we have to live, eat, think, and dream *nothing but fire!*"

3

On the ridge above Onion Creek, like a sickly new-born infant gasping in the cradle, the fire had barely lived through the night. In the chill that descended upon the mountains in the early morning it had cooled gradually until only a few glowing spots still maintained life. With the cold, the humidity of the air rose until it approached dewpoint, and the condensation of even the slightest film of dew would certainly have quenched the last coals.

As the chill deepened, however, the air along the ridge-top grew colder more rapidly than the lower air, and thus also becoming heavier, it began to slide gently down the steep slope. This draft came as a saving stimulant to the dying sparks. Moreover, this air was drier, so that a dew formed only on the lower slopes of the ridge where spray from the little brawling creek saturated the air. The fire thus continued to glow faintly.

At last, in the dawn, the glow seemed to fade out, but actually the fire was stronger, and inevitably after sunrise it grew stronger still. In the warmer, drier air it no longer had to expend its own heat in driving off the moisture from every pine-needle. During the night the fire had been like a shivering infant forced to expend the energy of its own food in merely keeping itself alive. Now it was like a well-blanketed infant, ready to stretch out arms and grow.

The sun, rising still higher, heated more rapidly the air at the lower end of the canyon. The warmed air began to rise, and since the trend of the canyon was toward the northeast, this new draft of air joined with and reinforced the prevailing southerly breeze.

The fire responded. Its six-inch line of dull red coals glowed with a more orange light. As pine-needle after pine-needle was engulfed, wisps of smoke, here and there, rose visibly to heights of half a foot, or even more, before being dissipated.

Yet the new breeze was a somewhat treacherous ally. During the night the downhill draft had blown the heat away from the upper edge of the fire and helped it stay alive only on the lower edge. The reversed breeze, however, could not revive the cold upper edge. As for the lower edge, its tiny flames consumed only what they had already seized upon; they could not lick forward to ignite fresh needles. Instead, they were now blown inward at the little patch of already burned ground.

So, after ten minutes, the fire again died down to a smoulder. Its chief vigor now centered at one end of a dry twig, half an inch thick; this twig was smoking vigorously. Looking big as a tree-trunk in comparison with the fire, it stretched out five inches into the unburned area.

4

As he walked along the corridor on the top floor of the Federal Building, Dave Halliday might again have passed for a civilian, if his gray Navy shirt and slightly rolling walk had not betrayed him.

On the right were the Administration offices; on the left, the Climatological Division. Ahead, on the glass door, he saw: *Forecasting Division*. At that point he felt a tingle within him, and knew that he had come home.

He flung open the door, and there was the Chief sitting at his desk. To see so much gray hair was something of a shock. But to see the Chief's face light up with the pleasure of recognition—that was good!

It was good to see Whitey and Mr. Ragan too, but what he really liked most was when the first flush of homecoming died down and he and the Chief could really sit down together.

"Hn-n?" said the Chief. "Just how long was it anyway? You went away a J. M. and a J. G., and here you are back a Lieutenant Commander, and—hn-n?—I guess we'll be paying you something more than that two thousand a year you started at."

"Well, what I'm interested in now is just where you're going to work me back into the Weather Bureau."

"Right here in San Francisco, if I have anything to say! But just now I have a temporary assignment for you. It won't be bad experience. You want to start work today, I understand."

"Well, as they say, a fellow has to eat. What's the assignment?"

"Fire-weather. One of our men had to go in for an operation, and our station at Suffolk in the Ponderosa Forest is running short-handed. You would be in charge. You have to make the special forecasts about fire-danger. It's ticklish work sometimes. But a man as good as you are—"

"Thanks. As I remember also, I'd have to go out to the big fires myself."

"Yes. There's a lot of tricky little stuff to work on—local conditions, terrain, up-canyon winds. You can't concentrate too much on what's happening along the Polar Front."

"Oh, I've learned that! When you're getting a wounded fighter back on deck, you worry more about today's little gust on the starboard bow than you do about tomorrow's typhoon somewhere over the horizon."

"Well, then, you'd better put out today. The man up there now isn't really good enough to carry the responsibility. You'll have to use public transportation to get to Suffolk."

"How about my jeep?"

"Good. I didn't know you had one."

"Yes. And, sir, you might be interested to know—her name is Maria."

"Hn-n? Yes, Maria, that's good! I understand you boys on the carriers used to give girls' names to typhoons too."

"Yes, and Susan was a terror. It's natural, I suppose, for young men—" And then he saw that the Chief was looking at him in that funny way.

" 'For young men' You know there's such a thing as being too much tied up in your work. A man shouldn't eat all his breakfasts opposite a teletype machine—although some women I've known are a pretty good imitation of one."

Dave Halliday was afraid he blushed a little.

"Anyway," he said, "the jeep is Maria. I had to get her painted, and I was going to get a good modest black until I realized that would make her a Black Maria. So I went whole hog the other way—guess I must have been prophetic. Anyway, she's a fine knock-you-down red. You could even say she's a fire-engine red!"

5

During twenty years, from the summer after his thirtieth birthday, John Bartley had been the Ranger of Barlow District. At first he had nursed ambitions to rise, some day, to be

Supervisor of a Forest, but as years passed, he cared less and less, for the Barlow became his world. And, paradoxically, the more he concentrated upon it, and the better Ranger he grew to be, the less fitted he was to face the problems of some whole forest, or to reshape himself to a new country.

And Barlow District was big enough to keep a man from ever feeling cramped. It spread over nearly a third of the entire Forest, much bigger than Suffolk or Rabbitbrush, bigger than Polkville and Sheba put together. It was too big, in fact, even though it attained a geographical unity by being the country drained by the South Fork. The Supervisor had plans laid to split it. Those plans, however, were now filed away until Bart should retire. To split the district would as good as break Bart's spirit, and he was so familiar with it that he could run it easily enough, even though a new man would be snowed under. . . .

In his office, paneled with straight-grained, knot-free sugar-pine, cut from the slope of Howell Mountain, Ranger Bartley heard a certain familiar ring in the voices. Liking people, he could not resist going out to see who had come in.

"Well, for cryin' out loud!" he said, tempering his language to fit the well-known reticences of the two young fellows he was greeting.

He extended his hand automatically, and was barely conscious of the fraction of a second the other hesitated before taking it.

"I thought you fellows had had enough of these parts," he went on quickly, covering up what would have been a silence. "You certainly always crabbed enough in camp about getting loose."

One of them laughed a little nervous cackle: "We're going to camp up by Poison Spring—hear the fishing's good."

"You don't mind waging war on trout, eh?"

The one laughed his little cackle again, but the other said, with dignity:

"It's not the same thing!"

"No, not by a long sight!" said the Ranger. "Well, you boys want a camp-fire permit, I guess. That's all right, and you, of all people, I don't need to warn about being careful with fire."

"No," said the one with the laugh, "we've fought too many fires. We don't want the Damon's Butte or the Peacock or the Kimshew again. If we see a smoke, we'll be out of this country so fast you can't see us."

The Ranger headed back to his office, leaving his clerk-dispatcher to issue the permit. "Pretty good kids those!" he was thinking, "hard workers on a fire line. Course, I don't approve of Conchies . . ."

Striding across the floor, the Ranger had been full of vigor. As he settled into his desk-chair, he looked older. His fine head and chest seemed to sink of their own weight, and his belt-line bulged. His bald spot looked more prominent. As his face fell into repose, its lines grew a little pudgy, as if the inner frame of the man had begun to sag a trifle, except when held up by effort of mind and muscle.

He heard the telephone ring in the outer office, and then the buzzer at his elbow. That would be his call from Headquarters.

"Bartley speaking," he said.

"Yes, Bart, this is—ah—Jones."

"Yes, Super."

"Say, Bart, are you free tomorrow afternoon?"

"Why, I guess so. Yes, certainly, if you need me."

"Well, this is my idea. I'd like to run up into the Basin with you. A lot of that timber up in there is getting pretty over-ripe, and there's a chance that we might do something with it."

Bart's jaw set suddenly, and he was again the vigorous strong man. But the Supervisor was still speaking:

"There's a good mill-site at Idylhurst. The chief problem is that steep road up Strawberry Creek. . . ."

"You know," said Bart, really breaking in, "that's an awful pretty country up through there, some of the nicest mature forest in California."

The pause over the phone was long enough to let Bart know he had registered his point, but the Super did not argue.

"How about leaving around eleven, take lunches along?"

"Good enough. While we're at it, would you mind going all the way up to Cerro Gordo? I've got a green lookout there, and she may need some bucking up."

"We'll try to make it. That's the girl Judith Something-or-other-Spanish, isn't it—took old Dick's place when he had to quit? I didn't see her when she came through."

"That's her—Judith Godoy's the name—college kid, pretty good-looking!"

"That's bad! When I put a woman on top of a mountain by herself ten miles from the nearest house, I like her old and snaggle-toothed."

"This one's no clinging vine, though—tall as I am, and got a square-set pair of shoulders would look good on a sergeant of marines."

"Well, anyway, I hope she knows enough to keep her eye lined up on where that lightning stroke hit. . . . Be seeing you about eleven, then."

As the receiver clicked down, Bart was out of his chair. His heels hit hard as he strode to the window and back again. There was a tightness in his throat. Twenty years now he had been Ranger of the Barlow. He knew it canyon by canyon, and ridge by ridge, from the shining granite and blue lakes of its high country, down through the fir and sugar-pine and cedar and ponderosa pine. He had climbed every peak, and fished every stream. "I love every tree of it," he said once to his wife. "Yes, even the miserable knob-cone pines, for they grow where the others won't."

And now this fellow Jones—the *Super!* Thinking up plans for a lumber mill—and in the Basin! A wild idea came into his mind. No Supervisor, no fellow who had come in from the outside only a year and a half ago, could last long if his old-time rangers didn't work with him. The Regional Office would know about it fast enough.

The idea hardly came in at one door of his mind before he threw it out by another. That was not a decent way of doing things; besides he hated to think of all the damage that might happen to the Forest itself in the course of such a fight. He was cooler after that thought, and he realized that the Super was not actually that bad—not bad enough to make the rangers stick together always. He remembered a talk three of them had had not so long ago, just when the Super was about finishing up his first year. Bart had been over at Sheba Ranger Station—he and Ben Roach of the Sheba and Jerry Barrett of the Rabbitbrush. Bart was the youngest of the three. Both the others were crowding retirement age, and when they had come to the Ponderosa the canyons hadn't been worn down so deep. There had been times when those two also had thought of being Supervisors—in the old days when a man was prouder of the way he swung a double-bitted ax than of a degree from Yale School of Forestry. But things had changed.

Anyway, they had talked about the Super, and finally Jerry had summed him up in that salty old-timer's way:

"Well, the Super's been here a year now, and there's three things I'll say for him. One, he knows forestry; two, he keeps his word; and three, he's a dangerous man to play poker with."

"Hell, Jerry," said Ben, "what more could anybody *ask* of a Supervisor!"

They had all laughed, but Bart knew (and knew the others knew) that there was still more that you would ask of a Supervisor if things got tough.

6

The girl on Cerro Gordo was having a quiet time, although all the time except for that hour of yesterday's thunderstorm had been, she reflected, quiet enough. She was getting into the swing of things now, and a very satisfying routine she found it, good for a troubled soul.

"Or at least, for her particular kind of troubled soul." She put the thought into actual words, but did not say them out loud, and she used the third person as if she were writing a composition for English 41. "The solitude would certainly have driven some people insane, but she found herself flourishing. Perhaps her decision to become a lookout had been motivated by escape. But if so, the escape had been partly successful. Already she realized [no need to mention names] he was a heel, and not worth worrying about any more."

No, not worth worrying about *much,* anyway. A girl on the rebound, as people said, was supposed to fall in love with someone else quickly. But she herself had rebounded differently. When the chance came to earn a little money and hold a romantic-sounding job for a few weeks and get away (this, most of all) from the whole problem of facing people and living with them for the rest of the summer—well, she had jumped at it.

"How'll you ever stand being alone?" they had wondered. She didn't explain that that was really the chief idea. Nevertheless after only two weeks she was already willing to admit that sometimes she was lonely.

Yet life on the tower was not altogether without human contacts. She had the telephone, the two-way official radio, and a small commercial set for getting ordinary broadcasts. Twice a day she reported in. During the evenings she gossiped a little by radio with other lookouts. The old codger on Horse Mountain talked like the Bible and acted crazy, but the motherly woman on Hamlin Point was nice, in spite of her addiction to soap-operas, which seemed to be a kind of occupational disease among lookouts.

Other contacts, at least she had come to feel them as such, were her descents from the tower—to visit the little house modestly set among the cedars, to get drinking-water from the spring, or to take a walk in the evening. She did not really care about going down from the tower, however. Probably she was not even getting enough exercise. It was not that she was afraid of rattlesnakes, or of bears either. It was just that the tower had already become home, perhaps in a more intense way than her real home had ever been. She had read about tank-troops in the desert, how even in a safe place they felt more comfortable when sitting inside their tank. So it was with her. When she climbed up through the trap door in the catwalk, and closed and bolted it, then she suddenly felt the calm of a great peace.

"The girl would have had difficulty in explaining this," she went on, still as if writing her composition. "First of all, it was the peace that went with freedom. It was like living in infinite space, like living in the sky. The closest things to her were the tips of the tall trees on the slopes of the mountain, and she even looked down upon them, as if they were little trees growing in a nursery. Far off, to be sure, she could see plenty of peaks that she knew to be higher, even Mount Shasta; but they were so far away that she had no sense of looking up or being dominated. Didn't people say, 'I'm on

the top of the world!' meaning they were happy? Why
shouldn't actually being on the top of the world really make
you feel that way? [And—oh, yes—what were those lines
about 'regions mild'?] She fumbled for some lines, and then
pulled them up, incorrectly no doubt, from somewhere in
her sub-conscious:

> In regions mild of calm and serene air
> Above the smoke and stir of that dim place
> Which men call Earth.

[Just a minute, though! Aren't you thinking all this is so
lovely and you're so happy, because you've run away from
things, and don't have to face people? Oh, forget it, and let's
get this composition written.]

"And next, it was peaceful because the little room at the
top of the sixty-foot stilt-legged [Professor Lehman will like
that] . . . at the top of the sixty-foot stilt-legged steel tower
was the most completely logical and ordered place that had
probably ever existed in the world, or could exist. It was
like the beautiful old Ptolemaic system of the universe. The
room was just fourteen by fourteen, glass all around, with
the narrow catwalk outside. Then it was oriented exactly to
true north-south-east-west, so that it must always be spinning
around with the earth in perfect harmony, just like the music
of the spheres. And for a center, right in the middle was the
circular fire-finder. In such a place you always knew what
direction was what and exactly where you were. And wasn't
that another condition of happiness and peace? To express
the opposite, people used words like 'lost' and 'confused.' "

She snapped out of it, and got practical by walking around
the catwalk for a careful look. There was nothing showing,
except two of her permanent smokes. One was Magna Mill
at 278, throwing up a big gray smudge, and the other was the
Suffolk town dump at 252, just barely visible.

Back inside, she played with the idea of having a visitor.
The visitor's book showed that there hadn't been any for
several weeks. The road was too bad for most automobilists,
and Cerro Gordo (official altitude 4565 feet) was not high
and exciting enough to tempt hikers. Still there might be—a
handsome young man, for instance. [Oh, that's it, is it? Well
as long as you're at the business, why not make it a movie-
star or the Duke of Berengaria.]

" 'Why, yes, Your Highness [Grace, idiot, Grace!] Why,
yes, Your Grace, I shall be happy to show you everything. . . .
Certainly, as you so aptly remark, that strange-looking brass
thing is at the center and we might well begin there. It is
called a fire-finder, and is a device for sighting through and
determining direction. If I place the indicator here and sight
through the wires, I am looking in the direction of true
north, and you will notice that the reading on the scale is
zero or 360, which is the same thing. . . . Ha-ha-ha, certainly
not, if it is a question of bank-accounts, very clever of you,
Duke! [Your Grace, idiot!] But to go on, as you thus look
north, the considerable chasm in the foreground is the canyon
of Potter Creek, then a ridge, and behind that the canyon
of Jacks Creek, another ridge and then the Middle Fork, still
another, then the North Fork, and that last ridge you can just
faintly make out is the one beyond the North Fork. . . . No,
not clever. *C'est mon métier.* (Your Grace speaks French, I
presume?) [I only got a C from Dr. Brenner, but I'll not
mention that.]

"Now let me take another sight. Here, about 60, between
northeast and east. Look closer. . . . Uh? [Even if he is a
duke!] . . . Would you kindly take your arm away? . . .
Oh, no, no offense I'm sure. . . . As I was saying, looking
through at 60 you see Reverse Ridge, so called doubtless because it runs counter to the general trend of ridges here-

abouts. Note the steep almost cliff-like drop-off on this side.

"Now here, at 65. Yesterday there was a lightning-strike over there, and I have to keep a sharp and continual watch for fear a fire may blaze up. . . . You're not interested? Well, to hell with you then! Who asked you to come anyway? You're probably a phony. . . . Oh, no, no, I. didn't mean it! *Not that!!* . . . God, he's jumping from the catwalk!"

[Well, I disposed of that duke all right. Bring on your movie-star.]

"Thereupon the girl, with remarkable *sang froid,* returned to her appointed work. She was much too busy to spend her time burying dukes."

By this time, she noticed, the sun was getting well into the west. The heat of the day was past, and the breeze rising up the slope from the canyon was cool. She made a round of the catwalk and started another, when—*wham!*

It was only the telephone, but smashing the long stillness of the afternoon it was like another thunderclap. *Long, short, short, short.* She grabbed the receiver.

"Cerro Gordo speaking."

"Hello, this is Bart. Say, did you have any visitors today?"

"Yes, oh, no—I mean no. Why did you ask?"

"Well, I was just gettin' you prepared, breakin' the news easy. You're going to have some visitors tomorrow—the Super and me."

"That's swell of you, Bart, letting me know. I'll have the windows washed and the whole place pitchfork-clean."

Bart laughed. "You're kind of a card at that, ain't you? Don't worry too much though. We ain't comin' to see you special, and we may not even make it. Won't be before two o'clock at best. . . . Say, you been watchin' where that strike was?"

"I have, all right!"

"Nothing showed up, eh?"

"No, nothing."

"Well, that's fine. Keep watchin' it!"

"But that's twenty-four hours old. Wouldn't it show up in this time? How long will it be?"

"Can't tell, baby! Some claims that a fire can lay as a sleeper through a whole winter—smoulder right under the snow. Plenty of 'em will lay for a week."

"All right, I'll keep an eye at 65."

"Yes, and don't forget the other three hundred and fifty-nine points either. Don't worry—I know you won't."

"What are you coming up this way for, if I may ask?"

There was a sudden pause, and she sensed something wrong.

"Oh," said Bart, "nothing much. Just an idea of the Super's! Tell you sometime. Well, maybe you and me and the Super will have a nice little get-together."

The sun was low, and the breeze was slackening. From the catwalk she looked out northeastward again. There was no smoke, but just a touch of haze in the canyons.

From where she stood, she looked down the furrowed eastern slope of Cerro Gordo. Bacchus Creek, Curran Creek, and all their little feeders—she could see the lines of their courses, but they were so deep in their ravines that she nowhere saw the water. Where did all the names come from? Bacchus Creek—that was a funny one. She would have to ask Bart about it. She followed its course with her eyes. It met the solid wall of the cliff-like southern face of Reverse Ridge. "The creek must be undercutting the softer rock," she thought, "and the lava on top stands up and makes the cliff. I ought to know some more geology."

East of Reverse Ridge she looked into the mouths of the twin gorges, where Onion Creek flowed out to join the North Fork of the South Fork. But nowhere could she see the streams—just ridge after ridge in what looked like wild confusion, with the hard shadows now making them stand out even more sharply. Here and there little knobs and peaks poked their heads up, but mostly they were the long, smooth-topped ridges, sloping away gradually toward the west and south, except where Reverse Ridge expressed its individuality by cutting right across the general trend. A strange way to live in a country—by knowing the ridges so well and having not the slightest idea of what lay in the valleys.

And now, just at sunset, as the heat oozed away and the breeze died and the haze shrank back to earth, she saw her whole world of peaks and ridges lie cool and calm and clear. There were ten other lookouts in the Ponderosa, and she could see six of them—her fellow watchers. Far off to the northeast she made out the tower on Sheer Rock, high at the headwaters of the North Fork. Swinging more to the east, she raised her binoculars, and picked up the white speck of the little house perched audaciously on the topmost pinnacle of The Butte, thirty-two miles away. Walking around by the southern catwalk, she saw Horse Mountain easily without binoculars, next Lovers Leap, and then Hamlin Point, off to the southwest. And that brought her round again toward the north where she looked across intimately at Humbug Point, her nearest neighbor, only eight miles away, across two ridges.

But the light was fading already, and when she looked again, she no longer could make out Sheer Rock. She lowered the trap door in the catwalk, bolted it, and was ready for the night.

7

Sometimes—so long ago that years mean little—there was an inland sea, and into it the rivers flowed and dropped their silt. And again there was dry land with volcanoes pouring out ash and lava. That was the beginning of that country, or as close to it as anyone knows.

There came a deep revolt of the earth. A molten mass poured from the center, and high mountains rose. The heat baked the older rocks into something different, and the mass itself cooled slowly into gray-white shining granite.

Time passed, some fifty million years, while the powers of rain and frost and wind warred against the granite heights, and wore them down until all that was left was a country of open valleys with gentle hills between. Broad rivers meandered in the valleys, laying down thick beds of red gravel, and with that gravel many shining particles of gold. Then other sheets of lava poured out, covering the gravels.

Once more the earth revolted, and a strip of land, a hundred miles wide and five times as long, tipped neatly upward along its eastern edge, thousands of feet into the air. The once level beds of the gravels and the lava-flows tilted to the west, and the streams of the broad rivers were cut off.

New rivers began, heading at the ridge. These were swift brawling torrents; as some millions of years passed, they cut down through the lavas and the gravels, and gnawed far into the granite, until each flowed in a deep canyon. But even so, the long ridge-tops between the canyons sloped away smoothly, still showing that they had all been once the surface of the level plain.

When at last the Spaniards came, they saw the shining snow on the highest crest, and called the mountains *Sierra Nevada,* "range snowed-upon."

To ANCIENT PROPHETS and poets on the shores of the blue inland sea, wildfire was a common thought. Their minds encompassed the idea, and turned to it for simile or symbol.

Though the rainless kingdom of the Pharaohs had no forests, the priests still told an age-old story, perhaps enshrining the memory of a moist era, that Ptah became king of the gods because he mastered the trick of fire—"When a tree on the mountains was lightning-struck, and the forest burned."

Moses saw it as no marvel that the bush burned—only that it was not consumed. His law laid down matter-of-factly the penalty: "If fire break out and catch in the brush. . . ." The Psalmist called upon his God to persecute his enemies: "As the fire burneth a wood, and as the flame setteth the mountains on fire."

To Homer, the Achaeans in their dazzling armor marched onward "as a ravaging flame kindles a boundless forest on a mountain's peaks." Lucretius assigned the discovery of metals to some time "when a fire had burned down great forests on mighty mountains." According to a famous tale, a blaze

35

kindled by some ancient shepherds burned for many days, and swept bare all the range of the Pyrenees.

Even England, in drier eras, knew that fury. The chronicler recorded glumly for 1032: "In this year came wildfire such as no one remembered before"; and again, "The wildfire did much damage in Derbyshire and elsewhere"; and still again, twelve years after the Conquest, "This was the dry summer, and wildfire came in many shires, and burned many farmsteads and towns." The names still testify to such an ordeal—Brentwood, Burntwood, Burntheath, Burnt Hill, Brantridge, Brindley—from Brent Fell in Westmorland to Burnt Oak in Kent.

In later centuries the rain fell more steadily, and woodlands were scantier. Then the English forgot. Neither Chaucer nor Shakespeare thought of forest-fires—unless we take the witches' blasted heath to be a flame-scarred moorland. Milton, almost by himself among English poets, used the figure, likening the fallen Archangel to the withered glory of a mighty pine, lightning-struck and standing as a blackened snag. The translators of the Bible must have found it almost sufficient marvel that the bush burned at all rather than that it was not consumed.

The English of those days knew little of forests and even less of fire in them. But those who were to plant the colonies in America would soon learn much of both.

2

Arnold Sorenson, the Dispatcher, put down the receiver, and leaned back in his chair to plan things. He was tall and powerfully built, with big hands. His blond hair and blue eyes showed Scandinavian blood—the son of one of those emigrants who had poured into the United States, and being woodsmen at home, had naturally headed for the great forests of the Northwest. The father had handled ax and saw; the son was a forester too, but he worked with subtler implements.

"Well," he thought, "we take off at three. That will give us plenty of daylight, and at that time of day any sleeper will be throwing up the most smoke it's going to. Better check the location again, though."

He got up, and turned to the large map on the wall behind his desk. It was mounted on ply-wood, and from it protruded the glass heads of eleven large push-pins, each fitted into a hole at the location of one of the lookouts of the Ponderosa Forest. Around each of the holes and pins was a neatly stamped circle, graduated into its three-hundred-sixty degrees. The Dispatcher took the pin at Cerro Gordo, and as he pulled it out, a thread which was held taut by a hidden spring followed the pin. Checking his memory from a written memorandum, he placed the pin so that its thread lay precisely upon the line of the circle marking sixty-five degrees to the east of true north. Then he pushed the pin into the board. Somewhere along this line would lie the location of the lightning strike, if the Cerro Gordo lookout had observed correctly.

Next he took the Horse Mountain pin, and with similar care placed it so that the thread lay at 320. He thus had a theoretical "cross" on the location of the strike, and he examined the map carefully at the intersection of the threads, so that he would be able to keep himself exactly oriented when flying.

The "cross" was clearly somewhere on the ridge between Wilson Creek and Onion Creek. But the exact spotting of a lightning stroke was difficult, because the stroke itself was momentary and startling, and because the observer was frequently not looking at the precise location. The old-timer on

Horse Mountain was one of the best in the business, in spite of being a religious fanatic. But the girl on Cerro Gordo was green, and might easily record a considerable error. On the other hand, the strike was likely to be on a ridge somewhere, not in a canyon. So it was probably on this particular ridge.

He studied the map for a moment. The ridge was the middle one of three which formed the southwestern base of Howell Mountain, sticking out like three toes. It was a dangerous place to have a fire start. The topography was bad, for at this season the prevailing south wind would sweep the flames up-hill, and they might easily make a run clear up Howell Mountain before you could catch them. The area was roadless area too, although a good horse-trail led down the south side of Onion Creek.

Next he pulled two aerial photographs from his file, arranged them beneath the stereopticon viewer, and bent above it. The whole ridge, even individual trees, leaped sharply into three dimensions. He studied the combined pictures. There were no sharp rocks or especially outstanding and isolated trees which would attract lightning. The whole ridge was well timbered in pine and fir, with a good deal of reproduction and underbrush between the large trees. He wondered whether it was Jeffrey pine or ponderosa. The difference between them was chiefly in the chemistry of their sap, and that did not show in an aerial photograph. Bart could tell him of course; Bart knew every ridge personally. But as far as picking up a sleeper was concerned, species of tree made no difference, and there was no need for him to bother Bart.

He stood a moment, bringing the facts together in his mind and considering other possibilities. He seemed to have done all that he could in preparation for the afternoon's scouting, and so he sat down at his desk and took up other work.

The girl with the fire-danger report came in.

"Good morning," he said. "How is it?"

"Down one point."

"Thankful for small favors."

She went to the dial. From blue, when the pointer was straight up, the dial was colored according to the rainbow until it became red when the pointer, revolving clockwise, again approached vertical. The blue was labeled "Low"; the green, "Normal"; the yellow "High"; the orange, "Very High," and the red, "Extreme."

The pointer stood in the middle of the orange sector. The girl moved it slightly, but the change was hardly perceptible.

"Might have a rain in a couple of weeks now," said the girl.

"Might have a lot of trouble in a couple of weeks too."

"How many fires this year so far on the Ponderosa?"

"Oh, a hundred and sixty-two, I think—if there isn't another one going right now."

"Haven't lost much acreage though, have you? The Ponderosa must be an awful good fire outfit this year."

"I hope so. Maybe, just luck." He picked up some papers on his desk.

She took the hint and went out. But her words had cut more deeply than she could have imagined. Were they a good fire outfit, or was it luck? That was the pay-off question.

They seemed to be good. They had jumped the fires fast, and hit them hard. Over a hundred-sixty starts, and the average burn was only—let's see—something under two acres. The total was 297 acres—away below the quota that the Regional Office allowed them, and even below the theoretical one-tenth of one percent which was the national goal.

Yes, they seemed to be good, but the season wasn't over yet. Were there any weak spots that he ought to bolster up some way?

The Dispatcher was not like the Supervisor, who had to keep a hundred things in his mind besides fire. No, the Dispatcher's full-time job was fire.

To look at his office you might have wondered. There was no ax or shovel or McLeod or back-pump in sight. But after all, you hardly find the office of the Secretary of War bulging with grenades and machine-guns. The Dispatcher had fought plenty of fires close-up. As the phrase goes, "He had commanded troops in the field." But now he fought his fires without smelling smoke, generally without even seeing it.

And if you looked at the office with more observant eyes, you noticed that it was not so innocent as it seemed. You saw the colored dial, for instance, and the map with its push-pins, and the stereopticon viewer. In the corner was a two-way radio. And on the desk was the ever-present telephone with which he could take reports and requests from the fire-boss, and in the other direction order up supplies and reinforcements through all the chain of command—Forest, Zone, Region—until in the final emergency the word might even go to the Chief Forester in Washington.

The Dispatcher heard a step, and saw the Supervisor coming in.

"Hello, Arn," said the Supervisor. "I'm going up in Barlow District. Be leaving pretty soon. Anything I can do for you up that way?"

"I don't think so; I hope not. Say hello to Bart for me."

"Anything this morning?"

"Not yet. Nothing shows from those strikes day before yesterday. I'm scouting this afternoon that one over by Onion Creek. Leaving here about three."

"I'll probably see you fly over then. Bart and I may be at Cerro Gordo."

"Well, say hello for me to that nice Godoy kid too."

"Sure.—Fire-danger about the same, I see. Maybe we'll get a rain in a couple of weeks now. I'll be looking for you."

"O. K. So long, Super."

Even he is thinking about fire more than anything else, the Dispatcher concluded. He wouldn't say so, but that's why he came in. Well, there's a chance the luck will hold for two weeks more; or else, if it really is a good outfit, it will keep on being good. "Always figure the worst possible is going to happen," that's the only rule for this job. You think you're good and you relax just a bit, and then—zowie!—it happens.

The Dispatcher was suddenly on his feet with the quick blaze of his imagination as to what might happen. The most treacherous thing on earth—a fire! You could kill it more times than a cat, and it still sprang at you again. Then he could hear in his memory the voice of old Ben Roach of the Sheba District; Ben had never been to school much, but he had the philosopher's way of summing things up. "Yes," he was saying, "a fire is no one thing. It's like a bunch of allies in the war, or maybe a team. There's wind and temperature and humidity and lay of the land, and cover-type, and accessibility. There's all the little things you'll maybe never even know about—but they make the breaks. There's the men too —the right man in the right place, or maybe the other way round. There's what happened to the men, maybe years back, to make them what they are now. If wind and humidity and the rest don't all work together—like maybe the Germans and the Eye-talians didn't always—why, you can go in punchin' and maybe think you're good. But if you get a hot dry afternoon and heavy timber on an up-slope and the wind decides to come in and help—God, boy, you better just run and hide, for there won't never be enough men and equipment got together in Region 5 to stop her!"

Yes, it was humiliating, but Ben was right. Only you didn't just run and hide. Ben knew that well enough too. You never quit. No, even with a blow-up like that, you worried it along the flanks, and fought spot-fires, and ordered up reinforcements, and planned a new defense-line. Then eventually the wind died down or there was a ridge with lots of bare rock. The allies weren't sticking so well together, and you went in punching again, and corralled her before there was another blow-up.

The Dispatcher was still on his feet and probably his excitement was showing in his face; he was suddenly aware of a young man standing hesitantly in the doorway of his office.

"Oh," said the Dispatcher, "pardon me for not noticing. I was thinking of something. Did you want me?"

"The girl out there told me to come in here, sir. I'm the new man to take over the weather station."

"Oh, yes," said the Dispatcher, extending his hand. Looks all right, he thought, about five-ten, slight, dark-brown hair and blue eyes, well enough set up, seems alert and reliable. (From long necessity in assigning men to their jobs on fires, the Dispatcher had practiced at making quick thumbnail appraisals.)

"I'm glad you're here, Dave," he went on. "They telegraphed me of course. (A lot of things come through this office.) So I know your name. We go by first names around here—mostly, at least. So call me 'Arn.' But I wasn't really expecting you before tomorrow."

"The Chief told me to get on the job, and I drove up in my own car—a jeep, that is. I asked for the Supervisor outside here, but they said he was out and for me to come in to you."

"That's all right. I'll be your chief contact man anyway. Yeah, the Super just pulled out."

"Maybe I saw him, at that. Somebody was backing out from the curb just as I pulled in to park—a very tall guy, driving a green car. He kind of looked me over, but I thought it probably was the red jeep."

"Well, he's tall, and he would look you over all right. But in this business you don't pick people by a green car! Most of us drive them."

3

Halfway up the steep canyon-side to the north of Onion Creek the fire still smouldered in the thick duff of half-decayed twigs and pine-needles. Vacillating in direction as air-currents shifted, eating ahead more rapidly here because of more combustible materials, held back or extinguished there, weakened at night by the cold and the moister air, quickened in the daytime by the heat and drying power of the sun, always tending to work up-hill because of the natural rising of heat—thus almost wholly at the push and pull of powers not its own, the fire had now burned a total area some four feet long and two feet wide, but of irregular amoeba-like outline. Each stubby arm represented a place where the fire on some two- or three-inch front had eaten more rapidly ahead under favorable conditions; each little gulf between the arms showed where the fire had moved more slowly, or gone out entirely.

The over-all pattern resembled an hour-glass. It lay diagonally up and down the slope, just at the base of the pine tree, a buttress-root of which formed the upper side of the waist of the hour-glass.

Measured carefully around all its sinuosities, the fire might have shown a perimeter of ten yards, but it was not actually alive except along a front of two or three feet. All the lower half of the hour-glass, near the middle of which had been the original point of ignition, was now burned out, and during the night had grown completely cold.

Well inside the upper half lay the white ashes of the twig which had once displayed the fire's chief vigor. As most of the fire had died under the influence of an unfavorable shift of air currents, the flames had worked along this twig. Blazing in miniature for a few minutes, as a great fallen tree-trunk may blaze gigantically for hours, the twig had let the fire work along the full length of its five inches and ignite the pine needles along its upper side. All of the fire now remaining alive sprang from the heat which had been transmitted through this twig.

Shortly before noon on the third day of its smouldering existence, the fire drew close to a dry pine-cone. As the heat grew more intense, the cone began to smoke vigorously. It was like a volcanic eruption in comparison with anything that had gone before.

In a few minutes the column of thick gray smoke was several inches in diameter. It rose some ten feet almost perpendicularly, opening up slightly, funnel-wise. Then the up-canyon drift of air bent it over and it spread out as a long drifting plume, failing now to rise sharply, and scattering rapidly. The general height of the trees along the ridge was a hundred-fifty feet. Any smoke particles which managed to rise to this height were so greatly dissipated that the most delicate optical instrument could not have detected them.

After a few minutes of vigorous smoking, the cone burst into flame. It was a conflagration quite unparalleled. Yellow flames, nearly invisible in the full daylight, shot upward for a foot or even more. There was a definite crackling.

Since the lower spines upon which the cone rested had been the first to catch fire, they were the first to burn away, and the cone settled downhill. Its central core, however, burned more slowly, and the slumping cone came to rest upon this support. After about ten minutes the cone was wholly consumed except for the still smoking core. The fire was again quiet.

During its life the fire had burned a number of beetles and other ground-insects. Its tiny column of rising heat had bounced, rather rudely, a passing pair of low-flying butterflies. The conflagration of the cone, however, had been noticeable enough to focus upon the fire, for the first time, the attention of a creature active enough to be interested, and intelligent enough to abstract the fire from the rest of the environment and consider it as an entity.

A good-sized pine-squirrel had sighted the column of smoke, and warily approached, leaping between the branches, to investigate. This was no blasé resident of a city park, but an unsophisticated mountaineer. In his two years of life he had never eaten a peanut; in fact, he had never seen a man, or a fire. He became intensely curious, but remained wary.

After some scurryings-about and false starts, he at last gained a branch of the pine-tree on the side away from the fire. He sat there a minute, chattering now and then, experimentally and provocatively. Nothing happened.

Bolder, with a sudden rush, he reached the tree-trunk. After a pause he stuck his head around. He was almost directly above the now slightly smoking fire, but he was fifty feet in the air. He could see the little smoke, but the drift of the air-current carried all smell away from him.

With a downward dash he gained the lowest dead branch of the tree, not thirty feet from the fire. He was rapidly losing his fear. Now he sat boldly on the branch, and chattered. He put anger into his voice, and indignation. He gave this intruder notice to be off. What was it doing in his forest?

A minute later, prudently keeping to the opposite side of the trunk, he descended to the ground. His enemies—marten, owl, wildcat—he knew, and this was none of them. Fear had dwindled, but not curiosity.

After two false starts he reached the blackened area at its upper edge. Scratching at it with interest, he put his right forepaw squarely upon a small glowing ember.

His reaction was so sudden that he sprawled over backward. Instantly recovering, he dashed for the tree-trunk and up it, not stopping until he was seventy feet high among the branches.

In this familiar world of the upper air, he sheltered himself in a crotch. Keeping prudent silence, he licked his scorched toes. The speed of his reaction had been such that he had suffered only an insignificant burn. Already he was hardly conscious of any more pain from it, but the smell of singed hairs was something new to him. Under the circumstances, it was also alarming.

From his reassuring height he again dared to look down upon the little fire far below him. He had an intelligent brain, and the memory of fire was now implanted among his store of experiences. He would willingly not get too close to it again. After a moment's observation, he ran out along a branch, favoring his right forepaw a little.

4

As Bart waited for the Super, he checked the form A-1103 which had just been typed in quadruplicate. There may once have been a time when rangers rode dapple-gray horses and spent their time posing in handsome young profile against a background of mountains; if so, that was a long time ago.

He heard a car drive up, looked out, and saw it was the

Super. Glancing at the clock, he noted the time at two minutes to eleven. He went out.

"Hello, Bart," said the Super. "The place looks fine. I like a Ranger Station in white and green occasionally instead of all that tobacco-brown we go in for so much. The lawn looks nice."

"Thanks. It's a pretty good dump. Got a better view than you got in Suffolk too."

The Super turned, looked across the clear stream of the South Fork, swirling between rocks, and let his eyes range up the two-thousand-foot rise of the opposite canyon-side.

"Yes," he said, "a better view. Say, Bart, when did they log that slope over there?"

"Oh, around 1902, before the Forest took over."

"She came back in fine shape—as pretty-looking a young forest as you see. Must be laying on quite a few thousand board-feet every season."

"Yes," said Bart shortly, "she's pretty." Then, as if pointedly changing the subject, he added, "That's the suppression-crew over there."

The Super looked at the half-dozen boys of high-school age who were pulling weeds on the lawn and trimming the borders.

"Of course," Bart went on, "that work on the lawn is really boondoggling. But I like to keep them pulled in here close this time of year. Then, if a fire breaks, they can get started quick in any direction."

"That's good."

"Well, had we better get going?—You don't mind takin' the pick-up?"

"Not a bit. You got the saw in it?"

"Sure have!"

Bart was secretly a trifle irritated. He was taking the pick-up truck so that he could have a cross-cut saw along to clear the tree from the road below Cerro Gordo, but he had not expected the Supervisor to click so fast on such a detail. . . .

They went about a mile past their turn-off so as to take a look at the Idylhurst Guard-Station. Idylhurst, such as it was, rated as the only settlement in all this part of the Forest, and was on privately owned land. It had been started as a resort, and named in that tradition, but now its cabins had been taken over as all-year homes by the families of men who worked in the Magna lumber-mill over on Potter Creek.

There were a dozen or so houses, pretty well run-down-looking. As the pick-up drove along, women came to the front porches, generally with small children tagging after them.

"There's hardly ever a car comes through here this time of day, and they come out to look," Bart explained.

He waved and spoke to them as he drove by:

"Hello, Jewel. . . . Hi-ya, Enid. . . . Afternoon, Peggy."

The women called back, "Hello, Bart!" and the Supervisor would notice each one tucking in a wisp of hair or straightening her flowered house-dress.

"How come you know them all, Bart?"

"Just comes natural, I guess. I like people." And then he added, as if defensively, "Of course, it's good business too. If they call the ranger by his first name, they ain't going to set any fires in his woods, just to be mean. This place is a pest-hole anyway—far as the Forest is concerned. God, it keeps me awake nights! Defective flues, trash-burning, cigarettes, kids playing with matches, God-knows-what!"

The Supervisor felt a sudden depression of spirits. You couldn't come out on any kind of mission without having to think of fire.

Beyond the houses they turned in at the Guard Station. Tony, the packer, was in charge there. He had everything ship-shape; the saddle-horses and the pack-mules all looked fine.

Driving back past the houses, they saw fewer women this time.

"Guess we rate only one look," said the Supervisor.

"There's Jewel again—*Hi-ya, Jewel!*—and she's sure been in and put on the lip-stick since we went by before."

"What about her?"

"Looks like a tart, if ever I saw one. But, matter-of-fact, far as I know, she's all right. Married to a fellow runs an engine over at Magna—no children though. Reads all the confession and movie magazines. No harm in her, I guess. Just takes it out in imagining."

They turned off to the right below Idylhurst, and went up the steep road along Strawberry Creek. Bart let the pick-up drop back to low gear. The road, they decided, would have to be entirely relocated before lumber-trucks could use it. They swung around the south end of Swayback Ridge, came to the low saddle connecting Swayback and Cerro Gordo, and stopped to look things over.

They could see down the winding course of Kelly Creek to the cliff-like face of Reverse Ridge four miles to the north.

"That's something!" said Bart.

"Yes," the Supervisor agreed, but he was appraising more carefully. To the right were a couple of big patches of worthless brush, scars of old fires, showing up as beautiful bright green stretches among the darker trees. But the rest of it, forming the eastern face of Cerro Gordo, was fine mature forest of mixed conifers. With practiced eye he picked out the different species—the orange-colored bark of the ponderosa pines; the dark, almost black, trunks of the Douglas firs, the red-brown fluted columns of the incense cedars.

"A lumber company won't like such big percentage of cedar," he said. "Otherwise it's a fine logging chance."

He waited a moment for an answer, and then turning to look, he sensed that Bart was standing there tense and hostile.

"Oh, come on, Bart," he said good-naturedly, "that's what trees are for, isn't it?"

"It's a mighty pretty stretch of trees. I've known it for twenty years. Why couldn't we just keep it for people to look at?"

"That's National Park stuff, Bart. You know that! We're a working concern. That stuff down there is crying out to be built into houses. As it stands, it's fire-bait. Think of all the down-timber in there. Look at the snags and the snag-tops. Why, right from here I can count—one, two, four, six. . . . Oh, no use even trying to count!"

"Yeah, quite a few dead trees."

"You know, Bart, it's funny. I guess most people agree with you. But still it's funny. Here's what I mean. When people pick out human beings to admire, they want vigorous young athletes, and juicy girls. Look at the pictures in any magazine. But when they look at trees, they admire doddering old things with gray hair and one foot in the grave, or paunchy middle-aged ones. Look at that cedar there! Maybe it's beautiful, but you know as well as I do that it's full of rot-holes. It's the opposite number of some sapless old guy who's maybe got a lot of property stored up but has his teeth all plugged with gold and his joints out of shape with arthritis. For myself, I'll take that vigorous young forest across from your ranger-station."

As the pick-up bumped and lurched up the steep grade toward Cerro Gordo Lookout, Bart was still silent. What the

Super had been saying, it made some sense—or did it? It was a lot, when you thought about it, like some guy saying to you: "Look here, Bart, you've been married thirty years now, and Jane's not what she used to be. Why don't you throw her out, and start chasing some peppy young thing?"

The Super, towering high up on the seat beside him, was silent too, and on this road, because of high fire-hazard, you couldn't smoke a cigarette to ease the tension.

Bart was glad when they swung around the hairpin turn, and came suddenly to the tree across the road. They looked it over.

It had been a hundred-fifty-foot cedar. The stroke had run well down it without much damage, and then in the unpredictable way of lightning-strokes it seemed to have exploded. Thirty feet high, the butt still stood, not much damaged, although without the foliage it was as good as dead. The upper part, splintered a little but really sheared off rather neatly, had fallen across the road. It lay mostly to the right, so that they had to make only one cut through the forty-inch trunk. Then they could roll the log off to the lower side, and the roadway would be clear.

Bart unlimbered the cross-cut saw, and they got to work. It was convenient enough sawing—about the right height and no need for wedging.

As the saw bit in, Bart began to feel a sudden satisfaction. The physical labor gave vent to what he could not say. He whipped the saw back a little faster. He felt the Super respond to the new rhythm, and whip his own end back a little faster too.

They rested, and when they began again, Bart set the pace faster. "Give that thing to me," he muttered to himself, as he jerked the saw back. Again he quickened the rhythm a little: "Give that thing to me. . . . Oh, you're trying to get it, are you? . . . No, you don't, give it here!" He liked to feel the sweat roll. He'd make the Super drag his tail!

Bart had weight and knew how to use it; he had the knack of the long-practiced woodsman. But as he now and then stole a glance across the tree he saw the Super still going strong. The Super had the leverage of long arms and legs, and he was fifteen years younger.

Bart pushed the rhythm up a notch still. The Super would have to cry "Uncle" soon; he was too much of an office-worker to take it.

But Bart himself was breathing hard. Then in a sudden awful moment he realized that the Super was now setting the pace. Bart took it back from him in two quick jerks that made the sawdust spurt. Then the tree itself settled matters by giving a loud crack and flopping down in the roadway with a three-foot splinter still on its lower side.

Bart relaxed gratefully, his lungs sucked air with relief, and without thinking, he began unashamedly to wipe his forehead. Then, as he looked across in embarrassment, he saw the Super doing the same thing. He felt a little foolish and small-boy-like. He wondered whether the Super realized.

The road ended not so far from there, and they had to walk the last hundred yards up a rocky trail.

"See!" said the Super, stopping to point. Looking a little pathetic, the sprawled length of a three-foot rattlesnake lay a few feet from the trail, its head thoroughly crushed. "Looks as if the lady could take care of herself!"

"I told you she could. If any guy wanders in here, he'd better not start to get fresh."

"She took the rattles too," said the Super, pointing to the severed tail.

Going ahead they followed the trail up a rock-slide, and

then saw the tower. The girl waved from the high catwalk.

When they had climbed up, Bart did the honors.

"Judith, meet Supervisor Jones."

"The Lookout is honored," said the girl, in a curious third-person way. Then she and Bart started chattering, even kidding each other.

Wearily, the Supervisor felt just a little out of it. He envied Bart that warm flow of feeling—for trees or for people—that made everyone happy. All he himself could do for the moment was to glance around, in a quick and unobtrusive way. The whole place was clean and neat as a pin—windows like crystal. Well, that didn't mean too much. The grapevine—Bart, himself, like as not—would have tipped her off that a brass-hat was on the prowl, and so she would have polished the windows. She looked all right just the same—tall and strong-looking, California type, light-brown hair but dark eyes, must be about five-feet-eight, as tall as Bart all right. She was wearing a dark-green man's shirt, open at the neck, and what looked like her best gray slacks—in honor of visitors. He saw what Bart meant by the shoulders, but there were good bulges below. A fine attractive girl!

She and Bart were still rattling on. Lookouts either seemed to forget how to talk, or else they broke out like a phonograph record.

Judith Godoy realized suddenly that she was not being polite to the Supervisor; after all, she was hostess. The best she could think to say was a silly: "I like Cerro Gordo," but she smiled when she said it.

It was an ice-breaker anyway. The Supervisor just said, "That's good!" but he smiled too. When he smiled she saw that he wasn't any longer a poker-face, or a sour-puss either. He had a good smile.

"I've got some coffee on for us. But I'd like you both to come out on the east catwalk. There's something I want to ask about."

Through the binoculars she showed them the puzzling little brownish-reddish patch on the hillside above Grizzly Creek. Of course, Bart knew it right off.

"That's the dump from the old Golden Queen mine. They worked it back in the seventies."

"What was it—gold?"

"Yes, that's all they get around here, and not too much of that any more, thank God!"

The girl looked so blank that the two men laughed, and she felt as if a little tension had eased between them.

"Yes," said the Supervisor, "there's nothing I hate worse than a lot of jippo miners mucking around in a forest. They take out five dollars' worth of gold—and what good is the stuff?—and they start a hundred dollars' worth of erosion. What would you do, Bart, if a dredger or doodle-bug moved into Reverse Meadow?"

"Me?—I'd probably kill someone with my bare hands!"

"And besides, miners can be careless with fire."

At the last word, all three of them suddenly glanced around. No, no smoke. But it doesn't matter, thought the girl, where you start, you end up at fire, in this business. She swung back to mining.

" 'Golden Queen'—that's a pretty flossy name!"

"Miners ran that way," said Bart. "Sounds rich. They were a superstitious bunch of—bunch of fellows. Always naming a mine after one that had been rich somewhere else—Gould and Curry, or Caribou. And they thought it was lucky to name them after something that had just happened. Look at the names of old mines over there. There's the Accidental, Cinnamon Bear, Spitcat, Broken Nose. A fellow saw a wildcat that morning he located the mine, and it stood and snarled and spit at him a second or two before it broke into the bushes. I used to know the old fellow that named the Broken Nose."

"Say, Bart," she heard the Supervisor saying, "all those mines must be close to where that lightning struck the other day."

"That's right!" said Judith Godoy out loud this time. "No matter how it starts, it comes back to fire. I can't see any smoke over there, but I wish you two would look—since you're here."

So the three leaned against the railing on the east catwalk, and looked out across the ridges, and were silent for a minute. Though they looked for smoke, thoughts also coursed through their minds. And though all three looked at the same trees and ridges, the thoughts were different.

The girl put hers into words, though silently, for she was one who thought in words. "This is my country, now," she thought. "Even if I never come back, I'll never forget it now. And yet I know it only by looking across the tops of the ridges. The flashing little streams in the canyons where the trout are jumping, all the glades and the meadows—they're mysteries. I know this side of Swayback and Reverse as well as I know my room in Berkeley, but their other sides I know as little as the other side of the moon."

As for Bart, the Ranger, he did not form words even silently, for the thoughts were vague and deep feelings more than thoughts which make sentences. But something drew tight in his throat, and his heart throbbed a little. Twenty years of his life were in that country, and in his throat and his heart-beat swelled up the old memories of fish he had caught and trails he had climbed, of sunrises and sunsets, of new moons and old moons, of deer he had watched without shooting and mink he had watched without trapping, of the rough bark of great trees where he had rested his hand, of fires he had fought, of rainstorms and snowstorms, of red dust rising and of horses he had ridden, of his wife laughing on a spring morning among cedars, of his son and daughter growing up taller every year like the young pines—and there was no end!

But the Supervisor, like the girl, thought in words. "It's a good enough stretch of country, grows trees pretty well. That's what we really should consider it, a farm. Some farmers grow wheat or cabbages; we grow trees. That's all there is to it. It takes a season to grow a good cabbage, and a century or so to grow a good saw-log. Yes, all this country out here that they call the Basin is over-ripe, and we ought to cut it, selectively, of course. Otherwise, there's likely to be a fire—Well, I guess the girl was right, we always come back to it."

Then he said aloud, "No, I don't see any smoke over there."

"Me, neither," said Bart.

Then in the pause all three heard the plane.

5

The air was rather bumpy as they flew low over the ridge. Then suddenly the gorge of Potter Creek opened up below them, and the Dispatcher saw the lumber-mill at its bottom, not sending up much smoke at the moment. Ahead, a little to the right and almost level with them, was the tower on Cerro Gordo.

The pilot was trying to speak over the noise of the engine. "What y'say, Jim?"

"Want to buzz the lookout, Arn? I hear it's a girl now."

"O. K.," said the Dispatcher, sounding cheerful, but with inward reservations. He did not really want to buzz the lookout. Jim had been a P-51 pilot, and what happened when he buzzed a lookout did things to the Dispatcher's stomach and nervous system. Still, he couldn't let Jim think so.

The earth rolled suddenly as the plane banked more sharply than necessary. Though it was only a slight change of direction, Jim had to get what kick he could out of flying a four-seater crate.

Now the steep western slope of Cerro Gordo seemed to be rising up to crash against them. It was an illusion that always bothered the Dispatcher a little, even though he had done a lot of flying over mountainous terrain. He spontaneously fingered his parachute harness, but a parachute was no use in such circumstances anyway.

"Look," said Jim, "she's got visitors."

The Dispatcher had a sense of relief when he saw the pick-up truck.

"Oh, yes," he said, "that's the Supervisor. He said he might be coming up here. Better not try any buzzing when he's there."

"Right! Wouldn't hurt to fly kind of close, would it?"

"I guess not."

The Super, Bart, and the girl, all of them were there. They waved as the plane went by—close to the tower, level with the catwalk. Jim wobbled the wings, and then jumped the plane with a little zoom.

For a moment the Dispatcher thought of asking Jim to circle the tower while he got into touch with the Supervisor over the radio. But he really had no message or question, and if the Supervisor had any, he would be on the radio himself.

The heavily forested and more gently sloping eastern side of Cerro Gordo was falling away beneath them now.

"That Lookout's not bad," Jim was saying loudly, over the engine-noise. "Bet she would make good cheesecake. When did you Forest-Service boys get the nice idea of having pretty girls for lookouts?"

"Oh, the war did it mostly, like a lot else. I guess right now pretty near half the lookouts in Region 5 must be girls—well, women, anyway."

"How about giving me the telephone number for that one?"

"That's easy! *One long, three short.* Find her at home any time. Only remember, half the lookouts in the Forest will be listening in. . . . But, say, change your course a bit. Patch of gray rock there on the ridge! Head over that, and you'll be about right."

The plane banked suddenly again, and a moment later— high enough so that it was not startling—they flew over the south face of Reverse Ridge. That face was so steep and dry that it supported only a thin growth of sun-loving ponderosa pines. The top of the ridge was largely bare outcroppings. But the better watered north slope, where the streams flowed down into Reverse Creek, was densely forested with shade-loving Douglas firs. Ahead, to the left, was the bright green of a big brush-field; tall blackened snags towered up high above the thick low-growing manzanita. To the right of the brush-field was the little grass-grown open space of Reverse Meadow, now looking more brown than green. In any color it was a comforting sight—about the only place in all this country where you had a decent chance to set a plane down, and live.

The Dispatcher pointed to the mouth of the gorge where Wilson Creek came out into the flat. Jim picked up a little altitude and went in level at 5100. This meant that they were a thousand feet above the creek and several hundred above the ridge to the south. But they were flying smack at the slope of Howell Mountain, and had to allow for room to turn.

This was what he had come for, and the Dispatcher watched the north slope of the ridge as they flew past. Scouting by air always sounded better than it really was. When you actually got there, you had to cover a lot of acreage with your eyes, and even at the speed of a slow plane you went over it too fast.

When they got close to the mountain, Jim swung around, and they went down the ridge. Since this was the most likely place for a strike, they kept close down to the tops of the trees. It was easy flying, for in this direction the ridge sloped down gently ahead of them and the wide-open low space above Reverse Meadow gave plenty of room for maneuvering.

The Dispatcher looked for a smoke, or for any tree that might have been struck lately. No luck!

As they came down over the snout of the ridge where it fell away sharply to the meadow, they were at 4600. They circled, climbed to 5100 again, and this time went up Onion Creek. The Dispatcher crawled to the seat behind Jim, and looked out to his left at the south slope of the ridge, now well below the plane again.

"If I had my old P-51," Jim yelled back suddenly, "I could fly right up these canyons just as well as down, and then climb out at the top end."

"We go too fast as it is. If you had your old P-51, we'd be going so fast these pine trees would look like turpentine!"

He wished that Jim had not said anything. Having to reply had diverted his attention for a moment, and at the rate a plane moved that meant the slighting of perhaps an acre of ground that might have been the very place for seeing a wisp of smoke.

Again they turned, uncomfortably close against the side of the mountain. This time they flew down the ridge to the south of Onion Creek.

After that they made all the four runs again for a double check. Nothing showed.

"Might as well be heading for home," said the Dispatcher. "No smokes, eh?"

"No smokes that I can make out," the Dispatcher corrected. "Of course, half the places, I can't really see to the ground under these big trees, and there's a fairly thick understory of bushes and young trees."

"Why don't you send a man in on foot then?"

"We don't know exactly where the strike was, and it would take him a month to scout as much country as we have this afternoon."

Well, it was a duty to be done, and he had done it. But the Dispatcher felt a little frustrated. Besides, the air over the ridges in late afternoon was bumpy, and his stomach and head didn't feel too strong.

"Let's get some altitude," he said. "I'd like a general look-around." And also, he thought, the air would be smoother.

At ten thousand feet—better than five thousand above the rocks on Reverse Ridge—the Dispatcher was happier. Some people would have said that from such an altitude the country looked just like a map. But that was fine with him. Much of his life was spent with maps, and he could get enthusiastic over a good one. From where he was, he could see Reverse Creek to the north, and Bacchus Creek to the south, both seeming to flow the wrong way. Where Bacchus ran into Onion at Onion Flat the two really met head-on.

All the ridges beneath, looking flattened from this altitude, stood out mostly in two shades of color—the dark green of trees, and the bright green of brush-fields. There was too much brush, and after every fire there was likely to be more of it. In a hundred years there might not be much else, if they weren't careful. Look what had happened, the professors said, in Greece and on the mountains all around the Mediterranean.

Besides the two greens he could make out the gray patches of rock on Reverse Ridge and Cerro Gordo, and the brown of the ripe grass in Reverse Meadow. Here and there a stream flashed brightly, or a red line along a ridge marked the course of a dusty mountain road.

Raising his eyes from what was directly beneath him, he looked northward. The blunt top of Lassen stood out clearly. A hundred miles farther still, he made out the two cones of Shasta; the lower slopes were hidden in haze, and the white tips just seemed to float in the sky.

The circling of the plane brought the eastern horizon into view, and he saw the main ridge of the Sierra; the boundary between Barlow and Rabbitbrush Districts. The Butte, rising a little over nine thousand feet, was the highest point in the Forest. It was black rock, but the other peaks stood out gray and glistening, reflecting back the rays of the afternoon sun. In that high country there were only patches of trees, but down around seven thousand began the solid forest of red firs. "Asbestos forest" they called it hopefully, because it was too moist and cold up there to burn well—at least, not very often. Still lower down and closer to him, he could half see and half imagine the infinitely irregular line where the firs began to thin out and the blue-green sugar-pines to take over.

But the plane still circled, and now he looked out over the flattish top of Cerro Gordo far below him. There was more haze toward the west in the lower country. Down there in the foothills the State boys were as usual having a few grass- and brush-fires on their hands. Still he could again half see and

half imagine the lines where mixed conifer gave way to ponderosa, and it again gave way to all the scrubby stuff of the
lower foothills.

His stomach felt better now. Partly it was the less bumpy
air. Partly also, he knew, it was this having had a look around.
He felt easier, for now he knew that during the hour in which
his assistant had been handling things no fire had blazed up.

"Well, Jim," he said, "let's get home."

8

Like the trees, the names also covered the mountains. They
too were rooted deep.

Oldest of all was that of little Waupomsy Creek, for it alone
carried a name that the Indians gave it, though no one still
remembered why.

Next came the emigrants of the covered wagons; from far
off they named The Butte, for it stood as a high landmark,
and there was none to compare with it.

Then came the miners, so feverishly in haste that they
hardly stopped to give names at first. So they said North Fork
and Middle Fork and South Fork, and North Fork of South
Fork. But later, they named the streams, because they followed
the streams and dug their gold there—Strawberry Creek and
Onion Creek and Rabbitbrush Creek, for what grew there;
Rock Creek, for the rock at the crossing; Buck Creek, for a
tall buck who stood and pawed the earth proudly at the dawn,
before they shot him; Grizzly Creek, for a bear seen at twilight, and to miners all bears were grizzlies. They named
mines for good omen, and streams after them—Sheba Creek,
Caribou, and Empire. Reverse Creek they named because it
seemed to flow against the grain of the country. Polkville,
they named for a president. Also they called streams for the
men who lived or mined or died there. (Happy thought—to

have a cool clear running stream forever as a memorial! And when the trout are rising, who cares what manner of man in his life was Kelly or Curran, or Hart or Jack or Potter?)

After the miners came the sheepherders. Like all men, they named the places which mattered to them—the springs and passes and flats and meadows. Poison Spring, they called it, because an herb grew there that poisoned the sheep. They named Bear Creek, not Grizzly, because they knew animals and were not given to overstatement.

After the sheepherders came the lumbermen. By Sawmill Creek you can tell them. They named Sugar-pine Point and Lodgepole Flat, for they knew one tree from another. They founded the town of Suffolk, but it was South Fork at the beginning.

Last of all came the foresters, and since they must always know quickly and surely where to send a crew to a fire, they named all that was left—the hills and ridges, the little creeks and lakes. The artificial townships they named artificially by the alphabet—Caaba, Cabbage, Cackleberry, Daadlar, Dabney, Dactyl—names to be easily distinguished even when the radio crackled.

There was humor in the names, as in Bacchus Creek—not the god of wine, but only a discreet spelling for a stream which seemed to run backwards.

There was memory of victory in Cerro Gordo. There was pride of a battle-hero in Barlow, though few remembered now the "boy-general," who charged at the Bloody Angle.

So, from the seeding of the years, from the men who had gone before, the names like the trees covered the mountains.

THE ENGLISH SHIPS dropped anchor, and the men of the cities and sheep-walks and plowed fields looked shoreward. Beyond the sand and the blight of the salt-spray, the forest rose wall-like, solid-fronted as a jungle. In their first homeward-carried tales was the wonder of the trees, and the poet wrote:

> The cedar reaching high
> To kiss the sky,
> The cypress, pine,
> And useful sassafras.

Later, when they landed and built towns and explored inland, the forest still went before them. "All the country," wrote John Smith, "is overgrown with trees."

If you could have flown high above that land, westward through a summer's day—in this manner the continent would have unrolled beneath. . . . First, as the sun rose behind you and shadows stretched far ahead from the ridges of the first mountains, you saw only the tops of the trees, unbroken broad-leaf forest of oak and ash, poplar and beech, chestnut and hickory. But later above the first flat lands, you noticed

64

little openings and meadows. They grew larger, until the prairies lay like grass-green lakes within the darker shore-line of the trees. Then, when the sun was hardly yet at noon, the grass-lands were no longer lakes in the forest, but the woods were islands in the grass. They shrank back into thin fingers reaching off along the stream-courses, westward. And as the sun swung ahead into the west, you saw the grass during the passage of an hour or two. There were trees again on the western mountains, but they were pines, and stood thinly, as if struggling against some stronger power; then at last came the sunset on the western shore, where the hills and mountain-slopes were forest-covered, but only grass grew in the valleys.

Thus by the intricate working of rain and snow, of lightning and fire, the pattern of trees and grass once lay upon the continent.

2

In the light of day the grayish-white smoke, rising in tiny billows and puffs, drifting off with the breeze, had been the chief evidence of the fire. In the darkness of night the smoke was invisible, and the line of glowing coals, where the fire was eating into the duff of needles and twigs, was the chief manifestation of its life.

A big owl, flitting ghost-like on noiseless wings, passed into the smoke unknowingly. The great eyes blinked, and at the pungent bite the lungs reacted in a sudden sneeze. Then the speed of flight carried the bird beyond the drift of smoke.

From the branch of a pine-tree, up-wind, a wildcat eyed the glow suspiciously. Like the squirrel, he knew nothing of fire, and did not even sense that his own eyes glared back at the redness with a strange reflected light. Unlike the squirrel he was incurious, and he was also hungry. He returned to his hunting, sniffing through the underbrush to pick up the scent of squirrel-nests or roosting birds.

The fire burned steadily and quietly. During the day it had eaten ahead some dozen feet through the duff, now and then blazing up as it ignited a cone or larger twig. After sunset it had done little more than hold its own, but nevertheless it was stronger than on the preceding night. Its front glowed in an unbroken though wavy line ten feet long. The fire was stronger because, having worked uphill and a little away from the tree's base, it had come to a spot where the duff was deeper, had now eaten down an inch or more, and beneath a little blanket of ash had found shelter from the dampness of the night.

Moreover, by growing only a little larger the fire enabled itself to grow larger still. Continuously, as its increased heat prevailed over the cold and dampness, its miniature flames reached out to more and more fuel. Thus the fire grew stronger still and larger, as a war, beginning with some frontier incident, augments and spreads, and in the end engulfs great peoples.

The fire had a look of tenacity and permanence—a beachhead force, after its first precarious days, now dug in and consolidated; an infection, once superficial and combatable by the natural forces of life, now eaten deeply into the tissues and awaiting only some favoring moment to spread throughout the whole body.

A puff of wind moved up the canyon. High above the ground, the tips and upper branches of the pines and firs swayed back and forth. Closer to the ground the air seemed scarcely to move faster. Nevertheless the dull red glow brightened to a luminous and more sinister orange, and for a moment even seemed yellow. Little flames licked upward. Then the upper branches ceased swaying, and the orange dimmed into a steady red.

3

Dave Halliday sat on a high stool at a high desk, worked at putting the last touches on his weather-map, and was happy. The early morning sun was bright outside; the teletype machine was clicking merrily. He was wearing a pair of old tan-colored civilian pants, and a gray Navy shirt, open at the neck. Thank God, the Forest Service didn't go in for spit-and-polish!

He hung back on the hooks the rubber stamps with their familiar captions: LOW, HIGH, cT, S/мРк. He gave the map a last appraising glance, and was ready to get to work on what looked like a not too difficult forecast.

This was Thursday, and since he was out of touch with the weather, he checked back as far as Monday. That had been a typical summer situation. A massive Pacific High dominated all the oceanic part of the map, and extended a long drooping nose into the continent, through British Columbia down into Montana. Northward of the high there was a weak storm in Alaska and another in Manitoba. Nearer home, California lay in a long trough of low pressure stretching up from the Mexican plateau. He looked closer, and saw thunderstorm-symbols recorded for some of the Sierra Nevada stations. That would be the work of some Gulf-of-Mexico air having its last fling. The isobars on the map showed him how that moist tropical air must have flowed up the Rio Grande valley, and cut loose with magnificent fireworks when it hit the mountains of New Mexico and Arizona. Not much energy was left in the little of it that got over those mountains and worked north along the Sierra Nevada. The few lightning storms it managed to release, however, certainly kept the boys worried around here—they were even jumpier than seemed necessary, though being a newcomer he shouldn't judge.

The Tuesday and Wednesday maps showed no thunderstorms; otherwise, no significant change for the region of his special interest. The two storms moved eastward. The trough of low pressure over California shrank back a little.

That brought him to today, Thursday. It looked, to tell the truth, remarkably like Monday, still showing the trough of low pressure over California, the massive high out at sea, and the two storms to northward. Of course, the storm now over Manitoba was the one which had been in Alaska on Monday, and the one now over Alaska was new.

But as he looked more carefully, he saw that there had perhaps really been a change. Any good meteorologist could have told at a glance that Monday had been a typical summer day; it might have been in July. But there was a touch of autumn about Thursday. That was a funny way to put it perhaps, sounded like a nature-fan looking at the woods. There was something in it, just the same.

The new Alaskan storm was what showed the change most. Its center was two hundred miles south of where the other center had been on Monday. In fact, this storm was really over the Gulf of Alaska rather than over Alaska. It was a somewhat more intense storm too—lower pressure, stronger winds. The curves of the isobars showed where it pushed southwestward, denting in the top of the Pacific High. That storm would bear watching, he decided. It might even be bringing in the rain that the people around here were waiting for, holding their breath.

Nevertheless, the summer weather would certainly hold for another day. He tapped off a local forecast which could have been adequately enough expressed in the two words, "No change."

4

Badger Hill Lookout picked up a smoke close to the Highway at 11:32, and a minute later got the report in. . . .

"Come on, you *bastards!*" yelled the Fire Crew Foreman at Suffolk Ranger Station. "Some *God-damned son-of-a-bitch* on the State Highway threw his cigarette out the window." They ran for the tanker. . . .

The Dispatcher had Barlow Ranger Station on the line. "Get down fast as you can, Bart. She looks mean!" He broke the connection, and said, "Get me Sheba!" without even hanging up. Then he heard the siren. "Pretty good getaway!" he thought, as from the corner of his eye he saw the big red tanker swing into the highway with a roar, the crew strapped to their seats along the sides and swaying with the roll. . . .

All over Suffolk and Sheba and Barlow Districts men were dropping tools between two strokes and cutting off conversations with unended sentences. They were running for trucks and starting engines. Radio waves were searching out after those beyond the reach of telephones. The siren let loose at Neva Lumber Mill. "Good *Christ!* A fire!" Far in the woods the buckers and fallers let their saws go dead. . . .

The Supervisor slid his wheels to a stop, and ran for the Dispatcher's office. He caught the Dispatcher between calls.

"Where is she, Arn?"

"In Gabbro! Right by the highway!"

"Smack in Deadman's Corner!"

"Merriam's Mill again, maybe!"

"Well, I'd better be gettin' there!"

And the Supervisor's long legs ran for the car again. . . .

5

All the lookouts had learned about the fire within a few minutes, and all of them who had any chance to see the smoke had lined up the proper angle and were watching.

From Cerro Gordo it would be at about 212, but a high flat-topped ridge blocked the view. Nevertheless in almost no time at all the smoke-column puffed up from behind the ridge. The jump that her heart gave really surprised her!

She had seen smokes already, but either they had been far away beyond the Forest boundary, or else they had been poor litle things which had never been very dangerous and had been jumped on before they could get going.

But this one was different. Even though it was close to twenty miles away, she could see the smoke billow up and rise higher as she looked at it. That fire was rolling!

But she learned more about it from the radio than from watching. They had orders to stand by on the radio so as to ease congestion on the phone lines, and she heard a lot that went buzzing back and forth on her wave-length.

No one could stop to tell a green lookout just what was happening, or likely to happen. But from what she knew of the general background of the Forest already and from the scraps of radio-talk, she soon pieced together a good deal of the picture.

They were particularly afraid of this fire because it was in what they called Deadman's Corner. That was the southwestern part of the Forest, and presented the worst fire-hazard because the country had been recently cut over, and the slash from the logging operation was still on the ground. Also this fire was close to the old Merriam's Mill burned area, and that made everybody doubly jumpy—a kind of psychological hazard.

She had already been long enough on the Ponderosa to know about the Merriam's Mill fire—or just "The Merriam's Mill" as they said. It had swept ten thousand acres, killed two men, and burned some houses, and a barn with horses and poultry. It must have been about eight years back, although she didn't know exactly. But she knew at least that among the personnel of the Forest it was a landmark like the *Mayflower*. Those who had come in since that time were new-comers; really to belong, you had to date back to the Merriam's Mill. There was even a long rambling song about it that they sang at picnics and other get-togethers.

But though she kept huddled over the radio a good deal, she also made her rounds of the catwalk, and kept looking, particularly toward where she had seen the lightning-stroke. Just because there was a fire in Deadman's Corner was no guarantee there would be no fire in the Basin also. And she was already enough of a lookout to feel that she would die of chagrin if Humbug Point or that old goat on Horse Mountain picked up a smoke somewhere under the nose of Cerro Gordo.

6

The Supervisor had made a fast run. He pulled in to the fire at 12:11, as he logged himself. The Suffolk ranger was on the job, and doing all right. The Supervisor decided to scout the fire himself, and went all the way around it. He was not noticeably tired when he got back; with his light body riding on his long legs he enjoyed a romp through the woods, even on a hot day. There was nothing special for him to do, and he would have liked to get out on the line with a shovel or McLeod, but that was bad for morale. If the men saw him working with a shovel, they would think things really had gone all to pieces. So he stood around and took it easy. He was something of a fifth wheel at a fire the Ranger was handling already. Still, there's a use for a fifth wheel sometimes. Not having anything to do itself, it can look around and see whether the other wheels are working all right. . . .

Bart pulled in from Barlow at 12:42.

"Hi, Super," he said, "you look as if you had things controlled. Guess I shouldn't have hurried!"

Without stopping to catch breath, Bart went in to the hottest part as a sector-boss. But at first he was a sector-boss with practically no crews under him, and he did a lot of ax-work himself, because no one else around seemed ever to have swung an ax. When more crews came in, they were good men, loggers and mill-workers from Neva, and Bart laid his ax aside. But the sector was long and full of ravines, and he had to chase back and forth all the time. The afternoon was blazing hot, and the smoke was rolling low. By two o'clock he was black with soot and dog-tired. . . .

Dave, the meteorologist, got to the fire about two-thirty. There was nothing very important that he could do, but the Dispatcher had advised him to go to it and see what a fire was like, close up. He found it very interesting, and spent some time watching the smoke, and studying its whorls, and billows. He took some rough observations on rates of rise, and on the spur of the moment he jotted down a trial equation for heat-loss by radiation from a smoke-cloud. Most of all he was interested in the way the fire seemed to affect the light local winds. That might turn out to be a more immediately practical matter for forecasting. . . .

Arnold Sorenson, the Dispatcher, did not go to the fire at all. Instead, he sat in his office at Suffolk, ready to bite his nails, wishing he could walk along the fire-line just once and let down his nervous tension by physical work. A fire seen was often not so terrifying as a fire imagined. But already this quick flare-up, running swiftly through slash and young trees, had burned three hundred acres at least; in part of one afternoon an absent-mindedly-thrown cigarette-butt had cost more acreage than the Forest had lost in the whole season up to then.

He had talked here and there by telephone and radio, until he felt like a spider sitting at the center of a web. By now he had put the whole Forest on a war-footing. Many men and pieces of equipment were already at the fire; more of both were on the road, and would get there in time for the night-shift. He had talked with Zone Headquarters and with the Regional Office in San Francisco. The near-by forests were alerted. By a single telephone-call he could now start men rolling in from the Tahoe, the Plumas, and the Mendocino. Five hundred miles to the south a transport plane was being held ready at Burbank Airport, to fly north with a fire-team from the Angeles.

Then, as so often happened, but as you did not dare to hope, things eased off. At 3:29 the Super himself telephoned in: "We've got a line around her. Maybe we've got her hooked."

"That's sweet music!" said the Dispatcher.

Then it was like the Super to ask: "You haven't got anything started somewhere else, have you?"

7

On the steep canyon-side the little fire that had sprung from the lightning-stroke still ate slowly ahead in the duff of pine-needles. . . .

When a baby, weak but tenacious of life, lies in his cradle in village or city, no fairy-godmother is needed to make some predictions for the future. Any sensible person can foretell that, barring great cataclysms, the child's early life will be shaped almost entirely by the immediate environment, though in later years he will grow to the strength and dominance of manhood, and may then in some measure determine his own career and even the history of his nation.

During its four days of life the fire had been infant-like, wholly at the mercy of its surroundings, but growing a little larger and stronger. It tended always to advance up-slope, but also to follow the path of the afternoon wind, which blew up-canyon, at right angles to the slope. As a result, the fire split the difference between the two forces, and went sidling up-wards.

The canyon-side was so steep that many needles and twigs were washed down it in the autumn rains, and the duff was therefore not very deep. Because of the wide-spreading branches, the area around the base of the tree was especially bare. By now, however, having eaten ahead some twenty feet from the base of the tree, the fire had come to the place where needles from the growing-tips of the branches fell to the ground. Into this thicker duff the fire ate more deeply, and somewhat farther ahead a scattering of dry twigs offered even better fuel.

Still a little farther on, the dominance of the tall pine tree no longer suppressed all other growth, and before the circle of dominance of the next large tree took over, there was a tiny opening into which fell thousands of seeds from the neighboring pines and firs. Every year many seeds germinated, and bravely set out to reach upward to the tiny patch of open sky far above. Some of these saplings flourished for a few years, but they gradually lost the vitality of early youth. Always shaded by the taller surrounding trees, they grew scanty in needles and spindly, and became infected with disease. One or two of them, however, had managed to reach a height of fifty feet and a thickness of six inches before dying.

On the side of the opening nearest the fire lay the fallen trunk of one of these largest saplings. It was half decayed, and its butt was riddled with the passages of a community of carpenter-ants.

Beyond this dead trunk was a fairly open space and then the clump of young trees ranging in size from mere sprouts to unhealthy-looking saplings ten feet high. They were growing so thickly that they interfered with one another. In many places their lower branches, mostly dead and dry, were interlaced.

The duff, the little dead tree-trunk, the gentle afternoon wind—these at the moment and for the obvious future determined the life and growth of the wavering fire.

So, for a baby in the cradle, the temperature of the room, the judgment of the mother, or a chance-borne microbe far outweighs all wars, droughts, and revolutions. But eventually the child, grown older, will be caught up, for good or bad, in the larger scheme of things. While he lies in the cradle, his future may already be linked with an unusual melting of the distant polar ice, with the erosion of a near-by hillside, with the slow rotting of a beam in some distant house. . . .

On the steep slope of the canyon-side, still far from the little fire and not even in the direction of its advance, a large cone was lying. It had grown upon one of the Jeffrey pines of which this particular stretch of forest was largely composed. At some time in the past season, having shed its seeds, it had dropped from a branch eighty feet above the ground, rolled some yards down the steep slope, and come to rest against a dry twig.

The cone was of the usual Jeffrey-pine type, and thousands of similar ones lay on the same ridge. It was about nine-inches long and nearly eight in diameter, thus lacking little of being spherical, and resembling in general form a fat acorn, or an old-fashioned wooden top with a blunt spinning-point. . . .

Six miles away, in a brushy spot near the top of Reverse Ridge, a good-sized rabbit was feeding. This rabbit had lived a peaceful and undistinguished life, and had never been more than half a mile from the spot where he had been born. He had spent his time in sleeping, feeding, escaping his enemies, and now and then begetting his own kind.

On this afternoon in September the rabbit was feeding in an open spot. Suddenly, with a quickness which resembled a nervous reaction more than an end-result of observation and conclusion, he dashed straight ahead, and in less than a second had covered twenty feet, and was sheltered beneath a manzanita bush. Actually there had been bushes to the right and behind which were much closer, but by means of his powerful and long hind-legs the rabbit could get moving so much faster in a straight line ahead that he saved time by not attempting any other direction.

If he had been transported to open country, he would have exposed himself to his enemies by such tactics. Within his own narrow limits, however, there was always certain to be some kind of cover within a few yards in any direction. Although the rabbit's sudden bolting thus might give an impression of senseless panic, it was actually an efficient means of survival.

The medium-sized hawk which had caused the disturbance viewed the rabbit's disappearance with accipitrine philosophy. He was really hunting mice, and though he might make a gesture at larger game, a full-grown rabbit was not his prey, even if not quite beyond his ambition. He flapped his wings lazily to regain height, and slid off down-wind. . . .

Far in the Gulf of Alaska the cold front of a storm swept forward above a five-hundred-mile line of white-caps. Behind the front a strong wind was blowing from the north, pouring out cold air which had recently lain over the Alaskan mountains and thus doing its part in the continually necessary readjustment of heat and cold between arctic and tropics. . . .

Still much more distant from the Ponderosa Forest, to the west and north, an incipient storm was developing over the Bering Sea, beyond the farthest Aleutians. . . .

6

Long ago the forest first began to cover the ridges and the mountain-sides. Perhaps that forest was of sequoias, as ponderous themselves almost as mountains. Except for a few groves they vanished.

After them came other trees, smaller but still gigantic, rooting themselves in the ancient gravels and in the weatherings from the lavas and granites.

On the canyon-seamed western slope of that great uplifted block of land, in a broad belt, the forest grew. Yet at the very foot of the slope there was no forest, only the grass-land stretching upward from the broad valley with wide-spreading oaks scattered thinly, park-like. Then, just a little higher, stood the gray-green digger-pines, shabby trees harried by fire, crooked and broken, grasping desperately for life on the dry hillsides, growing in thin stands, still not to be called a forest.

Higher still, where canyons were deeper and ridges higher and where winter rains fell heavier, stood the ponderosa pines in rich green. They were not like the cringing digger-pines, but rose straight and burgeoning—freemen among trees, like hardy frontiersmen, facing the edge of drought, but not overcome by it. And with them began the forest.

A little farther and higher, and the feathery Douglas firs and bright-green incense cedars stood among the ponderosas, and for many miles up the slope the trees mingled, sharing the forest in harmony.

Next, higher still, began the blue-green of the sugar-pines —greatest of all pines. From butts eight feet thick the giant trunks sprang upward, two hundred feet and more aloft, and from the tips of the level-held branches the long cones dangled delicately.

With the sugar-pines, also, the Jeffrey pines began to mingle, and with them both, the firs—dark, with downward-sloping branches, but cones upright like stubby candles. Then at last, suddenly, nothing was left but the gloomy forest of the firs, for on those heights the snows of winter were stronger than the droughts of summer.

As the ponderosa pines held the frontier of the forest against the drought, so the red firs held it against the snow. But as the digger-pines flung themselves as a forlorn hope against the drought, so a few twisted hemlocks, lodge-poles, and white-barks struggled for their hard-held outposts in the country of the snow. And above those outposts, on the wind-swept heights, naked beneath the sky, was only the clean and deathly beauty of snow and ice and granite.

In 1586, as Sir Francis Drake sailed alongshore northward from Florida, his chronicler noted "one special great fire, which are very ordinary all alongst this coast." Four years later, those attempting to find Raleigh's lost colonists steered hopefully toward a smoke; arrived at the spot, they found to their surprise, "no man nor sign that any had been there lately." Next day they set off toward another fire—to find only "the grass and sundry rotten trees burning." In 1607, freshly landed on the Chesapeake shore, George Percy noted "great smokes" of burning woods. Thus, even before they built Jamestown, the English knew that they had come to a land of fire.

During three hundred years the American went west with the smell of smoke in his nostrils. In the early days he looked on fire as an ally against the forest—the often sinister forest that gave ground grudgingly to his ax-strokes and then sent its saplings to infiltrate into the hard-won clearing. Also, fire seemed part of the natural cycle of the country, like flood and snowstorm. Ardent lover of the land that he was, Jefferson wrote without concern of "fires which traverse whole coun-

79

ties." In those days even the most thoughtful were likely to say blithely: "Burning is good for the woods!"

But now and then they wondered. Sometimes, from fires burning far away, the sky grew dark, and ashes fell from heaven along with discolored rain. Then beneath a sun of tarnished brass the people looked at each other's yellow faces, and thought of Judgment Day. May 19, 1780, was New England's famous Black Friday.

Or, if home and farmland lay in the path of flame, you did not talk glibly—when wildfire broke from the woods, swept the hayfield, burned barn and horses, and sent mother and children running from the smoke-engulfed cabin. Sometimes there was no place to run to. The Miramichi fire of 1825 straddling the line between Maine and New Brunswick left a blackness almost as large as Connecticut, and burned one-hundred-sixty people. A balladist saw God's anger against the sinning children of Adam:

> *In order to destroy their lumber, and the country*
> *to distress,*
> *He sent the fire in a whirlwind from the howling*
> *wilderness.*

In the drier pine-forest of the Lake states, the settlers rapidly came to have difficulty in seeing that fire was good for the woods, or for anything else. At least, the fifteen-hundred dead at Peshtigo in 1871 were beyond conviction, and burning had not been good for a deadened stretch of Wisconsin pine as large as Delaware. Ten years later a bit of Michigan equal in size to Long Island went up in smoke which darkened the sun over all the northeastern states. At Hinckley in Minnesota the death-list passed four hundred. Year by year, also, the thousands of smaller fires swept through the standing timber, or in their fiery whirlwinds wiped out the brave green saplings of the second-growth.

In 1910, smoke from the Idaho fires drifted across the continent; people as far east as Montreal, perplexed and troubled, worked by artificial light in daytime. Westward, five hundred miles off California, a puzzled shipmaster logged the smell of smoke and haze interfering with observations.

By this time economists were predicting a timber-famine, and historians were pointing to deforested mountains to explain the fall of Rome. A little frightened, the Americans were at last ready to do something serious about wildfire.

2

"Life for the girl on the lookout was not nearly so monotonous as she had at first feared [*expected,* really]—at first expected it might be. One day, for instance, she had watched the smoke of a large fire billowing up over the southwestern horizon. On the next morning that fire was no longer appreciably active, but the smoke of yesterday had now been blown along by the wind and rested as a great gray blanket [*Blanket* is not the right word, but you might use *blanketed.*]—and blanketed all the valleys and ridges to the east. Her landscape seemed to be divided, half and half. Westward, everything was clear. Eastward she could scarcely make out the profile of Swayback Ridge, and as for the . . ."

She snapped out of it. No way for a healthy-minded girl to be behaving! Too much alone, maybe! But even when Bart and the Supervisor had been there, two days ago, she had really not cared too much about seeing them, even though she did burst out with talk. Something had happened. Once she had held out her hand to the world, and the world had slapped it. She wanted to be alone, until maybe something would happen again.

But all this thinking was really worse than putting it into

words. She went out to the catwalk, wanting at least to keep a good watch to the west where there was no smoke-drift. Looking over the railing to the ground, she saw one of the chipmunks. It was foraging among the rocks, making its nervous little dashes this way and that. She had become very fond of the two chipmunks, and sometimes she focused the binoculars on them from the catwalk, and brought them up to close range. They were the only animals she ever saw during broad daylight. Toward evening, though, three deer sometimes came up out of the forest boldly enough, and browsed on the bushes which grew among the rocks forming the open dome-like top of Cerro Gordo. And once in the deeper twilight she had seen something that might have been a small-sized bear.

As for birds, she saw a good many, but the hawk was the only one she had got to know individually. Glancing at her wrist-watch she saw it was nearly eleven-thirty; he was a little late today.

Going to the east catwalk, she looked down the slope toward the canyon of Potter Creek. And there was the hawk! Near midday the south breeze and some rising heat currents, she supposed, made a good up-draft. As usual, the hawk was just holding his wings steady, dipping and banking a little, and letting the air-current take him right up the slope of the mountain. He was beautiful to watch!

She looked down for the chipmunk, but it had vanished of course. All the chipmunks had to do was to pop into any of a thousand rock-crannies, and they looked out for themselves so well that she had never seen the hawk even bother to make a pass at them.

The telephone was having a fit of activity, but it was not her call.

She watched the hawk drift by, fifty yards to the north of

the tower and about level with the catwalk. Then he re-adjusted his wings a little, and like a plane going in for a landing, he slid off down-grade, over the tree-tops on the northeast slope of Cerro Gordo, toward Reverse Ridge, barely visible through the smoke-drift.

The phone was ringing again, and it was her call.

"Cerro Gordo speaking," she said.

"This is Arn," said the phone.

"Oh—sure," she blundered. "You're the Dispatcher at Headquarters. I didn't expect to be hearing from anyone far off like you—thought probably it was Bart."

"No, Bart's still down on the Hart Creek Fire. I imagine they're working him hard."

"How's it going?"

"Everything's quiet now. I'm having a quiet day. Unless we have a blow-up this afternoon, it'll be all over.—But what I called you for (now that Bart can't do it) was to see what your visibility was like today. I'm checking lookouts."

"It's bad, that is, to the east and south, where all that smoke from the Hart Creek Fire is blowing in.

"What I was afraid of. How about northeast, out toward where that lightning struck on Monday?"

"I can't see much of anything there.—How long will this smoke hang around?"

"Chances are it will be gone by morning. Don't worry *too* much about there being a sleeper over by Onion Creek. Horse Mountain may still be able to see in there. I'll check with him next. Besides, Slugger O'Neill has a trail-crew in by Caribou Lakes, and they would see it before it got too big.—Say, you aren't getting lonely up there are you?"

The voice had suddenly changed from serious to light, and she answered in kind:

"Gosh, no. I like to talk to myself too much."

"How about a boy-friend?"

"No—I'm off men! My last one turned out to be a heel."

"Hmm? Your voice sounds a little serious when you say that. You must be all set for the next one then."

"Didn't you notice when you flew by, day before yesterday? If that pilot had flown any closer, I was all set to make a leap at him from the catwalk."

"If that pilot had flown any closer, he'd have brushed the hair on your lip, baby, and I'd be in a wooden box right now. Well, so long!"

3

Still eating its way ahead through the duff, the fire was within a foot of the half-decayed tree-butt which sheltered the colony of carpenter-ants. Already in the last few days the fire had destroyed many of their foragers, but the colony was adjusted to a considerable and continual wastage of ant-power, and if its queen and bureaucracy were not disturbed, the large loss of individuals was of no importance.

The fire, burning closer, gradually cut off more and more of the radiating paths along which the foragers were accustomed to march forth in all directions on their legitimate business.

As the individual ants came near the fire and began to feel its heat, they were strangely affected. Since their bodily activities varied with the degree of heat, they were accustomed to move slowly on a cool day, rapidly on a warm one. Coming closer to the fire, they were subjected to a more than natural temperature, and their rate of motion became phenomenal. If these ants had been magnified to the size of race-horses and their speed correspondingly maintained, they would have been galloping at five-hundred miles an hour.

Perhaps their mental processes were also similarly stepped

up, for they seemed to lose normal controls and pass into a manic hysteria. At their abnormal speeds they dashed this way and that; frequently, having started in the direction of the fire, the violence of their rush carried them right into it.

Some of the foragers, however, although moving with equal aimlessness, returned to the nest. Doubtless they could deliver no coherent account of what had excited and alarmed them, but they must have been able to transmit their own perturbation. More and more ants emerged.

The base of the log became well covered with ants They ran back and forth, or stood and waved their antennae helplessly. Even there, the heat of the fire was affecting them.

If this had been a cloud-burst or even a small flood, the ants would not have been so frustrated. Somewhere in their communal memory existed a cubby-hole of what was to be done when assailed by water, and they would have begun to carry eggs to safer places, and otherwise to labor for the preservation of at least the nucleus of the colony. But in the evolution of the carpenter-ants apparently fire had been but rarely encountered, and in these cases had ended in such complete disaster as to preclude even the memory of it. The ants, therefore, were like the citizens of a town which is being overwhelmed by such a diabolically supernatural disaster as completely to un-man them.

The fire was now so close that many ants actually on the log became over-stimulated and hysterical. They moved faster and faster, like the molecules of a heating liquid. Hundreds perished, and even more hundreds poured out from the nest. The log grew so hot that it began to smoke, and all the ants within a radius of some inches were shriveled. From beyond this death-line dozens of others kept dashing forward to their destruction.

The whole end of the log began to smoke, and in spite of

the rottenness of the wood some flame arose. The interior of the nest grew warmer, and the ants within it, in their turn stimulated, poured out in numbers which made all who had preceded seem a mere scouting-party. Thousands were burned, but other thousands were lucky enough to gain the still unsmoking up-hill side of the log.

Now at last, as when Pyrrhus and the dire Ulysses raged in the streets of Troy, the fall of the city was near. Smoke penetrated the interior galleries of the nest. The many ants still hurrying along the narrow passageways were quickly suffocated, and their bodies sealed in a living tomb the unfortunate queen, her household, and the thousands of her eggs, the only hope of posterity.

An hour later the butt of the log was nearly consumed and all the ants had perished, with the exception of a comparative few who, by good luck instead of by design, still wandered about beyond the destructive reach of the fire. These few, however, were completely helpless because of the destruction of the nest, and must soon perish also.

The whole middle portion of the log was now smoking vigorously. This smoke, spreading somewhat and dissipating, mounted high above the tree-tops, and there mingled unobtrusively with the smoke which had blown in from the other fire far to the southwest.

4

Arnold Sorenson, the Dispatcher, had had only two years in forestry school, and was the last man to claim to be a scholar. Nevertheless he liked to read books, had a certain philosophizing attitude toward his work, and remembered from years back in high school the crabbed rendering of a line from Caesar's *Commentaries*. It came from some passage describing the legions thrown into confusion by a sudden attack:

"By Caesar all things must be done at once." He used to quote it to himself and feel a sympathy with Caesar at times like yesterday when he was organizing a fire.

When he had told the Cerro Gordo lookout that he was having a quiet day, he spoke only in comparative terms. He still had more than two hundred men mobilized at the Hart Creek Fire, but he was already planning demobilization for the late afternoon, if the fire did not blow up. The telephone was still buzzing constantly.

In an off moment a slightly alarming thought came to him. The fire which had blazed up so suddenly yesterday was close to a stream called Hart Creek, and to comply with the regulations that each fire must be distinctly named, he had followed the usual custom of pouncing quickly upon the nearest geographical feature. The alarming thought was that in his engrossment with hundreds of details he had not checked his master-list and that there might possibly have been another Hart Creek Fire already this year. Such a duplication of names would cause confusions which would be embarrassing and time-consuming.

Quickly he turned to the big ledger-like book which held the basic record of all fires. On a back page were entered under initial letters all the fires of the current season. Under H stood only three names: Howson Creek, Horse Creek, Heelstrap. He let out his breath in relief, and entered Hart Creek beneath Heelstrap.

Someone knocked, though the office door stood open. Looking up, the Dispatcher saw Dave Halliday, the weather-man.

"Come in, Dave," he said.

"They said you wanted to see me, sir."

"Yes, I wanted to talk with you more about how you can help us out. Now on this Hart Creek Fire—"

"Oh, you name them! We used to name typhoons in the Navy, but you have so many fires I thought you might just number them."

"We've named them in the Forest Service since I don't know when—helps keep the records straight, and helps in giving orders when maybe there's a lightning-bust and you have thirty fires going all at once. If somebody over a telephone gets one figure wrong, it throws out the whole thing, but a name doesn't get mixed up that way. Same thing with townships. Most Forests stick by the old numbering system, but we have code names. Instead of having to stop and figure out a lot of numbers and letters, our lookouts just check the name on the map and report a fire in Ectoplasm or Cackleberry or Biennial."

"Pretty fancy names!"

"Don't compliment me—I did it. It's a system. *Adder* means that the township is the A row along the north edge of the Forest, and in the D tier, fourth in from the western edge. Besides, I picked words that wouldn't get mixed up in transmission. Maybe the radio contact is bad, but still if Cerro Gordo says Eelgrass, you don't get it mixed with Edification, or Deerhound, or any other adjoining township. Oh, well—"

The Dispatcher paused, knowing that his hobby had run off with him.

"Sounds sensible to me!"

"Oh, the other Forests make fun of it. They say that we let a fire take off once because the lookout was hunting in his dictionary to find out how to pronounce Ahasuerus. But every Forest has its little touches of individuality, and that's one of ours. Well, what about your weather?"

"No change again. There's a pretty good storm off British Columbia, but I can't tell yet what she's going to do."

"You're no bluffer, are you?"

The young man looked up and smiled quickly. "You seem to be putting quite a bit of study on me, sir."

"I have to study men, on my job. As somebody said it once: Men are the easiest of all tools to get out of order. Take an ax or a McLeod, or even a tanker or a bulldozer—they may go to pieces on you, but in general you know what they're good for. But a man it's harder to tell about, and maybe he isn't even the same this year that he was last year."

5

When a child lies in the cradle, a fairy godmother would know that its later life will be entangled, not only with things, but also with certain people—perhaps a child lying in another cradle, or a chemist at work in a far-off laboratory, or a fanatic preaching in an obscure market-place. So also the life of a fire is entangled. . . .

"Slugger" O'Neill was a Fire-Crew Foreman in the Ponderosa. That season he had charge of five high-school boys, and they had been kept for most of the time, strategically, near Caribou Lakes. Their daily work was trail-clearance, but their chief reason for existence was to be an advance-crew for quick attack on any fire in that isolated region.

The boys were having a good time. They had been sent to several small fires, and had enjoyed the excitement. They were either athletes or wanted to be, and constantly talked about how the steady work of clearing and rebuilding the trails put them into shape for the football season. They admired their thirty-year-old boss tremendously for his physical prowess.

"Gee! That's great!" they would say, panting, when Slugger had beaten them all and still continued doing pushups.

Lying around the camp-fire, evenings, one of them would pipe up: "Tell us about that time you KO'ed the red-head."

Slugger's career in the professional ring still won him local homage. That career had actually been brief and not too glorious, ending in a lamentable three rounds at the Oakland Auditorium in which a light-footed young Italian consistently dodged Slugger's rushes and haymakers, and punched his face to beefsteak. But the boys loyally told each other that they bet Slugger could have been welterweight champion, "If he had really wanted to go ahead with it."

He had deserved his nickname. That at least was true of him. He had been a straightforward and hard-hitting fighter, and now and then he had brought the crowd to its feet yelling. He had also, luckier in battle than in the ring, fought from Utah Beach to Nuremberg as a sergeant of infantry.

On this day Slugger and the crew were making a short-cut, and the boy who was leading paused before a thick clump of brush.

"Where's the best way to get around it?" he said.

"Hell," said Slugger, coming up, "you don't get around it. You go through it."

With a sudden rush Slugger burst into the tangle. Branches bent and broke before him. With yelps of enthusiasm the boys came after him. Slugger was a great guy, all right! They'd follow him anywhere!

As they came out at the other side, one of the boys had a bleeding cheek from where the stub of a broken branch had raked it.

Barney Zulik, ex-Seabee, worked for the Larkin Lumber Company. His chief physical trait was the one which had called forth a grim witticism at a moment when the outfit was in a tight place on some now-forgotten islet. "Hell, Barney," one of his buddies had remarked, "if the Japs take us prisoner, they can't cut *your* head off. *You* ain't got no *neck!*"

Barney was a cat-skinner—an amazing profession, and a word of interesting etymology. First, in the old days of the frontier, there were bull-skinners. This term arose, by double hyperbole, to denote men who drove teams of oxen and were supposed to ply their long whips so constantly as to strip the skin off them. Later, as ox-teams vanished, the word became mule-skinner. Mules also grew rare. Caterpillar-tractors took over, and by inevitable shortening came to be know as cats. Then, by analogy and complex humor, the operator of a caterpillar-tractor came to be a cat-skinner.

Some say that all cat-skinners are maniacs. Certainly, to watch Barney in the woods you would have said that he fed insatiable lusts for power and violence. He crashed along, crushing down bushes and toppling thirty-foot trees. With his bulldozer blade he assailed the butt of a four-foot log, and threw it to one side. Up and down impossible-looking slopes, over loose rocks or outcrops, he careened with clanking treads.

"Barney is sure tough," said an admiring bucker, as he rested against the handle of his saw. "He's built tight together and tough, like a solid rubber ball."

"He's three parts fool, though," said the other bucker. "Some time he's gonna roll that thing right over on hisself."

"That'll sure be too bad. It'll make a big dent in that nice cat."

Bo Fox, in the language spoken along Second Street in Sacramento, was a "wino," that is, he was addicted to going on binges by means of the cheapest and rawest of local wines. Bo Fox, in the languarge spoken by the Forest Service, was a "pogy," a word of forgotten origins denoting a casual un-skilled laborer, of the kind recruited in large numbers to fight fires.

Doubtless he had once had a more dignified name than Bo, but he had ceased to use it. On the rare occasions when he laboriously had to sign his name, he found it convenient to get the whole signature down in five letters. Anyone believing that names and people should correspond would have been happy to observe Bo Fox. Like his name, he was small and insignificant. Such an observer would also have easily imagined a certain furtive and fox-like quality to the pinched face, and a suggestion of being hunted—as if Bo Fox expected momentarily to hear the bay of the hounds behind him.

But the comparison is not fair to that intelligent animal who generally carries his brush high and knows what he is about. Bo Fox was really rabbit-like. Or at best he was like some runt of the vixen's litter, small in body and warped in brain, who has survived only by slinking and scavenging. Since babyhood he had been rejected, and now his mind was full of many fears—of policemen, of violence, of bad dreams. But most of all he had a vague fear of being trapped, of seeing a blank wall ahead and hearing the door click shut behind.

Walking down Second Street, Bo was inconspicuous among the other winoes. He stopped from habit in front of the Federal Employment Agency, and looked at the bulletins. Various possible jobs were posted, but he had paid in advance for another night at his flop-house and still had a little money in his pocket.

He went into a saloon, walked three steps toward the bar, and then looked back nervously as if afraid that someone had bolted the doors behind him or that the doorway itself had been metamorphosed into a solid wall.

6

The Supervisor was in a dilemma which was not infrequent with him. If he kept away from the Hart Creek Fire, he might give his men the impression that he was not backing them up. If he stayed there, they might think he was too busy looking over their shoulders. Of course, he reflected, he might have had no problem at all if he had been one of those easygoing mixers named Harry or Joe, or called Skin or Slim instead of Super.

Anyway, it looked as if he could leave safely. Things had smoked up a bit in mid-afternoon, but now at five-thirty everything was quiet, and lines of men were passing through the timekeepers, checking out. He went over to the headquarters enclosure, and spoke to Bart:

"Guess I'll be heading in to Suffolk, Bart."

"O. K., Super. We'll look after things here all right."

"Hope you get away before too late yourself, Bart. You look tuckered." Then he regretted saying that, even though he meant to be friendly, for he saw Bart bristle a little; old-timers never liked any suggestion that they couldn't take it any longer.

"Oh, I'm fine, Super!" said Bart. "Didn't get to bed last night of course, but an old smoke-eater like me is used to that."

After the Super had left, Bart was willing enough to admit he was tired when he talked with Ben Roach, the Ranger of Sheba District and his oldest friend.

"Sure, I'm tired," he said. "I wouldn't admit it to him, though. When do you suppose we'll get away from here?"

"All they need now is a skeleton-crew," said Ben. "Once we get the mess ordered up a bit, we ought to be able to get ourselves released—ten o'clock maybe."

"That'll mean way past eleven before I get to bed."

"I'll spend the night in Suffolk. Wouldn't get home to Sheba before too late. I'm tired myself."

"I make it from Suffolk to Barlow in half an hour. I'd rather get to my own bed. Wish I was there right now!" And Bart yawned. . . .

They were really released and at their cars not much after ten, but they did not get started for a while. They did not feel so tired as they had earlier, and these were always golden moments to talk things over and relax slowly.

Squatting easily on their hunkers, as only old woodsmen could do, they post-mortemed the fire. George had done a good enough job as fire-boss, even though he had only five years of experience on the Suffolk District. His Fire Control Assistant hadn't done too good—lost his head, kind of. Should have had more McLeods, not so many axes. The Super— well, the Super stuck his nose in a little, but that's what a Super was supposed to do, wasn't it? The fire sure burned hot in that slash. Did you see that new weather-man? Young squirt. Might know all about weather-maps, but could he tell you when the breeze was going to shift from down-canyon to up?

Then, at last, two cigarettes burned down at the same time, and there was a pause. Bart felt weariness roll over him again, and suddenly he would rather be in bed even than be talking to his old friend Ben.

"Better be going," he said.

Driving down the highway, Bart watched the ruby spot of Ben's tail-light. It was clear and plain on the stretches, and winked out sharply at the curves, or when Ben's car went over the top of a rise. But he saw it less and less often, and then not at all. That meant Ben was driving faster.

All right. Ben maybe wasn't as tired. What time was it anyway? Eleven-thirty. They'd talked longer than he realized. But that was the way it always happened. Gosh, he was tired. Up early on Thursday, sweating on the fire-line all that afternoon and all night, one little cat-nap, doing a thousand things today, and here it was nearly Saturday.

Ahead, the highway streamed steadily at him through the brightness of the headlights. Now he was passing through the old Merriam's Mill burn. Off from the edge of the road he saw the burned trees looming up in ugly desolation. Then suddenly he went in between solid walls of trees again, and knew that he had passed the burn.

Fighting sleep now, driving more slowly, he felt the road swing left and dip into the canyon. After what seemed a long time and too many curves, he came to the bottom, crossed the bridge, and at last drove through the empty street of Suffolk. Few lights were still on. Where the State highway turned left, he drove straight ahead and followed the narrower and bumpier road along the South Fork—his own river. Close to the water, with the down-canyon wind moving, the air was cooler than it had been on the ridge. The engine seemed to purr more smoothly, even though the road ran up-grade steadily. Below the road, to the right, he heard the deep murmur of the stream, and saw a vague whiteness as the water came down a chute between rocks.

Must be nearly midnight, he thought, glancing at the clock. Say, it really is just turning midnight, and here we . . .

. . . are with Saturday morning already begun, and not in
bed yet . . . cross the bridge above the glossy black of water
in the deep pool . . . up-canyon again, swing . . . go on
. . . rush of water on the left now . . . curves all the time
. . . could be asleep and drive this . . . well, nearly am
asleep . . . ah, swung that one a little wide, maybe . . . road
streaming in like a fast river through the headlight-glare . . .
LOOK OUT!

He was tramping hard on the brake. The tires whined, and
the car swerved, and the two deer which had been streaming
at him through the headlight-glare were bolting over the edge
of the bank, their rumps bumping.

He drove more slowly after that, shaking himself occasionally, blinking, consciously holding himself alert. He was dead
tired, and sleep was crowding in from all directions. He
counted curves to keep awake.

The old moon swung into view through a gap in the can-
yon-rim, and swung out of view again. He passed the boundary into Barlow District, and—WHAT?—smoke-smell! Quick
alarm brought him up sharply to the alert. He sniffed. No—
faint and stale—just drift from the fire he had left. . . .

He rounded the last curve, and saw the single bright light in the yard at Barlow Ranger Station. He turned in at the Station, switched off the engine, and let the car coast quietly to a stop beneath the light, its tires crunching on the gravel. He yawned, and got out slowly, leaving the car there.

Inside the house, his wife called to him from bed:

"Can I get you something to eat?"

"No, thanks. I'll get some of this soot and sweat off, and tumble in. I'm sleepy."

The warm water of the shower was like a blessing, and then he lay between the sheets on his right side with his knees pulled up a little to relax.

"Ahh!" he breathed, half-aloud, and let the air out of his lungs.

Yet he did not go to sleep just then. The road kept streaming at him through the headlight-glare, and there was always just one more curve to swing around. He lay on his back and tossed a little, and turned over on his left side.

"She sure ripped through some of those nice little patches of reproduction. Why don't I go to sleep? When I was younger—when, I mean, I didn't worry so much, didn't get so tired, let down faster. Say, I hate to see trees burn!"

But he had been carrying himself too long by nervous force, and that force could not relax quickly and let the body rest. He lay fitfully until after he had heard the clock in the hall strike one. Then at last he twitched a little all over, and suddenly it was as if something had hit him on the head.

2

The butt of the log, where the ant-nest had been, was a little mound of gray ashes. The middle of the log was also consumed, but its tip still burned quietly in the calm darkness of the early morning.

The conditions of the night were no more favorable than they had been on the preceding nights, but the fire itself had grown large and stronger. Now, instead of glowing faintly in dull red, it cast forth a strange and vivid pink. Its heat dried out the needles and twigs more quickly, and each one as it burned supplied more heat to ignite the next. The very lack of breeze allowed the heat to accumulate.

The fire had now advanced ten feet beyond the log, and burned on a front of thirty feet. Continually the pink glare was lighted up with little dancing yellow flames. The fire might still be said to creep, but now and then it seemed rather to take a little step forward, as a hotter burst of flame reached a few inches in advance and suddenly seized upon new fuel.

Within the already blackened area stood a foot-tall pine-seedling. The fire, eating through the fallen needles, had burned all around the tiny trunk, no thicker than a pencil. The thin bark was blackened, and had been heated past the boiling point of its inner layers. The needles had not actually taken fire, but had been desiccated and scorched. The seedling was fatally injured, if indeed it might not be called already dead.

Now along its upper edge the fire approached the clump of young trees, and the needles beneath another seedling began to glow. The heat of the nearing fire had already driven off the water from the needles of this seedling, and as the fire began to burn right beneath, the gums and resins vaporized. Mingling with the air, this vapor formed an almost explosive mixture. Suddenly as the heat grew more intense, the mixture ignited, and with a little hiss as of escaping air, a bright pyramid of flame rose to a height of two feet. The desiccated needles caught fire, and for five seconds the whole tree blazed; then the flames died down almost as quickly as they had flared up. The needles were all consumed, but for a few seconds more the tiny branch-tips glowed red hot, curling as they burned away. The tiny tree, too wet with sap to be entirely consumed, was left standing as a blackened skeleton.

By the aid of this sudden and intense flare-up the point of the fire had in a few seconds stepped forward another foot. Now it pressed upon the thicket of young trees, and flames began to shoot higher, crackling in the interlaced dry branches. In another minute the needles ignited, and the whole clump roared upward in a solid-looking pyramid of orange flame. A thick column of gray smoke ascended vertically. and stood high above the tree-tops, in the darkness.

3

Five-thirty? Do you think it's five-thirty? Judith Godoy, still healthily sleepy, got an eye open, and from her tangle of blankets peered around the lookout—that comfortably familiar little universe, with the fire-finder fixed and certain in the middle, just the way the earth was before Copernicus upset things and made everyone uncomfortable. Well, by the wrist-watch it was 5:28—light enough now to look around and see something, that is, if the smoke from the Hart Creek Fire had cleared away.

She swept back the blankets, came up sitting on the edge of the bed in her pajamas, stuck her feet into her warm slippers, stood up to stretch and yawn, and looked out south. Yes, the smoke was gone, just as the Dispatcher had predicted. She swung around to the east—and her mouth fell open! The familiar universe suddenly tottered. She blinked.

There, far to the northeast over Reverse Ridge, light gray against the dark background of Howell Mountain, rose a hazy, pillar-like smudge that had never been there before.

She ran for the catwalk. Through the binoculars the smudge jumped closer. Looked like smoke, all right!

(Check now, don't make a fool of yourself! Mist rising

from the creek? Dust from sheep being driven? Someone's campfire? Not likely, and can't take the chance. Hurry before Horse Mountain catches it! *God, maybe he has already!*)

She raced back, swung the alidade, lined up the crosshair through the peep-hole, and read the azimuth. Six-six-point-five! That settled it! Only one-point-five off where she had spotted the lightning-stroke, and might be smoke-drift to allow for.

Long-short-long. (Wait.) *Long-short-long.* (Listen. Why doesn't Bart answer?) *Long-short-long.* (Look nervously to see if smoke is building up.) *Long-short-long.* (Horse Mountain not on the line anyway.) *Long-short-long.* (Forgot to fill out the little blank, have the bearing anyway.)

4

Long-short-long. (Up from the depth of sleep as through water from a deep dive.) *Long-short-long.* (Break surface into half-consciousness, swing out of bed, blunder across room.) *Long-short-long.* (Should have had that line switched to someone else last night—oh, they'd rout me out anyway!) *Long-short—*

He jerked off the receiver, and spoke sharply, wide awake by now:

"Hello! Barlow Station. Ranger Bartley speaking."

"Bart, I got a smoke! This is Cerro Gordo speaking, I mean. *I got a* SMOKE *at* SIX-SIX-POINT-FIVE!"

"All right—that's fine! Now, not too excited, Judith. Wait till I write that down. *Six . . . six . . . point . . . five.* And the time is 5:31."

"That's right!"

"Vertical angle?"

"Oh, *Bart,* I *forgot!* I'll check!"

"No, stay put. It's behind Reverse, isn't it? You couldn't

see the base of the smoke anyway. That lightning-stroke, you think?"

"Just a point and a half off where I had it spotted."

"All right, now, Judith. Don't get excited up there by yourself, but keep watching it. If you have to change the bearing or report something important, call back. Otherwise, stay off the line. Good-bye!"

In spite of all his calm advice, Bart was breathing a little quickly. It was the girl's first fire, and he must be well beyond his first thousand—but even so! He breathed twice, and in the pause he heard the clatter in the kitchen as his wife pulled out the coffee-pot. Call Horse Mountain next—and then *long-short-long* again—and it *was* Horse Mountain.

". . . Wish to report a smoke, bearing three-two-oh. Same bearing as lightning-stroke on Monday. Base of fire not in view. Inconsiderable drift of smoke eastward. Well beyond ridge north of North Fork of South Fork. Estimate distance at ten miles. Southeast slope of Howell Mountain. Most likely in Deerhound, Section 12, or—"

"Wait a minute—you're not reporting Slugger's campfire, are you?"

"Mr. O'Neill's smoke is always very small, and is three points farther toward north," said the voice with a tone of reproach at having been suspected of a crass error.

"O. K. That's fine! Cerro Gordo has reported it already."

"Oh!" said the voice with a quick shift to let-down disappointment. Then it went suddenly into a high sing-song: *"Who is this that cometh out of the wilderness like pillars of smoke?"* and then added matter-of-factly, *"Solomon's Song,* three-six."

Bart clicked down the receiver, not knowing whether to be pleased or amused or irritated. The old guy on Horse Mountain was still a top-notch lookout, but getting daffier on religion all the time. Anyway, no time to worry about that just now.

He hurriedly got into slippers and his brown bathrobe, and started for the office. The loose slippers did not serve well for running, and as he scuttled across the hundred yards he looked like a middle-aged brown-robed monk trying not to be late for matins, his bald spot even serving as a good imitation of a tonsure. As he ran, he observed the sky—no great change in weather apparently. That meant bad enough, but not too bad.

In the control-room he flipped the radio-switch, and as he waited for the tubes to warm up, he turned to the wall-map with its push-pin for each lookout. Six-six-point-five for Cerro Gordo led out northeasterly, and three-two-oh for Horse Mountain, northwesterly. The threads crossed on the south slope of the ridge to the north of Onion Creek, but he would try to get another reading before he committed his crew.

He spoke into the microphone: "Z-17 calling Z-142. . . . Z-17 calling Z-142. . . . Come in, Z-142. . . . Come in, Z-142." He paused, hoping. Slugger O'Neill was not notable for brains, but any boss of an isolated crew should know enough to be standing by with his radio this time of morning.

"Z-17 calling Z-142. . . . Z-17 calling Z-142. . . . Come in, Z-142. . . . Come in, Z-142." He thought, half-panicky, of all the things that went wrong with radio-transmission. And then, so clear that he could recognize the bass tones of the voice, Slugger O'Neill spoke to him across twenty-five miles of canyons and ridges:

"Z-142 to Z-17. . . . Z-142 to Z-17. . . . Go ahead, Z-17. . . . Go ahead, Z-17."

Bart dropped the formality:

"Say, Slugger, this is Bart. We've got a smoke somewhere over by Onion Creek. I say: somewhere over by Onion Creek. You're the nearest crew. So get your men ready to hit it in a hurry. Get your men ready. You hear me?"

"I get yuh, Bart."

"O. K.—Get ready and stand by on the radio. I want to get a third cross from Hamlin Point, and then I'll be back with orders in a minute. Back with orders in a minute. Z-17 over and out. . . . Z-17 over and out."

The youngsters were yelping around him: "What's up, Slugger? . . . Who was it? . . . We got a fire?" They quieted as he straightened up from talking into the transmitter.

"Come on, you guys! We're alerted! . . . One ax, three shovels, two McLeods. . . . Canteens all round. . . . Two K-rations apiece. . . . Radio. . . . Get set! I'm standing by for orders."

The flurry of preparation hardly lasted a minute.

"Get the camp policed!" Slugger yelled from where he again crouched beside the radio, ear-phones in place: "Wet down the campfire!"

"Slugger, do we eat breakfast before we start?"

"We do *not!* But sling something together so we can eat on the trail."

Then the radio squawked: "Z-17 calling . . ."

They hit the trail at 5:42, the shadows still deep and cool. The boys shouted back and forth eagerly. Going to a fire was like a holiday from the steady work of trail-maintenance. In spite of their nondescript clothing they looked like a band of primitive warriors, shovels and McLeods like weapons for hand-to-hand combat, as they strung out in single-file along the narrow trail. Slugger led the way, carrying the double-bitted ax, like the chieftain. They had about two miles to go, and with Slugger setting the pace it would be a lot like a two-mile run.

Once Bart had got the crew started in, he relaxed a little. There was still much to be done, but it did not need to be done in such a hurry. He checked the aerial photographs, just to be sure, although from long familiarity with the country he knew already that the fire was burning in heavy forest on a steep slope. He called his clerk-dispatcher, and told her to get dressed and take over the office. He called Cerro Gordo and Horse Mountain and Hamlin Point again, and found that the smoke was building up some, as you would expect. (Horse Mountain quoted *Jeremiah*.) He considered the chances, and decided that a crew of five eager boys with a driver for a crew-boss ought to hit the fire soon enough and hard enough to get it well corralled before the heat and rising wind of afternoon made it more dangerous. Given any kind of break, that is. That was the trouble—the break might go the other way.

He rose nervously, and shuffled across the floor in slippers. The fire was in such an isolated spot that he had no other crew he could throw at it in a hurry. And Slugger, though he had his points, was no strategist.

At that moment the fire which was causing so much commotion throughout Barlow District was actually, on the spot, still far from terrifying. Grown suddenly intense by its engulfing of the clump of saplings, it had made the most of some good puffs of down-canyon wind just before dawn, and had taken off at right angles to its previous direction of advance. On a front of only a few yards it had made a quick run of some fifty yards diagonally up-hill, burning duff, underbrush, and an occasional clump of young trees.

By this very activity, however, the fire had also worked

against itself by sending up enough smoke to attract the attention of creatures whose racial experience, unlike that of the ants, included a familiarity with fire. Men did not merely stand and wave their arms; instead, they came swarming out with set purpose and weapons of offense.

As late as 5:53 a single active man with a shovel could have scraped away the duff from the front of the fire, and gradually extending his line could have contained the flames and let them burn themselves out. Since at that same time Slugger and his boys were little more than half-an-hour distant, anyone must have concluded that the fire was doomed. At that minute, however, one chance out of the millions possible contrived to change the situation considerably.

In its diagonal upslope advance before the down-canyon wind, the fire had at last reached the pine-cone which rested against the dead twig. Both cone and branch were soon blazing, and after a few minutes the twig, nearly burned through, broke at the point where the cone rested against it.

The cone toppled downhill, rolled two feet, wobbled— hesitated. (If it had been a long sugar-pine cone, it would have rolled uncertainly and have come to rest; if it had been the tiny cone of a Douglas fir, it would have lodged in some little roughness of the ground; but it was the almost spherical cone of a Jeffrey pine, eight inches through its shortest diameter.) It toppled again with the thrust of gravity and momentum, rolled a foot, then picking up speed, went rolling and bouncing and leaping erratically downward. The wind of its own movement made it blaze more fiercely. A flying ball of fire, it catapulted down the canyon-side, leaving a trail of sparks and burning scales behind. It struck a tree-trunk, ricocheted, rolled on again, caromed off a rock, and finally came to rest against a log, a good hundred yards from where it had started.

Many of the sparks and even some of the burning scales

smouldered for a moment and then went out. But many others ignited the tinder-like needles. A hundred-yard-long trail of smoke puffs began to rise. In thickly littered places the dry twigs soon blazed up. The tiny isolated fires reached out and joined. The log where the cone had come to rest began to smoke vigorously. Here and there a seedling flared up; underbrush began to crackle. All the heat combined to form an updraft, and the air flowing in from below blew up the flames.

In an inconsiderable time the fire had thus become several times more dangerous. Its area had not greatly increased, but because of the long down-hill shoe-string the perimeter which would have to be contained within a cleared line had quadrupled.

Still, the life-hold of the fire was by no means assured. If one man could have suppressed it before the cone rolled, six would now be adequate.

Slugger's crew was over the ridge. On the steep switchbacks the pace had told, but now they were on the headwaters of Onion Creek, and the going was downhill.

Slugger was still in the lead as the trail swung round a shoulder.

"There she is!" he yelled, halting. The boys came crowding up behind him, and saw, from well down toward the bottom of the canyon to a point more than halfway up, a faint line of smoke with a denser column at the top.

"She's not going places," said one of them. "We can catch her all right."

"Got a long front, if an up-canyon wind comes along," said another. He was the smallest and they called him Shorty; the pace had tuckered him out, and he was sweating hard.

But the pause was only momentary. As at the sound of the gong, Slugger had been used to rush from his corner head-on

at his opponent, so now he sighted across and down the canyon, straight at the nearest smoke, and his fighting spirit took
over. "Come on, you!" he yelled thunderously, and plunged
diagonally down the steep hillside through the trees and
brush. With yelps of enthusiasm the boys followed him. For a
moment, however, the smallest one hesitated. He was tired,
and glancing ahead he saw clearly enough that by following
the trail farther before taking the plunge a man should be
·able to get to the fire sooner and more easily. Then he went
with the crowd, sliding and scrambling downward, fifty feet
behind the others.

Ten minutes later they came puffing up the other side.
Slugger halted about twenty feet from where the smoke was
rising along the upper side of a log. Even he was blowing
hard from the breakneck downhill plunge, the fight through
the brush along the creek, and the steep climb up two hundred feet with sliding shale and slippery pine-needles for a
footing.

"Look—you-guys—" he panted. "Spread out—along the—
down-canyon side.—Say—who ain't here?"

"Shorty—he slipped—jumpin' th' crick. Hurt his knee—
he's comin'—but he's slow."

"Good Christ!—Can't a man even jump—a crick these
days?—Well, get busy, you four!"

"What about the radio?" said the boy who was carrying it.

"Well, s'pose I oughtta—call Bart. Ah, t'hell with it! It'll
take ten minutes. I'm goin' t'scout this fire first.—Get a dink-
line up that side first. I gotta see what—we're up against."

The theory of fighting a forest-fire is simple. Since there is
no way available for extinguishing the blaze, you merely con-
fine it within a fire-line, and let it burn itself out. An ordinary
fire-line is a foot or two wide. From it all duff must be scraped

away, so that the creeping ground-fire will die for lack of fuel. Above the ground all low overhanging branches must be cleared out, and in thickets this means the cutting of brush and saplings. The high branches of the mature trees are ignored, in the hope that they will not catch fire. If they do, the result is the cataclysm known as a crown-fire, in which flames tower up high above the highest trees, and pass from one tree-top to the next in complete disregard of fire-lines. Since heat, unless driven by a strong wind, rises sharply upward, the amount of conflagration short of a crown-fire that a narrow fire-line can stop is often little short of seeming miraculous.

In the files of the Forest Service are endless statistics showing how many feet of line a man can build under such and such average conditions, but as any Ranger or Fire-Crew Foreman can tell the world, average conditions never exist, and every fire is a special case.

Theoretically Slugger O'Neill had hit the fire at 6:23 with a crew of six. Actually, one of them had bumped his knee, and was not yet up the hill. Also, Slugger himself went off, as was right and proper, to scout the fire, taking with him the ax.

Therefore, four men with three shovels and a McLeod began to build line. All four were winded and tired from Slugger's pace-making over two miles of hard mountain trail, ending with the dash across-canyon. Just when they should have been at the height of enthusiasm they were really hitting their first slump. They got to work with a fair show of spirit, but the vigorous cursing showed that they were driving themselves.

Immediately also the problem of tools arose. "One ax, three shovels, two McLeods," Slugger had ordered, but shovels were not adapted to work on the rocky canyon-side. The McLeod—a foot-wide heavy hoe on one side, a kind of broad-toothed rake on the other—was just the thing for scraping away the duff until the unburnable raw earth showed through. Also they soon needed the ax, which Slugger had taken with him. But what tools to take to a fire and how to have the right tool ready at the proper time and place—these two problems have been the ruin of many a better fire-strategist than Slugger O'Neill, and can never be wholly solved, short of omniscience.

The McLeod-man worked rapidly up-hill clearing a narrow "dink-line" which would at least check the fire, and might be widened later. One shovel-man went along with him, doing what he could.

Two shovel-men, however, became involved with the smoking log. Actually that spot was no more dangerous than a hundred others along the perimeter, but the average human being has a strong tendency toward concern about what he sees before him, and toward lack of concern about what he does not see. The log was smoking heavily, and beginning to burn, along six feet of its length. To dig out a line all around a sixty-foot log just because it was burning along six feet seemed too much work. So they pecked at the burning part with their shovels ineffectually. They might have chopped it out, but Slugger had the ax. After some minutes the sixth man came limping up the hill with his McLeod. He manfully tried to scrape the fire out, but accomplished nothing except to get his McLeod hot enough to lose some of its temper. Then the shovel-men scooped up dirt from the stony ground, and threw it on the blaze. Though such measures did not put the fire out, they reduced it to temporary harmlessness.

By this time Slugger, having made the circuit, came sliding down the hill on the other side of the fire. Seeing three men puttering with one log while nine-tenths of the fire was still uncontrolled, he cursed them out, and sent two of them up to the upper end of the fire. The lamed one he assigned, with a shovel, to work along the lower point and watch for rolling cones.

Slugger himself went up along the front of the fire to clear out brush and saplings with the ax, where it was necessary. Under the stress of exerting his authority he forgot to set up the radio and report in.

By a quarter of seven Bart had eaten breakfast, and dressed, and been back in the office long enough to be feeling nervous. Slugger should have reported by now, telling what the fire looked like close up and whether he thought he could handle it with his crew. No news was neither good news nor bad news under the conditions. No news was simply no news. Still, that made a man nervous, just not knowing. A great many things could happen on a fire, and some of them usually did. The lookouts reported a build-up of smoke for a while, and then a gradual dying down. That ought to mean that the boys were getting some work done.

The Barlow suppression-crew had already started, but they were to set up their radio at the road-head on Onion Flat, and wait for orders before hitting the trail on foot. That was about all Bart could do at the moment, but he decided to call the Dispatcher at Suffolk. A little council of war wouldn't hurt.

The Dispatcher was feeling optimistic and even jovial, as indeed he usually was, as long as a fire was still a District problem and had not been dumped too heavily in his own lap.

"Hello, Bart," he said into the phone. "I hear you have a little trouble on your hands."

"Wish I knew if it really was little. Slugger don't report back."

"Well, you can't expect everything from one crew-boss.

He's in there swinging an ax, you can bet, and won't take time out to radio. From what Cerro Gordo says about the smoke, I'd judge he'll have it hooked in an hour or so."

"I wouldn't worry except that it's a tough place to get reinforcements in to."

The Dispatcher dropped his easygoing mood.

"I'll tell you, Bart. I'll order up the plane and take a look in there myself. Ought to be able to make it—let's see—by ten o'clock. Should I alert the paratroopers—any place to jump up there?"

"Gosh, I don't know. There's Reverse Meadow, but that's not so close. There're a couple of bare spots along the ridge, but I hate to ask anybody to jump into them."

"I'll alert them anyway.—Say, what's the name of this fire?"

" 'Onion Creek,' I guess."

"Can't be. Had one of those already this year, up on that Onion Creek that runs into the North Fork. What other names you got up there? There's nothing else on the map."

"There're all those old mines. Golden Queen—"

"Sounds like a perfume!"

"Spitcat, Broken Nose—"

"Oh, Spitcat will do! All right, Bart. Good Luck!"

Laying down the receiver, the Dispatcher took his pen, and matter-of-factly entered *Spitcat* in his log. There had been 163 fires already that season in the Ponderosa Forest; this was merely #164.

Inwardly the Dispatcher was congratulating himself that they had kept Slugger's crew up in that area, all ready for a quick attack. The far-planned strategy was paying off.

Dave Halliday, the meteorologist, saw the fire from farthest away of them all. To him it existed at an infinitesimal spot in an ordinary weather-situation. To him the fire lay between the 1011 and 1014 isobars, some two hundred miles to the east of the advancing cold front of a Pacific storm. As a result, the moderate south wind which blew toward the storm-center would dominate the region of the Ponderosa Forest during the day, growing stronger as the afternoon advanced. Some rain was probable in the night. He had committed himself to that forecast. What effect all this would have on the fire was the special business of the people charged with its suppression. . . .

The Supervisor had heard that there was a fire, but it remained a local affair as far as he was concerned. He had confidence that his Dispatcher and Ranger would handle the situation. And yet, he kept remembering that there was an uncontrolled fire, and in September. . . .

The Dispatcher also saw the fire at a considerable distance. It was his one-hundred-sixty-fourth fire for the season, and his capacity for worrying over every individual fire was badly impaired. The Spitcat did not seem especially dangerous. It was not building up. Its chief difficulty lay in its isolation— seven miles over steep trails from the nearest road-head. . . .

To Bart the fire was like a gnawing worry in the pit of his stomach, a kind of tiny focal infection which spread its poison through the body. He did not know what was happening, and was uncomfortable every moment. No matter which way the fire moved, it would burn a fine forest, and his trees were almost as his children. . . .

Judith Godoy on Cerro Gordo actually saw the smoke. But even to her the fire was small and far away. Now the smoke built up a little, and now it died down, but at most it seemed scarcely more than the smudge of a campfire on the horizon. In spite of herself she kept half wishing that the fire—her fire —would not be crushed out so young, but might grow and amount to something. But as often as the thought arose, she revolted from it consciously, as a disloyalty to Bart and the Forest.

Of all those in the Forest only Slugger O'Neill and his five boys had as yet been close enough to wince at the heat and choke at the bite of smoke in the throat. They had been working for an hour now. The brilliant sun struck hard against the slope; the breeze had fallen off, and a hot mid-morning calm lay on the canyon-side. From their scrapings and shovelings the impalpably fine red dust rose and hung in the air, settling all over them, irritating their nostrils and throats. The first flush of enthusiasm was long past. They were tired. Hands and faces were sooty and dusty, and streaked with the paths where sweat-beads kept rolling down. Already they were thinking of how fine it would be to get back to the routine work of trail-clearing.

Yet still they worked steadily and doggedly, and were in good enough spirits. They were making progress. They had run a line nearly all the way up the down-canyon side, the front of the fire. Another hour's work, and they might see the whole circuit of the line completed. Then it would be time for mop-up and mere watchfulness as the fire burned itself out.

They were tired, all right. Shorty was limping from his bruised knee. They were hot and grimy. Already they were sucking the water from the canteens, and wishing they had time to break out the K-rations. Still they had the satisfaction of knowing they were doing a man's job. Another hour, and they'd have her hooked.

The storm which on Thursday had been merely incipient had on Saturday grown well toward maturity. It now centered to the north of Unalaska, and was drenching Dutch Harbor with a heavy downpour. . . .

From the storm which had just crossed the Gulf of Alaska, the waves beat heavily all along the coast of Oregon, and spatters of cold rain were falling. The mountains of northern Idaho were white with new-fallen snow.

When he had arrived at the fire, Slugger had known nothing about the distant storm, and even if he had, his bull-like desire to charge right at the enemy would probably have prevented any finesse, such as an allowance for a wind-shift. As it was, he had acted in accordance with his own character, attacking straight on, at the point of gravest danger—tactics, indeed, which in warfare or fire-fighting are likely to be sound.

Even while the boys were at work, however, conditions were changing. The heat of the now high sun began to establish an up-draft in the canyon, and the approach of the storm-front reinforced this southerly breeze.

First came a little puff, and then a long sigh, as if something gigantic were letting out its breath. The smaller branches swayed gently. The tufts of flame wavered and spiraled, and then leaned over backward and stayed that way.

The boys looked at one another quickly. For a moment, from where they were working, it seemed as if the wind were aiding them, blowing the flames back upon the burned area. The fresh breeze was cool on their sweaty faces, and their lungs sucked gratefully at the smoke-free air. Then they remembered the other side of the fire.

Instantly, what had been the front of the fire had become its flank or rear. The wind no longer blew the heat toward the line which the boys had so laboriously cut through. Instead of advancing diagonally up-hill in a down-canyon direction, the fire shifted front by more than a right angle and took off up-canyon.

At this time of the wind-shift the fire had something of the shape of a long-barreled pistol, pointed down-hill, with the grip turned in the down-canyon direction. The crew had run a line along the under side of the barrel and part-way around the grip. But now the south wind fanned up the flames, and from all the upper side of the pistol-barrel the fire began to advance. In terms of a man walking, it did not move rapidly. Even a lame man or a child would easily have kept ahead of it. But in comparison with the rate at which six already tired workers could build fire-line, the speed of the advance was ominous.

Looking at one another, the boys for the first time felt a quick anxiety, almost a fear.

"God! She's outsmarted us!" said one of them. He was no poet, and he had never heard of *pathetic fallacy*, but quite naturally he personified the fire and attributed to it a malignant intelligence.

Slugger cursed violently to cover up his defeat. For a moment he hesitated, weighing the alternatives. Either he could fall back well up-canyon and try to build a line across the advance of the fire, or else from his established line he could hang on the flanks of the fire, keeping it from broadening its front, hoping to work ahead gradually and pinch it off.

Early in the morning he would undoubtedly have chosen the bolder strategy. Now he chose the safer.

"We'll flank her, boys! We'll catch her all right!" Then for the first time he tried to build up false courage. "This wind'll die down pretty soon!" And he added the rallying-cry of the hard-pressed commander: "They'll be gettin' reinforcements in to us pretty soon!"

"Sure!" said the boys. "Reinforcements! . . . Why don't they get us some reinforcements? . . . We can't fight this fire all by ourselves!"

Since he was clear at the top of the fire when the wind changed, Slugger was a long way from where he had left the radio. Again, on the grounds that it would take him half an hour to climb down the hill and back, he justified his own picture of himself as the heroic ax-swinging leader, not a fiddler with dials and frequencies.

"Come on, boys," he yelled. "We'll flank her on the up-side and pinch her off!" And with one Homeric ax-stroke he cut clear through the butt of a young tree standing too close to the line.

Bart called the Dispatcher again:

"Say, Arn, I'm starting in. Haven't heard from Slugger, but Judith up there at Cerro Gordo says the smoke is definitely building up."

"It's this south wind. The weather-man says it's going to get stronger, and may bring rain tonight.—But O. K., I think you'd better start in. Don't get out of touch, though."

"Who do you think I am, Slugger O'Neill? I'll keep the radio on!"

As he left the Station, Bart followed the same road up which he had driven through the darkness of that same morning. "Gee," he thought, as he steered around the first curve, "seems like I was swinging curves all night!" He felt dull in spite of three cups of coffee, and he had that little confused feeling a man had when he didn't really get enough sleep to make a clean break between two days and so wasn't quite sure whether this was yesterday or today or tomorrow.

After a mile, he turned off, crossed the bridge over the South Fork, and took the Idylhurst road. At first the shade still lay on the road, but soon the sun was higher, and hot. The dry furnace-heat of September beat in upon him; he smelled the faint pine-tree odor diffusing from the warmed needles. He longed for a cool breeze to snap him out of his lethargy and make him face the day with some enthusiasm.

An official notice affixed to his instrument-panel warned him against too fast driving even when going to a fire, but he interpreted it liberally. The road was narrow and twisty, but it had a smooth oiled surface, and he knew all the bad turns. His radio buzzed and squawked a little, and once he faintly heard someone calling a station that was not even in the Ponderosa.

Then at last (he was at the bend just before Idylhurst) he heard Judith Godoy's voice calling Z-112, his own car number. As he took the transmitter from its hook, he pulled to the side of the road and stopped.

It was just a brief message. She was relaying for the Dispatcher. He wanted Bart to know that things didn't look so good. On his own responsibility he had ordered the Barlow suppression-crew to start in from Onion Flat.

"O. K.," said Bart into the transmitter. "Thanks, Judith. Tell Arn for me that I'm nearly to Idylhurst and going on in as fast as I can."

He slowed down for fear of children and dogs as he came to the row of houses at Idylhurst. The women came bouncing out on the porches, and he heard one of them yell some question about fire. They would have seen the truck with the suppression-crew go by already, and living right next to the trees they would be nervous about a fire. Well, this one was a long way off, and going the other direction.

Bart pulled in at the Guard Station. Tony already had Betty saddled, and they took only a minute to get the neat-footed black mare into the horse-trailer. She snorted a little with excitement. Bart patted the sleek shoulder.

"You old girl, you like to go for a ride just as much as anybody."

Beyond Idylhurst there was no more oiled surface. The dust lay thick, and freshly imprinted into it, not yet marred by any deer- or fox-tracks, the double tire-marks of the truck led on ahead. The eight miles from Idylhurst to the road-head at Onion Flat were slower going, but Bart pushed as fast as the bumping horse-trailer would allow.

Here the forest was thicker, with taller trees, and the road was still partly shaded. Nevertheless, it was hot, and the trees shut off what breeze there might be, and the dust made everything seem even hotter. Dust—powdery red dust that, they said, had particles of gold in it—dust rose all about him and settled everywhere. It coated the wind-shield that he had washed before leaving. It floated in at the windows and seeped upward from the floor-boards. He felt his face grow dry and tight, as if someone were slowly shaking talcum-powder on him.

Yet he did not mind the dust. He was used to it, and it was only a minor irritating feature, like poison-oak and rattle-snakes, in a country that he loved. In fact, as he drove on, he grew more alert, and began to forget his weariness.

For now that he was actually getting close to the fire, his excitement rose. He found himself humming the tune of *Merriam's Mill*, that battle-song of the Ponderosa, and thinking the words as he hummed:

> *She called the District Ranger by help of radio,*
> *And said, "There is a smoke I see on bearing one-one-oh!"*

He felt himself split wide open. On one side he longed passionately for a call from Slugger saying that the fire was under control, so that he could relax suddenly, and make a wise-crack back. Then he would quit worrying about his trees, and turn around and head back for Barlow.

But on the other side a kind of diabolical suggestion rose

up, and he felt his sense of excitement urging it on. For if the
fire was a worthy opponent and too much for Slugger, then
by tonight he himself might be locked in battle with a gigantic enemy that knew neither pity nor rules of combat. He
felt the quick surge of the fighting-spirit:

> *Which also being sighted from the tower on Badger Hill*
> *Was soon triangulated as a mile from Merriam's Mill.*

To think of the blackened trees afterwards! And yet also
to think of trucks rolling and the cats crashing through the
thickets, the long lines of men and the councils of war: "What
about it, Bart? . . . Ask Bart. . . . Say, Bart, can you get a
cat up that ridge? . . . Bart would know about that!"

(So, in the old days, soldiers marched into battle, half in
anxiety and fear, and half in fierce excitement to hear again
the crashing volleys and the thud of charging hooves.)

And he hummed:

> *But the trees are black along the slopes*
> *of all of Bigler Hill;*
> *Ziegler's Station all is burned,*
> *and so is Merriam's Mill.*

The empty truck stood parked at Onion Flat. He pulled in
beside it, and took the transmitter again:

"Z-112 calling Z-17. . . . Z-112 to Z-17. Come in, Z-17."

But he could not get Barlow, being apparently in a blind
spot. So he called Z-3, and talked to Judith, who in turn
talked with Barlow. . . . No, no news from Slugger. The Dispatcher was taking off in the plane from Suffolk about quarter to ten. The smoke looked a little bigger. Lovers Leap
could see it now. Those were all the messages Barlow had to
forward.

"All right, Judith," said Bart. "Write this down and send
it in for me. 'Am at Onion Flat, starting in on horseback.

Have portable radio with me. Will call in when have chance.'
Repeat that back."

Judith repeated.

"All right. (Say, with your binoculars you'll probably be
able to see me going up the switch-backs in half an hour.)
O. K. Z-112 over and out. . . ."

As he forded the creek on Betty, Bart looked carefully up
the narrow gorge, but a shoulder of the mountain still
blocked his view, and he saw no smoke. With this wind it
would be drifting off to the north. Then the sure-footed mare
scrambled up the bank, and began the long pull up the
switch-back trail.

In half an hour, near the top of the last switch-back, he
caught up with the Barlow crew, lying down catching their
wind. He stopped to let Betty blow for a minute. From the
way the six boys were sweating, he saw that they had been
pushing hard. So, instead of making a wise-crack about their
lying down and taking it easy, he said:

"Don't rush too hard. It's a long pull ahead."

They grinned, knowing what he was thinking.

Higher up, the view opened out. Between the orange
trunks of two big pines he saw for many miles back down the
long straight canyon through which he had just driven. He
felt his heart leap suddenly, as it did when the space and
majesty of such a view pressed upon him. Far to the west
Cerro Gordo Lookout shone like a beacon, its windows reflecting back the morning sunlight. Closer at hand but far
below, Onion Creek foamed white over falls and chutes as it
came down the narrow impassable gorge.

The trail leveled and swung round on contour, getting
closer to the creek. He pushed Betty to a trot for a short
stretch. He came down-slope, forded the little stream of
Grizzly Creek, and followed the trail over a low pine-covered

rise. Then, as he came out into the open of Reverse Meadow, he saw the smoke. . . .

He had a tremendous sense of relief. As so often, fire actually seen was not so bad as fire imagined. This was no raging conflagration. He spoke to Betty, and with her quick walk she left the little meadow, and began to climb the steep trail which ran up the canyon, pointing directly at the fire. She had not gone far before she pricked up her ears, and then Bart too heard the plane.

He had been carrying the radio in front of him on the saddle. Now he dismounted quickly, found a small stone, twisted the aerial wire around it, and threw it over a limb. He set up the radio in a hurry and switched it on, and by that time the plane was in sight.

Bart stood in an open space and waved his arms up and down. When the plane was almost overhead, he saw the wings waggle. Then he went and put on the ear-phones.

From where he sat, he saw the plane circle over the top of the fire, and then go right into the smoke. He waited—too long a time, it seemed—feeling that little sickness which came sometimes when he saw a plane maneuvering so low over the mountains. Then it came flying right down the canyon out of the smoke, and he heard Arn's voice calling him on the radio. Arn's report was clear.

"Not too good, not too bad. Slugger's there all right. He's got a line up the back of her where it's not much use now, since the wind shifted. He and some others are flanking her along the top, but she's got two hundred yards open front, with two long stringers out ahead. She covers ten acres maybe. Get up to it as fast as you can. I'm going to send in the jumpers."

"Where you going to jump them?"

"The meadow is too far. I've been scouting that thin place

on the ridge. Looks all right—although, of course, I'm not doing the jumping. Any big rocks in there under the bushes?"

"Shouldn't be. It's a gravel-top ridge."

"Well, the lieutenant can decide. If he thinks it's too touchy, we'll have to use the meadow."

Radio contact suddenly became bad, and for a moment as the plane circled, Bart heard nothing above the sputtering of the motor-noise. Then he asked:

"You got one of our men to guide the army pilot in?"

"Yes—the Super!"

"Repeat, please."

"You heard me—the Super!"

"How come?"

"Well, he knew the plane might be going, and he said he'd never gone out with a jump-plane, and wanted to see how it was done. He cancelled an appointment with some big lumbermen. I think myself he just wanted to get up to see the fire—like the rest of us."

A little after ten o'clock, Bart halted on the trail just opposite the smoke. He found a good place for Betty, took off her bridle, and tied her loosely, so that she could follow the shade a little and reach a few bushes to chew at. He set up the radio again, and had no difficulty in making contact with his clerk-dispatcher at Barlow. Her voice was already getting squeaky with excitement.—Arn had landed back at Suffolk all right and had taken over. Ten jumpers were going in, and the plane ought to be starting any time now. Arn had ordered in twenty mill-men from Magna too, to take over the night-shift, and he wanted to know if Bart, now that he'd seen the fire, wanted any more men.

"Tell him 'no,' " said Bart. "Ten jumpers inside of an hour are worth more than a hundred men for the night-shift. But

I'll call back again as soon as I've got over there and scouted it."

He signed off, pulled down the aerial, and packed up the radio for carrying. As he looked across the canyon, he saw, here and there among the tall trees, little stretches of fire-line —the ground all black on the up-canyon side, everything green on the down-canyon side. This edge looked dead and cold already, but the up-canyon side was smoking vigorously, as the breeze carried the fire along.

There was no door on this plane in the place where a door ought to be, and the Supervisor did not like it. He sat opposite where a door should be, and held on to a bar behind him with both hands. The dark-brown lieutenant talking to the coffee-with-cream sergeant was standing nonchalantly close to the open space, holding with only one hand. Then the plane banked, and the place where there should be a door seemed to become part of the floor. Feeling about to slide out into space, the Super gripped convulsively, and pulled his long legs in. The shiny-black corporal beside him grinned.

"Not my racket!" said the Supervisor apologetically, through the engine-noise.

"What you doin' on this ride, big boy?"

"Oh, I know the country. I point out the place you jump into."

"Pretty soft! You point; we jump!"

But the little crackle of laughter that came afterwards did not ring very merrily.

"Where you from?" asked the Super, knowing that it was usually a safe question and waving his hand to take in the whole outfit.

"Us? Oh, lots o' places. Harlem, Chicago, L. A., Beale Street. (Me, I'm from Philly.) We even got a couple cotton-pickers right from 'lil ol' Joeja.' " He laughed again, at his own imitation of Southern dialect. "What your name, big boy?"

"Me? Oh, just call me 'Slim.' "

Then he noticed that the corporal suddenly grew quiet. He thinks I'm talking down to him, thought the Supervisor, but I couldn't say, "Call me Mr. Jones."

The plane bumped sharply, and the Supervisor looked at the ten men who were soon to jump. They sat, lounging, on the uncomfortably narrow metal bench which ran along both sides of the long compartment. They were in their jumping-outfits with only their face-masks yet to adjust. They were padded like super-football-players, and looked, he thought tritely, like men from Mars. Each had a coil of rope dangling from his belt. They sat silent, most of them smoking. They did not look at all happy, and he could see little beads of sweat on several foreheads. That might be the heat of the padded suits, or it might not be. The thought of having to jump into space on top of a country that mostly ran up and down could not be comforting.

The sergeant was pointing suddenly outside, and the Supervisor stood up and craned his neck toward the doorway, holding to a convenient little steel cable that ran along the ceiling —or whatever you called it—of the plane. Now they were flying over the fire.

"This *is* my racket!" he thought, and he made a quick appraisal. The fire was not crowning anywhere among the big trees. At the point of one of the long stringers was a hot-spot, and he saw the reddish flames lick upward where a clump of young trees was burning. Still, with one crew on the fire already, ten men about to jump, another crew getting close, and Bart on the job as fire-boss—with all that, he wouldn't grant that fire much of what the insurance people called life-expectancy.

Just beyond the fire—at least it seemed so from the air—he saw the thin spot in the trees.

He nudged the lieutenant with his free hand, pointed, and then realized that in that one gesture he had accomplished his whole function on the flight. The lieutenant and the sergeant both looked, and he could tell by their faces that they were not going to jump up and down and yell "Goody!" He saw why, easily enough. The thin spot was not to be called a meadow, even optimistically. Tall trees pressed in upon it, and some of the trees growing right in it did not look so small. It was really nothing better than a brush-covered opening with a suggestion of gullies beneath the brush. And as for slope, being just off the top of the ridge it did not slope as much as the rest of the country thereabouts, but that was about all you could say for it. He felt very unhappy at the thought of anybody jumping into a place like that. Even though it might mean trouble with the fire, he began suddenly to hope that the lieutenant would decide to head back to Reverse Meadow, and indeed he hardly saw how there could be any other decision.

"Christ!" said the lieutenant sharply, "that's no bigger than a barn-roof and just about as steep!" The Supervisor felt a quick relief. And then, suddenly military, the lieutenant snapped out, "Sergeant, take charge of the jumping."

"Yes, sir," the sergeant answered back in such a parade-ground voice that the Supervisor looked to see if he had snapped to attention. Fortunately he had not, for at that moment the plane bumped in such a way that if the sergeant had been standing at attention he would certainly have been tossed out head-first in a most unmilitary manner.

"Make it three-three-four," said the lieutenant cryptically, and then swinging from hand-hold to hand-hold he walked up to the pilot's compartment, to direct the pilot and give the signal for jumping.

The plane had flown past the bare spot, but now it began to circle back.

"Come on, first three," ordered the sergeant.

Three of the jumpers stood up, including the corporal. Each snapped a clip onto the convenient steel-cable to which the Supervisor had just been holding. They shifted their chutes nervously, making sure that everything was clear. Their face-masks were in place now, making them look more Martian than ever, but through the clear plastic the Supervisor saw the whites of the eyes flashing in a black face, looking inhuman and yet pathetic, like the eyes of a trapped and frightened animal.

He turned to the private who was now sitting beside him on the bench. "Do you get used to jumping, or is it always tough?"

"Don't know about the other boys, suh; but me, I get scared!"

The plane quit circling and straightened out. The three jumpers moved up closer. The sergeant looked out tensely. Suddenly a buzzing bell sounded.

"Ho!" shouted the sergeant, and the three men went out so closely together that they all seemed one.

The Supervisor had a feeling that his heart jumped up and went out of his mouth after the jumpers, but the sergeant still stood tensely, looking. From the cable three ropes dangled as if a gallows-drop had been sprung.

But the sergeant still stood tensely, looking, and as the plane banked a little, the Supervisor had a glimpse of a swaying green parachute afloat in the air.

The sergeant relaxed. Without asking, the Supervisor knew that all the parachutes had opened and that perhaps the sergeant had even seen the men land.

Watching the next three jump was not so bad, and as they

went out, the Supervisor saw a parachute on the ground squarely in the middle of the thin spot, and a man standing beside it waving.

As they went in for the third run, there was a tense moment when they saw one parachute hanging in a tree. But just afterwards they saw a rope dangling and a man sliding down it. The jumpers didn't carry those seventy-foot ropes at their belts just to look pretty.

Four men went out on the third run, and then they circled twice more, as the sergeant and the only remaining private pushed out bundles of tools and food and bedding attached to yellow parachutes.

After the last bundle had been dropped, the plane circled to head for home, and the lieutenant came back from the pilot's compartment. He and the sergeant settled down on the bench opposite the doorway, and lighted cigarettes. The Supervisor sidled up beside the lieutenant.

"Did all the chutes open all right?" he asked.

"What?" said the lieutenant, as if that were a funny question. "Oh, sure—they opened. Sure. Everybody got down fine."

Just the same, there was a glisten of sweat on the lieutenant's forehead, and he was not wearing a jumping-suit.

But the Supervisor felt a vast relief. Not only had they all got down safely, but also they would not take long to pull off their helmets and padded suits, grab their tools, follow down the ridge, and report to Bart. Ten fresh men on the fire-line would make a lot of difference, and they still would have a couple of hours to work before the hottest burning-period came, in the middle of the afternoon.

When Bart had got to the fire, he had seen immediately that it was out of control. Ugly as things looked, however, he did not seize a shovel and start to work. His job was to scout around the fire, and particularly ahead of it, and then plan strategy. So he merely told Slugger and his men to keep on doing what they were doing already; they were certainly not hurting anything, and no matter what they did, the fire was by now far beyond the power of six already tired men.

He had been scrambling through some underbrush when the big lumbering transport plane passed overhead. He heard it circling, and once from a clear space he saw three green parachutes suddenly open up right beneath the plane. When the plane headed home, Bart had just finished his circuit, and was mapping the fire on a form printed to show a section of land, with dashed lines for quarter-sections and forties. An ordinary person would never have been able to tell where imaginary lines crossed through this rough country of canyon and forest, but it was part of Bart's business to know, and he had had twenty years to perfect himself.

So without hesitation he wrote DEFINITE on the dotted line after TOWNSHIP, and marked 7 in the middle of the map, to show that this fire was in Section 7 of Definite Township. Then, starting down in the southwest forty of the southwest quarter, he drew a curving line northward, into the northwest forty, and then back to the beginning. The area enclosed within the line represented the burned, and burning, area—as nearly as he could figure it. (By now the fire had lost its pistol shape entirely, and looked more like a short dangling sock tattered at the top, with the sole and bulging heel representing what had once been the under side of the barrel and the pistol butt.)

But Bart was thinking of distances. The area was somewhat more than a quarter-mile long. It would be longer before they could control it, and allowing for breadth and irregularities he would have to figure on nearly two miles of line to construct and hold in addition to what Slugger's boys had already completed. For the whole job he had Slugger's tired crew, plus ten (he hoped) jumpers, plus the suppression-crew of six, who should be getting there in an hour or so.

He planned quickly. The rear was already held; two of Slugger's boys for patrol would be all it needed. Slugger and the three others could take the upper flank, where they were already, and he would reinforce them with the suppression-crew. That section of line would follow the ridge, where the fire was likely to burn low. He would throw the jumpers in along the lower flank. That was dangerous because of rolling cones and logs, and they would have to build under-cut line, well ditched to catch the rolling stuff.

Such tactics left the front of the fire wide open, but he was counting on the jumpers to work faster than the fire moved, so that they could get ahead and pinch it off. If not, the twenty mill-men would be getting in at dark when the fire was dying down anyway, and they should be able to close the last gap without difficulty.

With flames crackling ten yards away, Bart stood for a minute thinking. At best, any strategy for fire-fighting was only a balancing of chances. Some of them could be predicted with accuracy—length of line required, terrain and cover, number of men. You could make a fair guess at short range as to burning-conditions, and quality and condition of men. But beyond that, hovered the surrounding darkness of ignorance and the future. All you could do was to set a safety-factor against all those chances which might break against you.

Everything considered, the chances looked good. They ought to catch the fire—at best, some time in the late afternoon; at worst, not later than ten, after the mill-men had been on the line for an hour or two.

Now he heard the shouts as the jumpers came hurrying down along the ridge. He called back to them, and when they came up, he led them along, and posted them as he had planned, explaining the situation to the corporal.

It was a joy to him to watch the jumpers get to work. They were fresh; they were picked men; they had been specially trained for fire-work. Also, he guessed, any colored boy who volunteered for a jumper did it partly to show that he could do anything a white boy could do, and maybe better.

As he started to struggle up-hill again toward Slugger's crew, Bart looked at his watch. At the start of a fire, time always rushed by and left you standing, and now it was already twelve-thirty. The suppression-crew should be here any time. Also, he realized, the sun was not quite as hot as it usually was at noon. Looking upward, he saw a faint white veil of high cloud over the western sky, just beginning to dim the sun a trifle. He remembered a forecast of possible rain. Well, they could use a rain, and if the sun went under, burning-conditions for the afternoon would not be quite as bad as he had figured.

5

By mid-afternoon the Dispatcher at Weaverville in the Trinity Forest was wearing a grin that would not come off; half his lookouts reported rain. Farther inland, east of the ocean-fronting ranges, the storm was weaker; even so, the west side of the Shasta had rain at Mt. Eddy and a snow flurry on Billy's Peak. From the Klamath to the Mendocino fire-danger ratings were tumbling like stock-prices on Black Tuesday. A grass-fire in Colusa County, which had been running like a horse at noon, lay down and died of itself at two-thirty, smothered by rising humidity.

Working on his afternoon map, Dave Halliday was not grinning. Of course, from the scientific point of view which interested him most, a weather situation was merely that, and nothing either to grin or frown over. Still, two years in the Weather Bureau and four years in the Navy had taught him that the best scientist should also be a humanist. In meteorological terms the present weather-situation was nothing much —just an ordinary beginning of a California autumn. Even his old Chief in San Francisco would not consider it of great importance. But here in the Ponderosa Forest, to all these people who lived with fire in the back of all their thoughts, to his new friend the Dispatcher especially, the situation might mean everything, even life and death.

By now he had begun to realize his own place in the scheme. The others saw a fire as burning on a certain slope in a certain quarter-section. Or at most, like the Dispatcher and the Supervisor, they thought of a fire in terms of Forest and Zone and Region. But they turned to him—almost imploringly, it seemed at times, like villagers to a far-traveler—for news of the greater world. He must see a fire in terms of a spinning earth and a sun retreating toward Capricorn, of arctic against tropic and continent against ocean, of the flying spray from Pacific waves whipped up by winds and absorbed by thirsty air a thousand miles off-shore. Just when the breeze might eddy around in a certain canyon and give the signal for lighting backfires, any old-time ranger could tell better than he. But beyond the limits of his own horizon the ranger was helpless.

So now he studied the map. The front—that was nothing. It would doubtless bring some rain tonight, making good his forecast. Possibly it would douse that fire which was burning somewhere in Barlow District. But the front was a weak one, and after it had passed—would summer move in again for another month and heat go shooting up and humidity fall?

No—he hardly thought so. A much stronger storm, a genuine summer-breaker, was showing along the nearer Aleutians. It could mean nothing to the Ponderosa, however, for some days.

Letting his eyes swing again to the stations immediately behind the present approaching front, he noted light northerly winds, rather moist air, but—more strikingly—a sharp drop of temperature. Lookouts in the Trinity who could have sun-bathed in the hot early morning must now be wearing sweaters.

Then from the storm center in Montana he followed the blue line of the front southwestward. Over Oregon also, temperatures were dropping sharply as the cold air from the northern Pacific moved in behind the front, although barometric pressures had not risen much as yet. . . .

The forecast was a difficult one. After he had typed it and left his assistant radioing it out, he walked over to the Dispatcher's office. Arn was there.

"How's your fire?" Dave asked.

"Had a message through from Bart half an hour ago. He's got twenty-three men there now, counting himself. He's cheerful. Expects to get his line all tied in before so long, in time to get his backfires going before the main fire gets there. Then we figure that rain you're sending us will get here to make the mop-up easy. You're not renigging on the rain, are you?"

"No-o-o."

"You sound doubtful."

"Well, there ought to be some rain all right, but I'm wondering about tomorrow. I couldn't make a clean forecast. I'd like to talk to you about it."

"Go ahead."

"You see, I figure the pressure in eastern Oregon is the thing to watch. If we get a high in there, it'll mean we have a big dome of cold air lying over the plateau."

"What of it?"

"You know about water running down hill?"

"Read about it in a book once."

"Well, cold air runs down hill just the same way, and if a lot of it piles up in eastern Oregon, it's going to start sluicing down through these canyons until it fills the Central Valley of California like a bath-tub. And then—"

But he noticed that Arn was looking glum enough to eat worms.

"O. K.—Don't go on!" said Arn, "I know all about it from here in. We used to call it a Santa Ana on the Angeles, and a Mono on the Stanislaus. Up here it's not quite so hot, and that's about all. Just our luck to have a fire already going when she hits."

"Well, maybe she won't. Can't tell for sure yet!"

"She probably will all right. It's the right time of year. Our chance is to get this Spitcat Fire out, before the wind hits."

"There's the rain, you know."

"That's right!" said Arn, suddenly more cheerful.

6

All afternoon the jumpers had worked along the lower flank. The big cones of the Jeffrey pines were devils for rolling, and so the line had to be carefully ditched. Building an under-cut line was slow work, and during the afternoon the jumpers never managed to get clearly ahead of the fire. All they could do was to pinch it a little and force it diagonally up-slope toward the ridge.

The Barlow suppression-crew worked the ridge. There

were only six of them, but they did not have to under-cut, and so they kept up with the jumpers of the lower flank.

Slugger's crew was all told off now for patrol on the already held sections of line, except for the boy with the bad knee whom Bart had assigned to stand by at the radio. One rolling cone jumped ten feet across the line and started trouble, but the patrol set up a shout and brought two of the jumpers down on the run. By fast work they got a line around the slop-over before it really got going.

After sunset the wind which had been steady all afternoon fell off to a light breeze, still from the south. Soon afterward both crews managed to get a little ahead of the fire, and Bart judged that this was the moment.

The jumpers were tired now, but as their corporal yelled at them, they sprinted again and swung the direction of their line-building straight up-slope.

There was a gap of two hundred yards to link up. From above, Bart heard the clank of shovels hitting rock as the suppression-crew, swinging back at a sharp angle, came down slope to meet the jumpers. Only fifty yards off, the fire blazed up suddenly as a clump of young trees went off.

Bart scrambled up the slope with the corporal, pointing out where the line could be put through most efficiently. Then he sent the corporal back, and went on to meet the suppression-crew, knowing that he would have to build his back-fires from the ridge down.

When the suppression-crew had cleared fifty yards, Bart pulled a fusee out of his pocket. He held a match to the end, and the fusee flared with a bright pink flame. He stuck it among the twigs of a dead branch that lay four feet inside the fire-line. When the twigs blazed, he pulled the fusee out, and went along inside the line starting fires in the needles and twigs. "Fight fire with fire."

With the wind as it was, all the little fires blew toward the line, but moving only a few feet they had no chance to get big, and when they came to the cleared line they died. But on the other side, eating backward into the wind, the back-fires moved slowly. Still they moved, and as he watched, they spread sideways and gradually joined into a solid front. Then as the main fire grew closer, the back-fires caught the suck of the draft which the main fire pulled in toward itself against the light wind.

Suddenly the back-fires sprang to life, and went roaring through the underbrush toward the main fire. The two met about a hundred feet from where Bart was standing at the line. As in the head-on dash of two waves, the fires piled up. A clump of underbrush suddenly disappeared in white-yellow flames. Close by, a seventy-foot fir tree, its resins vaporized by the heat, exploded into a flame that towered a hundred feet upward. There was a long-drawn hiss that was almost a roar. For twenty seconds the dying tree stood out in the twilight, a white-hot torch of flaming gas. As it burned out, the tips of the level branches glowed red for a moment, and then the tall tree was nothing but a dark silhouette of branches against the fire-lit sky.

Bart stood watching. Unimpressed by the commonplace fireworks, he was trying to see what the sparks did. As far as he could tell, they went almost straight up and cooled to blackness high in the air without blowing across the line to spread the fire farther.

"Well, we got away with that one!" he said to one of the suppression-crew, and went on down to light the next section.

Before the two ends of the line were tied together, the fire was so close that there was no chance for a back-fire, and they had to hope that the line itself would hold. The fire jumped in one spot, but two of the suppression-crew, working almost in the flames, managed to hold it. One of them came out with a hole burned in the back of his shirt where a spark had lit.

Then, so suddenly as to seem queer, everything was quiet. Also everything was dark, for as they had worked, twilight had crept up, and now that the big blaze had died down, there was little light left.

In the excitement of the last few minutes the two crews had mingled, and now they stood, white and black, just as they happened to be, dog-tired, grimy and sweaty, leaning on their shovels, still watching but also letting rest soak into them. Inside the line hundreds of little flames licked up where cones and branches and logs were still burning, but they were all tiny by comparison and made little light and no noise.

The corporal scratched a match, and the flare seemed to light up the hillside. He lit his cigarette, gave a light to the suppression-crew foreman who stood beside him, and tossed the match into the burn.

Then, just as if to make things doubly sure, there was shouting from across the canyon and a show of lights, and Bart knew that the mill-men, fresh and twenty strong, had got up, and would be ready to take over for the night.

But as he started to relax, weariness hit him suddenly. It had been a long, long day. He remembered again that he had not really slept much since Wednesday night. He felt dizzy, and sat down on the ground for a moment to get hold of himself.

To THE MEN on the line the fire was red glare in the eyes and reaching flame, roar and crackle in the ears, choking in the throat, fierce heat on the face. The fire possessed them, and beat in upon their senses. Yet, actually, what was that thing called *the fire?*

Like a man, a fire exists in time. First as a tiny spark, it lives faintly. A breath of wind might blow it out; some drops of water, quench it. But, if born in happy circumstances, it feeds lustily and grows. It takes shape and develops structure, drawing in fresh air along the ground, throwing off smoke and consumed air skywards. Where once it scarcely crept, now suddenly it walks and runs. The vigor and power of youth rises within it. It grows adult, and casts out sparks to kindle new fires.

Yet, even as it sweeps ahead in power and glory, the shadow lies over it. "This too shall pass away." Failing to find food, rained upon, blown against by contrary winds, the fire loses vigor. Grown weaker, it searches less strongly for food, and so grows weaker still. It lies in the quiet of old age. At last, quickly or slowly, it dies.

137

The likeness to a man does not fully hold. Now a fire is more like a shape-shifting monster, stretching out long and encircling arms before it. Now a fire is like a nation, growing weak for a while, and then springing up with a new vigor, as millions of flamelets within it die, or as new flamelets blaze up. But—man or monster or nation—like them all, the fire is the thing-in-itself. It begins, and is, and ends; it is born, and lives, and dies.

2

After midnight an old moon was high enough above the shoulder of Howell Mountain to cast some brightness among the trees and let a man see something outside the range of his flashlight. Twenty feet off, Bart could now make out the form of the boy called Shorty, curled up beside the radio, trying to get a little sleep in spite of the cold of the mountain night. Bart himself had only snatched a few cat-naps; as sure as he settled down, some message came in over the radio or somebody clumped down the trail about something or other. Or even if there was nothing actually, Bart's nerves brought him up with a snap, just when he should have been settling deeper into sleep. There was no one else on the fire of sufficient experience to take over as night fire-boss.

He stood up to take a look. His improvised headquarters were at the bottom, just outside the lowest tip of the burned area. There was little to show that it really was headquarters —just the radio, and a few extra tools and two back-pumps which somebody had packed in and not used. The fire was all quiet, but Bart decided to make another round, now that the moon was up. He was weary, but it ought to be done.

He hated to wake the boy at the radio, but as he stepped closer, the boy stirred, and looked up of his own accord.

"Sleeping?" asked Bart.

"Not much. Too cold! We started in a hurry, and Slugger thought we'd be back in camp before night."

"I'm making a round again. There won't be any emergency, but write down the messages if there are any.—Here, put this jacket over you."

"You need it yourself!"

"I'll be walking.—Say, how's your knee?"

"Not hurting much.—Thanks for the jacket."

As he moved off, Bart felt chilly in nothing but his shirt, but he hated to think of a kid trying to sleep and just lying there shivering. That was the devil about fires above four thousand feet. The temperature might hit a hundred in the daytime, plus all the heat of the fire itself, and then in the early morning you were ready to freeze to death.

But, as he breasted the steep trail, the first line that Slugger's crew had built, Bart soon was warm enough, even though he took the stiff climb easily, because of his own weariness. He used his flashlight rather little, for the moon gave some light, and he wanted to see what the fire itself was doing.

You would have said at first glance that it was really dead, but as you looked closer, here was a little glow, and there a tiny flame, and since you saw dozens of such points, you knew that there would be thousands of them within the area enclosed by the fire-line.

Along here he must be very close to where the fire had started. In the morning, whenever he had time, he would look around for curiosity and find the tree that had been struck. Up ahead, he now saw a larger flame begin to blaze up, but he knew what that would be, and was not worried.

He climbed higher, stopping to pant now and then. After a while he came to where the line ran around in a half-circle. That, he realized, was testimony to how close Slugger's crew had been to choking off the fire in its infancy; the projecting knob showed where they had actually confined what had been the head of the fire before it took off up-canyon.

Just beyond this, Bart came to the larger fire he had already been seeing. Six loggers lay sprawled about, and they had just thrown a new log on a bonfire they had built inside the line to keep themselves warm. They had heard Bart scrambling up the trail, and as he came into the range of the fire-light, they turned or rolled over languidly to greet him.

He asked them how things were, and one of them said it was all quiet—only, he did not make that statement in such simple and concise form, but after the custom of loggers he elaborated the basic idea with conventional profanity and obscenity until the sentence was almost a paragraph.

Bart squatted down to catch his wind. A perpetual slow-paced conversation seemed to be going on among the men— like a slow fire, never quite kindling, never quite going out. One man would make a deliberate and potentially insulting remark to another, and after a while that other would reply in kind, perhaps involving a third. Then, just when Bart thought the matter had been dropped, the third one would languidly pick up the ball and toss it again. More than half the words, it seemed, were unprintable, and Bart wondered at the endless monotony of the ironclad rule which required that a man could not even turn to warm his other side without referring to Christianity, his neighbor's ancestry, and several bodily parts, functions, and perversions.

Having six men at one point meant that long stretches of the line were without patrol, but Bart said nothing. There was really little danger during the night, and he knew loggers. They would work like demons in an emergency, but at other times they responded to orders or ignored them according to whether the orders seemed reasonable in their experience.

By two o'clock Bart had followed the line that the suppression-crew had built along the ridge, and was at the head of the fire. Another group of men lay about another bonfire here, and one of them also said it was all quiet—adding the same elaborations that the other fellow had.

The moon had gone under clouds now, and actually the fire was even quieter than it had been. The overcast was low. The air felt heavy with moisture, and this moisture was smothering the fire, forcing it to use up its heat in merely driving the dampness away. Except for the nasty forecast of a high north wind in the later morning, Bart would not have been bothered at all. Even so, he was not really worrying.

By this bonfire he took out his map, and revised it. Coming up from the other bunch of men, he had counted his paces, and with allowances for climbing and other factors, he now had a better idea of size. He redrew his lines a little. The burned area now showed as an elongated slug-like form, wriggling in a mild double curve up from its base about two hundred feet above the creek to its upper point, where he now was, some four hundred feet higher. The length was about five-eighths of a mile; the average breadth, somewhat under two hundred yards. He estimated the area as forty acres, what the Forest Service would list officially as a Class C fire.

Actually, although Bart hated all fires desperately, he realized that this one had not done any great damage. It had wiped out the underbrush and small trees, but the underbrush would spring up fast and very few of the small trees would ever have grown to maturity anyway, against the competition of the big ones. Of the big trees very few had been killed, because the fire had mostly stayed close to the ground. The chief damage would be that the fire, eating at the bases of the large trees, had burned through the bark in places, and caused what the lumbermen called "cat-faces." Boring insects would work into these cat-faces, and in a few years there would be a lot of sick and dying trees.

Bart put the map into his pocket, and started to slide down the steep trail where he had set the first back-fire. Soon, having to pick his way with the aid of the flashlight, he was working along the undercut line that the jumpers had built. An occasional blackened cone lying in the ditch showed that it had not been labor wasted.

Halfway along he came to the six men of the suppression-crew, huddled miserably around a fire built inside the line, trying to sleep. They were cold in spite of the fire, and ready to sit up and talk. From lying where the needles had been burned, they had added soot to dust, and their faces were so black that you could hardly have told them from the jumpers.

"How's she look, Bart?" asked the crew-boss.

"Quiet. The dampness has her blanketed. We'll probably get a little rain any time now."

A general cry of protest arose, as if Bart could do anything about the rain. But to be rained on after a fire and to have the charred pine-needles dissolve into black mud and to be wet as well as cold—that was a final insult.

"What you crabbin' about?" said Bart. "The rain'll save us a lot of work at mop-up."

"Oh, sure," said one of them. "But I need some sleep. Those jumpers are the lucky boys. They just went back up the ridge to where the plane dropped their bed-rolls."

"Huh?" said another. "They can have their blankets, if they'll let me not have to jump!"

"You said it! . . . O. K., brother! . . . I'll take mine on the ground!"

An approving grumble ran around the fire, and then there was a pause. In the pause Bart heard a faint *whi-sh-sh* high in the tree-tops. He tipped back his head, and felt a tiny drop spatter on his nose.

"Here she is, boys, the rain! And I've got to be on my way."

Bart's mind was suddenly at ease. A fire that was already knocked down could never stand being rained on. But as he scrambled along the trail, he felt very little rain. It might be wetting the over-spreading canopy of pine-needles a hundred and fifty feet in the air, but scarcely any was reaching the ground. There was that bad forecast, too. But still with a fire looking as nearly dead as this one was, even Bart could not worry much. . . .

He was nearly back to his starting-point when he heard an unmistakable *click-clunk-squeak*. He felt a sudden warmth of comradeship. At times during the long day he had seemed to be a forgotten ranger with a few men, fighting a dangerous fire on a lonely canyon-side, alone. But that sound down the trail meant the coming of the pack-train, and that meant that he was not forgotten.

Somewhere during the long day people had thought of John Bartley and his men, and known that the K-rations would be running low. Then they had made sandwiches, and packed lunches in brown paper bags, and packed the bags into cartons, and packed the cartons into a truck. Then the truck had rolled up through Idylhurst, and on to the road-head at Onion Flat. And at some time Tony had loaded his mules into a truck and taken them also to Onion Flat. He had unloaded the mules and saddled them, and packed the lunches in the big saddle-bags. Then he had forded the creek —by now it was dark—and led the mules up the switch-backs, and along the contour above Onion Creek, and into Reverse Meadow, and on up Onion Creek, until he had seen the faint glow of the fire across the canyon. He had left the trail and worked the mules slowly down the canyonside and across the creek and up this side. And here he came now—*click-clunk-squeak*—with lunches for tired and hungry men, and with extra batteries for dying flashlights and headlamps, and with a first-aid kit, and a dozen other bits of this and that which men might be needing on a fire.

Bart felt something go out of him—a sudden inexpressible great love of the world and the people in it, and most of all of his own comrades. There were sudden tears in his eyes, all because a greasy-haired little Mexican mule-skinner was working three smelly mules up through the pine-trees.

"Why, Tony, you old son-of-a-bitch!" he called as he saw the dark moving forms. "Where the hell you been all this time!"

And he saw the shiny white Mexican teeth as Tony broke into a grin. . . .

When at last he came sliding downhill to headquarters, Bart was cold and damp. There were no messages written on the pad, and the boy was sleeping, curled up beneath the jacket. Bart lacked the heart to wake him up or take it away. He went off a few yards, inside the fire-line where a log was still smoking along its upper side in spite of the dirt that had been piled in against it. (The boys never seemed to learn that you couldn't put a fire out that way.) The log was giving off some heat, and Bart sat close to it. The rain had stopped; the wind, getting colder every minute, was shifting into the north already. Bart was stiff with the chill, but he was also dead tired. He sat all huddled up, and his head settled forward now and then as he dozed off, only to wake up again, tired and shivering.

3

That morning, across hundreds of miles of inland plateau, though it was only September, frost was glittering on the sage-brush. The air, cold and dry already when it had moved in behind the storm-front, had grown colder during the clear night, and having had most of its remaining moisture squeezed out as frost, it was also even drier than before. This dome of cold and heavy air, extending upward some thousands of feet, rested upon a plateau which was several thousand feet above sea-level, in eastern Oregon and the adjoining parts of Idaho and Nevada.

Only a few hundred miles to the southwest, in the low-lying Central Valley of California, the temperature had reached a hundred degrees in the afternoon, and had scarcely fallen below eighty during the night. The air was correspondingly light, and it rested on a surface only a little above sea-level.

Lacking a barrier, the heavier air must by the mere law of gravity, run down and replace the lighter air, and the only semblance of barrier between the two was the line of the northern Sierra Nevada. In ancient days, however, that edge of the tilting block of earth which had formed those mountains had been lifted only a few thousand feet above the level of the eastern plateau, and during the hundreds of centuries since its up-lifting the forces of air and water and frost had worn down gaps and passes which were scarcely a thousand feet above the sage-brush plain. The line of mountains, therefore, in comparison with the high-towering cold air, was little more than a picket-fence to ruffle the under surface. Before daylight a dry cold wind was beginning to pour through the passes and down the long canyons of the western slope.

Dave Halliday, still working beneath the green-shaded electric light, wrote 1023 on a free-hand circle covering most of southeastern Oregon, stamped HIGH inside of it, and leaned back to survey the map. The wind-arrows for the stations to the north and east of Suffolk already pointed southwest; well feathered, they showed winds at ten to twenty miles an hour. He would scarcely have to contrive what could be dignified by the name of a forecast; the thing was already upon them.

Outside, there was full daylight already, and through the window he saw the line of neatly planted young plane trees at the edge of the lawn. He was rather surprised that their big leaves were only stirring gently. That merely meant the wind had not yet quite got here.

Arnold Sorenson's big hands fumbled for the telephone automatically, almost before his eyes were open.

"Hello!" he said sharply, wiping the sleep from his voice. "Dispatcher Sorenson speaking."

He recognized the voice of Dave Halliday:

"Sorry to bother you—"

"Skip it, Dave. You aren't inviting me to tea, are you?"

"Well, there's trouble all right. Nothing but a little breeze here yet, but Reno has a twenty-mile northeasterly, and on my map I've got four isobars piled up between here and eastern Oregon."

"What kind of wind does that mean?"

"Twenty miles and up, in the canyons, hitting forty in the gusts along the ridges, and so dry she'll crack your lips in half an hour."

"Sounds sweet!" said the Dispatcher. Then he paused for a couple of breaths, considering. But there was obviously nothing worse that a weatherman could report, and so there was nothing more to ask. "All right, Dave," he said. "Thanks a lot." He hung up, jumped out of bed, started dressing. . . .

As he walked across to Headquarters there was a fairly good breeze blowing. It raised some dust from the dry vacant lot, and flapped the leaves of the plane trees. The sun, just rising, had a kind of hard brazen dazzle to it; though the breeze was cool, the heat of the sun was unpleasant, and the glare made him squint. Suddenly he disliked things in general. The sun, for instance, seemed personally hostile, and in the bare sky it looked indecently naked. He was licking his lips. Then he remembered, and tried to relax. That was what such a wind always did to people's nerves. He remembered an old story that in the early days a Californian who committed murder during a north wind could plead that as an extenuating circumstance.

In his office he turned the radio on, got contact with the stand-by on the Spitcat Fire, and asked for Bart. Bart sounded tired and sleepy, and he seemed rather unconcerned. That was, of course, usually the way of it—the man at the fire was either a lot more or a lot less excited than the man at Headquarters, because he saw the fire as it looked at the moment close-up, and you always had difficulty in making him realize that the general situation would soon be better or worse.

"Oh," said Bart, "I went all the way round her a while ago, and she looks awful cold. The rain—well, can't say we really had much rain—but the dampness, anyway, knocked her pretty flat. I've got two faller-crews in there—I can hear them right now—and they'll be getting the snags down pretty fast."

"How about wind?"

"There's a pretty steady wind—down-canyon. Don't seem too bad though. Once the sun gets higher there ought to be some up-canyon draft build up to check it."

"The weatherman thinks not. He's forecast winds up to forty miles on the ridges."

"Well, maybe. But he ain't been around this country as long as I have."

"Say, Bart, hold on a minute, will you? I've got something I have to do."

The Dispatcher got up and walked across the room. What he had to do was to think a moment.

"Of all tools," he was quoting to himself, "men are the most apt to get out of order." Bart was a good man, one of the best, but just now he was like a McLeod with a bent tooth, or a radio with a loose connection. His malady was what they called "first-slump-itis." You hit the fire all keyed up, and then when you got it knocked down, you had to relax. Moreover, Bart might be right. The fire might be harmless now, and young Dave Halliday could be wrong. But in this business the only safe way was to figure that the worst possible would happen.

"Look here, Bart," he spoke sharply into the transmitter, "you know what's going to happen if that fire takes off in a norther. Remember the Merriam's Mill and the Kimshew? That fire is pointed right at some of the best forest in California." (Maybe a little shock would help.)

There was a pause, and the Dispatcher felt that the shock was working.

"O. K., Arn. I'll do everything I can. You know that all right, don't you?" (The Dispatcher caught a faint pleading note in the voice, and he realized that Bart must be very tired.) "But say, Arn. What can I do, or anybody else, if this fire sets out to go places in a forty-mile wind?"

When he had signed off, the Dispatcher was in as much of a dilemma as ever. He could not set trucks and bulldozers and hundreds of men rolling to fight a fire which existed only as a future possibility. But at least he could call Cerro Gordo Lookout, which next to Bart was his closest present contact with the fire.

"How's the Spitcat looking, Judith?" he asked.

"Not much I can see this morning at all. Hardly any smoke at all."

"Well, I'll tell you, Judith. Keep watching it, and if anything happens—she blows up or anything, starts throwing a lot of smoke—call me direct. Understand?"

After that, when he had eaten breakfast and the time was a little more decent, he called all the Ranger Stations in the Ponderosa, and then Zone Headquarters. At least if he couldn't mobilize, he could get everybody alerted. He noted in the log-book, most carefully, the time of all his calls. If there was a Board of Review, his record would be clear.

He was anxious and nervous, tense with the dry north wind. Through the window he idly watched a scrap of newspaper being blown along. The wind lifted it, and dropped it, and then picked it up again, turning it over and over. Only when it had blown out of sight did he realize that the wind, to blow the paper like that, must be rising. And just then the Super stepped in.

"Hi, Arn," he said, "I'm early. Couldn't sleep—this wind, I guess. I was going over to Rabbitbrush today about some grazing permits, but I think I'd better stick around. How's that fire?"

But before Arn could answer, the girl with the fire-danger rating came in. (And she was early too, because she also, it seemed, could not sleep because of the wind.)

She went to set the point on the rainbow-colored little circle. The Dispatcher knew that there was bad news ahead, with a high wind like this. Nevertheless he started a little, when she stepped away and showed the dial-face. The point stood well within the red sector labeled *Extreme*.

During the night—like a man on his death-bed, drawing breath more slowly as the vital forces ebb—the Spitcat had grown weaker. At first, after the opposing rush of the back-fires had stopped its advance in a great upsurging wall of flame, the fire had for a while burned vigorously in isolated spots. But having consumed the fuel at hand and being unable to spread farther, it quieted rapidly. Minute by minute, one by one, the flames flickered out; red deadened into black. Nevertheless, the fire had spread to such a large area that even by morning it was still alive in some hundreds of isolated spots.

As, after some great gang of the underworld has been shattered, a few of the desperate and dangerous still sit nursing their hatred in hidden cellars and lonely rooms, hoping for the time when they may again go out to steal and kill, so in hidden and lonely places the fire still lived. From the lower side of a log, a faint smoke arose. Underground, a dead root smouldered. In deep duff, though the surface was black, a living fire still ate ahead.

More dangerous were the tall snags of the dead trees. As the fire had first rushed by them, it had ignited the dry moss around their bases. Aided by the upward draft of the heat, flames quickly ran clear to their tops, and for a little while they flamed like tall torches. Soon, however, the moss burned away, the passing of the ground fire removed the draft, and the fire in the dead trees died down.

During the night the fire was quenched in many of the snags, but it still burned in others—eating along beneath a slab of still clinging bark, hiding in the crotch of a branch, working through the holes of borers and all kinds of cracks and crannies.

The falling of the snags was too dangerous to be undertaken in the dark, but immediately after daybreak two crews had taken the guards off their cross-cut saws, collected their mauls and wedges, and moved in. Some twenty minutes later the first cry of *TIM-BER-R-R* resounded along the canyon-

side, and with a great thud which came echoing back from
the other wall of the canyon, the first of the snags came down.
As it struck, thirty feet of its top broke off, and a shower of
sparks showed that it had been still a hazard.

The dry northeast-wind had been moving down the canyon
of Onion Creek since before daybreak, but it was not very
strong. Nevertheless, aided by the quick rise of temperature
after sunrise, it rapidly dried up the moisture of the night.

New flames, almost invisible in the dazzling sunlight, licked
upward here and there. Smoke rose from spots where there
had been no smoke a moment before. And high in the air the
tops of dead snags again began to burn.

Yet, one might have said, the wind came only as a stimulant
which for a few moments revives a dying man, then to pass
away and let him sink more rapidly. The fire, contained within the line, could reach out for no new fuel, and the wind
merely made it burn out more rapidly. So after a while, the
flames and smoke began to die down again and to disappear
—except that the tops of a few snags were smoking heavily
and bursting into flame here and there.

The situation was still under control, although Bart was
worried again, as any fire-boss would have to be with a twenty-
mile dry wind and some snags still smoking. The crews that
had rested through the night were back on the job, and so he
now had thirty-eight men for patrol and mop-up. With the
northeast wind the down-canyon side was again the dangerous
one. He put the rested crews on that side, and scattered some
of them back into the underbrush to watch for spot fires. The
loggers and mill-men patrolled the rest of the line except for
those who were getting the snags down. The snags were all
that Bart was really concerned about, especially those that

were already flaming, even though they stood well inside the fire-line. Something must be done about them, if possible.

He hurried down to where a falling-crew was at work.

"How about it?" he asked. "Do you want to try those hot ones?"

The men glanced at one another.

"We'll take a look," said one of them.

One snag was burning at the bottom, and was too hot for the saw, even if you had had a salamander-crew to work it. They looked at another, appraised their chances with liberal profanity, and then got to work with the nonchalant air of men who were risking their lives and rather enjoying it. (After all, you didn't hire out as a faller at all, if you were interested in dying in bed.) Bart let them take the risk. If this fire ever jumped the line on a day like this, there would be a lot of trees burned and many lives in hazard.

While two men worked on the saw, another stood back and watched the burning top. Just as they finished the first under-cut he yelled, and they ran. A thirty-foot slab of flaming three-inch bark came falling through the air. They dodged behind trees, and the slab hit where they had just been working, with a crash that would have brained any man alive.

They kicked the burning fragments out of the way, and got to work again.

And still that great mass of cold air poured out, southward and westward, across the jagged tops of the mountains toward the hot lowlands. High in the air it was like a smooth and swift-running stream. But close to the ground, it eddied and swirled around peak and ridge and point, and ran turbulently as a mountain-torrent—here slower, here swifter, here built up into great gusts as surging waves of invisible air broke against mountainsides, funneled through gaps, or clashed one against another.

Dry at the beginning, that air grew drier still as it flowed down the slope, and grew warmer. It licked up thirstily the few drops of rain and the little dampness of the night. It robbed the plants of hard-won moisture sucked up from deep in the ground. Leaves wilted on the bitter-brush and mountain-lilac; turpentine distilled from the pines; on the forest-floor the needles were crackling-dry.

Nervous, feeling the pressure of the dry wind like an attacking enemy, the men wet their parched lips, and still the lips cracked. Suddenly they knew they were playing a desperate gamble. Around the fire ran a narrow line of cleared earth. Inside it, as the dry wind brought half-dead sparks to life, more and more flames licked up. Another snag where the fire had seemed dead, began to smoke; flames rose from its top, leaning off before the wind; sparks flew. And just beyond the line, everwhere the thick dry underbrush and the desiccated pine-needles waited for a spark in the turpentine-smelling air.

The fallers took longer chances. "TIM-BER-RR!" came the call, and another snag crashed down to the ground, where the gusts no longer swirled off the sparks. In the underbrush the scattered men with shovels and McLeods looked back and forth, watching the air for flying sparks, and the ground for rising smoke, wetting their lips, wondering. . . .

Then at last it came. From turbulences and pressures built up far away, a gigantic wave of air billowed and broke along the slope of the ridge, invisible, except as it wildly tossed the branches. From the slope of Howell Mountain another surging wave raced downward. The two met on the ridge in a great swirl.

The tree-tops bent suddenly like grass. In the power of the blast the flames at the tops of burning snags stood out stiff like flags. The quick wrench of the whirling air tore off bits of bark and rotten wood, swirled them upward for a moment, and then tossed and hurled them off.

Some cooled as they fell; some lit within the fire-line; but others blew across the line and fell flaming upon the tinder-dry needles. As a dog jumps from a platform and hits the ground running, so a fire took off from each fallen spark.

A strip of glowing bark dropped within ten feet of Slugger O'Neill. He jumped for it, as a flame licked forward three feet across the needles. With a single desperate scrape of his shovel he caught the running point and threw it back upon itself. In a few frenzied seconds he scraped a line around the spot-fire and contained it.

But other burning bits fell elsewhere. Flames ran across the surface of pine-needles for a second, and then flared up into the bushes. Working wildly, men shouted for help, but none came, for there were more fires than men. As you worked to hold one fire, another blazed up in the bush behind you.

Suddenly it was wide-open disaster, twenty spot-fires racing across the duff, smoke everywhere, underbrush blazing.

Bart, running down the line from where the blow-up had caught him, saw that the game was up.

"Get back out of there, boys!" he screamed. "Get back out of there! Head for the old burn!"

Some of them heard, and a white-faced youngster burst out of the underbrush, slapping at a spark on his sleeve. "One!" counted Bart. "Two-three-four-five. There's Slugger—six!" But there were still others somewhere in the already burning scramble of underbrush and trees that in a minute or so was going to blaze up like hell itself. Taking a long breath, he plunged in. If men were endangered for being where his orders had sent them, his job was to get them out, or else not go home and tell about it.

Fifty feet in, he came to a boy working so frantically around a burning bush that he did not even hear as Bart shouted at him. Bart grabbed his arm and shook it.

"Get back out of here! Get back into the old burn!"

"Christ!" yelled the boy. "Why don't someone come? We can catch this one!"

"You damn fool, get back before your pants burn off you!"

And then suddenly the boy looked around, and went white, and ran back.

Bart went on, shouting to the men ahead. Then all at once he knew that there was no going back into the old burn any more, for behind him there was suddenly fire everywhere.

He came to another of the boys, who had dropped his Mc-Leod and stood gazing about in horror at the blazes in front and behind. "Come with me!" said Bart. He was running now, edging off between the fires.

Paralleling what had been the old line, he picked up two of the jumpers. Far ahead, through rising smoke, he saw another of them running downhill in great leaps like a deer. He found two more—these were from suppression-crew—and then there was no more time.

With the five men following, he angled off, running downhill and away from the fire—but there were fires ahead too. Smoke was everywhere, blowing out flat before the wind. They coughed and choked with it, and their eyes watered and stung. The air was furnace-hot.

Bart heard one of the boys cry out sharply in panic, "We're goin' to burn here! I'm goin' t'run for it!"

Turning, Bart struck him with the open hand, full force on the cheek.

"Shut up!" he said. "I've been in these woods twenty years,

and I don't want to die more than you do! Stay with me!"

They went on for a few moments, the boy sniffling. Smoke shut off the sun and all landmarks, and Bart only kept direction by the feel of the slope. They choked so hard that they had to lean low to breathe closer to the ground, and their run faded off to a shuffle. The dry wind poured heat upon them. They hit a thick clump of young trees, and had to skirt it.

Maybe, Bart was thinking, the boy was right. Maybe I didn't want to run for it because I'm old and have a paunch on me. Maybe I should have let them run. But still panic was never good on a fire, and if you ran, you might get snarled up with thickets, or break a leg, or merely find that the fire—in a wind like this!—had swung around from somewhere, or blown ahead, and trapped you.

Just then right ahead through the smoke they all saw the glowing red-hot branches of a bush, and one of the boys let out the little scream of a trapped thing. But Bart was not afraid of panic any more. They were past that, and only wanting someone to tell them what to do.

From the sparks that came sailing by, he knew that fire was not far behind. Things would be decided now, pretty soon. He led on, through the thick smoke, toward the glowing branches in front.

It was a spot-fire—not very big probably, but it would have to do. It was scarcely burning along its windward side, where they were. Bart took as deep a breath as he could, threw his hands over his head, and dashed through the line of fire. The others followed. They had to slap out burning spots in their clothes, and their shoes were hot. But they were inside a little island of already burned ground. It was pitifully small-looking and they were certain to get extremely hot, maybe worse. But it was better than making a blind dash through the burning and smoke-filled forest, and short of some miracle such as the wind dying down, it was the best they could hope.

Their hearts were pounding; they were coughing worse than ever; they were half-blinded with smoke. They all lay on the hot ground, panting, and trying to suck up a little of the cleaner air that moved along under the smoke.

On Cerro Gordo that morning she stayed mostly inside the room. The wind seemed to shake the whole tower; she could scarcely stand on the catwalk.

There was only the faintest wisp of smoke over beyond Reverse Ridge. Then she just glanced in the other direction for a second—so it seemed, at least—and when she looked back, a great black column was towering up. Even while she stood for a horror-struck moment looking at it, the top billowed upward and rose higher. For another moment, as if reacting to some deep ancestral habit, she stood, making sure before she committed herself. Then she ran for the telephone.

This time she was cool as she rang the bell and waited; she was a veteran now.

"Hello, Arn?" she said. "Say, the Spitcat has blown up. There's a big column of smoke, rising fast."

After he got the news, Arnold Sorenson, the Dispatcher, paused only long enough to think once, "Well, here it is!" and then he went into action.

"Come on, Bud," he called to his assistant in the next room. "That Spitcat Fire has taken off! Call our rangers, and tell them to give us all they got. Fire-camp at Onion Flat."

He lifted the receiver, and heard the operator taking a call.

"Clear the lines, Jackie," he said. "We've got a blow-up!"

"Yes, sir," said Jackie, without even finishing her sentence to the other person.

"All right—get me Zone!"

Yet, as he waited the few seconds it would take to get that call through, the Dispatcher felt himself curiously calm and not particularly in a hurry. This was no flash-fire like that one on Hart Creek, where a minute's time lost in getaway might mean the difference between five acres and five thousand. It was not even like the Spitcat of yesterday where ten parachutists could turn the scale; now a whole battalion would not suffice. Today the job was not so much like fighting a battle as like building up an army. What yesterday had been a frontier-incident was now a total war.

The fire was blazing on both sides of the little burned area. The six of them lay close together, the four on the outside sheltering with their bodies the two who lay inside. One of these was hysterical, and the other had to hold him so that he wouldn't jump up and run, as he had tried once. Two of the boys had held to their shovels as they ran, and now they used the shovels to scrape dirt and burned needles and rocks from the center and pile it around the outside. The freshly cleared earth was a little cooler, but there were so many rocks that they could not scrape out much dirt, and the pile only served to shelter their faces. Every little while someone squirmed suddenly and started slapping at a smoking place on his shirt or pants where a spark had lighted. Now and then the hysterical one gave a scream.

So far, so good! Bart was thinking that he had been in as bad a hole as this a couple of times before—on the Nelson Point Fire, for instance. He had even seen men go hysterical. (He hoped the boy was just hysterical, and not really gone off.) So far, so good! The bark of the trees around them had been scorched in the first run of the fire and now it was smoking. If it began to burn, the place might get warmer than a

man could take. Or, the air might just burn out and let them
suffocate in smoke. Or, if the fire worked up into the tops of
the big trees and went roaring off as a crown-fire, burning
needles and twigs would come showering down, and the heat
would just get to be more than a man's body could stand.

Someone started "Our Father . . ." in a quiet voice, and
then someone else began with "Hail, Mary. . . ."

In a few minutes now they would know. So far, so good!

Humbug Point saw the blow-up, and Lovers Leap. Horse
Mountain reported, and signed off, quoting *Joel* 2:30—"and
in the earth, blood, and fire, and pillars of smoke." Far to the
north, Sheer Rock saw it suddenly above the high shoulder of
Howell Mountain. Hamlin Point saw it build up above the
round top of Cerro Gordo, like the towering smoke of a new-
born volcano. . . .

Ben Roach at Sheba Ranger Station stopped his car long
enough to yell to his wife, "I'm heading out. Bart's in
trouble!"

Jerry Barrett was pressing the throttle down to the floor-
boards, a mile out of Rabbitbrush, on the highway up to the
Pass. . . .

Already Forest had talked to Zone, and Zone had talked to
Region. In the Regional Office in San Francisco, two hundred
miles away, the Dispatcher was yelling for aerial photographs,
and telling his operator to put a call through to Los Angeles.

"Good God!" he was thinking, "that whole Ponderosa
country is a tinder-box today. We've got to hit that fire with
everything we can throw at it—and quick!"

Since the blow-up, the Spitcat had already run half a mile
down the ridge, and thrown out spot-fires even farther. It was
not a solid wall of fire, but was full of reaching arms, and

isolated spot-fires, and little islands of doomed greenery burning fiercely around their edges.

Now the great gust of wind had died down, but the fire burned more intensely than ever by its own piling-up of heat. The first rush of the wind had raced it along the ground, driving the heat low before it. But now the great mass of super-heated air rose upward. A small tree flamed, and then with a deep hiss a two-hundred-foot pine rose in a solid column of flame that towered a hundred feet higher. For half a minute the hiss deepened into a roar; the burning branches tossed as in a hurricane; then, as the tree burned out, the roar faded.

But already the heat had been too much for the next tree. It too towered into flame, and from it the fire spread onward to the interlocked branches of two others.

And now with a kind of slow majesty—when the end of the world is at hand, there is no need to hurry—the crown-fire moved down the ridge, leaping from tree-top to tree-top. The great pines and firs were burning like blades of grass in a prairie-fire, and the flames leaped up their hundreds of feet. Against that heat driven on by that wind, all the power of Forest and Zone and Region would have been for the moment no more than a few ants, futilely scurrying.

The camp-truck—it was always kept loaded—rolled out of the yard at Suffolk, three of the crew in the seat. . . .

A rumor was running on the grape-vine that Bart—no, it was Slugger—had been caught in the blow-up and burned to death, along with six men—no, it was eight. . . .

The Supervisor himself, a little pale, was nursing the radio, trying to get through to the fire. But everything had gone dead. All they knew about the fire was what came in from the lookouts. "Call for that scouting-plane again," he said.

"Say it's double emergency, may mean saving lives." And again he spoke into the transmitter. . . .

Walt Burnaby, trouble-shooter for the Regional Office on big fires, picked up his war-bag, and headed out for San Francisco Airport.

Lying there close to the ground beneath the worst of the smoke, Bart heard the long hiss and roar that meant a crown-fire. He raised his head a little into the smoke and fierce heat, and turned this way and that, trying to locate the sound. There was all the difference between life and death, depending upon whether the fire had crowned to windward of them, or farther down the ridge. Almost at once he was fairly sure it was down-ridge, and at the same moment a breath of fresh and cooler air, clean of smoke, low along the ground, swept across his face. And then, suddenly, he knew.

"Feel that, boys!" he yelled, or tried to yell. But there was so much smoke in him and his throat was so dry, that he merely moved his tongue and lips and croaked a little.

But they too had felt the cooler air, and as another whiff of it came across the ground, two of them raised their heads up. They looked at him, questioning. When they saw his face, they grinned.

The Supervisor quit fiddling with the radio. "I'm heading in," he said. "Who had I better take in the car?"

"Ralph and two of the girls are going in for time-keepers," said the Dispatcher. "Take them.—Say, who's fire-boss?"

"Why, Bart.—Isn't he?"

"Oh, Bart—yes!"

And then the Supervisor pulled out. . . .

The Modoc and the Lassen had no fires going, but their danger was so high that the Zone Dispatcher told them to watch their own backyards. He took five "overhead"—rangers and other trained men—from the Klamath, and ten from the Shasta, and the whole Trinity fire-team, including the Supervisor. . . .

On Second Street in Sacramento the loud-speaker began to blare: "MEN WANTED FOR FIRE-FIGHTING—TRANSPORTATION, GOOD PAY!—MEN WANTED TO FIGHT FOREST-FIRE!"

There was one thing about a hot fire—the hotter it was, the sooner it burned out. And also about a high wind—the faster it drove the fire along, the faster it cleared out the smoke and heat after the fire had passed.

One minute they were on the edge of roasting to death and suffocating while everything was ablaze just outside their little island. The next minute they were sitting up in a stream of fresh and fairly cool air. Once there was little fuel left, the force of the wind was actually blowing the smaller flames out, as if they had been matches.

The one that was hysterical suddenly stopped his whimpering, sat up, and seemed perfectly all right.

One of the jumpers discovered that when he had started to run his canteen was around his shoulder in its sling. In the excitement he had not even thought of it before, but now he passed it round. Each of them gargled a mouthful, and spit it out to get the smoke from their throats, and then drank a little.

Bart stood up, and got his bearings. From down-ridge came the crash and roar of the crown-fire; up-ridge—the way they had come in—many little fires were still burning, but they were isolated and the ground looked not too hot to walk across. He knew that it could not be far to the old burn. They seemed to have run a long way through the smoke, but actually they had not.

All at once he ceased being a man saving his life or even a crew-boss saving his men's lives. He was Ranger of Barlow District, and he was fire-boss of a fire that had gone rampaging out of control. His forest was burning, and he could actually hear his beloved trees going up in flames one after the other. Moreover, he was the key man, and until he got back into touch, nothing at all—or all the wrong things—might be done.

"I'm going out!" he said. "You can come with me or stay here—there's no more danger!"

As he thought they would, they all followed him. They were still shaken enough to want a leader.

The ground was hot to the feet, and Bart went at a run. He was so keyed up with emergency that he did not feel tired in spite of it all. As he thought, it was no distance at all back to the old fire-line.

No one was in sight, and Bart went scrambling down the steep trail, halloo-ing as he went. At the bottom, the fire had swept through what had been his headquarters for the night. The two back-pumps were scorched beyond use, and his radio was a lot of bare wires and blackened tubes.

He heard halloo-ing now from the other side of the canyon. He led his little gang down to the creek, crossed, and went up the other side.

A lot of men were sitting around at the spot where he had tied Betty the morning before. They were mostly from the mill-crew. When they saw Bart, they burst out into a chorus which was mostly profanity, but managed to express the idea that they thought he was dead and were glad to see he was not.

They were men without a leader, demoralized, merely watching the fire, impassively, as a spectacle. They had halted here apparently because this was where Betty had been tied, and that was a sort of official recognition. Tony had taken her out with the pack-train early in the morning, and nothing was left here but a trampled half-circle and two piles of horse-dung. But for men who had suddenly seen things flame up as if their whole world were going to pieces, this was enough for a rallying-spot.

Bart had so many things to do that he had no place to begin. First of all, he asked whether anybody had been burned. The men shrugged their shoulders, but at least they did not know definitely of anyone who had been killed. Where were the crew-bosses? They didn't know for sure—but after some questions it turned out that Slugger and another boss were probably down the canyon somewhere with a few men watching this side of the slope to catch spot-fires. (That was the first sign that things had not all gone to pieces.)

Then Bart saw the boy with the bad knee, and beside him was Slugger's radio, which the boy had had the sense to carry out. But in the excitement the aerial had been lost some-where. Bart sent two men across to the old headquarters to see if they could salvage an aerial. He sent four men to scout around the old fire line to look for the boss of the mill-crew, and bring back all the abandoned tools they could find. He sent four more to go to the top of the ridge, see what was happening on the other side, locate any men who were over there, and find out if they needed first-aid.

Step by step he brought order again, and the listless men came to life. He sent the rest of them down to join Slugger and help with spot-fires.

He had a chance now to look again at the five who had been with him in the fire. The two jumpers seemed all right; they were tough ones. He assigned the two shovels to them, and sent them down-canyon also. The boy who had been hyster-ical wanted to go too, but Bart knew he could not be trusted on a fire-line for a while, and told him to rest. One of the others had a bad-looking burn on the hip, and the fifth had a shoe that had gone all to pieces with the heat. Still, they might have been a lot worse off.

The two men came back with the aerial, broken in one place and black with soot. They set about rigging it. At least it might serve to get a message as far as to Cerro Gordo or Humbug Point.

Then at last Bart had nothing to do for the moment. He sat down in the dust of the trail. The sun was dazzling on his eyes, and the dry wind, warmer now, still came pouring down the canyon. The fire was crowning, a mile down the ridge. It was throwing a monstrous column of smoke, hot enough to rise high in spite of the wind, blackish in color because of all the charred bits of needles and bark that were being whirled upward.

As each tree flared, Bart saw the sudden towering flame, and a piece of himself seemed to go up with every tree. He felt suddenly discouraged, as if he might burst out crying like a little boy. For all he knew yet, several men might have been caught and burned. And then he felt so tired that he could not even keep his mind steadily upon how bad everything was, and as he sat there in the trail, his head tipped forward, and he dozed off.

By now, half the lookouts in the Plumas and Tahoe Forests could see the Spitcat smoke. From a hundred miles westward, lookouts in the Mendocino saw it rising above the haze that filled the Sacramento Valley.

It towered to twenty thousand feet, dark gray in the distance, leaning off to the south and west before the wind. The top was so high that its moisture had condensed and a fluffy white cloud rode like a cap on the smoke column. A few minutes before, that moisture had been part of the wood and leaves and pine-needles on the ridge above Onion Creek, it had passed as vapor through the fire, and now it was a chilly mist, close to freezing, a little below the boundary of the stratosphere. . . .

Flying at eight thousand feet, above Blue Canyon, the great four-motored plane was ahead of schedule because of the heavy tail-wind. One of the passengers sighted the far-off column of smoke.

"Look!" he said to his seat-mate. "Must be a forest-fire."

"Sure looks like it. You suppose they have men out there fighting it?"

"Must be a dirty job, in all that smoke."

A little wave of comment spread through the plane. Most of the passengers were interested enough to turn their heads in that direction.

"I hear they have women for lookouts now," said a girl. "It must be thrilling!"

Two men began to argue languidly as to whether the rising heat had caused the cloud or whether it just happened to be there anyway. But most of the passengers were now collecting their thoughts for their arrival in San Francisco. . . .

The heat of the fire was more intense than ever. In its midst the oxygen was actually burned out of the air over an isolated spot about an acre in extent. For a second the needles and twigs glowed red, superheated to incandescence like the fila-ment of an electric-light, unable to burn for lack of fresh air. Then as the wind burst in, the whole acre exploded, with a roar that was close to a crash. A tremendous whirlwind of fire and smoke spiraled upward two hundred feet above the tree-tops. In it swirled flaming twigs, strips of bark, and even whole branches, torn off by the tornado-force of the hot blast.

Now in the clear, now in the very edge of the smoke, the scout-plane bounced and tossed in the rising heat-currents. Pat Gilchrist, the Polkville Ranger, reported over the crackling radio: "She's a runaway down the ridge still, taking everything out clean. . . . Can't see that she's spotted across Wilson Creek yet, but there's enough eddy to the wind so she probably will. . . . Some men down there—look black, but may be soot on their faces. Don't dare go down lower to see. One of them's waving, but he don't make it look emergency-like. I don't think anybody's hurt. . . . Onion Creek side not so bad—quite a few men there, and the wind is keeping her a little away from the creek."

In Pasadena, five hundred miles to the south, the street was thick with Sunday-morning traffic as people converged upon all the churches. Suddenly the traffic shrank back to the curbs. A Forest-Service car, its siren at full blast, took the five-mile length of Colorado Street in five minutes, heading for Burbank Airport. . . .

On the skid-rows of Stockton and Reno, as well as in Sacramento, the loud-speakers were blaring, "MEN WANTED TO FIGHT FOREST-FIRE! . . ."

A stenographer of the Ponderosa had gone for a week-end with her family in Marysville. The call came that she was needed as a relief at the switchboard.

"They can't make you," said her father. "Tell them where to get off at!"

"But you see, Dad, there's a fire!"

And she began throwing her things into the suitcase. . . .

At Camp Far West many of the men were away on Sunday passes, but the sergeants swept the barracks of the unlucky ones.

"Turn out, you guys! There's a fire! . . ."

From the thick-forested ridges of the Klamath where men look out toward Oregon, from the brush-covered peaks of the Cleveland which meet the mountains of Mexico, from Los Padres canyons where the ocean-mist eddies around redwoods, from arid Inyo slopes where the last pines go out to meet the desert—from them all the men were coming.

When the camp-truck pulled in at Onion Flat not a single man was there. Bart's car with the horse-trailer behind it was parked along with the suppression-crew truck, and Tony's mule truck.

The camp-truck rolled to a stop at the little turn-around which marked the road-head, and the camp-boss jumped off and looked the place over. It was a good spot for a camp—a pine-covered triangular flat covering about ten acres at the point where Bacchus Creek came into Onion Creek. The camp-boss mapped the lay-out in his head—*Parking* on both sides of the road as it came into the south end of the flat along Onion Creek, *Timekeeper* next, and then *Supply* at the turn-around, *Communications, First Aid,* and *Headquarters* opposite *Supply* between the road and Onion Creek, *Kitchen* in the angle of the creeks with room enough around it for men to sit and eat, *Sleeping Grounds* out of the way over by Bacchus Creek, and *Latrine* up on the first slope of the hill.

Another truck with supplies and five more of the camp-crew pulled in behind the first one.

"All right, boys," barked the camp-boss, "get 'em un-loaded."

Steel stakes, ropes, shovels and McLeods tied in bunches, sharp double-bitted axes specially boxed for safety, mauls, wedges, rakes, cross-cut saws with guards for carrying, brush-knives, clippers, Pulaskis, grubbing-hoes, gasoline lamps,

headlights for night-work, the first-aid chest, desks for headquarters, bedding-rolls (they made a mountainous heap),
toilet paper, canteens, time-keeper's blanks—everything was
there, including a dozen sharpened pencils, neat stenciled
sign-boards for *Headquarters, Latrine,* and the rest, a box of
extra shoe-strings to call a man's bluff when he said he had
broken a lace and couldn't go out with his crew, and a little
American flag to fly over *Headquarters.*

But that was only at *Supply,* and over by *Kitchen* they unloaded stakes and ropes, camp-stoves, horses and planks for
long tables, chests of tin cups and tin plates and tin bowls and
knives and forks and spoons, a tent in case of rain, and a big
canvas fly to keep the cooks from working in the hot sun,
garbage-cans, crates of telescoped boilers and all kinds of
kitchen-utensils. And then the food—canned tomato-juice
("You can't fight a fire without tomato-juice!"), canned grape-
fruit-juice, canned beans, canned corn, canned peas, canned
peaches, canned plums, canned milk, sugar, salt, pepper,
catsup, coffee—for, if men are going to work, they have to eat,
and the better you feed them, the better they work.

By the time the two trucks were nearly unloaded, a third
one pulled in. It had the cook and the bull-cook, and all the
fresh supplies. The housewives of Suffolk were going to find
poor pickings on Monday morning, for the cook had routed
the three Suffolk grocers out of their Sunday-morning naps,
and swept the shelves of packaged bread, butter and margarine, apples and peaches, eggs, bacon and all fresh meat,
potatoes and cabbages.

There was a little confusion at first, and occasionally someone ran about looking for the precise thing he needed. But
soon there was the clanking sound of mauls pounding on steel
stakes. Then, as soon as the ropes had been run through the
rings on the stakes, the place was no longer a forested flat in

the mountains, but it was full of neatly marked-off and labeled squares and rectangles—like a village all laid out and waiting for its inhabitants. The Cook had his fires going, and would be prepared to serve lunch to a hundred men, or more in a pinch. The Supply-chief was ready to pass out tools at a moment's notice, and the Transportation-chief had his book ready to check cars and trucks in and out. You could almost say the room was swept and garnished. Though no one actually had any brooms out, two men were raking up the mule-droppings and clearing all litter from what would be the main paths, and two others were cutting bushes and small trees that would be in the road and were neatly lopping off all low branches, being careful not to leave sharp points for people to scratch against.

On Second Street the loud-speaker was still blaring: MEN TO FIGHT FOREST-FIRE! Bo Fox, the insignificant man who disliked a closed door behind him, followed the drift. He was out of a job and nearly broke. In front of him a man said to his buddy:

"Well, why not? They feed you good, and you can sneak off to the woods and ditch a lot of work."

They went in to sign up, and Bo Fox followed them, drawn along in their wake rather than swayed by his own decision. . . .

The smoke of the fire had now drifted down over Reverse Ridge, and obscured the sun. The rabbit, assuming that twilight was at hand, emerged from a manzanita thicket, and began to hop here and there, nibbling at grass and the tips of low-growing branches. . . .

Barney Zulik, the cat-skinner, was at a beer-parlor in Polkville when a foreman came looking for him.

"There's a fire up in the Basin, Barney. They need you in there with your cat."

"To hell with it!" said Barney. "Ain't it my day off?" And he added some diversified comments.

But the foreman knew the next move.

"Say, Barney," he said, "the guys that run those Forest-Service cats can't cut bacon up in the woods. They need a real cat-skinner in there!"

"Set me up another!" Barney yelled at the bartender, but he already looked uncomfortable, as the workman's sense of a job to be done began to stir within him. His bullet-head, set low on his shoulders, turned this way and that, as he glanced about to see what the others were thinking.

He began to speak again in expletives, but ended:

"O. K. I'll be there. Only don't try to rush me!" And with quick gulps he drained his glass of beer. . . .

Dutch Harbor was now drying out in a chilly and raw north wind. Having moved some hundreds of miles eastward, the storm was now discharging its rain chiefly upon the churning waters of the Gulf of Alaska.

The little congregation at Suffolk had a war-time look—women, children, and graybeards. Many of them were Forest-Service families, and besides, a crew of thirty-five locals was already on the way to the fire, and most of the suppression-crew boys were from Suffolk.

There was a haunting sense of fear in the little wooden church, and the preacher in his long prayer added a simple petition "for those of our loved ones who may be, this day, in danger." He had hardly done more than announce his text when he saw a girl come in at the back, walk up the aisle nearly to the front and whisper something to her mother.

From high in the pulpit, he saw the wave of the whisper spread outward. People leaned across pews to get the message. No one was listening to the sermon, and the preacher, a sensible man and humanly curious, stopped talking and motioned to one of his deacons to come up and tell him the news. Then he cleared his throat.

"In order that there may be no more confusion," he said loudly, "let me make an announcement. Ranger Bartley, who had been caught inside the fire with several men, has reported in. He and the others are safe, and all the other men of the original crews are now safely accounted for.—Let us join in singing 'Praise God from whom all blessings flow,' after which I shall, under the circumstances, pronounce the benediction and dismiss the congregation."

Sunday always made mobilization a little harder, but the Dispatcher was well enough satisfied. Men were moving, and not by dozens now, but by hundreds. Access was still the worst problem. The only way he could figure to get cats to the fire was to truck them in from the Sheba side to Parker Flat, unload them there, and have them walked in along one of the ridges above Reverse Creek. It would be slow, but on the south side the cliff along Reverse Ridge and the narrow gorge of Onion Creek made a barrier that even a cat-skinner could hardly force. But there was one thing! If they could not come to the fire, the fire was obligingly coming to them. It was burning almost directly toward the road-head at Onion Flat. This morning a man had to cover seven miles of mountain trail to reach the fire. By tomorrow morning he might not have to do half that distance.

The Supervisor took his time getting to the fire-camp. He could not afford to hurry or get excited. In front with him was the Chief Clerk going in as Timekeeper, and behind there

were the two excited girls, both in blue jeans, who were going
in as assistants. Twice he stopped and talked with the Dispatcher, by radio, and found that mobilization was going
along as fast as could be expected.

He had no special job on the fire as yet, and hoped he
would not have one. A big fire needed someone who could
keep the long perspective, and not be concerned with any
particular half-acre or half-day. Now that it was Sunday, he
wanted to focus his attention on Wednesday and on all the
little things that the others would miss, and to watch the men
themselves—needling this one a little, commending that one.

At the moment he was concerned about the road-markers.
You could never have too many of them. He stopped the car
where a track ran off toward the right.

"I don't suppose anybody would make a mistake here, but
you can't tell at night. Signs are cheap. Let's put up another."

He picked up a sign. It was designed:

so that the arrow could be pointed right or left and the sign
still be read. The arrow itself was of a glittering ruby-color
to reflect back the headlights at night.

Having tacked the sign to a convenient tree, the Supervisor
drove on with the comfortable feeling of another detail made
safe.

Timekeeper with his two girls had barely got set up for business when the first crew pulled in. During all the afternoon they came.

Twenty-one (21) mill-men and loggers from Magna. They toned down their speech a little when they saw the two girls.

Thirty-five (35) local pick-ups from Suffolk—small ranchers, day-laborers, and the town bum.

Ten (10) Power-and-Light men with Johnny Martley as crew-boss.

Twenty-five (25) of the Zone Hot-Shot Crew, professional shock-troops, fit as athletes and specially trained for night-fighting.

Forty-four (44) from a crew that had been grubbing wild gooseberry on Blister Rust Control.

Three (3) loggers with a lumber-company power-saw.

Forty-five (45) Reno pick-ups, the worn-down survivors of many a skid-row brawl and bender, with missing teeth and broken noses, and here and there a finger gone or only a shrunken lid where once was an eye.

All afternoon also the overhead poured in—the men of the Forest Service with their pine-tree badges, ready to officer the crews.

Bart threw the reins to one of the boys, and hurried toward Headquarters. Men seemed to be milling around all over Onion Flat.

His face was black with soot and smoke, and smeared where he had wiped it with his sleeve. From the blackness his bloodshot eyes shone with a kind of glare. There was dried blood on the back of his hand from a scratch. One shirt-sleeve was torn into tatters, and the back of his shirt was burned in three places. Hat and jacket were gone. He limped as he walked.

All over the Flat the impact of his coming surged and eddied.

"There's Bart. . . . The ranger. . . . Now we'll be going. . . . Hi, Bart! . . . Tough time of it! . . . Knows all this country like a book. . . ."

Ben Roach was slapping him on the back. Jerry Barrett had grabbed him by the arm.

Bart felt the warm wave of confidence and friendship rising up around him, almost like a physical support in his weariness. These men were his comrades; they trusted him; yes, they loved him. By God, they would go back in there, all of them together, and they would put out that fire like a couple of matches burning. But when he came to Headquarters and saw the Supervisor, he was cold for a moment, and then something inside him boiled up hotter. For in that first glance of the Super's eyes Bart saw no love, although there was no hate either. But they were level, deep-searching eyes, and they seemed to be asking merely, "What about this Ranger? Can he do the job?"

Then the Super, who always seemed to be looking down from the eight inches difference of height, stretched out his hand at the end of his long arm, and what he said was nearly the same, in words, as what Jerry Barrett had said:

"Hi, Bart! Well, I'm glad to see you got out of it all right!"

Bart held his own hand back. "Thanks, Super," he said. "Say, my hand's all messy."

But then he put his own hand forward, and took the Super's.

"Bart, you must be tuckered out."

Ten minutes before, Bart had been ready to fall right to the ground but now that something which boiled inside him brought new drive and strength.

"Say, Super, us old-timers can take it. This ain't nothing for an old smoke-eater. You shoulda been here for the Merriam's Mill."

The Supervisor looked up and glanced around, and though he said nothing, his glance cleared out of Headquarters all the rangers who were standing there, so that he and Bart were alone.

"Say, Bart," he said, "how is she?"

"Pretty bad, all right. But I think we can catch her tomorrow morning."

"You *think,* or you *hope?*"

"I said *think,* didn't I?"

"Yes."

There was a pause, and then the Supervisor said, and his voice was almost hesitant:

"Look here, Bart. I've been figuring. You got called out on that little Hart Creek business back on Thursday. This is Sunday afternoon, and I know you haven't had much let-up. You've been through a hell of a mess today. How about my putting Ben Roach in as fire-boss, and you getting some rest?"

The blood-shot eyes in the blackened face seemed to glare more brightly; the thick jaw-muscles set hard.

"Of course, Super, if you want to throw me out, all right. But this is my District that's on fire, and my trees. I know the country."

The Supervisor thought for a very long moment:

"O. K. She's your baby."

Bart organized it as a three-division fire. Division I was the north flank, the Wilson Creek side; Division II was the south flank, the Onion Creek side; Division III was the front. Bart picked an Angeles man as Division-Boss for I, and a Trinity man for II, but for III he picked Ben Roach, who was his friend, and an old fire-fighter, and an old-timer on the Ponderosa. Also he picked Jerry Barrett of the Rabbitbrush for Chief of Staff.

The Division-Bosses were assigned their Sector-Bosses, and the Sector-Bosses their Crew-Bosses, and the Crew-Bosses got the names of the dozen men who formed their crew.

The crews lined up and were issued tools, and head-lamps, and canteens. About sunset they began to cross the log footbridge, and start up the switch-back trail.

The Supervisor got out of Headquarters, so as not to be in Bart's hair. After he had looked over the kitchen, he went and sat in his own car. Things seemed to be moving well enough, but he wondered what a general would think having to send into battle an army which had been thrown together in half a day, in which officers were assigned to their troops and moved them out to the battle-line in the same half-hour.

The decision about Bart had been a hard one, and as he thought it over, he again weighed one side against the other. Bart knew fire, and he knew the country better than any other man, and those of course were the chief points for him. On the other hand, Bart was tired, perhaps too tired, and besides he was too much tied up in his feelings with the country. He said "my trees," and when he said "I think," he should perhaps have said, "I hope." To fight a fire you had to be clearheaded, even if that meant pulling back and letting a thousand fine trees burn today, to save ten thousand tomorrow.

So far the *pro* and *con* balanced. What had really swung him was the knowledge that through the Forest, and even up and down the Region, men knew and liked John Bartley, and called him Bart. And if he himself, whom men called the Super, had used his power to replace Bart, there would have been an ugly taste in men's mouths and a feeling of doubt and uncertainty. And men did their best job of fire-fighting only when they trusted their leaders.

After dark the Maps-and-Records man, one of the Shasta rangers, was working on his first map at a field-desk beneath a flaring gasoline lamp at Headquarters, and he gloomily derived a kind of inverted pleasure from a careful plotting and calculation of the day's burn.

On his township map he had outlined Saturday's burn in red. It was insignificant-looking, about forty acres wholly within Section 7 of Definite.

From the reports of scouts—in the plane and afoot—he had lightly sketched in pencil the outline of the present day's burn. Enormous by comparison, it spread across the township-line, now stretched in a broad belt across Sections 12, 13, and 14 of Deerhound, and was already encroaching upon other sections. It had swept the whole ridge between the two creeks, and having crossed Reverse Creek at the end of the ridge, was burning now at several points in Reverse Flat. It was roughly three miles long, and was nearly a mile wide. There was also a spot-fire to the north, where the fire had jumped Wilson Creek. He outlined the day's burn with an orange-colored pencil.

Estimating as carefully as possible, he put it down as totalling 1085 acres, or something less than two square miles.

THE SIMPLER PEOPLES have no doubts; the fire, for them, is living. It understands speech—so say no ill in its presence; it grows old and feeble, no matter how well fed, and must once a year be re-kindled; the fire-sticks are man and woman, and the spark is born between them; the reaching flames carry the seed of life, and a virgin lies close at her peril.

The old words linger, and make us half believe. We *feed* and *tend* a fire, as if it were horse or child. It *eats, devours, runs, spits,* and *roars.* It lies as a sleeper, springs to life, and dies. Its dwelling-place, the hearth, stands for man's dwelling-place, the home. And *ashen pale* is the color of coming death.

Quench once meant, both to put out a blaze, and to kill a man; *kindle,* to light a fire and to give birth to young. And even yet, as spelling shows, our *kin* and our own *kind* are those *kindled* from the same ancestral fire.

2

At Cerro Gordo the girl was still on the catwalk after midnight. Far off, beyond the vague black mass of Reverse Ridge, the fire lit up the sky with a violent pink, like no color she

179

had ever seen. "Forest-fire pink—our latest!" she could imagine the advertisements saying. But who would want to wear it? You thought of pinks as mild and washed-out, but this vehement glare was more dominant than scarlet or magenta.

The night before, even though she had known where to look, she had seen no brightness. The fire was too far away, burning too mildly behind too many ridges. During the day she had seen only the gray mass of the smoke-column, but with evening the glow had built up as the light faded. The old guy on Horse Mountain had shouted out something about a pillar of cloud by day and a pillar of fire by night; he was getting so excited that he was cluttering up the air with Biblical quotations.

Perhaps she herself was the one to be getting excited. As she knew from the map and from the wind and from the pink glow itself, the fire was driving right toward Cerro Gordo. To start with, it had been twelve miles off, now it was not more than nine.

But nine miles was a long way, and the brightest part of the glow, which showed the actual line of flame, still made an arc of only six degrees on her fire-finder scale, a mere spot on the horizon. Besides, all day her squawking radio had blurted out memoranda of the mobilization. Region 5 was throwing a thousand men at the Spitcat. Somewhere—even now, perhaps—they were closing in for the kill.

And she also was one of them, even though she wielded no shovel. She felt the quickening sense of comradeship. Sometimes it rose with a tightness in the throat.

All day they had been calling by telephone and radio. Familiar voices spoke: "Say, Judith, what's that smoke looking like now?" Unfamiliar voices spoke: "Cerro Gordo Lookout? . . . Relay this message for us. . . ."

By day and night, now faint and now loud, she heard the

conversations, sometimes both ends, sometimes only one, those strange conversations in which someone repeated himself or said the same thing over in different words because he was not sure that the man at the other end could always hear.

Now it was the Chief of Staff talking to a Division-Boss:

"Has she spotted across the creek yet anywhere? Has she spotted across the creek?"

"Not that I can see. I don't think so. No, I don't think she's spotted across the creek."

Now it was a scout reporting from in front of the fire; he must have been going a hard clip through the woods, and his voice was gaspy:

"No—nothing beyond—me—from where I am now—that is—west—I mean. Nothing west—of me. Lot of reproduction —thick stuff—in around—here.—Y'hear me?" (Silence, as her radio did not pick up the reply, and then the scout went on.) "O. K.—As I'as sayin'—lots of reproduction—she'll burn hot. Well, I better be on my way."

Then he had signed off quickly, and there was only silence. But she could imagine him as he pulled down his aerial and gathered up his equipment and took another nervous appraising look at the advancing fire, and then crashed on through the thick growth of young trees.

"The girl was happy that evening—" she suddenly put the thought into unspoken words, and then checked herself. Yes, she was happy in spite of the fire—really, to be honest, because of it. For with the fire she had suddenly come back into the world again. She was no longer a girl by herself on a mountain-top, in flight from what she had not faced; she felt herself now again to be a part of humanity. High on the lonely tower, cool in the night-wind, her thoughts were with the men who sweated on the fire-lines, in danger of death perhaps. With them she fought a common enemy. This was no time to make up words in fantasy, to seek refuge inward, like a half-grown schoolgirl.

There had been smouldering and ugly memories, and she had never quite dared to look at them. She had gone to a mountain-top, she had killed a rattlesnake—to show how strong she was. But she had not dared to look inward.

But now the glow beyond Reverse Ridge was like reality itself. You could not wish it away. If you closed your eyes, it was there when you opened them. You could not fool it, or cajole it, or browbeat it, or trick it into signing on the dotted line. It held no truce and gave no quarter, but it was honest. With a thousand others, she marched outward to grapple it.

Then, all at once, she looked into her own mind. Strangely, the ugly smouldering things were like light and cold ashes, as if a fire had burned them.

Suddenly, along with being very happy, she was lonely too, needing someone to share her happiness.

3

After nightfall the Sacramento Valley had grown cooler, and though the broad current of air still flowed down the mountain-slope, it was no longer like a raging torrent, but like a smooth and swift river. As the wind had fallen off, the flames from each burning tree-top had begun to rise more sharply upward, and before long a tree burned without igniting the next one beyond it. From this gap in the blazing front the arms of cooler air worked outward in both directions, and the gap grew wider. The fir trees, their gums vaporizing, their thick-set needles holding back the heat, still went up in sheets of flame, but the thin-foliaged pines were more fire-resistant. Just as they let the winter snow sift through to the ground, so they let the columns of heat and even the flames pass through them and reach the upper air. Their slender needles held little gum, and even when they burned, they did not tower skyward with an explosive roar.

Since most of the forest was of pines, the fire thus ceased to crown. It was very far, however, from sinking back into the weakness of the preceding nights, and it advanced steadily through the duff and underbrush, shot up in higher flames at every clump of younger trees, and occasionally still it roared clear to the top of a big fir. It burned on a front of more than a mile, and from two square miles the heat still rose from burning snags and logs, like the heat of a thousand furnaces.

As in some nation two races may live at peace before a hatred is kindled between them and grows hotter until they fly at each other's throats, so it was in the forest. The oxygen of the air and the carbon of the needles and wood, in ordinary times, lived quietly. But now, heated by the approaching fire, they rushed together, and by their flaming union released more heat to spread the fire farther. Constantly indeed the heat drained off into the air, upwards; at the same time, cooler air was sucked in at the base of the fire. But though the heat was thus kept within some limit, the current of cooler fresh air brought fresh supplies of oxygen. Like some great insensate monster, the fire thus seemed of its own strength to breathe and feed and to consume the forest for its own sustenance.

Soon after midnight the southern corner of the fire came to the edge of Reverse Meadow. The dry grass flared up; the front of fire swept quickly across, and soon was burning in the forest on the other side.

4

After midnight the three of them got together at Headquarters—Bart, the Supervisor, and Walt Burnaby, trouble-shooter from the Regional Office. They pored over maps and aerial photographs, and hastily studied the reports which the scouts had radioed in. All evening they had been like a General Staff which sees its troops drained off to minor theaters of war. Division I had called for men to fight a spot-fire beyond Wilson Creek and keep it from crossing the ridge. Division II had needed fresh men for patrol to replace the worn-down mill-men and paratroopers who had been on the line since Saturday.

But Bart had doled reinforcements out sparingly. To stop the fire he must meet its attack head-on as it came rolling across Reverse Flat, and so for Division III he held back the best crews for a striking-force. More than two hundred men were concentrating in the vicinity of Reverse Meadow. Except for the stiff climb up the mountain-trail, they were fresh. They were under the command of Ben Roach as Division-Boss, and were organized under Sector- and Crew-Bosses, well equipped, with head-lamps for night-work. In addition, two cats were about to start in from Parker Flat.

The problem, essentially, was simple. The crews of Division III must close a mile-and-a-half gap and get the back-fires going before the main fire reached the line. But beyond that, the problem grew more and more complex, as factors of time and wind and cover and human fallibility appeared.

"We'll radio to Ben to put her through here," said Bart. From a point to the southwest of Reverse Meadow he drew a line northwesterly across the front of the fire, leaving a good quarter-mile of leeway.

"How much of that line is through trees and how much through brush?" asked Walt Burnaby.

"Half and half," said Bart, drawing on his memory of the country.

The Super was checking the aerial photographs. "Better

than half is through brush—thick manzanita," he concluded.

"Not much more!" Bart snapped, and then he noticed, with a faint irritation, that the Super was doing a multiplication problem on a sheet of paper. . . .

The Super's problem was much like those he had once had to do in school arithmetic: "If A builds ten feet of fence in an hour, how long will it take . . ." Only the problem was a great deal more complicated than even an eighth-grade one. Take a mile and a half of line on the map, but that gets to be at least a mile and three-quarters on the ground, because you can't run a line straight across country. Then a man will build so many feet of line in an hour, but not so much his second hour, because he will be a little tired, and even less in the hours afterwards. He tends to work faster at night because it's cooler, but slower because he can't see so well what he's doing. Line through manzanita is much slower and has to be built wider. Two cats can punch a line through manzanita like nobody's business, but two cats in the woods aren't two cats on the line. And then on the other side there was the question of how fast the fire would advance. Some of its points were a long way out ahead, but you could send a crew in to hot-spot the points and hold them back. If you really tried to write an equation for all that, you had correction factors stretching across two pages, and yet if you didn't look at some real figures, you merely made a guess, or believed what you wanted to believe. You studied fire-fighting all your life, and then every fire was different, and you had to adjust what you thought you knew.

The Supervisor straightened out his long body from where it was bent over the desk, and came up with an answer. How much the answer was from figuring and how much from hunching—just as Bart hunched—was hard to say.

"Well," asked Walt Burnaby, "what's the verdict of higher mathematics?"

The Supervisor could not tell whether Walt was smiling or not, but he was sure about Bart.

"The mathematics says we're all right, but I'd like a bigger safety-factor." He paused a moment. "Bart, you might give her a little more room. All that would burn would be the brush-field, and it's no use anyway."

He saw the stubbornness set on Bart's face.

"You know, Super, that brush-field is old, and the young firs are poking right up through it. Give us ten-twenty years, and the brush will be dying out. Burn her now, and she'll come up solid manzanita again. . . . You know, we got to decide *something.*"

For another moment the Supervisor thought of all that might go wrong—a leaking oil-line on a cat, the carelessness of a Sector-Boss. Bart took the transmitter and glanced up for a word or a sign. The Supervisor remembered suddenly the story of some general who kept silence and refused to confirm or to countermand a charge. Bart began talking into the transmitter.

Well, thought the Supervisor, that was it, and they had made a decision. In war, the saying ran, a bad decision was better than no decision at all. Perhaps it was the same with a fire. But there was this difference. In war, even a rash decision, so long as you did something, might disconcert or confuse or frighten the enemy; your very rashness might surprise him and catch him off balance; you might even expect him to make some mistakes. But no matter what you did, you never bluffed or bothered the fire. You thought of it sometimes in human terms, as vindictive or treacherous, but actually the worst thing about it, and what most shook a man's nerves, was its wholly inhuman calm, its unbreakable imperturbability.

5

Bo Fox did not mind being crowded into a bus with some thirty other winoes. In fact, he rather liked being close to the man on the seat beside him. He got a little alarmed when the bus-door was closed with a bang, but he soon found that he could open the window. That made him feel better. After a while, as they began to get into the mountains and it was night, the air got so cool that the others made a fuss and he had to close the window. Still, knowing that he could open it, and even crawl through it, made him feel less like being trapped. The old bus ground along slowly, up-grade, around many curves, and he heard through the darkness the rushing sound of a river.

Barney Zulik ran his cat down the ramps from the truck, and zoomed his engine for a moment. The Forest-Service cat-skinner came across to speak to him. Barney had never seen him before, and had the usual disdain of a lumber-company cat-skinner for a Forest-Service one, but he shook hands, and he even agreed that he would follow the other cat. After all, this was a Forest-Service show. The other fellow was yelling various things over the roar of the engine, and Barney got the general drift:

"Easy enough . . . five miles or . . . open, mostly pine . . . five-hundred feet up to the . . . steep pitches down on the other. . . ."

Barney did not bother to hear or remember everything. All he had to do was to tag after the other cat, and he was ready to guarantee that in any game of follow-the-leader he would go as far as the other guy would, and farther too.

The lights of the two cats glared whitely in the little open space at Parker Flat, reflecting back from the light-colored bark of the big pines. The roar of the engines blotted out the gentle night-noise of the wind streaming through the pine-tops. Barney's swamper climbed up beside him. A Forest-Service man moved up-slope ahead, scouting the way on foot. He stood out sharply in the lights, his long shadow bobbing about as he moved.

The other engine suddenly roared louder, and the cat lurched forward, crushing down the bushes. Barney gave her the gun, and followed the tracks.

6

The Dispatcher did not even try to go to bed. Mobilization was still rolling, and there were a hundred things to watch after.

The night was cool enough, cooler than any they had had lately, but in some way it seemed hot. The dry wind blew steadily, with the smell of dust in it—and sometimes, he thought, the smell of smoke.

He was still tense and nervous. That was, he knew, partly from the wind. But it was partly, also, from being so far away. Except when there was a blow-up, a man on the fire-line never worried much. The closer you were to the fire, the smaller part of it you could see, and when you were right there, it often seemed to be merely crackling around in a few bushes, no bigger than a trashfire in your own backyard. Often, if there was a chance, a man lay right down by the line or leaned back against a tree, and went quietly to sleep. Men at the fire-camp worried more, but they saw the reassuring movement of crews up to the fire-line. They rolled up in their blankets and lay on the hard ground, and slept through a lot of noise and confusion and men blundering over them in the darkness.

But a dispatcher back at Suffolk, if he had any imagination, worried and worried. If he went to bed, he lay in all the comfort of box-springs and sheets, and instead of sleeping, he tossed. He saw the fire, not as a few bushes burning, but as a nightmarish monster—miles around, blazing redly, engulfing a whole township. The men and equipment, even though they passed through, seemed mere driblets, and he never saw them massed into power, as they were in the fire-camp.

Though he was not even trying to sleep, the Dispatcher began to think of a wind-shift that might carry the fire off in some new direction, and of men trapped in brush-choked ravines, and of run-away crown-fires that roared through the night.

He stepped to the little porch outside his office, still keeping within sound of telephone and radio. The stars were bright, but they were unfriendly, as the sun had been. They looked indecently naked. *Glitter* was the word for them, and there was no mellowness or benevolence, and no real beauty in them. They looked—he thought of a film he had seen— like diamonds sparkling on a hard and mean-looking woman.

But over a large part of the northeastern sky, no stars were showing. That was where the smoke-column stood up.

An old bus came lumbering by him, and slowed to a stop at the gasoline pump. He clicked it off in his mind; it would be the one from Sacramento which had been delayed on the grades by an overheating motor. The men piled out, yawning and stretching, cursing aimlessly, lighting cigarettes. Beneath the brightness of the floodlight, the Dispatcher saw that it was an average bunch of pogies. They were the despised and the rejected of civilization—weaklings, morons, alcoholics, perverts. Half of them were gray-haired. He felt a quick resentment that these were the basic material from which he must build a fighting-force. Scarcely a man in the load but would have been rejected in the draft as over-age, or physically unfit, or mentally unreliable.

Yet, as an honest man, he would give them their due. They could take cold and heat and dirt and smoke, and sleep under a bush, and eat emergency rations. They expected little. At best, fire-fighting was a nasty job, and where a high-class workman would have thought he was being intolerably abused, the pogy would take things as they came. Sometimes also a crew of pogies would dig in and do a job to make you proud of them.

"O. K.!" he heard the bus-driver yelling. "Pile in!"

The first one back into the bus raised the window and leaned out. For a moment the Dispatcher thought the man was trying to crawl out the window, and being a little shrimp he probably could have. That was a funny note, a pogy wanting a window open! Usually the inside of one of their buses was hot and stuffy, smelling of tobacco, cheap liquor, and bodies.

He heard his telephone begin to ring, and with a sigh he went in to answer it.

7

And still to the camp at Onion Flat the trucks and buses kept rolling in.

Ninety-nine (99) soldiers with a First Lieutenant (1) in command. "Hope to God that Looey goes out on the line with his men—the last one just stuck around camp!"

One hundred (100) sailors with two (2) Warrant Officers. "Christ, they're wearin' black oxfords again—don't the Navy *never* learn at all!"

Two (2) volunteers who had been fishing up by Poison

Spring. "Say, you boys was in that C. O. camp last year, wasn't you?"

Five (5) overhead from the San Bernardino, not quite at home among the tall trees and thick forests of the North. "Hello, Bax. They sure must be scrapin' the bottom of the barrel to send *you!*"

Sixty (60) pick-ups from Sacramento in two buses. "Sure, I'll make out the slip for you. . . . California Hotel? . . . Just put an X here."

Fifty-eight (58) Mexican Nationals, lifted as a unit from the San Joaquin harvest-fields. "Adios, amigos! Moocho goosto! Pancho-Villa-cucaracha-trace-cohonies-la-rancho-grandy! . . . Sure they understand me!"

Thirty-two (32) professionals from the State Division of Forestry, sent to give a hand in the emergency. "Say, why don't you Federals hold a fire sometimes where the hills ain't so steep!"

There came a sudden humming mutter, as the generator-truck took over. Electric lights, strung from tree to tree, came on all over the central part of the camp. At *Headquarters* and at *Timekeeper* men turned off the hot and flaring gasoline lanterns.

By two in the morning the camp had sunk somewhat into inactivity, but it was still far from dead. Three men worked at *Headquarters*. The radio stand-by sat at his instrument, fully alert. The timekeepers were busy. *Supply* issued bedding-rolls as new crews came in.

Three camp-fires were burning quietly. After the men had their bedding-rolls, most of them went over and stood by the fires for a few minutes, smoking cigarettes, spitting into the coals, relaxing. Even away from the electric lights the moon shed a little brightness through the canopy of pine boughs, and as the men left the fires, they had enough light to guide them to the sleeping-ground. There—huddled beneath a bush, stretched straight upon the pine-needles, half-curled around the base of a big tree—everywhere were the rough mounds of men rolled in their blankets, catching a little rest, hoping to sleep the few hours before they went on shift in the morning.

8

The heat of it that night was in the big brush-field which covered most of Reverse Flat, where Division III was running a line to hold the front of the fire. Ben Roach had the best crews there—the Hot-shot veterans, the blister-rust boys, some mill-men and loggers, the Suffolk locals.

The fire was not exactly racing across the brush-field, but it was moving steadily, and making a clean sweep. Sometimes it leaped from bush to bush in a good imitation of a real crown-fire. As the thick leaves distilled their oil, the hissing sheets of flame were white hot; they looked hotter even than the blaze of a fir-tree, though they rose only to twenty or thirty feet in height. More often the fire did not spread directly from bush to bush, but after one bush was burned, the flames died down as the fire crept forward through the ground-litter. Then the heat of the burning litter ignited the lower branches, and the next bush flared up. Here and there a vigorously growing young fir had managed to get its head above the manzanita, and each of these also, as the fire came to it, went up in a sheet of flame.

A difficult place to work, and a dangerous one! "Look out for your men," Ben Roach warned his bosses. "Always be sure there's a way out for them." Not that the bosses needed any warning. They were experienced men themselves, knowing and respecting manzanita. It was jungle-like in thickness, but had nothing of the soft green lushness of a jungle. The tough twigs bent back stiffly as you pressed to get through, and if they snapped, the broken points stuck out dagger-like.

First went the ax-men. At each thick-set bush they swung with the flats, breaking the twigs and little branches. When they could reach in to larger branches, they used the edge. It was slow work. The moon was not bright enough to do much good, and the bobbing headlights were not all you could ask for swinging an ax. The manzanita-wood was hard and tough; even sharp axes in skilled hands made slow work of it. To come to one of the fir-trees was a relief. A good lumberjack could send the chips flying cleanly from the butt of one of these, and bring it toppling down after a few strokes. But even a good lumberjack left a manzanita branch looking chewed and haggled.

"It's as bad as the stuff we used to have in Burma," said one of them.

After a few minutes of work the sweating pair of ax-men moved back, and other men went ahead to throw the litter of branches into the brush on the side away from the fire. Then the ax-men moved ahead again, and from behind came the men with shovels and McLeods, scraping away the smaller branches and twigs and the litter of dead leaves until the red dirt showed from beneath. A narrow line is no good in manzanita, and so they cleared to an eight-foot width. It was a lot of hard work and little to show.

Before long a kind of recurring chant began to go up: "Wher're the cats? . . . Say, a cat could plow right through this stuff . . . Why don't they get some cats?"

There was a long stringer reaching out ahead of the main line of the fire, and getting dangerously close. Ben sent the Suffolk locals in to hot-spot it, and hold it back. They worked close up to the point of the stringer, running a dink-line around it, like troops flung out to fight a delaying-action, both flanks in the air.

9

Right where the nose of the ridge began to fall away, the cat-skinners got their first good view of the fire—not only the main fire in the brush-field, but also a lot of the isolated blazes where snags and down-logs were still burning along the ridge that the crown-fire had swept over.

They stopped a moment to consider. The Forest-Service cat-skinner said they were about two miles from the nearest point of the fire-line, and he figured they could make it by daybreak.

"Christ! Let me take the lead," said Barney. "I'll get us there before that!"

The other cat-skinner did not like the tone, but it was Barney's turn.

"Take it over then, if you want to get your Boy-Scout badge! Hell, it's no treat for me!"

Barney gunned his engine, worked his levers, spun the cat about, and walked it through the bushes to a place ahead of the other one. The peculiar madness of cat-skinners was rising up within him, and there was a dash in the way he swung it around. They started down the steep nose, a four-hundred foot slope ending in some almost level ground, an arm of Reverse Flat.

In a few minutes Barney found he was going no faster than the other fellow had. The trouble was with that Forest-Service guy who was walking in front scouting out the way with his flashlight.

"That bastard with the brass-plated pine-tree!" Barney was fuming, "I'd like to put it where it belongs, and him too! If

he'd get outa my way, I'd slide this bunch of junk down to the
crick faster than he could follow after it. You get out—" he
turned to his swamper, "and point me out the way, and we'll
forget that bastard!"

They went a little faster then. The nose of the ridge was
fairly open forest of big trees with much brush beneath them,
and some rocks. The two scouts thrust ahead this way and
that, feeling the way, and almost before they had time to
signal, Barney's lights were close upon them, and the cat came
roaring down, crushing bushes, toppling small trees, its treads
crunching and scraping and sliding on the rocks.

There was a steep open place, and for a hundred feet ahead
Barney's lights showed up nothing but a smooth expanse of
brush. He gave her the gun, and the big cat, its blade raised
high, lurched forward. The two scouts jumped aside, out of
the way. The cat crunched down the slope. Then suddenly its
treads ran out along the tops of the bushes, and as the cat
tipped forward the treads had nothing but bushes beneath
them. Barney jumped and went flying through the air. The
cat dropped on its blade, toppled, went upside down. Then,
the whole thrust of its momentum driving it downward, it
turned again—lazily as a rolling elephant—and came to rest
upright.

They rushed to pick up Barney's body from where the cat
had rolled over it, but he came up from the underbrush
cursing. Short-necked and thick-set, he had merely curled up
and lit in a clump of manzanita like a rubber ball. The stubs
of broken branches had torn his clothes and clawed his face,
and he looked as if a harrow had worked over him. But having fallen about two feet from where the cat had rolled, he
was not even limping.

The cat, being at least as tough as Barney, was probably not
much injured either. They hurried to look it over. Barney got

the engine started, but the control levers were bent beyond using from having had the whole weight rolled over on them.

When they examined the place, they found there was a six-foot sheer drop-off. The brush had grown up higher below the ledge, so as to make the slope look about even. It was a natural tank-trap.

The cat rested broadside to the slope, tilted at a silly angle, up to its ears in brush. The moonlight lit it up, and the lights from the other cat were playing squarely on it. Barney sat on top in all the blaze of light. The blood oozed from his scratched face, and he cursed steadily. He shoved and yanked at the hopelessly jammed controls.

10

The old moon was high when Ben Roach made a hurried inspection of the first half-mile of line and told the Sector-boss to start burning it out. This had been the easiest part, before they came to the brush-field. Here the line ran through an all-aged forest of mixed conifers—ponderosa pine, incense cedar, and Douglas fir. But even here the line-building had been no picnic. There were gullies, and thick clumps of bitter-brush and young trees, and patches of squaw-carpet that held the earth in a mat of wiry roots. There were big fallen trees, half rotted, and you either had to take the line around them or else use up time in sawing a section out of them. Where a dead snag stood close to the line, you had to set a man to scraping a line around it, in hopes of keeping the fire from getting to it and running up to its top.

Still, this was all moderately open as compared to the brush-field, and a good eighteen-inch line was enough. Moreover, the Sector-boss started to light his back-fires without any fears for his men; the forest behind them was open enough for a get-away, if necessary. But the brush-field was a different story. In many places a man could hardly move through it at all, and the bosses always had to plan first for safety.

The Suffolk locals had managed to hold back the point, but the main fire was getting too close for comfort. The men's faces were sooty with smoke. They stopped to cough more often, or stood blinking their eyes to get the tears out and to see where to strike. They sucked at the canteens to ease the choking in their throats. Now and then someone slapped quickly at his neck or hand, where one of the tiny but very hot specks of burning manzanita leaf had fallen. As every man worked, in the dancing half-light of the nearing fire, he had the uncomfortable sense that these sparks were also falling beyond the line. Twice, little spot-fires puffed up on the wrong side, but men breaking their way through the brush controlled them before they took off.

The unfinished gap was less than two hundred yards now, and the men of each crew could look ahead through the already paling moonlight, and see the bobbing headlights of the other crew and the severed branches being thrown aside. But off to one side the fire was not so far away as the distance to the other crew.

"Listen!" yelled one of the men. As the clump of axes and the scrape of McLeods ceased, they heard the crackle of fire and the sigh of wind, but cutting across those sounds, from off to the north, came the muttering roar of a big Diesel engine.

A little cheer went up. "There she is! . . . About time! . . . That's sure a cat!"

They suddenly relaxed a little. They stood leaning against shovel-handles, and mopped their faces with bandannas. One of them spoke the thoughts they had not dared express:

"Say, it's lucky she got here. We'd never have closed this gap in time."

After that they hardly worked at all. They knew that their axes were dulled and their muscles tired, and that the cat could punch the line through so fast that a few feet more or less made no difference. The noise of the Diesel swelled up. When the cat-skinner struck the cleared line, he made even better time. With blade still raised high, he bucked and plunged along.

"Christ! Look out—here he comes!"

With fine unconcern for human life, the big cat came careening down upon the men. They scattered to both sides, crowding back into the brush.

The machine took over. It lurched to a stop at the head of the line. It paused a moment. The roar of the engine grew quieter, as if the monster—saying, "Permit *me* to manage this affair!"—were now considering the situation. The two men on top of it began to work levers, but they looked like mere slaves of the machine. The real power lay elsewhere.

As the men worked the levers, the big steel blade sank lower and lower. The swamper switched off the lights, useless now in the dawn. The cat-skinner stood up and looked ahead at the lay of the land. The fire was so close that he decided to swing the line back in a little loop.

The engine roared louder; one tread scraped and slipped as the cat changed position a little. Then, as one-hundred-fifty horsepower took over, it lurched slowly forward at the dense thicket ahead.

Even above the roaring motor there was a sudden crackling noise as the blade sheared into the manzanita. The bushes at which the men had labored so slowly were no match for the concentrated power of the machine. Twigs bent back; whole branches snapped; four-inch stems were sheared off or uprooted. A forty-foot fir tipped, and went over. The cat moved

ahead through the thicket as fast as a man could follow at a
slow walk.

Now and then indeed it paused. Perhaps the brush had
piled up too high ahead of the diagonally slanting blade and
must be pushed to one side. Perhaps, meeting the resistance of
some larger, deeply rooted bush, even the power of the cat
was equalled, and the treads slid for a moment, tearing the
earth. But always the monster, backing off for a fresh start,
changing angle a little, came in again and swept all before it.

Behind the machine, the men moved in as mere scavengers.
They picked up the litter of broken branches, threw them
aside, and got to work with shovel and McLeod. But they
could not even keep up. If there had been another cat to
follow the first, clearing the litter, scraping down to the red
earth, the work would have gone much faster.

By now it was full light. The blaze of the fire was no longer
as dominating as its smoke. The cat finished punching through
the line, and made contact with the other crew. Crashing into
the brush, it swung around, and started back to mop up the
line. The swamper lowered the blade, and it scraped the top
of the ground, sliding all the litter off to one side, shaving off
the top-soil. Crunching and banging, it tore out rocks or
scraped over them. After it passed, the high places showed red
dirt and the low places were filled with litter. Merely by the
two passings of the cat, the trail was cleared out and leveled
so that in a pinch a car might have been driven along it—
where, a few minutes before, the brush had been so thick that
a man could not even walk. Except for the raw earth and the
piling up of litter on the sides, the fire-line was like a country
lane, with the bushes on each side standing up higher than
a man's head.

In one spot the fire was only twenty feet off. As a bush
flared, the cat seemed almost to move through the flame. The

swamper hung over the side, sheltering himself behind the seat. The cat-skinner shielded his face behind an arm.

It was now or never, and behind the cat came Ben Roach with a lighted fusee. By good luck the back-fire caught quickly, and roared up to meet the advancing point.

But there were dozens of others. Or rather, the line no longer met merely the threat of advancing points. There was danger everywhere. From one side the heat came like a steady pressure. The men worked, sheltering their faces.

The heat of the first back-fire died down. No sparks had jumped the line, but the line itself had been too hastily cleared and a point of fire had worked across it to the other side. The heat was still furnace-like, but two Hot-shot men rushed in, caught the point of fire, and threw it back across the line.

As they came running out, their shirts steaming, Ben Roach lit the next stretch of back-fire, and on the other side his Sector-boss did the same. Between the two back-fires the danger was too great, and so no man must be left there. That part of the line now had to take care of itself.

To be anywhere along the line was dangerous now. On the unburned side the brush stretched away, so thick that a man trying to penetrate it must often climb over the tops of the bushes rather than walk on the ground and push his way through. Once the fire burned up to the line or a back-fire was lighted, no one could stay in the cleared line without being burned, and if he went into the brush and the fire jumped the line, he might be caught.

The only way to light back-fires without trapping the men was to begin at the middle and work outwards in both directions. The rear-guard was the post of honor. A Sector-boss from the Inyo Forest held it on the north end, and Ben Roach held it on the south. . . .

Ben Roach had fought many fires, and he knew that this was a tough spot. Blazing fusee in hand, he retreated step by step. With luck it might hold, but the cat had got there a little too late, and there had been only one cat. The sun was up now, and that meant that the wind would blow a little harder. As he fell back, he made sure that no men were left behind him, and then he went along sticking the fusee into the dead leaves or among the twigs of some dead branch All the while he listened for the shouts from behind. With a couple of miracles they might hold her. A billowing curl of smoke came down right over him, and he coughed and shut his eyes, and slapped out a spark. His last back-fire blazed up finely, and he stepped off to get away from the heat.

Then suddenly came the long whoop from behind.

He swung around. "Beat it, boys!" he yelled. He flung his fusee into the bushes, and ran.

Ben was not young any more, and he was heavy-set. He could not run as fast as he once could, and also he had to look around as he ran to be sure that no one was left behind. But the only ones he could see were two youngsters ahead of him, and about all of them he saw were the rising and falling soles of their shoes as they widened the gap.

There was a cooler stretch. A buck leaped out of the brush on the fire-side, took two jumps down the trail, and then went off into the brush on the other side. (He'd take care of himself probably; a deer could go through brush where a man would stick.) Ben was panting, and it was hot and smoky here. He hoped that the Sector-boss, or whoever it was, had not waited too long before yelling. A wood-rat, fur ablaze, scuttled across. (He would probably spread the fire, but no matter now.) Then, just ahead, smoke and flame seemed to be blowing right across the line. (Anyway, the boys must have made it.)

Ben stopped, blowing hard. He was too much of an old-timer to get rattled in a tight place. He might try to go back and out the north end, or chance it through the brush, or build himself a back-fire, or just wait for the blaze ahead to die down a little, as it might. But things did not look too bad ahead. He wrapped a bandanna around his nose and mouth, pulled his felt hat low, took a long breath, and dashed in.

For the first dozen jumps it was bad. Flames were reaching across the cleared line. But just as he wondered, he came out into an open space. He fell down, and rubbed his smoking clothes against the dirt. Then he was up and dashing into the bad spot ahead.

It turned out to be not so bad, and in a few seconds he came through to the Sector-boss and a few men on the other side.

All the Sector-boss said was: "Well, Ben, I see you made it." But from the looks he was getting Ben knew that his clothes and face must be a sight. There was a smell of singed hair about him from where a flame had swept under the brim of his hat.

"Yes," he said, "I made it, but I won't need a neck-shave soon.—How about all the others?"

"Everybody made it, I guess. But a couple of them sure got hot pants. Sorry I didn't give you more time. She came fast all of a sudden."

"How about the north end?"

"Haven't heard any shoutin', and you can still hear the cat, if you listen, though that might just mean they'd pulled her back."

"Don't make much difference now. The line's all gone to hell anyway. Get on your radio, and tell 'em to pull out before they run into trouble. I'll get to mine, and tell Bart about it. Check with your crew-bosses, and be sure everybody got out."

"It's tough. If both the cats had got here, we'd of held her

. . . Say!" The Sector-boss held up his hand for silence. "Listen. They've cut off the cat-engine. . . . And now hear 'em yell!"

11

The cat-skinner, finding that he was likely to be in a hot place, had merely shoved the brush back in several directions, and then when the yell came to abandon the line, he just swung the cat into the open space, cut his engine, and ran for it. A cat thus protected would ride through a lot of heat.

What happened on the north end was about the same as what had already happened on the south end, except for the doings of one man. The Forest-Service men on that sector were largely from the Inyo. They had been on a fire in another northern forest, and had been sent to the Spitcat without even going home or getting their clothes off. (Now the Inyo is an east-side forest where rain is scanty and big pines stand widely spaced on dry mountain-sides and even brush grows thinly.) They were rather appalled at the thickness of the growth in Reverse Flat. As a result, most of them were over-cautious, but one of them was foolhardy, because he kept feeling that the brush at any given point must be unusually thick and that it would be normally thin just a little way off. Also he was a cocky youngster, who had never yet been in a bad fire.

He had gone a few yards into the brush to catch a spot-fire, and he was there when the shout came to abandon the line. Looking back, he saw the cat-skinner run along the line and then the Sector-boss, but the Sector-boss did not see him. Thinking for himself, he decided that by the time he scrambled back through the brush to the line and then ran along the line, he might be in a bad way. Looking the other way, he saw that it was no great distance to where some firs stood up high from the brush, and on the east side brush never grows thickly among trees. The smoke was drifting down heavily upon him from across the line, and he realized—all this took only a few seconds—that he was in a bad spot either way. As any man must, he made his decision in the light of his experience. He turned away from the fire, and began battling through the brush toward the fir-trees.

(It was like that old nightmare. You work and strain till the blood beats at your ears, but still your legs seem to have lead weights bolted to them; your chest is tight, and the very air seems thick, as if you tried to struggle forward through deep gray ooze.)

For ten feet he crashed through an easy place. Then swinging with his shovel, he broke away some branches ahead of him. There was a solid front of branches next, but on hands and knees, dragging the shovel, he started to crawl beneath. A dry branch snapped, and the sharp stub caught his shirt. For a moment he wriggled like a hooked fish. He lunged hard. The shirt tore, and he felt the branch-stub gouge at his back. With a twisting roll he broke through, and came out at the other side of the bush, panting, having advanced six feet. Standing up and jumping hard, he let his weight crash him through the next barrier. He felt his back bleeding.

He came up squarely against a big dead bush, a whitened skeleton with sharp points reaching outward like a hundred deer-antlers. All he could do was to go back, swing to the right, and try again.

He had gone no more than a hundred feet, but his heart was pounding so violently with the exertion that he had to stop for breath. Looking to the right, he saw that the fire had already jumped the line. A point had run ahead almost even with him.

"Don't get excited," he thought, and looking ahead, he saw that the fir-trees were not so far. The brush must be thinner from there on.

He plunged ahead once more, again trying to slash a path with his shovel. It worked, but progress was too slow. Smoke was getting thicker and lower. He could hardly tell which way he wanted to go. The fire must have jumped the line behind him too.

There was a sudden easy place—a deer-trail perhaps—and for a twisty thirty feet he almost ran. Then he stopped short, for it had bent toward the point of fire on the right, away from the direction he wanted to go. Getting his bearings with difficulty on account of the smoke, he again plunged at the tangle.

A new wave of smoke rolled over him, making him stop and yield to a fit of coughing. But what really struck panic into him was the heat. The fire must be closer.

He abandoned the useless and impeding shovel, and with a fit of energy flung himself upon the tops of the bushes, almost as a swimmer upon water. He worked forward for some yards, but it was like swimming in a morass, or floundering across quicksand. The branches broke beneath his weight, and the broken points caught in his clothes, holding him back. They scratched and tore his skin. One shirt-sleeve was dangling, and he ripped it off.

Standing up, he tried to walk across the tops of the bushes with his feet breaking through the twigs and finding some solid support upon the heavier branches beneath. This also worked, but it was too slow.

His energy was failing. He had worked hard during the night, and now he was like a man trying to swim against a swift current, or setting out to sprint a hundred yards and finding he must go a mile. He was dizzy with fatigue, and the smoke cut him off from even the comfort of pure air for his heaving lungs.

He stopped a moment for breath, crouching down low for cleaner air. He calmed his rising panic. "Got to play this clever," he thought. He looked about shrewdly for the easiest passage-way between the interlacing branches. He found one, broke through it without too much trouble, found another, went on. But such progress was always sinuous, and he struggled ahead twenty feet to gain ten feet toward safety.

He slapped at a spark, and in new panic at the thought of spot-fires, stood up to look ahead. Smoke was rising from a spot-fire well in front of him, to the left. But he felt sudden relief when he saw that the closest fir tree was scarcely a hundred feet away. Energetic again with the thought of safety and rest, he plunged ahead, just as a white sheet of searing-hot flame went up from a bush not thirty feet behind him. He burst through bushes, climbed and walked across them, crawled beneath them. His face and hands, and his bare arm, were crisscrossed with bleeding scratches. He kept his eyes half-closed to protect them from smoke and from twigs. Almost blindly, in an animal-like intensity to live, he struggled on, keeping direction by the drift of the smoke.

Then suddenly, as he reached ahead, his hand came upon something soft and comforting to feel, not the harsh and hostile stubs of manzanita. It was the branch of a fir-tree!

He had a quick sense of thankfulness and relief, and then as he looked up, his heart sank even lower. The tree, some thirty feet high, rose from a solid mass of brush. The downward-sloping branches of the fir intermingled with the upward-reaching branches of the manzanita. The dense brush pressed upon the tree, as closely as the water of a lake laps around an isolated spire of rock. Here was no safety, and no hope of easy progress.

He was so exhausted that he lay still, with one hand clasping the fir-branch, and failed to react quickly. He was like the runner who has run his mile, not to win a medal, but to find safety beyond the broken tape. Then, when he had broken the tape, there was no safety, and he had spent his strength on the final sprint.

After half a minute he roused himself and stood up, shakily. He was not in complete panic. Still, he reasoned, where the trees stood more thickly, the brush must be thinner, since it could not thrive in shade. Straight ahead seemed still the best way. The long running point of fire on the right was ahead of him, and the spot-fire on the left had advanced and grown much larger.

He was just about to try skirting the fir-tree when another cloud of smoke enveloped him. He closed his eyes; his throat gagged; a paroxysm of coughing shook him. Suddenly—from smoke, or exhaustion, or panic—he was faint. Swallowing nausea, fighting blackness, he collapsed, sinking down almost comfortably upon the soft fir-branches. He lay dazed, unable to recover quickly because the smoke was still choking him.

Like cold water dashed in his face, a sudden blast of heat brought him to alertness. The tip of the fir-tree was tossing. A gust of wind had blown up, and the fire was making a quick run. A bush, only twenty feet on his right, was going up in crackling fire.

Quite calmly he knew that he could not out-run this fire. Even when he had had a good start, the thick brush had been too much for him, and now he was exhausted, and half-overcome with smoke. For a moment he thought of trying to make a cleared space around him or of digging a hole and covering himself with dirt. But even if he had still had his shovel, there would probably not have been time, and with his bare hands it was clearly impossible.

Yet he was a young man, scarcely more than a boy, and he could not merely lie there and let the fire burn him. With a final desperation he began to climb the fir-tree. Once he had reached the trunk, he found the branches in ladder-like arrangement, and he went up rapidly. The thick and sloping branches were almost like a sheltering roof to keep out both smoke and heat. He thought hopefully that the fire might sweep ahead beneath him. He was barely conscious of a faint resinous smell.

Then, as a bush blazed up beside it, the distilled gum of the fir-needles exploded into a hissing flame. As the fire towered high above the tree-top, something tumbled from the branches, and fell inertly to the ground.

12

A day of disaster, with one bit of bad news close behind another!

Bart had got to bed—crawled into a sleeping-bag without even taking off his shoes—about two o'clock. In spite of all his tensions, he was so tired that he went solidly to sleep, only to be raised out of it cruelly at four-thirty, when the siren went off.

As the day-crews, cursing the siren, came crawling out of their blankets, Bart pulled himself together, crawled out too, and blundered over to Headquarters.

The first thing they told him was that some fool cat-skinner had run his cat off a cliff and put it out of action until some major repairs had been done. Then, after an hour, came the word that the whole line in Reverse Flat—partly of course because that cat did not get through—had gone all to pieces,

and let the fire go racing across the brush-field. Then, to top
it all, a man was missing. Things were still too hot for anybody
to go in and look for him. There was a chance he might
merely have out-run the fire and still be wandering around
in the woods. But he was more likely dead. Worst of all, he
might be lying somewhere, badly burned and dying in agony
for lack of care.

Bart himself looked like disaster. He had not yet changed
his shirt with the hole burned in it, or got all the soot off his
face. There were bags under his eyes for want of sleep.

Before the news of losing the line had come in, the day-
crews had lined up and eaten breakfast, and got started up the
steep switch-back trail. Bart had to send a man on horseback
to recall a lot of them. They would not be needed in Reverse
Flat from here in.

Yes, it was a day of disaster, and of retreat. Yet in some ways
it was not so bad as the day before, when the original blow-up
had sent the fire crowning down the ridge. That had been
complete rout. Today at least it was retreat in good order.

The three of them held another council of war, but it did
not take long this time.

"I played it too close up," said Bart. He felt that he had to
say something, and he felt so bad about the man and about
all the trees that were going to burn that he cared little about
himself.

"You'd have been all right," said Walt Barnaby, "except
for that crazy cat-skinner. He wrecked his own cat, and of
course that held up the other one for a while too."

"There wasn't enough safety-margin," said Bart.

"We know that now, Bart," said the Supervisor, "but nobody can tell for sure in advance."

Still, Bart remembered how the Super had said that they

maybe ought to give the fire more room, and let the brush-field burn. Just then the news came in that they had found a shovel with the handle burned away, and that did not make him feel any better. You could say it was just an industrial accident, as if you told a man to take a truck down to Suffolk for supplies, and he had a collision and was killed. Just the same, Bart had ordered the line run through, and the loss of that line and of the man were tied up together.

There was no argument, though, about where the line should go this time. They all agreed that the top of Reverse Ridge was the place, and there was hardly need for Bart to state the case:

"It's a natural line of defense—ridge-top, and rocky, so that the trees are scattered. In a lot of places rock-ledges crop right out. Where you don't get rock, the ground is pretty level on the ridge, and it's good cat-country. That ridge would stop lots of fires, just by itself—I don't mean a fire like this one!"

They agreed. And then came all the problems of reorganization and redeployment.

From a three-division fire, they reorganized it as a two-zone fire, with five divisions. First Zone would be all the north side. The Angeles man would take over as Zone-boss. There would have to be a new fire-camp. ("Arn Sorenson can fix up the details.") Second Zone would be the south side. Its Division I would run from the northeastern point, near where the fire had started, down along Onion Creek; that was mostly cold line now, and would not need many men. Division II would run from Reverse Creek along to the top of Reverse Ridge at the head of Waupomsy Creek; there would be a lot of fire along that line; it would be mostly a flanking-job, but still Division II would need plenty of men, and at least one cat— two, would be better. Division III would take the line straight along the top of Reverse Ridge; it would have to meet the fire head-on; that Division-boss would get first call on men, and should have all the cats he could use ("Tell Arn we need a lot more cats!"); if the cats could clear out a way, tankers might even be able to get up to the ridge and fight the fire with water. ("Arn's got to see that the tankers are in the right place.")

The other zone included the other two divisions. It had nearly as long a total line as Zone I, but it was cold—or nearly cold—or else would be a flanking job. Division IV ought to have two or three cats. ("Make a note for the Dispatcher.") Division V could get along without any.

There would have to be a wholly new fire-camp ("Tell Arn to pick a place."), and maybe a drop-camp somewhere on Division V. ("Tell Arn, either that, or else get another pack-train going.") And, oh yes, an advance gasoline- and oil-dump for the cats ("Tell Arn!"). Maybe we need a spike-camp over at the road-head there by Cerro Gordo. ("Make a note for Arn on that too.")

From here on, the Angeles man in charge of Zone 2 would be practically an independent commander. The fire was so big that no single Fire-boss could get around to all parts of it and plan the strategy in detail. The fire-camp for that zone would have its own independent supply-lines coming in from the north. The two camps might be seven or eight miles apart —by direct air-line, across the mountains—but they would be a lot farther than that by any trail, especially now that the fire was burning between them and would block trails. By road you would have to go thirty-nine miles back to Suffolk, then seventeen to Polkville, then twenty-seven more to Sheba, and then over a twisty mountain road twenty or twenty-five miles more. It would be a good part of a day's driving.

But Zone 1, particularly Division III, was the hot spot. There you wanted the men you could trust most, and work with best. So Bart kept Ben Roach for Division III; there was nobody better than Ben for close-up command.

Accessibility had always been the first problem with this fire. It had started in one of the most out-of-the-way spots in the forest. Now it had burned so as to separate the two zones and make any shift of personnel almost impossible. Now indeed the fire was getting much more conveniently close to the Onion Flat camp. But still there was the problem of getting the men to the line.

From Headquarters Bart had to tip his chin back to see up to the top of the steep mountain-wall beginning just across Bacchus Creek. It was a six-hundred-foot rise to where he could see, and beyond that was a gentler slope of four hundred feet before you got to the crest of Reverse Ridge. To get up the face of the Ridge by trail you would have to walk three miles up Bacchus Creek along the bottom of the cliff, and then two miles up Curran Creek. And then you would have to walk back along the top of the Ridge.

But to a man who knew the mountains, the face of the Ridge was not so formidable as it looked. In most places the cliffs fell off sheer, but in between there were gaps where the rock had broken away. There were talus-slopes, and chimneys, and water-courses—you could even see trees—along which any active man could scramble up or down. From the camp to the crest of the Ridge was a thousand-foot climb, but not over a mile of distance. All that was needed was to have each Sector-boss take his men along the trail until he saw a likely-looking place, and then lead them up to the top.

Bart heard a nervous little laugh, and turned around to see one of the boys who had come in for campfire-permits the week before.

"Wher'd you blow in from?"

"Oh, we'd been fishin' up by Poison Spring. We saw the smoke, and thought you might need some help. So we came in and volunteered—even if we are Conchies."

"You mean," said Bart, grinning, "you smelled smoke, and couldn't keep away!"

The boy gave his little laugh again: "Yes, I guess so."

"What crew you in?"

"Mostly loggers."

"That'll be a good crew, but don't learn too many bad words from 'em!"

The boy gave his little laugh, and went on. But to Bart the meeting gave a definite lift. This fire-fighting was nasty and dirty and exhausting, and yet it made you feel good inside. He didn't know that he blamed a Conchie too much for not going out to kill people. You might have to do it, but it couldn't ever be a thing to feel too happy about. A Conchie who would come in and volunteer—especially after he'd been fighting fires under orders for three years—was all right.

The crews who had been ordered back from the trail to Reverse Flat, now that the line was lost, were coming into camp now. They were a motley crowd, but Bart suddenly felt a great human love for them all. They fought a common enemy, and not a lot of other men much like themselves. In a war, you had to teach men the causes, so that they would hate, and not trade tobacco and chocolate between outposts. But once let a man see a crown fire, and you didn't ever need tell him it was an enemy of all men. The crews came streaming across the flat—loggers and millmen, linemen from Power and Light, soldiers and sailors, Conchies, two store-clerks from Suffolk, field-laborers from the Valley, pogies and winoes, a young Mendocino ranger with a Master's degree, who might be Chief Forester before he died. The two girls working with the timekeeper were students at Berkeley, and a buxom Idylhurst woman helping in the kitchen was reputed to have led a professional career in San Francisco before she was married.

Among the pogies there was a good scattering of Negroes, two Filipinos, and a slant-eyed fellow who must be half-Chinese. Among the loggers, three dark and short Indians, remnants of a slaughtered local tribe, walked beside the tall, blond-haired Scandinavians. The brown-faced Mexicans talked musically in a language the others could not even understand.

A Sector-boss called to his men, and jumping the narrow stream of Bacchus Creek, he began to lead up the steep ascent beyond.

13

By folklore, it was supposed to blow for three days, once it got started. Dave Halliday was not at all impressed by folklore about weather. A wind like this might blow one day or two days, or maybe four days. His morning weather map showed that it was certainly going to continue for its second day. Pressure over the inland plateau had fallen somewhat, but there was still a mass of cold and heavy air which was bound to come pouring out toward the California valleys. The Ponderosa Forest just had the bad luck to lie between.

Studying the map and checking back to Sunday's map, he decided that the wind would probably blow its traditional three days, and very likely a fourth for good measure. The storm which had brought in the cold air was moving slowly east across the Dakotas. The next storm behind it was squarely in the Gulf of Alaska. Between the two a tongue of polar air was poking down across Canada.

He found himself wanting to see a weather-map of the

whole world, instead of this miserable little rectangle which was only a few thousand miles each way. Though there were no intense storms and nothing you could call remarkable, yet he felt a drama in the making. It was the turn of the seasons. The forces of the South were at last in full retreat; those of the North, advancing. The sun was drawing back; the frost was creeping down from the Pole. Now, during the clear nights on the high plateau, the heat that drained off into space was more than sun could supply during the day. Yet the storms moving from the west were still weak. Between a dying summer and an unborn winter, the west winds faltered.

It was hard on the Ponderosa Forest. But even if you had a World Weather Control, would they decide to shut off this particular little flow of air? Perhaps it was just the safety-valve needed. The situation which was burning trees in California might be strengthening the hands of fire-fighters in Washington and British Columbia. And what about the forests in Russia and India and East Africa? He smiled a moment at the thought of what a thankless task World Weather Control would have. Just now every pressure-group in California would be bombarding it with telephone-calls: "This is the Governor of California speaking. Shut off this north wind. It's an outrage!" . . . "Sorry, sir, but unless we drain that air off from the plateau, the European hay-crop will be ruined by too much rain." He was glad that he only had to forecast weather, without being responsible for it.

And yet, in spite of his world-view, he had a curious kind of loyalty to the Ponderosa Forest. If he had really had the power, probably he would have turned off this wind. Being just a person, he was too conscious of what was happening right around him, and his cracked lips were uncomfortable. That would be the trouble with WWC, as they would call it. Whoever ran it would have to be a real citizen-of-the-world of infinite wisdom. He would have to keep cruising in the stratosphere above all the changes of weather, or else in a windowless air-conditioned room where he could just push buttons and not hear complaints of farmers being ruined by drought or screams of children in a house crumpling before a hurricane. Or better perhaps, you would have to perfect human nature before you took the weather over.

He went in to speak to Arn about the forecast. The Dispatcher's office was a hum of activity. Arn was like the caricature of the big businessman, using two telephones, and a radio in the seconds between. He seemed to be setting up a new camp, and ordering in a scouting-plane, and doing something with the coroner, and talking with the Regional Office, and getting a transport-plane for dropping supplies by parachute, and emphatically telling a lumber-company official to get those cats moving fast.

When things calmed a little, Dave told him the forecast and said he'd like to go and have a look at the fire closer up.

"Sure," said Arn. "Cerro Gordo Lookout would be the best place. I'd take the jeep. The road is not much."

"Thanks," said Dave. "The lookout won't mind, will he? Is he a good guy?"

"Oh—yes—" said Arn, in a funny way. "I forgot you were so new to the Forest. No, the lookout won't mind, I imagine. I shouldn't be surprised if you two would hit it off pretty well." And then, although Dave could not imagine why, he added the curious comment, "You know, Dave, you're quite a handsome fellow!"

14

By mid-morning the fire was rolling, pressed forward by a gusty northeast wind, on an unbroken front of more than a mile.

On the right flank it had entered that part of the brush-field where many tall snags (killed in some old fire) still tow-ered gauntly above the manzanita. As the fire came to each of the dead trunks, it ran quickly up the dry moss-grown surface until the snag flared clear to the top. Then, as the wind dis-lodged bits of burning bark and wood, the blazing fragments sailed forward on the wind, and in their slanting fall reached far ahead. The fire thus raced along rapidly.

The snag-patch itself was an inferno. From the ground-level the flames rose white-hot from the thick manzanita. Flames licked up along the towering dead tree-trunks; a hun-dred feet and more in the air the tips of the dry snags blazed in the wind, smoke and flames streaming off like flags. Through the thickly drifting smoke you looked up to see the dull red disk of the sun, and through smoke-eddies the tips of the snags like torches blazing wildly in the sky.

On its left flank the fire was also entering a new phase. So far it had burned mostly along the level or downhill, but now it was beginning to breast the slope leading up to Re-verse Ridge. Cut steeply into the Ridge, facing almost north, the canyon of little Waupomsy Creek, funnel-like, scooped up the wind. The rising heat also swept up along the canyon. With this new aid of terrain the fire burned more intensely among the undergrowth and small trees, although it seldom crowned in the taller trees. Gigantic, the column of gray smoke sloped off toward the southwest, spreading out as it rose, until above twenty thousand feet it felt the westerly drift of the upper air and spiraled off eastwards.

In spite of all the labor and energy expended against it, the fire had grown steadily larger. In the general collapse of the line across Reverse Flat, flames had jumped the little stream of Bear Creek and were burning to the north of Reverse Creek. All morning there was a desperate flanking fight to keep the fire from taking off up-slope, and to edge it back to the south of the creek. The abandoned cat, scorched but still workable, was brought out of the burned brush-field. Another cat also came to the rescue, and the newly organized Zone 2 flung the best of its man-power on this critical half-mile.

On the other flank the problem was simpler. Since there was obviously no stopping the fire where it roared in the funnel of the canyon, the strategy was merely to give ground, take the line up the nose of a ridge, and be sure that the fire nowhere jumped across the watershed.

Far away along the top of Reverse Ridge two cats and two hundred men began work.

15

The rabbit on Reverse Ridge was considerably disturbed that morning. He had never before seen or heard a man or a machine. The breaking of the underbrush, the clamor of voices, the scraping of tools, the roaring of engines—all worked together to confuse and alarm him. He retreated into his thickest brush-clump, near the corner of the line where Division III and Division IV joined. There, not fifty feet inside the line, he lay quietly. After a while, since no harm came to him, he grew less alarmed.

16

The bus in which Bo Fox was riding continued to have an overheating engine. Finally at Idylhurst it was stopped, and the men were loaded into a truck. They were then taken along the road which skirted the slope of Cerro Gordo, and unloaded at the new spike-camp. They were assigned crew-bosses and issued tools. Then the bosses led them up the steep and narrow trail toward the top of Reverse Ridge.

Bo Fox looked about him with a continual, though furtive,

apprehension. He saw nothing in particular to arouse anxiety. He had never gone so deeply into the mountains before, but the presence of many men comforted him, and the crew-boss gave orders in such a way as to relieve him of any strain of making decisions.

The trail zig-zagged up a steep talus-slope which formed a break between unscalable cliffs on either side. As the crew climbed higher, Bo looked more nervously in both directions and saw what seemed to be continuous walls of cliff, except for this one gap where the trail ran.

His tension grew somewhat. The gap was comfortably broad as he looked at it, but when he moved his glance along the line of cliffs, the gap seemed a mere narrow entrance, the only break in a solid wall. If anything should contrive to block this door, the place might be a trap, for on the other side he could see nothing but the unbroken front of smoke.

17

This noon the base of the smoke-column covered twice as wide an arc on her fire-finder as it had on the day before. By its very look it seemed closer too. From scraps of talk over the radio she knew that it was on this side of Reverse Flat by now, and so was only about eight miles off. The smoke was less of an unvaried gray. She made out more whorls and convolutions. The sun was high overhead, but even so, it shone only as a red disk through the smoke. ("The red sun was pasted in the sky like a wafer." Who wrote that, about some battlefield? She remembered it from English 130C.) Although she could still cast a shadow, the light had a sinister yellowness. Then, as she stood on the east catwalk with her hands on the railing, something light and fluffy and white settled gently on the railing by her right thumb. It was a bit of feathery ash, the first she had seen!

With the falling of that bit of ash, the fire seemed to jump closer. Now as she looked, she saw yellow tones, as of reflected flame, along the base of the smoke-column, just above Reverse Ridge. She decided also that the peculiar feeling in her nostrils was not wholly from the dry wind but must be from smoke in the air—a faint permeation which had come so slowly across the miles and spread so universally that it could not be isolated as a smell.

With the dry wind and the close atmosphere, it looked like an uncomfortable afternoon ahead. She thought of going into a halter and shorts, but that was hardly the costume for an official representative of the Forest Service, who was even theoretically empowered to make arrests. That ought to be headlines—a girl pinning her badge on the halter and dashing out to give someone a ticket for breaking fire-regulations! But besides, during a fire there might be a lot of rough characters around, and a costume like that might seem a come-on. Finally, however, she decided she might as well be comfortable. She didn't think there would be any man she couldn't handle, particularly with the aid of that loaded pistol which Bart had insisted she keep handy.

When she went out on the catwalk again, she looked more like Carmel Beach than Cerro Gordo Lookout. She had even done up her brown hair in a yellow handkerchief to keep the smoke and ashes out of it, and she was wearing dark, sloped-up glasses, for by now the sun was getting far enough to the west to be out from the smoke.

The fire was certainly moving in on her. Plugging along the road which skirted Cerro Gordo she heard still another truck. She could not see it on account of the trees, but she knew that it was making for the newly established camp. Looking through her binoculars she clearly made out yet another long line of men carrying tools, climbing up the steep trail through one of the gaps in the cliffs.

Then suddenly she was enveloped with thousands of little flying things. Often before, she had been impressed with the insects which she saw from the lookout, for she had thought of insects as fluttering low along the ground, not as sailing high across the tops of peaks. She caught one of the thousands, or millions, that were now filling the air. It was like a little winged ant. They must be termites, which swarmed after the first rain of the season, and were on their way to establish a colony in some fallen log. They would eat and digest the wood and thus return it to soil; then from the soil another tree would be nourished, which after five hundred years might fall as another dead log and nourish the far descendants of these same termites. According to the Termitic School of Philosophy, she supposed, the object and divine purpose of forests was to supply food for termites.

There were other flying things too, dark little beetles. Once she slapped hard when one of them lit on the back of her neck and bit her viciously. Unlike the termites, which drifted with the wind, these beetles seemed to be making purposefully toward the smoke. These must be what Bart had called smoke-beetles, which lived by burrowing into charred wood. For them a forest fire was a bonanza, a regular opening of the Cherokee Strip.

So much was happening that she had little time to be conscious of that feeling of exaltation which had come over her as she looked at the red glow through the darkness of the early morning. Yet when she stopped a moment, she still was happy, and was also happy with that sense of loneliness and wishing to share happiness with someone.

Perhaps, she realized, that was why she listened intently

when she heard a motor puttering somewhere on the tree-covered slope below her. It sounded closer than the main road, as if it might be on the steep pitch up to the lookout. As the sound got closer, she was sure.

She dodged back from the catwalk in a slight panic, and considered pulling some jeans on, and a shirt. Then, peering through the glass, she saw a sudden flash of color from among the trees, and a bright red jeep came right up the slope where there wasn't even a road, and stopped in full sight. There was only the driver in it. He was not wearing a Forest-Service uniform, but he did not look like a rough-neck either. The gray pants looked like the Navy, and the open-necked plaid shirt gave him a collegiate touch. He had no hat, and his wavy brown hair had been blown in all directions by the wind. He looked sophisticated enough not to mind a girl in halter and shorts.

Maybe he was sophisticated, but he didn't know much about the etiquette of lookouts. Instead of calling up to ask permission, he just started to climb the steel stairs, and she could hear him whistling softly. Of course she could close the trap door in the catwalk, and make him explain his business first, but that seemed like timidity and a bad start. She was really excited, pleasantly.

She stood at the corner of the catwalk. The first thing she saw of him was the wind-blown hair rising up through the trap-door, and then the back of his neck and the plaid shirt. When that much of him had come up, he stopped, looked back over his shoulder, and saw her.

At first there was just sheer amazement in his face, and then after a full second he blushed red. She stood enjoying it, as what girl wouldn't! Then she had pity.

"Come on up," she said. "I'm Judith Godoy, the lookout."

"O-o-h," he said in a long-drawn exclamation, "I *beg* your pardon!"

"No harm! Come on up."

"You see," he said, still without moving, "**Arn Sorenson** didn't tell me there was a girl here. I've just come to Suffolk, and I thought lookouts were men."

"I see."

"I'm awfully sorry. All Arn said was he thought the lookout and I might get along pretty well."

"Oh, that's it! That's what passes for a good joke in this part of the country.—Well, come on up, and have a look at my fire."

But when he came up, she was pleasantly conscious that he was not looking altogether at the fire. All right, she thought, it's no crime, and there's nothing about my figure that's too deformed.

18

Bart was in the saddle once more, and the black mare took the narrow trail along Curran Creek with quick strides. Behind, followed a boy with the radio, riding a bay gelding. The trail was steep as they came to the place where two big cedars grew close together, and Bart had his chance.

He pulled the reins in, and swung himself to the ground. "Let them blow a minute," he said to the boy, and then without saying anything more he went off through the underbrush.

The place was not a hundred feet from the trail; yet, as with many another place of beauty in the mountains, few people had ever seen it. The tourists flocked to high points where they could see for miles and miles without being really close to anything; they stood on the edge of canyons, and uttered senseless exclamations. But Bart never passed along this trail without stepping aside to look at what he merely called The Glen.

Ice-cold and clear, fed from unfailing springs, the little stream dropped in gentle falls over clean rocks from pool to pool. Where the high water of springtime swept them, the rocks were shining gray, and above that they were deep in moss kept always green in the dainty spray of the tiny waterfalls. Farther back from the stream, where the air was still moist, the azaleas grew, and in the spring the glade was spotted thick with the faintly orange blossoms. Out of the carpet of azaleas rose the red-brown fluted columns of the cedars, and high overhead the canopy of branches let the sunlight pierce through in long rays.

Even on hot days, the Glen was cool. On windy days it was quiet. Only, at early morning and late afternoon, air moved gently up or down the stream, as if the place itself were drawing breath.

Without thinking, Bart took off his hat. Moving carefully among the azaleas so as to break no branches, he went forward to a tiny pool, and knelt by it. The little rainbow trout darted away, as he leaned over to drink.

As he rose again, he stood and gazed around. He breathed deeply. As when he had looked out from Cerro Gordo, profound feelings surged within him, inexpressible longings for beauty, and vague hope that all things might live together in love.

Now, scarcely a hundred feet away, he made out the doe. She was standing in the shelter of a bush, looking out at him with grave curiosity. He saw the sleek curve of her neck, and the wide liquid eyes, timid and yet not really afraid.

"Hello, old girl," he said quietly, for he had seen her there often before, and she was almost a friend. Her fawn must be sheltered somewhere close by.

With a last look, he shuffled back through the azaleas, moving carefully. This at least, he thought, was secure. The trout were too small to tempt fishermen, and no lumberman could afford to send crews into such a narrow ravine just to take out a few cedars. The doe might grow old and die, but her fawns would still haunt the glade. Trampling tourists would never come to admire the view. A six-foot waterfall, some little pools, moss on the rocks, azaleas, a sleek doe—that was not enough for a national advertising campaign and bus-loads of exclaiming vacationers. The place was secure to the man who loved it. From beneath the cliffs the springs would send forth their icy water, until the years of God had run.

He had scarcely been gone a minute. As if with faith renewed, he came back to the trail, swung into the saddle, and started on, the boy on the bay gelding still following him.

Nature might rule in the Glen, but on the top of the ridge men were at work. Bart shifted too, and changed to leader of men.

As he rode along, he was like a general inspecting the ridge-top where his troops built fortifications against the headlong sweep of the approaching enemy.

"That's the Fire-boss! . . . He's the works! . . . See, the guy on the black horse!"

He heard them, as the crews drew back to let the horses through. Though he was on horseback and though the radio-boy might pass for an orderly, there was nothing of the fuss-and-feathers that hedges a general about. His pine-tree badge was his only symbol of authority. His shirt was dirty and torn and had a hole burned in it; his face was shaggy with a sprouting black beard, speckled with gray.

"Hi, Bart! . . . 'Bout time you got here! Been sleepin' late? . . . Where'd you get that cayuse, Ranger?" The Forest-Service men called out as he rode along.

To a man who loved power there would have been intoxication in the air. A little more than forty-eight hours before, he had scrambled across a ravine and come to an insignificant fire on a canyon-side where Slugger O'Neill and his five tired boys were the only crew. By now, on Division III alone, three cats roared back and forth, and where their treads had passed, the trails were already deep in dust. By now three hundred men, still being reinforced, were mopping up behind the cats, and the bosses were from half the forests of California.

Coming to a high spot along the ridge, Bart dismounted and climbed a rocky outcrop. Six miles to the west, away from the fire, Cerro Gordo Lookout stood out white on the round mountain-top. Close below him, over the curve of the slope to the southeast, the fire-camp was hidden from view. To the north and northeast, all was fire. Through the smoke he could barely make out the three parallel, toe-like ridges running out from the base of Howell Mountain. The two northern ones were blackened and fire-swept, and smoke was still rising from them. The thickness of the smoke cut off the view of the brush-field in Reverse Flat, but he knew that it was all fire-swept, and that the snag-patch was still blazing. Just along the left-hand edge of the smoke-column he barely made out the sector of Division IV where the fire had jumped to the north side of the stream. By latest reports that fight was going well, and from where he stood, it looked as if the fire had been edged in along the flank and finally crowded back to the creek.

At best, that was only a victory in a local engagement. It was important as confining the fire and keeping it from widening its front, but it had not met the fire head-on. The main fire over there was south of the creek. It had moved fast through the snag-patch, and had thrown a long arm ahead. Division IV might still be in trouble if the fire jumped the creek again and headed up-slope. (And that was typical too.

No matter what wise plans you made, the fire always decided
to do something else.)

Right below him, however, on the north slope of Reverse
Ridge, was still the main front, a good mile wide. As he
watched it, the fire was not racing rapidly, but even from so
far away it seemed to advance with a terrifying inevitability.
As a gust of wind struck, it made a short run forward, and
engulfed a clump of small trees. He saw the flames shoot up.

Yes, with the dry wind tending toward gustiness, conditions
were still at the emergency-level. He had a pang at thinking
of all the trees that would burn, but it would be too dangerous to put men in front of such a fire as it came funneling up
those canyons—useless too. For there the fire, with the cumulative heat sweeping up-slope, would have every chance of
jumping any line that could be put in front of it. And if it
crowned in the tall Douglas firs, it would merely roll on, as if
no line were there at all.

The ridge was the only place. It was a strong position, for
at that point the rising heat would be carried off into the air
above the tops of the trees growing on the downward slope.
Moreover, he had been able to mass machines and men along
the ridge. Yet, as he watched the smoke and flame, his heart
was sick for the burning trees, and he was far from confident.
The very cumulative enormousness of the fire was sickening.
By now the perimeter stretched out to many miles. Every
minute millions of sparks were flying upward, and any veering gust, even a whirlwind generated by the heat itself, might
carry a spark across the line. There, in the crisp dry wind, the
spark might take off before anyone saw it, and become a running fire that a hundred men could not catch.

By this time the boy had got the radio set up, and was in
touch with Zone 2. Bart talked with the Zone-boss. He con-
firmed, what Bart thought he could see, that they had

squeezed the fire back across the creek. But they were having a bad time keeping it from jumping again farther up; he needed more men for Division IV.

Bart called the Onion Creek camp, and it turned out that the Super wanted to talk to him.

"Hello, Bart," said the Super. "Say, they found the body."

"The body?"

"Yes."

"Oh! . . . Say, was the guy married?"

"They say he was."

They signed off, and Bart looked down the slope again to where the fire was burning. Suddenly it came in his mind to be a vile and ugly monster, raging wantonly among his trees. He had a quick and wild thought that he would gallop along the line to rally his men, and with a wild cheer they would dash down the slope against the fire, and charge upon it and stamp the life from it.

Then he realized that the boy was staring at him, and that he himself was staring into space and probably moving his lips.

"You sick?" said the boy.

"Naw, I'm all right," said Bart, but it was an effort.

"Must be tough to be a fire-boss, lots o' work and no rest."

"Not that," said Bart. "But when you've watched a forest for twenty years and then see this happen, you'll know what I mean. This big stretch of Douglas fir down there now— God, by tomorrow afternoon it's going to be nothing but a lot of blackened snags."

19

The Super went to the chow-line late that evening. Balancing his tin plate and cup, he stood between two pogies, waiting for a cook to ladle out stew.

"How's she look, Ranger?" asked a pogy.

"Not too bad," said the Super. He had felt suddenly warm when the pogy had called him "Ranger," but of course the pogy did not even know his real name. To a pogy any man with a badge was a ranger.

The Super helped himself to catsup at the long table, messy with spilled sugar and salt and dirty spoons. Then he walked to the base of a tree, let his long legs fold up beneath him, and sat cross-legged, eating. Two Forest-Service men—from the Stanislaus, he thought—were eating near him, talking and laughing. He thought that perhaps he should have joined them. He would have liked to, but he was afraid they might stop laughing, and call him Super.

The throbbing of the generator-truck began, and in the dusk the electric lights came on. Well, this was another day, he thought, and about as bad as a day could be. They had lost a man, and half a mile of line, and had a big runaway fire on their hands. It looked fairly good for tomorrow—lots of men and equipment, well-placed lines. Yes, it looked fairly good, barring accident. Bart—well, Bart knew a lot about fire. If he just didn't get so sentimental about trees! Sentiment never was good for fighting fires; the fire itself never showed sentiment. As soon as you began thinking from somewhere inside your stomach and guts instead of from your head, you made mistakes.

Why be sentimental about a tree? It was just a lot of lath, and siding, and two-by-fours, that still happened to have roots on one end and needles on the other. If a lumber-yard burned, you figured the loss in dollars and cents, but you didn't weep tears.

Then, as had happened before on a big fire, the Super became almost indignant at conifers. They were senseless help-less creatures, who had let themselves get into such an evolu-

tionary box that there was no reason in it. Generally speaking,
they refused to grow except in a region with a long dry season,
and then by shedding needles and twigs and bits of bark they
converted their whole forest into a powder-magazine awaiting
the first spark. Besides, they stored up highly inflammable
gums in their needles. The only insurance they deigned to
carry was the thick non-conducting bark about the bases of
the bigger trees, but this did not suffice.

20

Beneath the electric lights at Headquarters the Maps-and-
Records man again performed his melancholy rite of totaling
up the burn. In the last twenty-four hours the fire had swept
diagonally across the center of Deerhound, burning most of
Sections 21 and 22 and smaller portions of seven others. The
area, as he outlined it tentatively in pencil, was highly irregular in shape, each bend and angle mutely eloquent of some
shifting fortune of the battle. A sharp bump stood out at the
northeastern corner, where the spot-fire to the north of Wilson Creek had spread fast until caught by a hastily built line
along the ridge. A notch toward the southeast showed where
the first half mile of line across Reverse Flat had held, thus
saving the fine forest that covered the southeast quarter of
Section 22. At the western end of the fire a long tongue reaching forward was a startling evidence of how the snag-patch
had aided the run of the flames. The most discouraging feature was that the fire, aided by the wind blowing directly up
the diverging watercourses on the face of Reverse Ridge, had
actually in the twenty-four hours doubled its front.

With his dividers set to half a mile by the scale on the map,
he measured the perimeter of the burn, and ended by counting, "Twenty-six." That meant that merely to walk around
the fire would be a journey of at least thirteen miles. Even

though the fire was still uncontrolled, the amount of necessary and useful work accomplished was already tremendous. More than ten miles of line along the flanks had been constructed and held.

Considering that his outline accurately represented the scouts' reports, he methodically traced with a yellow pencil inside the course of the black line. The whole shape of the three days' burn stood out suddenly on the map, in red and orange and yellow, like the snout and head and shoulders of some monstrous crocodilian rearing up from the slime.

He worked out the area of the last day's burn as 1,955 acres, a little over three square miles. That was almost twice as much as had burned on the two preceding days, and the acreage of the total burn now was slightly more than three thousand acres.

As SYMBOL, fire is the opposite of water, as dryness, its nega-
tion. Water stands for release and fruition; dryness, for steril-
ity; but fire, with its heat and red flame, for all the drive and
passion without which nothing would need release or demand
fruition.

The words are as much of common speech as of poetry—
fire of life, flame of love, glow of genius, spark of imagination,
blaze of indignation, burning wrath and lust and zeal, con-
suming jealousy, kindled ire, ardent desire, smouldering hate.

The prophet and philosopher would lack much, lacking
the symbol. The Buddha preached his Fire-sermon. Jeremiah
cried: "Ye have kindled a fire in mine anger, which shall burn
for ever." Paul wrote shortly: "It is better to marry than to
burn." Empedocles thought fire one of the four elements.
Heraclitus, going further, declared the other three to be only
its manifestation, and fire itself to be the soul and even intelligence.

But also fire is the purifier and the destroyer, that welcome
bringer of the last release. Then at the end of the world the
mountains burn and the seas are consumed. Loki brings the

232

flames to high Valhalla. So also each man goes through the final fire. Then crimson flame and sooty smoke pass by, leaving behind the quiet ashes, clean and cool and white.

2

Once more, in the darkness before moonrise, she looked out from her mountain-top toward the glare beyond the dark mass of Reverse Ridge. Again the fire had taken a long step toward her. It still showed in that violent pink, but there was a deeper crimson shade along the lower edge and now and then a faint flaring of yellow. Where on the night before the glare had been a little spot and low on the horizon, now it dominated the northeastern horizon, and was twice as wide, and towered high into the night. Through the binoculars the pines along the ridge stood out in intricate silhouette against the vibrating pinkness.

There was no sound, though it seemed there should be. She could only imagine the crackle and roar of flames. She was, her thought ran, like a person who sees sheet-lightning flicker in the sky from far across the horizon, or like some horrified villager who, too far off to hear the explosions, standing in calm and quiet, watches the bombing of a city.

Then, faintly at first, over the easy murmur of the wind in the pine-tops, she heard the grinding of a truck coming down-grade. It grew louder fast, roaring in crescendo, magnified out of proportion by the stillness of the empty mountain-side. She saw the glare of its headlights, now low among the trees, now suddenly lighting up the pine-tops as the truck bounced on the rough road. It passed by. The sound and the glare faded out, as the truck crossed the little stream that was the head of Bacchus Creek, and swung downwards around the shoulder of the mountain.

In the silence she looked out again toward the fire—and

caught her breath! Against the pinkness flared a luminous yellow point of living flame. There was no arguing now! She was in the presence of the enemy.

Her imagination flared quickly like the flame itself. She thought of bale-fires and beacons. The Apaches are over the river! The Northmen have landed! The topsails of the Armada are bearing down the Channel!

But after the first moment of alarm, she relaxed. The bright spot she was seeing did not mean that the fire had raced suddenly ahead and swept to the ridge. On the lookout she was high enough to command a partial view down the north slope. Just now, on some isolated point, a tall snag had flared up, and the flame had risen into her line of vision.

In a few minutes, indeed, the point of light died down, flickered once or twice, and disappeared. She saw again only the pink glow, vibrant along its lower edge with the hint of tossing flames below the pine-shaggy ridge-line.

She was happy still. There were no bad thoughts from which she fled into fantasy. That was a nice boy who had been up here in the afternoon. TAH-*ta*-ta-TAH! Take a girl on the rebound, and then put her alone in a lookout! TAH-*ta*-ta-TAH! He was coming back, said it was the best place to observe winds. TAH-*ta*-ta-TAH-*ta*-ta-TAH!

3

In the unfriendly blackness Bart lay in his blankets. He was so tired that he twitched now and then, but he could not sleep. "Old nerves!" he thought. "Come on now, relax! Never used to be this way!" In his weariness the yielding pine-needles felt comfortable as a soft bed. He was used to sleeping on the ground. It was not that! (Come on now. This is Tuesday morning, and what between Hart Creek and this fire you haven't had a good sleep since last Wednesday. If you don't sleep, you'll go to pieces!) But the harder he thought of sleep and longed for it, the more he kept sleep away. He was like a mouse, and sleep was the cat stalking him. And though he wished to be caught, yet at the last moment always some power deeper than he could control kept him alert to scurry away just as the cat pounced. Once the soft paws caught him for a second, and then he jerked into wakefulness again.

After a while the thoughts began to race so swiftly that even his heart beat faster, and he merely lay there thinking. The Super now! Ought to be running a lumber-yard, not a forest. Figuring on paper! Beat his face in some time! Of course, they had lost that line across Reverse Flat, and one guy—no, don't think about that! But that was because of that crazy cat-skinner. All cat-skinners are crazy, but you couldn't figure a cat-skinner would do that. Lucky he didn't break his god-damn neck. *Always figure the worst is going to happen.* (God, it sure had, this time.) But the Super!

In the unreasonable imaginings of the darkness, in the guiltiness of his own failure, his fingers grew tense and hooked and his chest swelled. He gripped a tall lithe man by the throat, and the man struggled and writhed mightily, and then the long legs crumpled and folded and the thin hard-muscled body went down.

His heart pounded and he was wide awake. "What an awful dream!" he tried to think. But he knew that he had not really been asleep.

Then the Super faded from his mind as the fire filled it—a red and reaching monster, treacherous and destroying and foul. Wiping away the gracious beauty of the pines and the cedars, leaving death and blackness, burning the deer and quail, burning—(no, don't remember!).

Once he had thought of the fire, there were a thousand parts of it to think of. That narrow canyon where Reverse

Creek came down! What if there was a slop-over, and some men there, and the fire took off up the slope behind, and cut them off? With a quick movement he half threw back his blankets. He would go to the radio and call Division IV, warn the boss about it! But he lay back again. No, that was mere panic.

But Division I now! They hadn't called for anything all day. That boss up there, that Eldorado man, maybe he just wasn't watching things, didn't realize how bad a fire could burn up in there. What if it jumped Onion Creek after all now, after they'd fought so many spot-fires, and managed to hold it on the north side that day of the blow-up? Just because an Eldorado man didn't watch out!

This time he actually sat up before he realized that what was driving him on was only unbridled fantasy. Division I— why, the Line Inspector had been all along it this afternoon and reported it was in fine condition, mostly cold! Calling the Division-boss now would merely make him wonder why you didn't trust him.

Oh, yes—and now he remembered why he was worrying about Division I. It was the old joker. Division I covered that part where the fire had first taken off, where he had first come to it, and seen it burn hot. When a fire-boss had seen a fire grow up, the place he had first fought it came to be a fixed thing in his mind. If he didn't watch out, he got the feeling that to hold that place was to hold the fire everywhere. And so he might send in more men there, even though that part of the line was all cold and men were needed somewhere else.

But Division V now—maybe that was being forgotten. Or IV? No, III was the bad one! Then he thought of trucks running off the narrow roads and piling up in ravines, and of men caught beneath falling snags, or hit by carelessly swung axes, or stumbling over cliffs in the dark.

And then suddenly he really was out of his blankets, and on his knees with his head against a tree. Though he almost never went to church, he was praying quietly and simply:

"O God, watch those fellows up there by that canyon, and don't let them do anything crazy. And God, help us stop that fire along the ridge. (Tomorrow about noon, will be the time.) And keep the front tires of the trucks from blowing. And don't let the little quail get mixed up and fly right back into the fire the way they do sometimes. And help me get through tomorrow. And—ah—amen!"

As he got to his feet, he looked around into the darkness, a little nervous lest someone might have noticed. He felt better, and yet prayer was not included among approved techniques in the *Fire Control Handbook*.

Picking his way, barefooted, among sleeping men, he went off toward where the lights glowed brightly at Headquarters. Two Ponderosa men were on duty, one of them acting as Night Fire-Boss.

"Hello, Jake," he said. "How are things?"

"Everything quiet, Bart."

"What about that narrow canyon up on Reverse Creek?"

"Nothing special. Zone 2 sent a message over a while back. Here it is—we logged it at 3:22. Says everything is O. K. They wanted some more batteries for the headlights, and said they'd released Ike Selsby of the Mendocino and sent him out, because a message came through his wife was having a baby."

"How about Division I?"

"Why, nothing at all. Were you looking for something?"

"No. Just wondering."

"I can get them on the radio just in a minute if you want me to."

"No, not necessary.—Guess I'll get back to sleep."

"You better, Bart. You look all in."

Then he walked back toward his blankets. He had said "get back to sleep" because he did not want to admit he had not slept. By now he could make out just the faintest glimmer of dawn among the trunks of the pines. The wind seemed to have risen; he heard it moving through the tree-tops high above.

He climbed into the warmth of his blankets again. His beard tickled as he lay against the jacket folded on top of his boots which served him for pillow. As he rubbed the tickliness, he felt the beard so long that it was soft instead of scratchy.

Well, he thought, I laid my troubles on the Lord, and then I checked with man. Guess I can sleep now.

But he really knew that he would not sleep at all now, and would lie quietly waiting for the siren. It would not be so long now. Then he would get up without any break between two days, without the lift and the new life that comes with sleep. Dull and tired, he would face the daylight. Everything would look doubly hard. He could only hope that luck would break with him this day, and that he could get through till evening.

4

The rabbit, being mostly a night-feeder, had nibbled busily during the hours from dusk to daybreak. By now he had become accustomed to the clatter of tools and the voices of men and flashing of small lights which continued to stay at a little distance and did not approach his cover.

Just at daybreak, however, the deep roar of a Diesel engine grew closer, along with all the clank and crash of the working bull-dozer. The rabbit was a little alarmed, and was already fed to satiety. He hopped off to his favorite covert in the center of the thicket. Ears laid back, eyes glancing about, he rested there alertly. The noise of the bull-dozer rose up to a peak. Then, as it died down again, the rabbit relaxed. . . .

The storm-front now lay across the Alaskan panhandle. Behind it, a cold and dry wind poured down from the mountains upon Juneau; ahead of it, a slanting rain from the south drenched Ketchikan.

5

Bo Fox and the other pogies had spent the night at the spike-camp which had been set up on Curran Creek, where the road skirting the lower slopes of Cerro Gordo came to an end at a little flat. The crew turned out at four-thirty, ate breakfast, were issued canteens, lunches, and tools, and set out to relieve the night-crews.

Along with the others Bo jumped the tiny stream, and began to climb the steep trail which went up by many switchbacks. Again looking apprehensively both ways, he saw no other break in the face of the cliff. Looking up and ahead, he noticed that the smoke was thicker and closer.

By now, having been together on the line for a day, the men were feeling some comradeship. There was calling back and forth, and shouting of friendly obscenities. As they paused to catch breath on a steep shale-slide halfway up, the man beside Bo took a suck at his canteen, and said something about wishing it was stronger.

Thus encouraged, Bo spoke what was on his mind.

"Jesus, this must be the only way up to this place!"

The other man looked languidly one way and then the other.

"Yes," he concluded agreeably. "Looks like it, but there might be lots of others for all I know."

Like most casual laborers, he was not interested in geography; he assumed that someone else showed him how to get there and back.

But the steep slope was sheltered from the wind and was quiet. The third man down the line had heard Bo speak, but had not made out all the words. He asked the next man closer:

"What'd they say?"

"They say this is the only way up here."

The man who had asked the question was not without independence of judgment, but as he looked along the line of the cliffs, the statement seemed reasonable. For lack of anything better to do at the moment, he passed the word on to the next man, unconsciously changing it to a direct statement.

"You know, this is the only way to get up here."

Each man had just enough interest to wonder what was being said above him and just enough love of showing off his knowledge to pass the word on. It ran along through five men, and then came to a skeptic.

"Is that so!" he said belligerently. "Who says it is?"

Taken back, the other blustered in his own defense:

"Why, everybody says so! It just come down the line. The Ranger up there musta passed the word back."

But the skeptic was not really interested in cliffs, and the mention of the "ranger" gave him a new approach.

"Good Christ! Is that all that bastard has to worry about. And if it is, what of it? You wanna go another way t'see the view?"

By his shift of attack, however, the skeptic had tacitly admitted the truth of the original statement. At the same time the men farther down the line had noticed the argument and wanted to know what it was about. The word thus rapidly spread down clear to the last man. Growing stronger and simpler as it went, it ended as an official statement passed back

along the line from the boss at the head, that this was the only
way up. They were simple and ignorant men, not given to
viewing the larger scope of affairs. They did not question or
wonder why the "ranger" had seen fit to pass this information
along. Nevertheless, among all the men behind Bo Fox (and
he was well toward the head of the line) the idea was implanted as a fixed point of reference: "This is the only way
up through the cliffs."

6

As Arnold Sorenson, the Dispatcher, was fond of saying, a fire
was like a team or an army of allies—wind, humidity, terrain,
and many others. Among the most important of the allies was
always the forest itself, which offered different burning-conditions according to the size and type of its trees.

The Spitcat Fire had started at an elevation of about 4,500
feet where the forest was of Jeffrey pines with an intermin-
gling of highly inflammable white firs.

When the fire, however, had burned down over the nose of
the ridge and had raced across the meadow and the brush-
field, it came to a forest which was growing at a level five hundred feet lower and was therefore a different forest. Here the
commonest trees were the ponderosa pines, and mingled with
them were Douglas firs and incense cedars. To a forester
walking there the three kinds of tree would have been as different as Chinese, Negroes, and Indians in war-paint. Without
even raising his eyes to the needles he would have distinguished the scaled yellow-orange bark of the ponderosas, the
corrugated dark gray, almost black, of the Douglas firs, and
the fluted red-brown of the cedars.

Before fire had entered it, it had been a gracious and beautiful forest of spacious vistas—the trees of all ages, from this
year's tiny green spikelets to stalwart veterans of the centuries,

six and eight feet in diameter. It was a forest where the impression was of air and light, not of tangled darkness. The larger trees were broadly spaced, and beneath their shade even the smaller trees seldom formed thickets. The canopy of foliage was nowhere dense. Sunlight poured into the glades, and filtered through the thinly spread needles of the tall pines. The yellow-orange bark reflected the sunlight, and seemed to carry it clear to the ground. This was no dim forest of the story-books to be haunted by bears and witches. Its sun-dappled glades were more like the settings for merry men in Lincoln green, and nut-brown maidens, and jovial foresters trolling:

What shall he have that killed the deer?

This was before the fire had run through it.

After the fire the forest was black and ugly. Fire had even licked up high around the trunks of the larger trees, leaving them covered with charcoal and soot. Except for a few little islands which the fire had capriciously skipped, every blade of grass, every green leaf on the undergrowth, every needle on the smaller trees had been reduced to ashes; the trunks and branches were left standing, blackened and dirty.

Yet the forest had been open enough so that most of the big trees and even those of medium-size had lived through the cataclysm. Each glade and gap had been a chimney letting the heat drain off skywards, and even when the flames had managed to reach upward, the tree had usually burned without igniting the next one. Thus, in spite of the steady dry wind, no all-devastating crown-fire had swept through the upper foliage.

Higher up toward Reverse Ridge, however, came a change of forest. Here, on the north slope, the summer sun beat less fiercely and the shadows stretched out sooner. In this damper ground and cooler air the pines and cedars could not compete with the Douglas firs. As the yellow-orange and red-brown trunks became fewer, the forest grew darker and gloomier. After the habit of Douglas firs also, the trees grew more closely together. The black boles rose high without branches, and then at last shot out into a dense canopy. In the continual shade almost no young trees sprang up, but the underbrush was a thick and deep tangle of fern and berry. The trees themselves competed ruthlessly, and here and there stood dead snags showing where less vigorous trees had been shaded out by their fellows and killed. A criss-cross of fallen trunks testified to the next chapter of the story.

Little light penetrated the overspreading foliage, and the black tree-trunks enhanced the dimness. This was like that grim and gloomy forest of the story-books where the horror-stricken traveler finds himself benighted even at twilight, and meets only a black-faced and boorish charcoal-burner, if not a wolf or an ogre.

The fire, entering the thicker forest about mid-morning, soon began to show the difference. It roared fiercely in the thick mat of dry fern. The criss-crossed fallen tree-trunks smoked, ignited, then burned hotly. The fire ran up the dried bark of the snags. By then, no one could have complained of any lack of light in the forest.

At the same time the thick-spread canopy of foliage prevented the easy escape of heat. As in a furnace with its outlets clogged, the temperature soared. The needles withered and shriveled as their water was driven off; they began to smoke. Then suddenly, not in a single tree but over an acre at once, the tree-tops burst into fire. With a deep roar, flames and dark smoke rose some hundreds of feet, whirling upwards the blazing twigs and needles and strips of bark. Tree-tops rocked and swayed in the blast of hot air. A rot-weakened snag tottered, cracked resoundingly, and went down with an echoing crash.

When the piling-up of heat was thus relieved, the fire died down somewhat. Once it was established as a crown-fire, however, it remained so. The dry wind still blew into the funnel-like mouths of the three canyons which seamed the north slope of Reverse Ridge. Terrain, dryness, wind, and the thick forest thus combined to make the fire more intense.

The ground-fire and the crown-fire advanced together. The one burned close to the ground; the other, high in the air. Between them was a region where the branchless trunks afforded little fuel, so that the two fires seemed to burn independently. Yet they advanced with equal steps, and were not so isolated as they seemed. If the ground-fire for a while ran ahead, its rising heat dried out the canopy and speeded the advance of the crown-fire. If the crown-fire gained the lead, burning debris fell among the ferns and bushes, and hastened the march of the ground-fire.

Between the two, no living tree or bush or fern or herb was left. The advance was not rapid. Even struggling through the tangle of ferns and scrambling over the fallen trees, a man could have easily kept ahead of it. But though the advance was not rapid, it was steady. It seemed inevitable and inescapable. The towering line of flame appeared massive and heavy, rolling onward by the power of its own momentum.

Ahead lay the upward slope and the thick forest; from behind the dry wind pressed steadily. Advancing in solid front of fire, points ahead in the canyon-bottoms where the wind funneled more strongly, the Spitcat moved terrifyingly against the line of Division III.

7

Bo Fox's crew had been the first, that morning, to leave the spike-camp on Curran Creek. On gaining the top of the ridge, they had been headed eastward along the fire-line, and had passed along through the men of the night-crews, tired now, and mostly lolling about, waiting to be relieved and to get back to camp for breakfast.

Bo had steadily grown more apprehensive. On his left hand rose a curtain of smoke, pressing ever closer; on his right, he knew, lay the line of the cliff. In the last half hour he had heard various men speak of the trail as being the only way up through the line of the cliff, and he did not realize that this report, now coming back to him as if official, had really originated in his own mind. The idea was thus firmly fixed and had become an established fact, and the farther he walked eastward the more he felt himself walking into a trap. If the fire burned across the trail anywhere behind, it would be like a door clicking and he would be caught.

Bo was no leader. On all occasions he docilely took his boss's orders. Thus, although he grew more nervous, he merely kept glancing to right and left, and made no protest. When the crew stopped, however, to let a roaring cat pass them, Bo spoke to the man next to him.

"If it burns up across this trail, we can't get out of here."

"That's so," said the man, agreeably. "This trail is the only way up through the cliff."

He also looked at the fire and then toward the cliff and back along the trail, sizing up the situation. But he was phlegmatic, and no worrier like Bo. The fire did not seem very close. Having looked, he merely let loose a few conventional obscenities to express an opinion of life in general, and relaxed.

After they had walked about a mile along the ridge, the crew came to their assigned position. Their boss reported to the Sector-boss, and was assigned the portion of the line for which he was responsible. The night-crew, thus relieved, quickly filed off toward camp and breakfast.

Since three cats had been working all night with crews cleaning up behind, the line was already eight feet wide and in excellent condition, and needed only the finishing touches.

"Come on, men, let's get her marcelled!" said the crew-boss.

Under his direction the men began to work along the sides of the line, cutting back the higher bushes, chopping down the young trees, and scattering any piles of debris which would be likely to catch sparks. The dry wind swept steadily across the ridge. The glittering sun, unpleasantly hot, was still so low that it shone in from the east below the overhanging column of smoke.

When they had worked for an hour or two, the men became conscious that the fire was burning hotter. Less than a mile away, down the slope, great flames spiraled skyward. They heard the crackle of fire, and the resounding crash as a dead tree went over.

"She's crowned!" said one of them who had been on fires before.

Even from so far away, the fire was frightening to look at. Several of the men glanced back along the trail where they had come in.

One of them spoke to the crew-boss, as several others listened:

"I hear this trail we come in by is the only way up through the cliff."

The crew-boss was not a Ponderosa man, but he knew something about rock-formations, and this one did not look as if it would be unbroken and unscalable.

"That so?" he asked. "Who said so?"

The man talking had really thought that the crew-boss himself had said so, but finding that this was not true, he called back along the line:

"Say, who said that about there was no other trail up here?"

"Why, the ranger did!" someone called back.

The crew-boss, who was not a ranger though the men thought of him as one, assumed that some Ponderosa ranger must have said so.

"Well, it must be so then, I guess," he said.

The man to whom he was talking became a little confused, but also decided that the source of the information must have been some other ranger, not his own boss.

The crew-boss himself did not think the matter of enough importance even to investigate, and he did not really believe it. He did not think that any fire-boss would put a dozen crews in a position where they might be burned to death.

The fire burned closer and hotter, and the flames seemed to toss higher. The sun disappeared into yellowish smoke. There was a growing restiveness among the men, and they looked backwards now and again. At one end of their line they mingled with the men of the next crew, infected them with their nervousness, and passed their creed on:

"This trail is the only way up through the cliff. The ranger says so."

At the other end of their line the men of the crew mingled with those of another crew who were based on the Onion Creek camp. These men had actually come up through another break in the cliff, and walked westward along the ridge. Hearing the casual talk about only one way up, they did not compare notes; in their general unfamiliarity with the country, they assumed that the one way was that by which they themselves had ascended. Moreover, their boss was young and much impressed by his responsibility for the safety of his men. Looking at the crown-fire, he was nervous.

Once the rumor had made the jump, it ran along the ridge eastward, and men of those crews also began to look nervously backward, although they looked eastward, not westward, for the one way by which they must escape.

Downslope, half a mile away by now, the crown-fire sent up sheets of flame from the tree-tops.

8

By this time the fire-organization was so large and complicated that even the Dispatcher could have given, off-hand, only approximate figures on men and equipment—at the fire, in transit, and being mobilized. The totals were growing continually, and it would have been a useless labor to keep them always neatly summed up.

By now there were about sixteen hundred men on the fire, and more coming. At the work of transportation there were more than a hundred trucks, buses and cars, three pack-trains, and a cargo-plane. Twelve cats were on the lines, and three tankers were ready to go into action if ever the fire got where they could reach it. A scout-plane was on call. The main fire-camp, for Headquarters and Zone 1, was still at Onion Flat. The camp for Zone 2 was at Parker Flat. There was also a spike-camp for Zone 1, mostly for Division III, at the road-head on Curran Creek. Clear off at the other end of the fire, where the paratroopers had jumped, there was a spike-camp kept stocked with supplies dropped by parachute from the cargo-plane which kept shuttling back and forth from the base at Redding. A work-crew of convicts had a camp of their own down the road from Onion Flat. In addition there were various isolated dumps for supplies, and for oil and gasoline to keep the cats and trucks working.

As always with a large fire, more and more men were tied up with staff- and supply-work, and never handled a shovel or McLeod. There was the Dispatcher himself; except for flying over the fire that first morning, he had never got closer to it than his office in Suffolk. There were headquarters-men, time-keepers, cooks, camp-crews, tool-sharpeners, radio-repair-men, truck-drivers, mechanics.

The sheriff came in for a while, just because seeing his badge might keep any tough characters from playing it funny. A reporter came in, but did not like the steepness of Reverse Ridge, and never got beyond Onion Flat.

There was a purchasing agent who never got closer than Sacramento, but was on the job to buy whatever was needed for the fire and see that it was sent in. There was a tall pro-fessorial-looking author working on a book, and a bright young man from the Regional Office doing research on fire-organization and viewing everything in scientific and objec-tive calm.

Sweating it out in his familiar office, the Dispatcher would have preferred to be really at the fire, but probably he knew more about what was happening than anybody else did.

9

The fire was still closer. Bo Fox grew more and more restive. Drifting wisps of smoke came across the line; the men coughed, and their eyes watered. The heat beat upon them. Ashes and bits of blackened bark were falling. A man rubbed his face, and some soot smeared out behind his finger, leaving a black mark across his cheek, giving him a strange and wild look. Seeing it, Bo trembled a little, and looked back along the line. He tried to see whether the fire was closer to the trail there. He thought that it was.

But looking at the crew-boss, Bo felt less jittery. The boss seemed calm, a refuge and strength.

The crew-boss actually seemed a little calmer than he was, but he was more excited than disturbed. Meeting the thrust of such a big fire as this was likely to be touchy. He had seen some good-sized fires, and was not alarmed for his own or his crew's safety. At the very worst they could take shelter in some of the rock-outcroppings and let the fire go over and around them. There must be, he thought to himself, some pretty shrewd old cookies who were running this fire, and he was ready to trust them.

From his own experience he could guess what was going to happen with the fire. He knew that his men were getting nervous, and he considered telling them, explaining things to them. But the crew were taking his orders and seemed to have confidence in him. If he told them what was going to happen, then it might not happen that way, and the men would merely lose the confidence they already had, and things would be worse.

And now still another disturbing report began to work along the lines.

"Yesterday . . . yes, morning, they say . . . got caught . . . Jesus! . . . Is that right? . . . Fella told me that seen a guy . . . dead as they make them . . ."

It was an ugly idea, especially when you looked at the fire getting closer, and remembered that there was only that one way up through the cliff.

A gray-haired, snag-toothed old fellow spat his tobacco juice and considered the question of death with dismal gusto.

"Yes," he said, "he was burned to a *crips*—yessir, to a *crips!*"

"Hell, there ain't no such word. You mean he was burned to a *corp!*"

"You guys! Christ, you're *both* nuts!"

But at least there seemed no doubt as to the fact itself. Someone had met a horrible death. The knowledge made no one less nervous.

As the climax neared, Ben Roach set up headquarters on a rock-ledge close behind the line and just about the middle point of Division III. His radio-man had rigged a good aerial, and communication was excellent. To the rear he could talk with headquarters at Onion Flat, and he could also reach the Lookout on Cerro Gordo whom he had told to keep a close watch for spot-fires puffing up anywhere behind the line. Ahead, he could talk to his three Sector-bosses, who were carrying walkie-talkies. On the flanks he could keep in touch with Divisions II and IV. From the ledge also he could see east and west along a quarter-mile of line, and could watch the fire below him.

To his practiced eye, the fire was already changing. The ridge was comparatively flat on top, and once the fire reached leveler ground, it lost that part of its vigor which sprang from the up-slope and the funnel-effect of the canyons. Moreover the top of the ridge was in full sun, and the soil was dry and thin and rocky. Ponderosa pines again replaced the Douglas firs, and even they were somewhat stunted and were scattered more thinly. There was underbrush, and some clumps of manzanita grew in places. With a dry wind pushing it, the ground-fire would race ahead rapidly through these, but the crown-fire would almost certainly puff out, once it passed the edge of the thickly growing Douglas firs.

This was what he could sense, rather than see, was happening already. An unpracticed eye would have thought the fire

as strong as ever, but Ben could see little weaknesses in the
front.

The whole strategy had been planned for this event. For
this reason they had not tried to run a line along the slope.
The crown-fire would have walked across an eight-foot line
without even knowing it was there, and no one could start a
back-fire among the tree-tops. But now it might all be over in
a little while. He had seen roaring fires met squarely—and
half an hour later they were nothing but smoking mop-up
jobs.

He checked with his Sector-bosses to make sure that they
had plenty of fusees handy and understood the tactics. From
here on, they would be on their own.

He called Cerro Gordo: "Keep looking. The next half
hour will be it!"

He called Bart.

Bart jumped when he knew it was Ben. He had been waiting for the call.

"How's she look?" he asked.

"Not so bad," said Ben.

"I wish I was up there with you."

"Not a thing you could do, Bart. You know—you're doin' a
lot more back there where y'can be in touch all round.—But
say, we'll be lightin' back-fires pretty soon. The crown-fire is
droppin' down. Just the last few minutes there's a lot of gaps.
The next half hour will be it!"

"Golly, Ben, I wish I was up there with you!" And suddenly
Bart's voice broke. "I can't stand it down here waitin'—I
can't stand it!"

There was a pause, as if Ben were perplexed by the vehemence. Then his voice came again, almost wheedling.

"Now, looky here, Bart. Ain't *nothin'* you could *do* up

here, and besides you *ain't* here. (So don't worry.) And you hadn't oughta talk like that—might be some pipsqueaks hear it. Don't worry now. Things look good. S-1415 to S-1493— Over and out, over and out."

Bart suddenly realized that Ben had signed off quickly to keep the Fire-boss from saying anything more over the air. He had slipped! The radio stand-bys all around the fire would have heard, and would be saying to the next man: "Gee, Bart is worried. Things must be bad!" For that matter, the Super and Walt Burnaby right here at Headquarters had heard him, and they were not saying anything, but he thought they looked a little disturbed.

Judith Godoy and Dave Halliday, close together, leaned against the railing on the east catwalk. She was wearing khaki trousers and her dark-green man's shirt, open at the neck to show her throat. The yellow handkerchief around her hair was more for work than looks today; it was already smudgy with ashes and soot. And if her mouth was a red blob of lipstick, that was more for protection too; the air was drier than ever.

The broad towering column of smoke was rising from just beyond Reverse Ridge. It was plainly full of eddies and billows now; its grayness was shot through with yellow tones where it reflected flames and sunlight. Even from six miles off, though they could not look quite to the base of the fire, they continually saw great reddish flames lick upward.

"I'm just a Greek chorus," she said.

"What's that? I'm just a meteorologist."

"I mean, I see everything that happens on the stage and make comments, but I just stay put and don't take part in the action."

"Your comments affect what other people do.—Well, what

about me? I keep looking at that storm on my map, and making comments on it, but I can't make the storm bring us rain to douse the fire."

"What do you think?"

"I can't even forecast it yet. If it keeps far enough south, we'll get rain. If it keeps north, there won't be rain, and there'll be another dry north wind behind it."

"That'll be bad!"

"That'll be terrible! The only sure thing is to get this fire hog-tied before the front comes in, and we haven't got forty-eight hours to go."

"You heard him. He said the next half-hour was it."

"That's fine! That's a lot off my back. On a carrier they can always decide whether to send the planes out or not to, but you just fight fires any weather. I don't know that I like being a Greek chorus."

"It's another thing we have in common, anyway," she said simply, and then was in a fright for fear she might have said too much. But he was only smiling at her nicely.

"There's another bit of ash," he said, and started to wipe it off her hand. But in some way or other it seemed more natural just to let his hand stay on top of hers.

A back-fire is a powerful weapon, but two-edged. It is highly effective, and equally tricky. Its effectiveness, and its trickiness, change with wind, cover, terrain, and all the other factors affecting the main fire itself. No experienced man begins backfiring without the secret fear that his own weapon will turn in his hand and strike him.

A steady wind was blowing, so that the back-fires, if lighted close to the line, would not work back into the wind effectively. But if they were lighted well inside the line, the wind would bring them sweeping down upon the line almost as dangerously as the main fire itself.

The situation thus called for the trickiest of maneuvers, and the one which above all requires the closest timing. A large fire sucks air in toward itself from all directions. Thus at a certain distance ahead of itself the fire neutralizes the wind, and at an even closer distance reverses the wind. The back-fires were thus to be lighted at the moment when this reversed current of air became effective. Perfectly executed, this is the grand slam, re-doubled; it is the hole-in-one; it is the home run with the bases full. Some old rangers, however, will tell you that approximately one hundred things may go wrong; others say two hundred.

Watching from his rock ledge, Ben Roach felt moderately confident. The line was clean, and in many places had the backing of the rock outcroppings. The growth in front of it was not too high or thick. He saw the crew-bosses begin to scatter some of their men back from the line to guard against spot-fires. The main fire had now dropped from the tree-tops entirely, but was still burning fiercely along the ground. It was getting close enough and was throwing out an almost in-tolerable heat. Ben felt the wind fall off to a lull, and then slide gently against his other cheek.

At the same moment, the Sector-boss in the stretch below him lit his fusee. As its pink flame blazed up, he thrust it boldly into a carefully piled heap of dry brush. Thin smoke rose up, and then flames leaped and crackled. The fire built up fast. Two men watched to see that it did not jump the line. The Sector-boss ran off to start the next fire.

In a few minutes Ben saw smokes rising from the line far-ther east. The reverse of the air must have come later to the west, but after a while he saw the smokes there too.

By now the back-fires were roaring off and forming a solid front, twenty feet high. In a few minutes they would meet the main fire in a sudden dashing up of flame, and the worst would be over. Everything looked fine.

A ranger who knows the country and has fought fire during thirty-nine seasons, who is sturdy of body and unwarped in mind, who feels behind him the strength of all his comrades —that is one man. It is something else to be a pogy who has never fought fire before, small and insignificant, with a mind harboring strange bug-bears. Bo Fox, one might have thought, had nothing to live for, but most emphatically also, he had nothing to die for. There was thought neither of home nor of Fatherland, and not even pride in himself, to sustain him.

To Ben Roach looking from the rock-ledge the back-fires roared off magnificently. To Bo Fox, half a mile down the line, the back-fires crackled too close to his ears, and threw off a terrifying heat against which he covered his face. The line seemed pitifully narrow and ineffective. He did not realize that the flames were actually moving away from it. Glancing back along the line where he had come in, he saw everything blotted out with drifting smoke, but he saw the crew-boss standing firm, and that steadied him for the moment.

The reversed air-current was only close to the ground, and once sparks had been whirled upward, the prevailing wind blew some of them back across the line. A wisp of smoke curled up, but two men sprang to take care of it.

The back-fire reached the advance of the main fire, and at their meeting the flames leaped high. Men cowered before the heat. Bo glanced behind him, and at that moment a little bush on the wrong side of the line flared up.

He felt the click of the door behind him, and with the high-

pitched scream of a terrified animal, he dropped his shovel
and ran!

The crew-boss saw him and shouted, and then ran to stop
him.

The others looked, and saw a man running in panic, the
crew-boss running and shouting, and a fire across the line. On
the other side of them the fires roared up.

"Run for it!" someone yelled. "It's the only way up
through the cliff!"

They dropped tools and ran.

"Jesus, we're trapped!"

Swinging round, the crew-boss tried to block the trail,
standing with his arms out, calling to them, cursing. Like
stampeding animals they swept by him.

"Christ! Hurry! It's the only way out!"

The men of the crew farther east looked up and saw the
others running, and their own flank in the air.

The line was lost! Something frightful must have happened! They glanced behind them nervously, and remembered about only one way up through the cliff. Hell, the line
was lost and there was no use being a hero! They oozed back
uncertainly.

Their young crew-boss, worried about the responsibility
for his men's lives, considered hastily, half in a panic. If the
other crew was running, there must be some reason for it.
Perhaps the whole line was being abandoned, and in the confusion orders had not got through to him. He made the
decision:

"Come on, let's get out of here! Bring your tools!"

Having the tools made it look like an orderly retreat, but
once started there was no use going slowly. The men began to
run, glancing over their left shoulders at the fire. Their mo-

mentum swept up the next crew, and most of these ran unashamedly, dropping shovels and axes and McLeods.

In the other direction, it was sheer rout. Crew after crew looked up as they heard the babble of frightened men. They saw scared men running. The panic infected them, and they imagined some disaster, all the more terrible for being unknown. They too began to run. And once a man had started running, his panic grew. There was no use doing things by halves, and so he ran fast. As he ran, justifying himself, he babbled out words of disaster and terror to men whom he passed.

This was no trained army, disciplined through months of maneuvers. The officers were not empowered to shoot the first man who retreated. Yet they were set against an enemy which was horrible and implacable, and worked upon primitive fears. As they ran, they felt the heat. At every bend of the trail, they feared to see the red fire already licking across it.

Some of the crew-bosses, really thinking that some disaster must have occurred, joined in the flight. Most of them stood their ground, and usually a man or two of the crew stood with them. A Sector-boss, trying to block the flight, was knocked down by the running mob.

The rout surged by the rock-ledge where Ben Roach stood, helpless to stop it. His jaw dropped. He had seen panic before, and recognized it now.

"Good God!" he said, turning to his radio-man. "You make allowance for wind and slope and cover and all the rest, and then the *men* panic on you!"

"We gettin' out of here?" the radio-man asked nervously.

"Naw, this place is safe as church.—Get me Bart."

Toward the west the panic continued until the men came to the top of the gap through which the trail started down.

By that time they were blown and tired, and they had got to
the place which had become associated with safety in the back
of their minds. Even Bo Fox sat down and panted, no longer
apprehensive.

Toward the east the panic rolled along until it came to the
line held by the crew of convicts. These trusties might not
rate high socially, but they were tough babies. They enjoyed
mightily seeing the honest men run, and they stood by the
side of the trail and jeered obscenely.

The men who had been scattered back from the line to
fight spot-fires started to run also, and most of them ran right
away from the fire. Once they were running, they seemed to
feel the fire hotter and hotter on the backs of their necks.
When they came, by twos and threes, to where the cliff
dropped off, they went sliding down steep places and jumping from ledge to ledge, taking many more chances than
they would have with the fire. They all got down safely except for one who piled up on the last slide with a broken leg
crumpled under him. Actual trouble rather stilled the panic;
one man stayed with the injured fellow, and another went off
for help.

Much of the line had been constructed so that bare outcroppings backed it up. The little blaze which had startled
Bo Fox merely burned itself out against the rock. But a long
stretch of line was left empty except for a scattering of bosses
and the few men who had stuck by them. As the meeting of
the fires threw up high stabbing spirals of flame, the upper
wind caught sparks and swirled them across the line. Here
and there, as was only to be expected, wisps of smoke curled
up. Like all spot-fires they started small. Some burned themselves out against rock-ledges; the few remaining men got to
some of them. But other fires had puffed up in the long

stretches where no men were left and in the gaps between outcroppings. In the dry wind the little fires built up rapidly, and raced ahead.

10

Then suddenly, when that news came, Bart had a horrible vision—as if what had once been a beautiful young girl was stripped and ravished, horribly mutilated and fouled with dirt and black blood, and left thus to lie open to the gaze of all who passed by.

"God!" he said only half aloud, and there was terror in his tone.

He saw the Super and Walt Burnaby jump a little as he said it. Startled, they looked at him; then quickly, at each other.

By that time they were getting some idea of what had happened. Ben Roach had kept them in touch for a while, and then:

"Getting too hot here. I'm going to crawl into a rock-cranny now, and let her go over me. Over and out."

After that their chief reliance was Cerro Gordo. The Lookout had a good view, except for the smoke, of all the south face of the ridge. From her reports it looked as if all the center of the line was holding by its own natural strength. But to east and west the fire was across, and reaching out in two broad tongues down the steep slope, the points moving fast. On the cliff-like slope the growth was thin, but the wind could carry everything ahead two or three times as far and as fast as on the level ground.

"God!" he had said all at once, with terror in his voice, and the others had looked at him.

"What is it, Bart?" he heard the Super saying, and the voice sounded far away.

But perhaps he himself was far away, he thought, for though he knew he was standing by the high desk at Headquarters, he heard the crash of flames in the cedars, he felt the bite of the thick smoke and the fierce heat, and he saw the azaleas wilting and the moss turning brown and the water flecked dirtily with ashes.

"Yes—what is it—Bart?" he heard Walt Burnaby's voice this time, and it too came from far away, and it spoke slowly, forming the words distinctly, as you talk to a child.

Then Bart came back slowly from where he had been. He put his hand on the planks, and steadied himself. He was there in Headquarters, and was very tired. But it was not so much the being tired as all the horror that was soon to be. (There was something dashing this way and that through the bushes, trapped.)

"Why, yes," he said, and he thought his voice was steady. "Yes, Walt, I'm here. What is it?"

"Don't you think, Bart, you ought to get some rest? You've been going a long time."

"Hell, I've gone longer than this, lots of times—that Mendocino bust in '44."

"That wasn't your own district." It was the Super this time. "You're worrying now."

Suddenly, when it was the Super talking, something oozed up from inside, and Bart was strong again.

"Yes," he said, and his voice was firm. "And why shouldn't I worry! This ain't just a lumber-yard to me! I'm Fire-boss here. That line would have held if the men hadn't panicked. Nobody can allow for that!"

"Nobody has blamed you, Bart, for that—or is going to."

But as Bart looked up at the tall man who towered above

him, there were wild ragings inside of him. (He hoped they did not show in his face.) He hated the younger man because his days of strength lay ahead, and because he thought of trees as lumber, and figured fire-fighting on sheets of paper.

Then he shook himself, and turned to the map. He was Fire-boss! He drew the point of a finger along on a line a little up the slope from Curran Creek.

"We'll put a new line along there," he said.

Even as he was saying it, while he leaned over the desk, he knew that they glanced at each other again across his back. He would have been angry, if he had not felt so tired again, and if the memory of that horrible vision had not still smouldered deep inside him.

"Say, Bart," said Walt Burnaby, "that's playing it pretty close up, isn't it?"

"Maybe, but there's some awful pretty country we got to save in there—that glen along Curran Creek. We can hold that line, if we don't stand around makin' long faces! We got to believe we can do it!"

But again he knew that they were looking at each other, and that one of them was probably making that little movement of the head which means to step aside somewhere and talk this over.

"It can't be done," said Walt Burnaby.

"That's right," said the Super. He was holding the piece of paper in his hand. It was full of figures—man-power and transportation and line-building, against distance and rate of spread. The fire won, unless you figured in a miracle on the other side.

"Well," the Super went on, "I suppose we'd better tell Bart so." There was silence. "Hadn't we?" he added, almost hopefully.

"No use!"

"What do you mean?"

"You know what I mean."

"I guess so, Walt."

"When a man starts talking about 'if we just think we can do it!'—Maybe you can fight other people that way, but you can't, a fire!"

"Well, it's my job!"

"You're supposed to put it in writing."

"Good God, not unless somebody makes me!"

From where they had drawn aside to talk it was not more than a hundred feet to Headquarters. That seemed a long, long walk. But even so, it was not long enough to let him think of a good way. Everybody liked Bart! He himself liked Bart, even though Bart didn't like him. He wished he were the kind who could do something the easy way with people— not just run head on. Some people could jolly around for a bit. If only he were the older man, and not the other way round!

He came to Headquarters. Probably the boys must know what was going to happen. As he stopped and stood still for a moment, the Chief of Staff and the Maps-and-Records man and the others about Headquarters looked at him, and they caught something in his glance. They faded away, out of ear-shot. Bart stood facing him, his back against the high desk. You could see he was waiting for something, as a wounded animal waits for the knife or the club.

"Say, Bart," he began, "you know, you were on that Hart Creek fire, and you've had a pretty rough time here. You're getting pretty tired, I guess—"

He paused.

"Yeah—" said Bart, not helping him out.

"You see, Walt and I have been talking. We think maybe

you better—don't you think it would be a good idea?—if you took some time and got rested up?—"

He paused again, and the sweat flowed.

"You mean," said Bart in a level voice, "you mean you're throwing me out of bein' Fire-boss."

"Well, Bart, you've had a tough time—"

Suddenly he saw Bart's eyes blaze; at least he was going down fighting.

"Super, you got to give that to me in writing!"

"All right, Bart, if you want it the hard way."

And yet it seemed really the easier way. This at least was a man taking it, not a wounded animal.

The Super was calm now. He took a writing-pad, found a piece of carbon-paper, and adjusted it. With pen pressing hard to be sure the imprint carried through the carbon, he put down the date, and looking at his wrist-watch, added the hour and minute. Then he wrote:

Ranger John Bartley is hereby and as of this time relieved of all further duties as Fire-boss of the Spitcat Fire.

He signed it, and beneath his name wrote *Supervisor, Ponderosa N. F.* That was official enough to pass any Board of Review.

"Here," he said.

Bart was still defiant as he took it, but as he looked, he seemed to crumple. He folded the paper once, and put it into his shirt-pocket. Then he turned and walked away.

11

Like the wolf Fenris who has broken his bonds, with ever-reaching fingers like the hundred-handed Briareus, the monster of withering flame and choking smoke again ranged loose

in the forest. The fire rolled ahead through two broad breaks
in the line.

If there had really been a solid wall of cliff as the men imagined, the bare rock might have blocked the march of the
flame. But actually, down every steep brush-covered slope in
the gaps between sheer rock, the fire ran fast. With wind behind and steep slope in front, each spark fell far ahead.
Burning cones and debris rolled and tumbled. As spot-fire
after spot-fire flamed up in advance, the fire no longer merely
crept along the ground, but moved in quick short steps.

On the sun-baked and rocky southern face of the ridge, the
forest was so thin as hardly to seem a forest at all. Sun-loving
ponderosa pines grew sparsely, like trees planted one by one
in a park. Here and there ancient gnarly junipers clung to the
cliff-side, their roots anchored deep in the rock-crannies. Between the scattered trees was only a thin growth of underbrush among the rocks.

Sending up little flame and smoke, the fire seemed to be
rushing through to seize richer spoils, as men cross a desert
to reach gold-mines beyond. Its rush was all forward. Often,
splitting at some rock, it sent two arms ahead, to unite farther
on but leave between them a long spindle-shaped patch of
unburned ground. So also the front of the two breaks did not
widen much. Instead, each seemed to pour over the steep
slope following the breaks in the cliff, as if a dam had broken
and water were cascading downward.

As when an army-front collapses before a swift thrust and
in the confusion, by platoons and companies, men fight as
best they can, so on the broken front of Division III, each
sector-boss and crew-boss fought the fire as he saw it. Here
two bosses and three men labored heroically to contain a

spot-fire. At last, exhausted and panting, they saw it die down, and then found that another one had leaped the line behind them so that all their work had gone for nothing. But elsewhere, thirty men without a leader merely stood and watched a fire escape when they might have controlled it.

Gradually order came again. As the heat died down, Ben Roach climbed out of his rock-cranny, and got his radio working. Cerro Gordo Lookout, in spite of the smoke-curtain, plotted the general front of the two advancing points. Scouts, hurried out from the fire-camp, reported more exact findings by radio. Sector-bosses radioed that they had rallied what few men they had left and were hanging on along the flanks of the break-throughs.

12

In the log-book stood the simple entry, "2:11 Supervisor Jones took over as Fire-boss." That was all.

He had expected a certain sense of resentment, of opposition even. He had replaced Bart who was everybody's friend, and he himself was merely the Super. Nobody called him Slim.

But there was no sullenness. The fire burned a man in the brush-field, or the fire wore a man down and broke him by piled-up weariness and worry and horror. But where the man dropped out, the line united and faced the fire still. There was no surrender in this war.

Again it was a flanking job, and he organized rapidly. In the emergency he turned out the night-crews two hours early. If they could hold the flanks and prevent the swift downward-running tongues from getting any wider—that would be enough for the present. On the down-slope there would be no chance of stopping the run, and there would be little chance of stopping it at the bottom. Now in September the water in

Bacchus Creek was down to narrow ribbons between the
pools. From the steep down-slope sparks would blow across
the narrow ravine to the steep up-slope. Spot-fires would pop
up everywhere, and then with the dry wind still behind, and
duff and underbrush crackling dry, the fire would sweep off
up-slope again with the combined forces of wind and rising
heat to drive it. All anyone could do was to flank it on the
up-slope and slowly pinch it out, or else fall back to a ridge
and build a strong line along the crest.

Again, he thought, it was like fighting a war. A general
figured it would cost so many dog-tags to cross the Rhine.
Thank God, a fire-boss didn't figure in lives of men, but he
had to sacrifice trees here to save more trees farther on.
That was part of Bart's trouble; he didn't want to admit that
any trees had to burn.

Now as he tilted his head and looked up the steep slope
beyond Bacchus Creek, he saw the actual running front of
fire. It had come over the crest and through the line of the
cliffs, and now was sliding down the precipitous slope even
as he looked at it. There was a curious crab-like quality to it,
for the smoke and flame rose up, and the line of fire moved
down. Here and there through the smoke he caught the flash
of a swinging ax. But the men were merely hanging on the
flanks, having an easy enough time of it there, but wholly unable to work around in front.

The Camp-boss came with his inevitable question:

"Shall I start pulling her out?"

The Super looked at the fire again and estimated time and
distance. He figured a minute on his pad—man-power and
rate of line-building. Yes, it looked as if they could throw a
line around the camp and hold it, but such tactics would call
for many man-hours of labor, and there would be some risk

in any case, both to thousands of dollars' worth of property and to men's lives. Shifting camp might be more expensive in time and labor, but at least it was safe and sure.

"Go ahead," he said to the Camp-boss, "pull her out."

"There's no flat place big enough this side of the Guard Station at Idylhurst."

"Make it the Guard Station then."

Suddenly at the order men came hurrying, and trucks roared out of the transportation park and backed into place, and all the tons of material that had been so recently brought in and stowed so neatly with so much labor were broken out again and loaded.

At the kitchen they quickly dumped the great kettles of half-cooked stew and the coffee-pots and the boilers of hot water, and they loaded kettles and pots and boilers still hot onto the truck. They doused the fires, and dismantled the stove-pipes and let the stoves cool a little, and loaded them while they were still warm. They loaded the mountainous heap of supplies—the sacks of potatoes, the boxes of oranges and apples, and the crates of cabbages and peaches, the margarine, the eggs, the bacon, and the packaged bread, all the high-stacked pile of canned goods. They loaded the chests of tin cups and tin plates and tin bowls, and the knives and forks and spoons, and took down the big canvas fly and rolled it up and loaded it, and all the garbage-cans and kitchen utensils.

The Timekeeper and his two girls loaded their own records and supplies, and piled into a car, and got off easily.

But at the supply-dump they loaded the grind-stones and all the hundreds of axes and McLeods and shovels that were not out on the line, and the high heap of bedding-rolls.

Even while they worked, the fire was rolling down the slope beyond the creek, and the smoke came drifting across the flat in little wisps. Then from off to the left along Bacchus Creek came the high whining roar as a pump-engine started. Another joined in from far off to the right on Onion Creek. The pumps could throw water from the creeks, and wet down things close to the stream. They might work in along the flanks and narrow the front, but there was no hope that they could keep the fire from jumping Bacchus Creek. Two pumps in front of the Spitcat were no more than two machine-guns against the break-through of an army-corps.

A starter whished, and an engine took hold, and the first truck lumbered out past the Transportation-boss, and started down the road toward Idylhurst.

A car got off with the women who had been working in the kitchen. (That was good; it was no time to be looking out for women.)

Just then came a thicker whirl of smoke as a gust of wind eddied down the narrow canyon. After that came the long whoop that they had been waiting for, from over on the slope by Bacchus Creek. It turned the blood a little cold. Someone was yelling for help, and you knew that the wind-gust had thrown a spark across the ravine and it had lit in the dry needles and taken off with a rush up-grade in the wind. With luck they would catch this one, but there would be a dozen to follow it.

They were still working at Headquarters, but the canvas fly was gone from above them, and everything was packed except the painted planks that served for desk and a few maps and pads, and the log-book. If you laid down a pencil, somebody picked it up and packed it. Men were gathering round to grab the desk-planks too.

Men unstrung the ropes from the steel rings, and coiled them up and loaded them. Mauls clanked against the steel stakes, knocking them loose in the ground. Men came carrying the brightly-painted red seats from the latrine, and the box of toilet-paper. They came with the wash-basins and the long planks from the wash-stand down by Bacchus Creek; the wash-stand had almost been forgotten in the rush, and the fire was so close over there already that the tin basins were hot to the hand and the men had to grab the stuff and run.

There was another long whoop, and then another. Two more trucks pulled out. At Transportation five grunting men hoisted a gasoline-drum into a pick-up truck and got it going. (That was nothing to have around when sparks were falling.) The Transportation-boss ran up and down his line, checking that keys were in all the cars. Mentally he checked the cars against the men left to be sure that they all had drivers.

The flag came down at Headquarters and the radio aerial.

"Keep close to me," the Super said to his radio-man. Then he said to his Chief of Staff, "Let them get our stuff loaded now. Go on back, and get set up at Idylhurst. I'll be along after a bit."

"Aye, aye, captain! Last man to abandon ship, eh?"

The Super grinned. Hardly anything as heroic as abandoning ship—but that was the idea at least!

He had hardly stepped back from the desk before some men picked up the planks, and another one shinned up the tree and started knocking down the neatly stencilled sign HEADQUARTERS.

He walked across the flat, his radio-man dutifully trailing him. The camp—camp-site you would call it now—showed all the pathos of things without people, like an evacuated village or a ship abandoned to founder, with the water already sloshing deep in the hold. The ground was ripped and torn where feet had tramped and stakes had been pulled up.

At the kitchen the sloppy messes of dumped stew had spread out along the ground; in the center they still steamed a little, but along their edges flies were gathering already. A sack of fine Oregon potatoes had been spilled and lay scattered about. In the confusion of broken crates lay one that had been left for empty, but was still half-full of unopened cans of tomato-juice. A shiny tin cup lay there. Someone had tramped on it and ruined it, but a tin plate near by was good as new. Farther off among the trees lay a blanket-roll that had been missed. Somebody's jacket hung limply from the stub of a limb. The sign LATRINE with an arrow beneath it was still on a tree. But all these made nothing to worry about. Fire-fighting was a wasteful business at best, almost as wasteful as war, and you couldn't stop to count pennies.

The Super walked on to the meeting of the two creeks. The rapid-fire high-pitched sputter of a pump was close. Just across Bacchus Creek he saw flames tossing in the bushes, close enough to be hot against his face. Up Onion Creek the clean flat arch of water from the pump was playing across at the other side of the ravine. It should be no trick to hold the line of Onion Creek, for the wind was nearly down-canyon, and the rushing stream was ten feet wide. Men were scattered along on the side opposite the fire, as they should be.

But looking up Bacchus Creek, he saw that it was another story. Smoke was rising thickly on both sides of the little trickling stream. Whether the fire had jumped the bushy ra-vine or whether it was a big spot-fire made little difference. Already the Division-boss must have had to pull his men out from this side, and be merely trying to flank the fire on the west side as it ran up the slope. As he himself had planned, the area of the camp was now abandoned to the enemy, and the fight would be made on lines farther back.

Suddenly he felt lonely and exposed, as if he were cut off from all help and about to be surrounded. This was no man's land!

"Let's get out of here," he said, and he saw that the radio-man looked unusually happy to be going.

As they crossed the camp-site again, a spark had fallen from somewhere, and a little fire was quietly burning in the needles near where the kitchen had been. Running before the wind, widening its front as it ran, it had already left a blackened, wedge-shaped mark, twelve feet long. One edge of it licked along the mess of spilled stew, and sent up a faint smell of burning meat.

Even without a shovel, just by grabbing up the abandoned tin plate and scraping a few needles away, he could have stopped that fire. But there was no use.

He walked on. There was only one car—his own—left at the parking space. He and the radio-man got in. He pressed the starter button, hoping it would work. The engine started easily, and then he gave one last look. The little fire had spread noticeably farther. He swung the car out of the parking space, and started down the road for Idylhurst.

The air was crisp and hot, but he seemed to hear the gurgle and swish of water, and to see the bow of a ship settle down deeper to meet a wave.

13

The old man was going crazy, certainly. From the whining radio she heard the high chanting voice of the lookout on Horse Mountain.

"Thus saith the prophet Joel," it ran on. "Yea, *the fire hath devoured the pastures of the wilderness, and the flame hath burned all the trees of the field.*"

Even on the catwalk, alone now and looking out through

the darkness toward the blazing face of Reverse Ridge, she
heard him:

"Repent ye, yea, repent. Thus saith the Lord through the
mouth of Jeremiah, *I will kindle a fire in the forest and it
shall devour all things round about it.*"

Well, the old guy might be correct! Jeremiah and the Lord
were doing a pretty good job! She had seen the dramatic
break of that afternoon, and now the southern face of Reverse Ridge, in full view, was still blazing up before her
eyes. Two nights ago she had seen only the violent pink of the
reflected fire; last night she had seen merely an occasional
tip of flame; tonight, half the world seemed to be ablaze.
Even on her high catwalk there was glare enough to cut
through the darkness of the night. It reflected from the windows, not flaring up and down like the light from a single
bonfire, but vibrating with a long and slow pulsation as now
one part of the vast fire blazed up or another died down.

"Woe unto us!" cried the voice. *"The mountain burned
with fire unto the midst of heaven, with darkness, clouds, and
thick darkness."*

He was a little off, she thought. That should be a daytime
quotation. But the mountain was burning to the midst of
heaven all right. She thought of the line of the old song that
her grandfather used to quote:

Fire on the mountain, run, boys, run!

When she was a little girl, she wondered whether the boys
were running to put the fire out or to get away from it.

Well, she might have to do a little running herself before
this was over. Step by step, day by day, the fire moved closer
and closer. First it had been a tiny puff of smoke—twelve
miles off. Then it had come—nine miles, seven miles. (Like
the poem about Sheridan's ride she had read in American

Lit.) Now it burned in full view at the very base of her own mountain, four miles away.

"Thus saith the Lord God," the voice was chanting, high-pitched and ecstatic. *"Behold I will kindle a fire in thee, and it shall devour every green tree in thee and every dry tree: the flaming flame shall not be quenched."*

"Sign off, Horse Mountain," another voice was saying in irritation. (It sounded like Humbug Point.) "Sign off! I've got to get a message through."

There was a moment's pause, and then Horse Mountain said in a matter-of-fact voice, just for the record apparently: *"Ezekiel,* 20:37; *Ezekiel,* 20:37," and signed off.

The other message was merely something being relayed through from the Zone 2 fire-camp, nothing of interest.

As she looked out now through the binoculars, she saw individual fires. A tall snag suddenly flared clear to its top. She even saw, or imagined, its flames stringing out westward with the wind. (It was shifting more into the east as Dave— oh, Dave—yes, as he had said, this afternoon, it would.) With the more easterly wind she could see that the fire, having slid down to the bottom of the steep slope, was sending out a long stringer westward through the thickly grown ravine along Curran Creek. What must be a patch of brush in the ravine was going up now in an intense flame that was more white than yellow.

And there he was at it again! She heard the high-pitched voice in sing-song:

"A fire goeth before him, and burneth up his enemies around about. His lightnings enlightened the world; the earth saw, and trembled. The hills melted like wax at the presence of the Lord."

Oh, she thought, come now! It was a lightning-fire all right, but she hadn't heard of any hills melting.

Then again she was suddenly happy. Maybe something inside her was what had melted. (Dave, oh, yes—Dave.) Being a part of all that was happening along with so many people had made something break or unloosen inside—well, *melt* might be the right word.

She heard a truck grinding up the road below her. She listened—yes, there were two of them. The glare of the lights tossed and shifted among the trees. There were many more trucks on that road this evening. The fight was moving in closer to her, and she was more a part of it than ever. Again she knew that she had lost the old tenseness and fear, and was moving out from herself once more, one among many comrades. "Melted like wax," she thought. "Yes, melted like wax."

14

Except that the trees on the flat at the Idylhurst Guard Station were mostly oaks, the new fire-camp looked a lot like the old one. There was again the mutter of the generator at work, and the electric-light wires that had been hastily pulled down at Onion Flat had been as hastily run up again at Idylhurst.

Beneath their glare at Headquarters, the Maps-and-Records man was trying to total up the day. As always after a bad break, reports were fragmentary and conflicting, and he could not tell very accurately just where the fire was burning. The shape on his map, as he outlined it in green, grew into an epitome of the day's events—the solid mass where the crown-fire had crashed up-slope, the two separate arms running down the other side. The southeastern arm, which had burned to the camp-site, had narrowed as it stretched out; the pumps had kept it from crossing Bacchus Creek along a front of a good quarter mile. But the southwestern arm had widened, and was more dangerous. A shift of wind toward the east had sent it up the ravine of Curran Creek, and headed it threateningly for the low divide into the drainage of Potter Creek. Toward the south, although the reports were vague, this arm had certainly jumped Curran Creek in several places. There was also a well-established spot-fire over on that side.

Drawing several scallops to show the points of the fire and making a little circle for the spot-fire, he finished his outline, and then with his dividers measured the perimeter. Because of the highly irregular outline, it had jumped tremendously. Even with no allowance for the scallops, he figured it roughly as a good twenty miles, as against thirteen for the preceding day.

By means of the township- and section-maps, he estimated area. The fire had burned clear across Deerhound. The tip of the southeastern arm was in Eel-grass and the southwestern was half a mile into Daddy.

The day's acreage worked out at 2,765. Again, within twenty-four hours, the fire had nearly doubled its area. It totaled out roughly at 6,000 acres, or about nine square miles.

Although he still derived a little melancholy satisfaction from keeping the score, the Maps-and-Records man was getting disturbed. This inevitable quality by which the fire seemed to double its area every day would have to stop soon, or by the laws of mathematics the results would be cataclysmic.

As THE WOLF was before the dog, so also man knew the wild-fire before the hearth-fire. Like a maddened beast it roared in the thicket, and writhed, and devoured. He ran, and cowered among the rocks.

Centuries later, his mind grown keener, he placed it for the shape-shifting demon it was—cruel and uncontrollable, striking without hands, running without feet. Grown cleverer still, he schemed to placate it, and vaguely he worshipped.

When he had tamed the hearth-fire, he knew a kindlier demon—nourisher, protector, comforter. It allowed no familiarity, quick to run wild, to scorch, smother, and destroy. So still he could not help but worship. In it he saw the symbol of his life—its tenuous and untouchable flame, that soul of his in which he now believed.

Then too, since hearth-fire was hard to come by and its loss a disaster, the family tended it dutifully, entrusting its care to the daughters. Before long, as often happens, what began for use came to be mystical, and perpetual flames burned before altars tended by high-born virgins. "The fire," ran the law of Moses, "shall be burning upon the altar; it shall never go out."

277

So the fire-gods took shape from the vague demon. Agni of the Aryans—"steward of both worlds," his triple form declaring earthly, heavenly, and solar fire! Moloch—grim king, delighting in the savor of children! When the hearth-logs crackled, the Greeks said, "Hephaistos laughs!" and the Norsemen, "Loki beats his children!" Atar, Vulcan, Xiuhectli, Ho Shên, Brigit, Grannus—the muster of the fire-gods is of many lands!

Old ways die slowly, or change and do not die. Long after Brigit became St. Bridgit, chaste nuns tended the fire before her altar at Kildare, church of the oak-tree. Calling "Granno!" French peasants waved torches on the day of their ancestral fire-god. Even we may light a Yule-log, the very name commemorating a heathen mid-winter rite of fire. So, too, candles still burn in churches, and undying flame flickers at the tomb of the Unknown Soldier.

2

And now, after midnight on the fourth day of the dry wind, the Spitcat Fire still crackled and blazed in the bushes, and roared up in the clumps of young trees, and now and then (even in the coolness of the night) sent a tall tree towering still taller in a searing blast of hissing white-yellow flames. Its threat was worse than ever. If its outreaching arms stretched to the south and united, they would doom all the rich forest that covered the rolling country between Swayback Ridge and Cerro Gordo. But with an east wind the fire might sweep across the low divide into the drainage of Potter Creek. An unexpected shift of the wind to south or west could be even worse, for along the many miles of lightly held line the blowing of a single spark might send the fire off in a wholly new direction.

Because of the accumulation of heat and the ever-increasing

length of line and the heightened possibility of accident, danger had grown even out of proportion to size until now it assumed a nightmarish vastness. The fire, instead of growing weary and middle-aged, sprang upon each new clump of bushes with youthful vigor and enthusiasm, like a wild beast seizing its prey and growing stronger by what it feeds on.

3

In the Weather Bureau at Suffolk, Dave Halliday worked beneath the brightness of the electric lights, bringing his map up to the minute. The crisis, he saw, was at hand.

At one in the morning Seattle reported steady rain. (That probably meant the end of the fire-season in the Puget Sound area.) The storm center which he had been watching for the last four days was now somewhere in the interior of British Columbia, and the long front stretched southwestward far to sea. A ship, two hundred miles off the mouth of the Columbia, reported low overcast and drizzle.

Twenty-four hours would bring the storm-front in, and tell the tale. He studied the map, but even at no more than twenty-four hours' range he could not be sure. As so often at this time of year, northern California lay just on the edge. If clouds broke over Alberta, if the hurricane off the Louisiana coast intensified—any little unbalancing of the meteorological scales a thousand miles away might swing the tip of the rain belt a hundred miles north or south and make all the difference between triumph and disaster on the slopes of Cerro Gordo.

Actually the wind would today be worse than at any time since the first outbreak. High pressure over the northern Rockies and a storm developing in Kansas (yes, even the hurricane in the Gulf) were combining to create a broad westward-moving river of air. Flowing now from the east as it had formerly from the north, it still surged through the passes between the jagged peaks, and slid ever faster down the long canyons of the western slope.

4

Reading the emergency weather-forecast that had been telephoned in from Suffolk, the Supervisor was pleased with its honesty. The fellow as much as said he didn't know. Things might be going to be a lot worse in twenty-four hours, or a lot better. As far as the Supervisor, acting as Fire-boss, was concerned, that made everything easy. He merely had to prepare for the worst.

His plans were already well under way. Because of the new breaks, he had reorganized in three zones and eight divisions, and he was re-deploying his men. The panic yesterday had developed because the critical Division III had been manned by inexperienced pick-ups, while the crack fire-fighting outfits were mostly off on parts of the line which had once been dangerous but were now quiet and cold. Half-scared pogies, city-bred soldiers unused to handling tools, sailors in low shoes—even though their numbers ran into the hundreds, they could not match the trained efficiency of the Hot-shot men and the regular suppression-crews.

When three buses rolled into camp and stopped for a minute to let the men rest, the Supervisor went over to see them. Even in the semi-darkness, from the way they got out of the buses and stood around, he could tell that they were veterans. They did not glance about, half apprehensively, as men unfamiliar with the mountains would do; they did not stand stiffly. He could tell them by the way they stood loose-jointedly at ease, or squatted.

He picked out the Hot-shot crew, and the loggers, and the locals from Suffolk. He saw the thick-set silhouette of Slugger

O'Neill, his boys trailing him, one of them walking with a limp. Then he jumped, as from the semi-darkness someone called:

"Hi, Slim!"

He snapped around and saw shining whites of eyes in a dark face. Behind the Corporal stood the little group of paratroopers.

"Hello, Corporal," said the Supervisor. "How've you boys been making out?"

"Not too bad! We got run out in that big blow-up, and damn near got the shirts burned off us, but then we fought spot-fires on the Wilson Crick side, and held her from jumpin' the crick. Since then we been mostly just patrollin' and sittin' around.—Say, I didn't know when I saw you up in that plane that you was the big boss!"

"That's no matter! But what I want to know is whether you and your boys are looking for more trouble."

"Sure! We're all rested and ready to go!"

While they had talked, other men had come crowding around. ("That's the Super!" the word had run through the crowd, "He's Fire-boss now!") From his height the Supervisor looked down upon the many faces, raised to look at his. Close in front were the paratroopers; to right and left and farther back he saw the Hot-shot men, and the loggers, and the locals, and Slugger's youngsters. Before he realized it, he was making a speech.

"Look here," he said. "We lost that line yesterday because the crews got scared and ran out."

There was a groan of derision, and a logger let out a cat-call.

"Well, they were just a bunch of pick-ups, and they didn't know fire. I want you men to go in at the head of the fire, and do a job—"

He could feel a little surge of feeling among the men. "Let's go!" someone called.

"There's half a mile of front up there where the fire heads right for the divide over into Potter Creek. We've got to run a line across there and get her burned out. It's a tough country and the cats can't help much. I'm counting on you boys to do it."

That was all he said. There was a little cheer as he turned and walked off to Headquarters. He heard the Corporal calling, "O. K., Slim!" and some others joined in.

5

On a quiet sector of Division IV, near Reverse Creek, a man now and then conscientiously patrolled back and forth along two hundred feet of line, and in the intervals sat and talked with the man who was patrolling the next section. The two were neighbors and friends, small ranchers from the dry foothill country below Polkville, who had come to the fire for the honest motive of earning a few dollars.

(No comets streamed in the sky; no beasts and birds reversed their natures; no ghosts walked. Only the deaths of kings demand such omens.)

When he had finished a patrol-tour, the man came back to where he was accustomed to sit with his friend. In frugal backwoods fashion he rolled himself a cigarette, lighted it, and carefully threw the match across the line into the burned area.

A hundred feet in from the line no fire at all showed on the tall snag, but in the hollow base, out of sight in a dip of the land, the fire ate redly. Minute by minute, the heat weakened the tough fibers of the pine-wood, and the fire ate through them, as if a man with a dull knife slowly frayed the hard strands of a cable. In the wind the snag swayed back and forth, and as the base weakened, it swayed occasionally an inch or two farther.

(No smell of death went out from the man like an exhalation. His thoughts were not gloomily foreboding, for he was no second-sighted Gael to sense when his weird was upon him, but only an American, knowing what eyes saw and ears heard.)

He talked with his friend about the probable price of steers. He drew easily on the cigarette, and spat into the ashes.

High overhead the tip of the snag swayed westward with the wind-pressure behind it. As it leaned, more of the over-heated fibers snapped, and its tons of weight pulled hard at the weakened base. But once more the fibers held, and being bent out of their natural shape, they reacted elastically. All the tons of the tall tree-trunk came slowly to a halt, and then at the pull of the fibers swayed back into the wind at the majestic rhythm of a pendulum nearly two hundred feet long.

The cigarette was down to its butt, and the price of cattle was talked out. The man flipped the butt between his fingers, and sent it flying surely in a flat arc well across the line.

"That's so," he said. "And I guess I'd better be going along my beat again."

High overhead the snag was swaying with the wind, farther still this time. Fibers broke again, but the elasticity of the bent wood pulled back hard. Then a slight veering of the wind twisted the tree-top, and deep within the base a whole strand of wood separated from another with a muffled crack.

But, conscientious as he was, the man knew that patrolling this stretch of burned-out line was little more than a formality. He found it pleasant to sit with his friend, and he lingered a moment, saying nothing.

The twist and the breaking loose of the strand of wood had suddenly upset the whole balance of forces. As the tree leaned only a little farther, its many tons of weight felt the earthward pull more directly. On one side of the base, the wood crumpled into waves under the overwhelming pressure. On the other side fibers snapped by thousands, and the whole base of the tree split open, with a long and resounding crack.

In horror the men heard, and with freezing blood they looked up to see, uncertainly, vague against the dark sky, the imminent and real shadow of death. To run, not knowing which way the tree was falling, would have been to dash toward danger as probably as away from it. Instinctively each sprawled out away from the other, asking the shelter of the ground, pitifully rolling up tight to be small, as if seeking the first safety of the womb.

With a crash and a concussion that shook the ground, the tree-trunk struck the earth between the two cowering men.

("Then shall two be in the field; the one shall be taken, and the other left.")

As the echoing noise died out and the forest was silent, the man who had sprawled to the right felt himself uninjured, and stood up, weak with shock and terror. The one who had sprawled to the left lay crushed, bloodily, beneath a projecting branch.

6

Far off at Barlow Ranger Station, as the dawn was breaking, Bart slept dreamlessly at last. It had not been like those other times, those many times through all the years, when he had come home from fires. He had been as tired before, and as dirty, and just as scratched and burned. But always before, the fire had been out, or at least controlled. Now he had remembered the crinkle in his pocket where he carried the note.

He was not angry at the Super any longer. The Super had

merely done what had to be done. Bart was shaken in himself. What had happened? Was he getting old? Or was it just because the fire had burned, devastatingly and agonizingly, across the country of all in the world that he loved best?

He had bathed, but even the luxury of the sluicing warm water had not relaxed him. His wife had dabbed antiseptic on his scratches, and stuck bandages on the worst of them. Then she had come with a glass of water and a long white capsule in her hand.

"Take this," she said.

He took it. As a ranger's wife should, she knew first-aid, and there had to be something in the medicine chest to ease the pain of a burn or of a dislocated shoulder, while a bouncing truck, serving as ambulance, covered the long miles down to the doctor.

It had not worked. Through the evening he lay on his bed and tossed. He did not want to be Fire-boss any more, but he wanted to be back on the line somewhere. She gave him another capsule finally, and he lay more quietly. Half awake, half asleep, he had that horrible vision again—of the violated girl, mutilated and bleeding, lying horrible in the sun. And again something dashed this way and that trying to escape.

But at last the sharpness of the vision dulled. He dozed, fitfully at first, waking now and then with a jerk. Later he slept more deeply, and the horrible imagining that was half dream and half vision faded out.

As the dawn broke, he slept soundly at last. While he slept, the foul imaginings of his symbols were becoming real.

After the fire had jumped Curran Creek, all that country of narrow, thickly grown ravines was doomed. The fire reached out clutching fingers around the little glade where the red-brown fluted columns of the tall cedars rose up, and the azaleas bloomed in the spring, and the clear water came down in miniature waterfalls over moss-grown rocks.

Yet all during the night the Glen had been like a quiet countryside in the midst of raging war. High overhead, smoke drifted through the cedar-tops, but close to the stream the air was still fresh and even moist. The shifting red glare of the not-too-distant fire cast uncertain shadows back and forth. Now and then came a resounding crash as a burned snag went down, but the lines were so far away that even the roar of the working bull-dozers was only a muttering undertone through the darkness.

Almost as on any other night, the doe moved here and there, browsing upon the bushes, followed closely by the fawn. Now and then she raised her head and looked about nervously as some louder noise disturbed her, or as the glare flickered more sharply, or as some eddy of the wind brought the acrid smell of smoke. Once she sniffed suspiciously as the wind brought the scent of a bear; and again, of a strange buck. There was an unaccustomed populousness around the Glen. More rabbits scurried in the bushes; a coon, business-like and knowing what he was about, trotted across the glade and into the forest on the other side; a mink, moving in graceful, undulating leaps, came up along the stream; even more owls than usual were flitting about.

All this disturbance was not without its contagious effect upon the doe, but she lacked experience and generalizing power to know that the fire was sweeping the animals before it, even more effectively than a thick-posted line of beaters could have done. But since the doe had not actually felt the near approach of the fire, the effect of her nervousness was to make her stay closer to the bed-ground in the thicket, from which she never, even on ordinary nights, strayed very far.

Well before daylight long stringers of fire had crossed the

ravine above and below the Glen, so that it was in a deep pocket. Just at dawn, an up-springing of the wind suddenly brought the fire surging closer.

The doe looked nervously about, and stood hesitant. Then, in full sight, a clump of bushes roared into flame, and for the first time thick smoke rolled low across the Glen. The doe broke in panic. For the moment forgetting her fawn, she dashed through the azaleas, leaped the stream, and went sailing off up the opposite slope in long jumps. The fawn followed valiantly, but after a few jumps he lost sight of his mother's bobbing tail. Also in panic, he accidentally sheered off at a different angle.

Halfway up the slope, the doe realized that no fawn was following her. As panic and maternal love clashed and neutralized each other, she paused uncertainly. Even on the slope she saw the strange flickering redness not far away. But once she had paused, all the strong drive of motherhood forced her back toward the bed-ground where she might find the fawn. Trotting uncertainly, pausing to eye the flames, she went downhill. At the stream she stood, bleating. (But the fawn was out of ear-shot, and even more panic-stricken than the doe, was dashing about near the ridge-top, hopelessly lost.)

The doe, in growing alarm, leaped back across the stream and through the azaleas, and came to the bed-ground. She found no fawn. The heat struck terrifyingly upon her; in the eddying smoke, she coughed. But having left the bed-ground and come back, she felt it more than ever her place of safety. She ranged about in a small compass searching the fawn, bleating. Though terrified with heat and glare and smoke, she lingered.

Except for the mink still swimming lazily in a pool, the wave of larger animals had given place to smaller ones. A chipmunk, drunk with smoke and dazed with terror, ran chattering back and forth. Dozens of wood-mice rustled in the grass.

As the doe lingered, an arm of fire ran along the opposite slope, almost completing the circle. Then, close-by, the edge of the thicket which enclosed the bed-ground rose suddenly in flame. With this final link to safety sundered, the doe again leaped up the slope. After a dozen bounds, she came up sharply, snorting, at the line of fire directly ahead. In full panic she swung to the left and met fire again. There was still an open gap, but the doe was incapable of finding it. She dashed again toward the bed-ground, and almost into the flames, before the heat drove her back.

By now the fire was close to the glade on every side, and the heat was intolerable. The azalea leaves were wilting. Even along the stream there was no sense of moisture or cool-ness. Trembling, the doe stood in the water for a moment. Then, as a spark lit on her back, she dashed off in uncon-trollable fright at the sharp pain and the smell of burned hair. She came to the wall of fire, but in her panic the fire seemed also to be pursuing her from behind. With a wild leap, she sprang into the flames.

Her very speed might have carried her through with no more than a singed coat; but as she leaped, her lungs de-manded air, and through wide nostrils she sucked in a full breath of white-hot flame. She ran a hundred feet, and then as her seared lungs failed, she collapsed. Crumpled, she lay on the forest-floor, where the fire still burned quietly at the criss-crossing of some fallen branches.

The fire now roared on all sides, and with the steady east wind blowing up-canyon advanced swiftly across the glade. Now the azalea leaves smoked, and flared up. The heat ig-nited the moss and the dry bark of the cedars; the flames licked high up on the red-brown columns until they seemed to stand knee-deep in fire. No spray rose from the little water-falls, for the dry hot air licked up all droplets of moisture. The moss on the rocks was steamy hot, and turning brown at the edges.

Now a holocaust of white-hot fire rose up from the thick covert of young cedars, leaped higher, and ignited the high crown of the mature trees. There was the sudden scream of a chipmunk, quickly stilled. In the intense heat the mink drew even his nose into the pool and lay submerged. The surface of the water was dirty with charred needles. The dried-out moss on the rocks burned like dry grass. The rocks themselves flaked and scaled in the white heat.

As in a furnace which reflects heat from all sides, the temperature leaped up. Even the mice in the rock-crevices shriveled, as the heat seared their lungs and sucked the oxygen from the air. In the intensity of white light the skeletons of the azaleas stood out luminously for a moment, and then collapsed into ashes. Hot scales of rock mingling with the ashes of the moss slid down, and sizzled in the pool. Even the water grew luke-warm, and the very trout sought the rock crannies at the bottom.

The intensity of the fire burned it out all the faster. After little more than a minute had passed, the heat fell off, and the white dazzle deepened into yellow.

The ruin of the Glen was complete. It was a place of desolation and ugliness and death. From the bottom of the pool the mink emitted his breath in a chain of bubbles; rising cautiously, he broke the surface with his nostrils and refilled his lungs. Along with the trout, he was left alive.

7

At the ridge-top he reined in the little black mare, and listened and looked.

Sounds poured in upon him. Close at hand he heard the

click-clank of hand-tools rasping at the earth and knocking on stones. There was the slow *clunk . . . clunk . . . clunk* of an ax. Farther off he distinguished the rumbling of a truck, and the angry roaring of a cat. Suddenly the staccato of a power-saw burst out, stuttered for a moment, and then took hold with a crescendo.

From the canyon below him and to the east, the great column of smoke still poured up, but he noted with pleasure that its front seemed all to lie within the two ridges. His strategy was working.

"Come on," said the Supervisor to his radio-man, and the two rode down along the ridge. A cat had been through just once, but still the trail was easily passable for the horses. The first men they saw were the Hot-shot crew.

The Supervisor was not a fine figure on horseback. He had lengthened the stirrups, and his feet hung down awkwardly beneath the line of the mare's belly. His height, commanding when he stood, was ungainly in the saddle.

Nevertheless the Hot-shot men greeted him with exclamations which were almost a cheer. They had been up all night, and had worked through most of it, but they were still going strong and were set for the day-shift too. They recognized the emergency, and wanted to be in on it. The crew-boss came up grinning.

"Well," he said, "we stopped her in the flat over there and ran her up to the ridge like you said—us, and the colored boys, and some others."

"Good job!"

"Think we'll catch her today?"

The Supervisor paused a moment, and suddenly all the mountain-side seemed full of the roaring of power—trucks and cats and saws, and even, he thought, a pump.

"*Sounds* as if we ought to catch her," he said. "Got enough machines and a lot of men too. But you know what a big fire is!"

Next, the paratroopers were working ("Hi, Slim!" they called), and then came Slugger O'Neill's boys, and the Barlow suppression-crew.

Just beyond, a cat was barging around. The burly thick-necked cat-skinner was death-like gray with dust, and the whites of his eyes rolled wildly. He rammed at a thirty-foot pine tree, toppled it over, backed off for a better bite, went in low and pushed the tree to one side, roots and all.

A four-foot tree-trunk lay across the way. The cat-skinner hit it hard and shoved it a foot, and then his treads slid. He backed off, and stood up a moment to look the thing over. He went in again slowly, caught the tree-trunk at the proper angle. The engine roared and the treads grabbed, and the tree-trunk slowly revolved about its own base until it lay to one side. Then the cat, without seeming to pause, slowly toppled forward and went clanking down into a ravine. "All cat-skinners are crazy!"

Next the Supervisor saw the cat-skinner rooting out a four-foot boulder. That boulder seemed to make little difference to the line one way or the other, but the cat-skinner was having a fine time, and the Supervisor knew there was no use arguing with him. As they rode by, the horses shied a little at the roaring cat, or maybe it was at the cat-skinner.

The staccato hammering of the power-saw paused sud-denly, and very faintly from far-off came the long cry, "Timm-ber-rr!" Then he heard the crash. That was one more snag that would never blaze like a high torch and send sparks scattering far down-wind.

Almost immediately he heard another one go down. With half a dozen power-saws working, the snags would be drop-ping like ten-pins. This time he was giving the fire plenty of room, taking no chances on losing the line, that is, at least no more chances than you had to take.

From a point where the ridge fell away, he had a better view. Far to the east he saw with satisfaction that little smoke was rising from the northern point of Swayback Ridge. The arm of the fire that had run across the camp-ground at Onion Flat had been flanked in and pinched off during the night, and was now all held within the line and well burned out. Closer below him, in the long canyon that Bacchus Creek had worn in the eastern slope of Cerro Gordo, the main fire still burned on a curving front of a mile or more. It was running through a fine forest of mixed conifers, crowning here and there, putting up a heavy smoke-column. The wind was funneling up the canyon; the point of the fire was well ahead along the stream, and moving fast.

Let it move! His strategy was working, and with any luck he had the fire in a pocket. By throwing the weight of his best crews during the night he had stopped the fire in its dangerous rush toward the divide and the Potter Creek drainage. Now it burned only in the canyon of Bacchus Creek, well confined between two sharp ridges. All he had to do now was to flank it along the ridges, and finally meet its onset along the flattish and rocky and thinly forested top of Cerro Gordo. That meant letting two or three square miles of good forest go up in smoke, but he had taken the responsibility for the sacrifice, and it was the safest plan. That afternoon should tell the story, and they would know whether they had won or lost before the change of weather came.

From his lookout point the smoke-column dominated his view; opposing it, he could only make out two little patches of dust on the other ridge, rising from the working cats. But when he listened, he grew more confident. Any crackle of fire was wholly drowned out by the noise of the machines. The

roar of cats and power-saws ruled the air. He heard snag after
snag come crashing down. The fury of the fire might still be
terrible, but against it was mobilized no despicable force.

Though the fire was horrible because it had no feelings and
could never be frightened, yet at the same time, he thought,
the fire was blundering and stupid. Otherwise it would have
thrown reserves in, and smashed through for the divide to
Potter Creek, only a mile away. Now it had stuck its head into
a bag.

Then he shrugged his shoulders. What was that old one
about catching a bear in a fox-trap? What if the bag didn't
hold? Yet, as he heard another snag go down, he had confidence—if they didn't get another bad break.

8

In the tiny settlement at Idylhurst there was little enough to
do or talk about, ordinarily. The fire had been a godsend, for
gossip. Most of the men were off with the lumber-company
crews on the fire, but that happened once a summer at least,
and the women did not worry. The smoke-cloud drifted high
overhead, and though it shut out the sun, the air was so hot
and crisp that a sheet dried out on the line almost before
you turned your back. Now and then you could smell smoke.

Old Mrs. Dawson talked about when her town was burned
in the big Idaho fires of 1910. Young Mrs. Swenson told about
her cousin being run out at Bandon in '36, when eleven
people burned to death.

Even on Monday they had been getting nervous, and on
Tuesday afternoon there was suddenly more smoke than ever.
(Mrs. Dawson said the smoke smelled just the same as it did
in Idaho in 1910.) Then the camp-crew came streaming back
like an army in full retreat, and set up the camp at the Guard
Station. The Idylhurst women who had been helping in the

kitchen told some highly exaggerated stories about how they had been run out of Onion Flat with the fire on their heels, and the tension around Idylhurst rose to a delightfully high pitch. Jewel Magnus was charmed to have so many men around; she put on lipstick till she looked more like a tart than ever, and went where she could see the most men, and be seen.

The Camp-boss told them there was no danger, but Mrs. Nelson telephoned her sister at Suffolk about staying there with the children if they had to leave Idylhurst, and Mrs. Axelrod, who was always nervous when her husband was away, made her children go to bed with their clothes on.

The next morning Mrs. Axelrod could not smell much smoke, but she had not slept very well and was more nervous. She decided she would take the children, and go to her cousin's place in Polkville. At first her idea was that she was just going to make a visit, but then it seemed foolish to leave all her belongings to be burned up, if the fire really did come, and so she started loading a clothes-basket with this and that.

When Mrs. Bushnell next-door asked her what she was doing, she had to defend herself, and she remarked firmly that she was not going to stay there with her children:

"—and be burned like rats in a trap!"

There was something memorable in the phrase, and it ran up and down the row of houses from Mrs. Axelrod's. No one considered whether you customarily burned rats in traps, but it sounded convincing. Mrs. Axelrod came out carrying her beautiful bridge-lamp, the one with the pink shade and fringe all around, and she carefully packed that in the back of the car, which by now was getting rather full.

Middle-aged Mrs. Ralph said the thing she really would want to save most was her refrigerator, and since she couldn't pack that in a car by herself she guessed she might as well stay where she was.

Young Mrs. Swenson told what her cousin told about Bandon in '36. She told it so convincingly that she convinced herself, and suddenly decided to pack up her own car.

Jewel Magnus, with lipstick wonderful to behold, said she thought she would leave too—but she really had no intention of leaving, as long as there were so many men around.

Most of the women were good solid daughters and wives of lumberjacks who had lived in the woods all their lives and were not going to run out because of some smoke in the air. In fact, only three women were really loading anything into their cars, and one or two others had shoved some of the heavier pieces of furniture out to the front-porch so that they could be carried to safety easily, if the time came. It was really a matter of little importance, and would have been of no moment at all, if just at that time the news-photographer had not happened to drive in.

He had been hanging around the fire-camp off and on for two days, but the pictures had not been so much, and the editor had not used any of them. Now the photographer came driving down between the two rows of houses, and the first thing he saw was a clock and a portable sewing-machine sitting on a front porch. His mind clicked like his own camera-shutter, and he knew suddenly that his editor was going to love him better. "Human interest!" he said to himself. "That's it!" He knew human interest when he saw it, and so did his editor, and human interest is what sells papers.

(A few miles away many hundreds of men fought with the heat of the fire on their faces. The axes swung, and the cats plunged back and forth, and the power-saws ate swiftly through the tree-trunks, and the smoke towered up against the sky.)

Human interest thrives on women and children and household goods. The photographer quickly arranged a picture by pulling Mrs. Axelrod's best lamp-shade part way out through the window so that it showed. (She would never have driven off with it like that, and she had really packed it very carefully—but of course it hadn't shown.) He took several pictures with Mrs. Axelrod standing by holding her four-year-old boy. The boy was frightened by the photographer's jumping around and snapping things, and he was ready to blubber. You would have sworn the fire was burning in full sight and scaring him to death. It made a wonderful picture.

But Mrs. Axelrod was squat and big-waisted, and you need glamor along with human-interest really to hit the big time. Then the photographer looked up and saw—just a gift from God—Jewel Magnus, lip-stick and all! She had a figure, and that kind of big blowsy handsomeness that shows up well in a newspaper cut, even if the ink gets a little thick.

He herded her to a porch and sat her in a rocking-chair against a background of a console-radio and a vacuum cleaner. It was Mrs. Palmer's porch, and the household goods were hers too, but it was a fine background. Jewel was carefully dabbing at her lips, and looking in her compact-mirror, for she had read her magazines and knew that girls got contracts in Hollywood when people were impressed with their pictures in the paper.

"Say," said the photographer, "where's your baby?"

That was a temporary set-back when it turned out that Jewel didn't have any baby. But he borrowed Mrs. Martin's. (He couldn't use Mrs. Martin of course; she had a face no editor would print.)

He pulled the vacuum-cleaner to one side so that it would show. With a good professional skill he slipped in a flashlight bulb to overcome the shade of the porch. He looked through his finder, and then he paused.

"Say," he said, "a little bit—you know—" and he pulled at the knee of his trousers.

"Oh, cheesecake!" said Jewel, who read her magazines. She obliged.

"No, no," he said. "Down a little!" After all, there were limits to what an editor dared use.

"Fine!" he said. Even he could see that Jewel was not holding the baby the way a mother would, but everything showed up well—as much of everything as you could get by with. He popped the flash-bulb.

In the end things settled down at Idylhurst. Nobody left except Mrs. Axelrod, who wanted to go to visit her cousin anyway. But the pictures of Jewel and the baby were excellent.

9

The perimeter of the burned area was now more than twenty-five miles. Merely to encompass the whole of the fire-line, plunging into ravines and climbing out of canyons, would have been beyond the power of a strong man to accomplish in a whole day of walking. Much of this line was burned out and seemingly cold, but patrol still had to be maintained against the chance of accident. A considerable portion, moreover, although the fury of the fire had long since passed away from it, offered a definite threat; smoke, and even some blaze, still rose from where fallen tree-trunks lay crossed, or from dry stumps, or from the cracked and splintered tops of snags.

The Sector-bosses maintained an active warfare against all these threats. They sent in falling-crews to bring down the snags. Other mop-up crews separated the burning logs, so that no draft could be maintained between them and each would burn itself out.

Unburned areas within the fire-line constituted another threat. Like most large fires, probably because of air-currents generated within the blaze itself, the fire had failed to make a clean burn everywhere, and a few little unburned islands remained.

Such a small island, largely of thin brush, remained near the line at the western end of Reverse Ridge. It was a threat, since it might blaze up suddenly in a gust of wind, just when it would be most dangerous.

A crew therefore went in and began burning it out. The ground-litter kindled readily, but there was no appreciable danger that sparks would be carried across the line and start a spot-fire on the other side.

The rabbit, hidden in the center of the brush-patch, had been thoroughly frightened on the preceding day, but by lying close and burrowing down into the earth and litter, he had escaped becoming more than uncomfortably warm, as the fire had swept around his covert.

Now, however, he heard a number of men come tramping about, and in a few minutes the strange crackling noise and dancing light which he had first experienced on the preceding day began again to surround him. He burrowed closer, laying back his ears in alarm, glancing around nervously, and sniffing with his sensitive nostrils at the odor of smoke.

This time the fire did not roll past him, but came quickly closer from various directions. His alarm increased. This was not like the swoop of the hawk or the rush of the fox which were to be escaped by a sudden unloosing of the elastic spring of his powerful hind legs. Nevertheless, aside from this mere cowering in the center of his brush-patch, the quick spasmodic dash forward was the only means of safety and escape known to him. His legs were tense and ready beneath him, and his feet rested firmly on sure ground for the push-off. His mind could hardly be said to think. His whole body was more like a coiled spring, set for release, as by the tripping of a trigger, when his eyes and ears and nostrils had piled up tensions in his brain to the snapping-point.

The fire burned nearer; flames flared close beside the rabbit, engulfing him with sudden intense heat. As at the swoop of the hawk, his leg-muscles contracted frantically, and he shot straight forward.

Fire was ahead of him too, but once committed to his dash, he did not stop. Through the burning litter he rushed. His own fur ignited, and he came out the other side as a smoking ball of running fire.

The speed of his own rush whipped up the flame. Half blinded by his dash through the fire, he still rushed straight ahead in wild panic. Six jumps took him across the fire-line, and as he ran, his burning fur ignited the dry leaves and litter.

He made a hundred yards in a few seconds, and then collapsed miserably, most of his fur burned away. The fire which he had kindled by his own passing blazed up around him to bring death which was only mercy.

The panicked and burning rabbit had taken not more than a second to emerge from the fire and disappear into the cover beyond the fire-line. None of the crew had happened to see him during his momentary passage, because their attention was focused upon the burning of the brush-patch. Only when its smoke died down a little did their crew-boss suddenly sense that there was more smoke.

"Christ, she's over the line!" cried the crew-boss, and sent up a long whoop for help.

He led his men to the attack on the run, but the new fire had already stretched out along the ridge, and was moving rapidly, out of the control of one crew.

10

In those former years when battle had still something of pageantry left in it, men thought in terms of the Grand Assault. At the final hour, when the armies lay spent with combat and even the guns were stilled, then The Guard moved forward. Regiment by regiment, their own music marshalling them, flags bright above the ordered lines, not deigning to break the rhythm of parade-ground step, majestically terrible, The Guard advanced toward victory or death. . . .

Hemmed in between the ridges on either side of Bacchus Creek, the fire (you might have thought) at last was confined. Again and again, tongue after tongue of flame had surged up either side, only to meet a descending back-fire, rise up in a roaring blaze, and then die down. If any spark swirled over the ridge, half a dozen men were ready to pounce upon the little smoke that first came curling up.

Yet the front of the fire still crashed ahead along the stream-bed, and of the hundreds of men who watched from the ridges not one sympathized with it as a trapped and dying creature. Still burning on a mile of front, roaring on before the pressure of the dry east wind, sweeping ahead ever the faster because of the steepening slope—the first was terrible and majestic. It would give no quarter, and ask none. Facing that inexorable advance, even the Hot-shot veterans glanced now and then over their shoulders. There was power and danger still in the unbroken front of flame. . . .

Like The Guard that dies but never surrenders, the fire pressed steadily to the assault on Cerro Gordo.

Dave Halliday was watching the sky and the feel of the wind. Things were as close as that now. The barometer had fallen by a hair's breadth. Wind or rain—it was still a toss-up.

But mostly he wondered if he shouldn't jump into the red jeep and start for Cerro Gordo. That was a wonderful place for watching wind-currents. (But the wind-currents were, in some way, not drifting smoke gigantically across canyons or swaying tree-tops, but were causing little ripples in wisps of brown hair that stuck out from under a yellow handkerchief.) Well, why not? I'm as much use there as here anyway, he thought.

"I'm starting for Cerro Gordo," he called to his assistant. "Call me if anything important comes in on the teletype."

"They'll be abandoning Cerro Gordo pretty soon now," said the assistant, "The new fire-line runs right underneath it. Things will be getting hot there."

Dave felt a sudden alarm which had nothing to do with air-currents.

"Well," he said, "I'll report in to the Dispatcher by whatever radio I'm nearest."

He went in a hurry, but as he was getting into the jeep, he looked at the sky. The air was just as hot and dry and glary and uncomfortable as ever, and there was a slight acrid smell in it. High overhead the smoke-drift covered most of the sky. But at the edge of the smoke, south and west, he picked up a single thin mare's-tail of cloud. High cirrus, he thought, and damn high too! Well, wind or rain? Funny, two thousand men were working on that fire, and yet they were just so many babies in comparison with what that cloud might mean. Funny, too, that with the air hot and uncomfortable the cloud which he could see so clearly was so cold that it was nothing but a drifting wisp of tiny ice-crystals.

He got in and started the engine. Then, as he looked at the sky again, the cloud seemed already just a trifle bigger and solider-looking.

Long-short-long. She rang, and waited. *Long-short-long.* The receiver against her ear was deathly quiet. *Long-short-long.* The receiver was still silent, too silent. She hung it up and rang no more. (That's that!) The telephone-line was gone, burned out somewhere down the slope. Of course the radio was still working, but she felt a new sense of isolation. Closer and closer the fire was pressing in.

Now from the lookout the fire dominated everything. Only a mile away she saw the flames tossing up and the tree-tops swaying as the draft of the fire struck them. Above the flames the smoke belched out, eddying and swirling, rising up in a broad yellow-gray column. Its drift covered all the view to the east and north, obscured all the familiar outlines of the ridges. Even to south and west the smoke was thick enough almost to isolate her. Except for occasional dashes she stayed inside, for on the catwalk there was a continual rain of ashes and charred bits of needles, and now and then a still-warm ember. The once bright-yellow handkerchief around her head was rumpled and grimy. The air, too, was better inside, for on the catwalk she coughed and choked, and her eyes watered, as swirls from the main smoke column, drifting not so far overhead, dipped down and swept past the tower like wisps of fog.

"Thus saith the Lord God," blared the radio in the high-pitched ecstatic voice. *"Behold I will kindle a fire in thee, and it shall devour every green tree in thee and every dry tree. The flaming flame shall not be quenched."*

Below her on the slope the fire was licking forward through forest that seemed to be growing in three levels. From a thick undergrowth of small trees rose middle-sized trees to fifty or a hundred feet in height and above those again towered the mature trees fifty or a hundred feet higher again.

The fire was sweeping ahead, wiping out the small trees.

As she watched, it leaped from small trees into middle-sized ones, and the flames stabbed up high above their tops. The old trees stood as if wading deep in fire. Their dead branches were burning, and dropping to the ground. An old cedar ignited, and even from on the tower she heard the roar. It seemed incredible that all the big trees did not burst into flame.

She had orders already to abandon the tower whenever she felt it advisable. She did not feel lonely, in any case. All the activity of line-building was in full view from the tower. In fact, she had a grandstand seat.

Two cats were plunging back and forth along the half-mile of line that the lookout commanded. Behind them the neutral gray-brown of dead pine needles and the green of saplings changed to an eight-foot strip of raw earth. Men by dozens swarmed out after the cats had passed. They cleaned up the debris, throwing it back on the side away from the fire. With brush-clippers they cut back the intruding branches which had bent aside to let the cats go through. With axes they chopped at the young trees close to the line. Down the slope, getting closer all the time as the fallers retreated, she heard the machine-gun roar of the power-saws—three of them, she thought—and almost minute by minute, it seemed, she heard the faint cry of "Timm-ber-r-r!" and heard the crack and long resounding crash. Now and then glancing up hurriedly she even saw the snag tip and go over.

And now a three-man crew with a power-saw came into view. They quickly set up the saw at the base of a tall snag which she remembered as part of her view ever since she had come to the tower. When the engine started, she went out on the catwalk and focused her binoculars on the crew. The chain-saw ate into the tough wood as she watched, burying itself out of sight almost before she realized it had started.

Then suddenly, as she stood on the catwalk, she was hot with a beating heat that was not from the sun.

She went inside hastily, coughing. It was not so hot inside, but the eastern windows were warm to the touch.

"The girl stood on the burning deck," she quoted out loud, *"Whence all but she had fled!"*

Well, not exactly, when she could still hear the saw and the cats, and had only to look out to see the men on the line. In fact, two men on horseback had just come into view, and she recognized the Supervisor by his long legs hanging down and making the horse look too small.

She might as well be getting out of here—if the fire made a rush, or crowned badly, she wasn't just sure how hot it might get suddenly, or if the flames would actually sweep the stairway.

Yet she hated to run out. All at once, she found herself wishing Dave would come to tell her what to do.

The Dispatcher, this morning, had little to do except to pace back and forth. He had mobilized two thousand men, and sent in their equipment, and organized the supply-lines. Everything was working at last. More men would only get in one another's way, and complicate the problem of supply. His office would hum with activity again when demobilization began, but now there was a quiet moment between, something to be thankful for, if you were not worrying about the fire and not being able to be there.

One thing was good anyway. You didn't need to think about the bills. The standing instructions were to put out the fire, and Uncle Sugar would honor the checks.

The Supervisor set up field-headquarters among some big boulders that stood out along the flattish top of Cerro Gordo like the backbone of the mountain sticking through. The line ran along the edge of the boulders, so that they formed a secondary defense.

He had chosen the place because it gave him a good view. Southward he looked along half a mile of line to where the tower stood up against the sky. Smoke was drifting low, and sometimes obscured the tower. (The girl, he supposed, must be out of there by now.) Westward he looked over the convex forested slope of the mountain-top until it fell away into the deep gorge of Potter Creek. Northward, through a haze of smoke, he still could see the smoke-column being thrown by that new slop-over or spot-fire which had jumped the line on Reverse Ridge. How it had happened, no one seemed to know; it was just one of those accidents which you expected to happen somewhere on twenty-five miles of line. It was not too bad, although it would add a hundred acres or so to the total acreage. It was a division-job, not even calling for re-inforcement from zone.

But to the east—all was fire and smoke. Closer now, the fire surged up against the line. One power-saw was still at work, but the cutting of the snags was about finished. The line—looking both ways, he saw nearly a mile of it—was clean as a swept sidewalk, and even trimmed back neatly along the edges. Everything was finished, and with just a little time to spare. The division-bosses were getting ready to light back-fires.

Now where the fire burned, there was no longer any running water. High on the mountain-side, under the shade of the trees, only little dry water-courses seamed the slope, where after rains the rills came rushing swiftly and tumbling in waterfalls. But now there was no water.

The flame and heat and smoke, rising, pressed close against

the steep slope, and the pressure of the dry east wind held them in ever closer. Far ahead, the bushes withered. Then they flared up, and after the bushes the clumps of little trees, and after the little trees the larger ones.

Yet one thing was missing. On all that slope not a single snag burned torch-like. Neatly toppled, they lay on the ground, their smooth butts showing the fresh tooth marks of the chain-saws. Where they lay, they burned hotly, but they cast no sparks forward, high in the wind.

Three deer trotted up the slope, keeping their distance ahead of the fire, now and then stopping nervously, not liking to be driven from their homes and toward the sound of men along the crest. A brown bear shuffled along, often close to the deer but paying them no attention. Of smaller animals, rustling through the underbrush, leaping from branch to branch, there would have been no counting. Two owls, driven from their roosts, flitted about, half-blindly.

Still with steady step and ranks unbroken, sweeping all before it, The Guard moved forward in the Grand Assault.

Then suddenly on the tower everything was almost quiet. The last snag had gone down, and the power-saws were still. She saw a crew carry their saw across the line and place it for safety among the boulders. The cats had withdrawn behind the line also. She could see one of them, but its idling engine brought no noise to her. Even the men seemed quiet.

A deer—two, three—loped easily out of the forest, across the line. They passed close to groups of men, not seeming to mind. It was good, she thought, that they got away before the back-fires were lighted.

And now she was conscious of a new sound filling the air. It was not so dominating as the roar of engines and the crash of falling snags, but it was low and sinister and all-enveloping —the hiss and crackle of flames.

Maybe better be getting out of here, she thought. Even inside the glass-walled room, she felt hot. Thick smoke drifted close overhead now. Often it swirled around the catwalk.

Looking downward, she saw beneath the smoke along the line. Men were lighting fusees now. They ran along, setting fires inside the line.

The back-fires, it seemed to her, hardly wanted to burn. The wind leaned their flames over toward the line. Still, slowly, they ate back through the duff. Here and there a bush or sapling flared up.

From her grandstand seat, she watched in fascination, except once when the drifting smoke settled lower and enveloped the whole tower. She shut the door quickly, for at the moment more smoke than fresh air came in. She was frightened, but did not like the idea of trying to rush down the stairs and be overcome with smoke. But then, even before she could make a hasty decision, the smoke lifted high, and everything was safe again.

The air even felt fresher. She went out to the west catwalk. The gorge of Potter Creek was mostly filled with smoke haze, but she gave it a good looking-over to be sure no smoke was popping up from a new fire. Just because there was a big fire going was no assurance that there would not be another fire start. And that was what a lookout was for!

The telephone-line was certainly dead, but she could still report by radio, or merely yell from the catwalk.

She wished Dave would come. He had said he would be up again. He could tell her just when she ought to leave the tower.

A scrap of glowing bark lit on the east catwalk. *That* would have started a fire all right. She looked north and south from her vantage-point, trying to see if any spot-fires were already popping up. Today she would earn her pay.

Already the Sector-bosses had scattered most of their crews back to watch for spot-fires. A few men would be enough to watch along the line itself. The back-fires had eaten in thirty feet from the line by now. They had spread and grown together except for a few weak places. Very soon they would begin to feel the back-draft of the main fire and go roaring off to meet it.

One of the men saw something come bursting out of a thin place in the back-fires: "See! A bear!"

Looking neither right nor left, he trotted by within ten feet of a man, paying no attention. His brown coat was singed. He shook his head fretfully, and blinked his watering eyes, and as he went, he whimpered softly to himself, like a baby, at the pain of his blistered feet.

Two miles down the road there had been a truck parked in the middle of it, and a tall mountaineer on guard.

"No equipment allowed past here," the guard had said to Dave. " 'Tain't safe. Zone-boss's orders."

"I'm the weather-man, and this is my own car."

The mountaineer had spit and contemplated:

"I guess I was jest to stop Forest-Service equipment, not damn fools—go ahead."

Past that point he had really driven fast, with a sense of urgency and alarm. Of course Judith would be down out of the tower by this time, but he wanted to see for sure.

When he came around the last turn and up to the crest, he was suddenly face to face with the magnificent show. The back-fire had met the main fire, and everything was going up in high and solid masses of flame. As he looked at the tower, he saw the smoke drifting thickly all about it, and then through the glass he just had a glimpse of a yellow handkerchief bobbing about.

"The little fool!" was his first thought. "Why didn't she get out when the getting was good?" Then he realized with a quick pleasure of excitement that he was going up to get her himself—or try to go!

He jumped from the jeep and ran toward the base of the tower. The heat of the high flames beat hard on him, but the air was good, being sucked in hard toward the fire. As he ran, he figured chances. All the upper half of the tower was in thick smoke. But a man who had spent his years studying air and the way it behaved to make weather—*he* knew that along that leaning edge of smoke there would be pockets and whorls of rising fresh air, the backlash from the air that was being sucked in toward the base of the fire. The thing to try was to hold your breath in the smoke, and grab some more air when you came to a pocket.

Six ten-foot flights up to the top! The first two were easy. Then the smoke was close above him. He took a long breath, made eight steps with his eyes almost closed, saw clear air again, and got half a lungful before the smoke closed again. He had to make that do him clear up to the fourth landing. Two more flights to go!

He lay flat on the landing, just able to breathe a little. His heart was pounding faster than he could count. (Rushing four long flights would be hard work, even with good air.) He dared not try the next flight without more oxygen, and for a moment he feared he was blacking out.

Then the smoke eddied again. The air was hot, but he breathed quickly three times, pulled the last one in deep, got to his feet, and rushed the last two flights.

Staggering, feeling himself close to going out, he made the catwalk, flung open the door, stepped in, and closed it behind to keep out the smoke.

He was just ready to drop to the floor, but the air inside was better, and his head cleared.

"You—little—fool!" was all he could think to gasp, and then it seemed the most natural thing in the world that she was sobbing against his shoulder and he had his arms around her and was patting her back.

That must have been only a moment, for suddenly he knew that it was too hot to be staying in this glass box. There was smoke all around, and snapping sharply, a window-pane cracked with the heat. A wedge of glass clattered to the floor, and smoke poured in through the gap. Then in all the whirling smoke and confusion a sing-song and unreal voice began to cry out: *"There are three things that are never satisfied, yea, four . . ."*

"Come on!" he said and pulled her toward the door.

". . . grave; and the barren womb . . ."

Thick smoke poured in at the opened door:

"Take a deep breath and hold it!"

". . . and the fire that saith not, It is enough . . ."

He had his arm around her, and knew she was holding her breath. The first flight down was easy, running. Halfway down the second it was getting hard, and then he felt the wind-shift. He stopped her by the pressure of his arm. The air was suddenly good. Thick smoke was blowing by, so close still you could almost put your hand out into it. He breathed gratefully. The air was cooler and there was even some moisture in it.

"Relax!" he said, and he loosened his grip, though he still kept his arm where it was.

"I can go on down all right."

knew suddenly that it had happened. The heat beat less intensely; the flames tossed less wildly, and had faded from white to yellow; the front of the fire had breaks in it.

Even as he looked, he felt the heat ease off still more. He stood up, only sheltering his face a little behind his arm. The flames puffed out on a stretch fifty feet long in front of him. For a moment the branches still glowed redly. As they faded to black, he took his arm from in front of his face.

And now, instead of a wall of flame, there was only a blackened forest with fires burning here and there. The heat eased off, as if someone had turned out the gas in a stove.

He climbed to the top of the boulder, and looked back and forth along the length of critical line. Everywhere the fire had died down, and he saw men standing idle and looking at it.

That had been a last outburst, the furious raging of the dying beast. The wind was freshening now from the southeast, and swiftly clearing the smoke away. Across on Reverse Ridge he saw that the new slop-over also was throwing scarcely any smoke at all, and must be under control.

He let out a long breath, and then breathed easily. From his pocket he drew his note-book. He glanced at his watch, and started at seeing that it was only three minutes since he had looked before. Then he wrote firmly:

"2:52 P.M. Fire under control."

The southeast wind was rising gustily, but its reinforcement had come too late. (Against the heights of Cerro Gordo, The Guard had already launched its attack, and died.)

On the ridge above Onion Creek where it first had burned, in the brush-field of Reverse Flat, in the snag-patch, on the face of Reverse Ridge, by Curran Creek and Bacchus Creek, on the slope of Cerro Gordo—everywhere the great fire was dying.

In one place or another it still blazed in hundreds of isolated spots, but it nowhere advanced in solid front to seize more forest.

As once the fire had grown hotter and stronger and larger as it encroached upon new supplies of fuel, so now it grew colder and weaker and smaller, as it burned out its fuel and could spread no farther. As once it had grown strong and so grown ever stronger, now it grew weak and so grew ever weaker. Where once a fierce blaze had drawn air toward itself and made its own draft, now the weakened blaze could not maintain the draft, and so shrank back even from the wood it had already seized.

Minute by minute, heat radiated off; the woods and rocks and earth grew cooler. Acre by acre the great fire was dying.

THE MEN on the line, as the hours passed, had thought of fire only as an enemy. Evil, malignant, and scheming, it came against them. They stood and fought, and fell back, and stood again and fought—and in weariness and danger and terror they hated fire.

Yet all the while fire also was good. As friend, it worked for them. Fire lent its heat to the coffee that lifted their hearts in the morning chill. Fire sent forward the supply-trucks, and powered the crashing bull-dozers, and sustained the scouting-plane. The smouldering fire of cigarettes gave comfort in the breathing-spells. In the piercing cold of the mountain nights, the men warmed themselves at the glowing logs. And when the right moment came, the back-fire was their best ally.

(So from the ancient past, fire has been at once—comforter but mischief-maker, blessed but baleful, preserver of life but its destroyer, purifier but annihilator. It gives and it takes away.)

Yet, in the end, all this good and bad was only in the mind of man. The fire, like a storm or river or star or sun, felt

315

neither love nor hate, knew neither good nor bad. The fire burned—and made no judgments.

2

All through the evening they had still been anxious. A fire controlled was not a fire out! As darkness had fallen, hundreds of glowing red spots had stood out, like the eyes of cats lurking in the night, where flames still licked up from between crossed logs, or embers glowed in a punky stump, or red-hot coals still lived in the shattered top of a snag. In spite of the hundreds that had cooled and winked out, hundreds remained, awaiting only the sudden rush of a dry wind to burst out again. . . .

At Suffolk, his work finished, Dave Halliday slept soundly. There was rain already on the north Coast Ranges, and drizzle clear south to the Bay. And also the front was sweeping in cold and heavy air from the Pacific, to fill the Sacramento Valley and block any dry wind that might try to rush down from the north or east. . . .

There were no stars that night, but the men on the lines knew that cloud, not smoke, stretched across the sky. From the southeast, veering toward the south, a moist wind blew steadily. In the dark of early morning the rain began—a drifting mist at first, and then a steady drizzle, and sometimes a gentle shower.

Suddenly damp and cold and miserable, the men huddled about, turning up their jacket-collars, drawing close to the shelter of the trees. After a while they pulled charred logs from the burned area, and started bonfires just inside the line. Underfoot the deep dust, where the cats had passed back and forth, changed to soft and slippery mud; inside the line all the charred pine-needles disintegrated into sticky blackness.

To sit was to lapse into pig-like squalor. The men stood by

the bonfires in the steady rain, turning one side and then the other, steaming gently, weary with long work, unnerved with the passing of tension. Utterly let down, they grumbled unceasingly—at the rain, at the bosses, at the food, at one another. . . .

The rain fell upon the red embers and the little flames. Where each drop struck, a sudden spot of blackness showed in the red glow, or the flame fluttered. As thousands of drops fell, the blackness grew and encroached upon the red, and the flames wavered and winked out. Only here and there, deeply hidden where the drops could not reach, a few red glowing points still shone through the darkness and a few flames licked up.

At Headquarters on the flat beside Idylhurst Guard Station the Maps-and-Records man, with lugubrious satisfaction, summed up the fire for the last time—or at least, he hoped.

With skillful pencil he outlined the last day's burn. It differed from any of the others in that it lay in three isolated areas. On Reverse Ridge a full hundred acres showed where the slop-over had raged until two hard-working cats and a hundred men had brought it under control. No one seemed to know what had happened, but most of them thought it had been from a rabbit or wood-rat. Far to the southeast, another area of some two hundred acres showed where the fire, after burning out the camp, had run up the point of Swayback Ridge; two good-sized spot-fires stood out as small circles on the map, totaling some ten acres. But the main drive of that day was displayed in a broad and long-reaching tongue of burned area stretching off to the west. A sharp north-south line showed where the picked crews in their desperate fight had blocked the rush up Curran Creek. Thus narrowed, but still a mile wide, the fire had pressed on for three miles with the stiff east wind behind it, up the canyon of Bacchus Creek and clear to the crest of Cerro Gordo.

He outlined the three areas in blue. Estimating by means of quarter-section boundaries, he put the day's burn at 3,770 acres.

Now the whole irregular shape of the fire lay revealed to him. The crocodilian monster which had once seemed to rear head and shoulders from the slime, had now grown a foreleg, and dragged a cumbersome tail behind. From nose-tip to tail-tip, gigantic in more than antediluvian measure, the monster stretched out for twelve miles. The perimeter, now equalling the length of line constructed and finally held, mounted up to the total of thirty-two miles—an impressive accomplishment, considering that most of the line was eight feet wide and had been built in four days across mountainous country, far removed from roads and sources of supply. To the Maps-and-Records man, as he looked, every twist and sinuosity and angle of the perimeter was eloquent of terrain and wind-shifts, of the strategy and tactics, of success and failure, during the five-day battle.

Even from the map he could see that the Spitcat had died hard. On the final day of burning, with a steady wind behind and a rising slope ahead, it had pressed on, unspectacularly but without pause, and burned more acreage than on any preceding day. Adding its total to that of the other days, he wrote down the figure at 10,032 acres, almost sixteen square miles. Later estimates, more carefully compiled under less pressure of haste, would change his figures somewhat. "Call it ten thousand, roughly," he decided, and laid the map aside.

It was as if some running conflagration had swept from Spuyten Duyvil to the Battery, leaving two-thirds of Man-hattan Island in a blackened swath behind it. Yet the Spitcat

Fire would not be very memorable even in the annals of Region 5. Any old-timer could recall a score of greater ones, and would only expect that the years to come would bring many more. In comparison with the Tillamook, which in eleven flaming days had wiped out 311,000 acres of the best forest in Oregon, the Spitcat was a mere waste-basket blaze.

Even so, the costs of suppression alone would run well over a hundred thousand dollars. Two men had been killed, and a score of others had suffered injury. The value of the burned trees would pass a million dollars, figured at current prices and with no allowance for timber famines of the future.

Yet the damage could not with justice be calculated merely in terms of the present. Already the turbid streams showed that even the light rain was washing away the earth. Where previously pines had just been able to find root on the thin-soiled ridges, now half-bare rocks might be left, where only gnarled junipers would cling.

Though the Spitcat had burned for only a few days, yet its effects could be reckoned ahead in centuries. Looking across the country from a peak, an unskilled observer would have seen many tall trees still standing green, and might have thought that surprisingly little damage had been suffered. But many of those trees had been fatally scorched around the bases, and many others were so damaged that they would soon fall prey to boring insects.

And everywhere the small trees had been wiped out, as if a plague had swept through a nation, sparing some adults but killing all the babies and children. In the next few years the still-standing older trees might reseed the ground beneath them, but once they had been logged off or fallen from disease or mere old age, only tiny saplings would remain—not vigorous young trees reaching up fifty or a hundred feet already.

But that would be the best that could be expected. Where

the crown-fires had raged, no trees were left to spread seed, and brush would spring up faster than forest. Once established, it would remain for many years, perhaps for centuries, yielding only foot by foot as the forest pressed in around the edges. Indeed, some said pessimistically that the forests of California had established themselves in some wetter cycle of centuries and that the brush, once rooted, would remain until some wetter cycle returned.

The flaming disaster of those few days would not be undone in a hundred years. Even after five hundred, a skilled forester might still be able to trace the scar of that old burn.

More also had vanished than any man could assay in dollars. There had been a green and gracious forest, full of the rustle and movement of life, beneficient to men. Now there was only blackness and ugliness and desolation, and over it all a heavy and terrible silence.

In the Glen the trunks of the big cedars were charred and blackened. The scorched and swollen body of the doe lay singed of hair, the lips drawn back from the teeth in a grimace of death. No fly buzzed about; not even an ant crawled on the staring eyes.

The burned azaleas raised up pitiful charred stubs. Though the air was again wet, the brown and dead moss could absorb no moisture and turn green. The once-clean rocks were smeared with ashes and charred needles, sticky with rain. The little stream ran dirty-yellow with mud, foul with floating blackness. It poured uncleanly over the waterfalls, and even the foam was gray. From the washing-in of ashes after the rain, the water was sour with lye, and in it the poisoned trout floated belly-up. The mink had passed on, hunting a stream where he could find living fish and pure water and the shelter of bushes. High overhead all the overarching cedar-tops had burned away, and gray sky loured over naked and blackened earth.

3

Even the long-cynical editor had difficulty in stomaching the picture of Jewel Magnus. "My God," he said, "Ike is sure getting corny!" Still, he reflected, readers like human interest, and there was not much doing at the moment. He ran it on the third page.

Thus, from all that happened on the Spitcat Fire, what made the city papers was a brief story of the "evacuation" of Idylhurst, and a picture of Jewel awkwardly holding a baby not her own, with her skirt up to her knee, against a background of a console radio and a vacuum-cleaner. This is because, in comparison with such things, the roaring to the sky of a crown-fire and the struggle of two thousand men are not considered to be "human interest."

4

At Idylhurst fire-camp, long strings of men were going through the timekeepers. When they had got their final time, they stood around waiting for the trucks and buses that would take them home. Under the gray sky they were heavy-eyed and chilled and miserable. Their faces were sooty and mud-smeared and scraggly bearded. A dozen campfires were going, and around each men stood in a circle, getting what comfort they could find.

They would draw their pay and go back where they had come from, and nobody would give them thanks or make speeches. Yet they had done a good job, and they would have the memory. Sometimes in the future two of them would meet; then they would speak of what they had seen and done by Wilson Creek, and along Reverse Ridge, and on the slope of Cerro Gordo, and they would be like veterans of the same battle.

During the fire they had all fought a common enemy. No one had cared who worked beside him, as long as he worked well. Now that they no longer faced the attack, the men drew apart.

At one campfire the paratroopers had gathered, and the other Negroes drifted there to join them. The Mexicans stood in another ring. The two Indians smoked together. The Hot-shot men and the pogies kept their distance.

Down the road rolled a truck bearing the convict-crew. Two days before, the convicts had held the flank on Reverse Ridge when the others had run. Now the men in the trucks looked at the men around the fires, and the men around the fires looked back. But a ban lay between, and no one spoke or called good luck.

5

At Forest Headquarters in Suffolk, Walt Burnaby had ten minutes to wait before his plane would be ready. This early rain had not extended far south, and now there was a flare-up on the brush-covered mountains of the Cleveland Forest, behind San Diego. He was needed there.

Arnold Sorenson was busy with demobilization, but he took a few minutes with Walt to hold post-mortem on the Spitcat.

"At least," he said, "we couldn't have done anything to prevent the lightning from striking."

"No, the Board of Review won't hold anybody for that."

"Maybe, though, I should have spotted it when I flew over, two days later. Then this all would never have happened."

"It wasn't showing then, probably. I think myself we should have caught it with that first crew. That boss—'Slug-

ger,' you call him—may have made a mistake, but you can't
tell now for sure. Mostly it was just low humidity and high
wind, and country that was hard to get men into."

"How about Bart?"

"Poor old Bart! He played her too close in Reverse Flat—
but you know about those things better afterwards than before. And about that panic on the ridge, no Board of Review
will ever find out what really started it, not if they sit for a
month."

"Well, it was a tough break for the Forest, just at the end
of the season."

"Yes, ten thousand acres. But maybe we're lucky! It might
have been forty thousand!"

Jackie called to say that the plane was ready, and Walt
headed for the south, without taking time to change his shirt
or catch a shower. With resignation, Arn settled to the job
of getting two thousand men and a lot of pieces of equipment
back to place again. As far as he was concerned, it had been
just another fire.

6

On the slope above Onion Creek a tiny heap of indistinguish-
able ashes marked where the burning pine-cone, after rolling
downhill, had come to rest against the log. Already, in the
never-ending cycle, the fertilizing elements of the ashes were
mingling with the soil to nourish new growth. . . .

On Reverse Ridge the rabbit's body lay, half-roasted.
Stretching off in every direction, a hundred acres of black
devastation supplied a funeral monument that an Assyrian
king or Tartar khan might have envied. . . .

Far over Nevada the storm-front, grown weaker but con-
tinuing to advance eastward, still labored at its task of mingling warm and cool air.

7

When the old fellow on Horse Mountain all at once had reported three towering smokes that nobody else could see and had then gone out of communication entirely, two men rushed up from Barlow to see what was the matter.

They found him running about at the base of the tower, wearing only his untrimmed gray beard. As they came close, he faced them, and threw up his arms toward the sky, crying out: *"If I be a man of God, let fire come down from heaven and consume thee and thy fifty!"*

At his vehemence the men paused as if they felt a hovering over their heads. But no fire fell from heaven, and, as they paused, the power seemed to ooze away from the old man, as if his God had denied him.

"Come on, pop!" said one of them. "This fire's been too much for you. We're going to take you where you can get some rest."

When they came up to him, he was quiet and gentle.

8

At the now almost deserted fire-camp Slugger O'Neill's boys gathered round to say good-bye to him.

"Gosh, Slugger, it's been a great summer! . . . Won't ever forget all this! . . . Thanks for everything!"

(They had made the first attack. Twice they had seen the fire almost caught, and had been run out in the big blow-up. After that there had been only four of them, for the one with the burned hip had been sent out. They had spent two easy day-shifts on Division II, patrolling and mopping-up. Then with the veteran crews they had been shifted quickly—by trail and truck and trail again—clear to the other end of the fire, where they had ended by efficiently holding a small stretch of line near Cerro Gordo Lookout.)

"Well, so long, boys!" said Slugger. "You're a swell bunch o' fire-eaters! . . . Don't worry about your stuff you left back at Caribou; I'll see it gets sent to you."

They climbed into the waiting bus, Shorty still easing his knee a little, though it was better now. Then they leaned out of windows to speak to Slugger again.

"I'll remember that straight-arm trick you showed us; she ought to be good in a broken field. . . . Gee, I hate to go back to the old school grind! . . . See you next summer!"

The bus pulled out, and they looked back a last time at Slugger making them a thumbs-up sign.

"God, even Slugger looks all in," said one of them suddenly, as they were whisked out of sight.

"You ain't so daisy-fresh either," said another one. And then as they looked at one another, they all laughed a little glumly, for they had scraggly adolescent beards of six day's growth, and though they had washed as well as they could, their hair and skin, and their clothes even more, were streaked and coated and smeared with red dust and gray dust and yellow dust, and with black soot to boot, all caked into red and gray and yellow and black mud where sweat had rolled or rain fallen. Their faces were scratched and their eyes bloodshot, and their hands blistered, and their finger-nails broken. Their clothes were torn and had holes burned in them, and their shoes were broken out or had soles flapping or heels missing. In fact, they looked like anyone who has just spent five days fighting fire, mostly at hot-spots.

Yet, though they were so tired they were about to fall asleep in their seats, they were all happy boys, for they knew they had done a good job among men.

"It's a great life!" said one of them, yawning. "Makes a man of you!"

"Yes," chorused another, "and Slugger's a real guy! Bet he's the best crew-boss was on the fire!"

"You bet!" said two of them heartily, and even little Shorty, nursing his knee, said, "Ye-ah—" with so slight a touch of doubt that the others did not notice.

But since he was the smallest of the lot, he had to use his head more, and sometimes he had wondered just how things might have been if Slugger had kept them better in hand at that first attack and had remembered that the wind would be due to change after the sun got a little hotter.

By now so many cats had passed back and forth that there was practically a two-way road along the ridge. Shoving and yanking at the brand-new control-handles, Barney Zulik walked his cat back to Parker Flat, where the truck was waiting.

"How'd things go, Barney?" said the truck-driver.

"Where's the first place I can get a beer?" said Barney. "Christ, I worked forty hours straight up there on the ridge. They was one o' them Forest-Service bastards was tryin' t'run things till I told him—Say, why the hell don't we get goin'?"

"O. K., Barney! Bet you really showed them!" said the truck-driver, but as he spoke he was taking in the new control-handles with the corner of his eye.

The pogies were in a bus again, and Bo Fox sat by his opened window.

(They had been on a quiet sector for the last two days, and had spent much of their time at dodging bosses and sleeping in the woods. They were more dirty than tired.)

As they swayed around the sharp curves below Idylhurst, Bo's seatmate spoke to him.

"Yes, sir, sure was lucky we run that time! Guess we'd all been burned!"

Bo did not bother to pick up the conversation. He had drifted to the fire for no particular end, and now he was drifting back toward some other end, equally unparticularized. To him the fire had never been anything more than a miscellaneous burning of some trees and bushes. He was innocent of the knowledge that his panic had enabled the fire to double its size, and he would have been overcome with the embarrassment of the limelight if anyone had told him that for once in his insignificant life he had been a very important person.

9

Bart came driving into camp neatly shaved and in clean clothes. There was nothing melodramatic about the meeting, and neither of them said anything about what had happened.

"Hello," Bart said. "I've had a good sleep, and I thought maybe you could use me for something."

"Thanks, Bart," said the Supervisor. "As a matter of fact, I *would* like you to ride up along the line with me. I want to see where this all started."

The trails were muddy, and made heavy going for the horses. Where the two big pine trees framed the view was a natural place to stop and let the horses blow. At the same place Bart had stopped on that day when he first rode up to the fire. That seemed long ago, and yet at first glance the view did not seem to have changed very much. He still looked off along the straight canyon, and down into the gorge of

Onion Creek. The familiar roll of the ridges was just the same. But when he looked closer, things were different.

Cerro Gordo Lookout still stood up sharp against the distant western sky, but it was no longer a shining white. Below the lookout he saw the long blackened swath on the face of the mountain. Closer at hand was the burned top of Reverse Ridge, and then clear off to the north again he saw the burned brush-field, and still farther, the ridge above Onion Creek where he had run from the big blow-up.

Then he thought, with a sinking heart, of something else, and he looked back toward the west. Reverse Ridge hid the canyon of Curran Creek, but he knew where the Glen was— or had been! It would never be the same again, not while he lived, or any man who was living now.

Yes, a lot had changed in six days, and he himself was an old man. He could run the routine of the District all right, but they'd never trust him with a big fire again. The Spitcat had been too much, and something had broken. All the men knew it. He wouldn't even trust himself.

What he was thinking must have showed in his face, for he heard someone saying:

"Don't take it too hard, Bart. It's just part of the way things are!"

And when he looked across to the man on the other horse, Bart saw that the Supervisor was trying to smile at him.

"Yes," the Supervisor went on, "where there are pine trees, there's also going to be fire, because if there's no dry season, you'll have a hardwood forest. You might say if there weren't fires, there wouldn't be pines."

"I'm thinking of some of the places I used to like to go."

"It's hard to tell about it all, Bart. The way a rabbit thinks, a brush-field must be the Garden of Eden, compared to a pine forest. In nature—whatever that means—a raw gullied canyon-side may be just as good as a fine slope of trees. The difference is in our minds."

"That's a big difference to me," said Bart.

And then, as they rode on, with the horses' hooves slushing in the red mud, the Supervisor felt the old wall again. Things, he understood and could manage—land, trees, even fire. Yes, fire, he knew—but would he ever know men? Sometimes the wall seemed to be growing weaker, even to be crumbling —as when the paratrooper called him "Slim!" and when the Hot-shot men put up their little cheer. This fire had meant something to him; perhaps he had taken a step forward. The men knew he could stop a fire for them, and they would honor and respect him. He had met the test that the new Supervisor had to meet. But would men break into grins when he came suddenly upon them?

Awkwardly, his long legs dangling, he rode along.

It was a tedious pull up the trail along Onion Creek. The sun had broken through and the trail was drying out; but the horses still slipped and slithered.

On this side, the forest was rich and green; on the other, where the crown-fire had raged, there was only the desolation of black trunks and branches. Sick at heart, Bart recognized the kinds of trees automatically, even from their skeletons. Here was a clump of young Douglas firs, their branches looping gracefully upward. Here the level-held branches showed pines, and again he saw the white firs, with their branches sloping downward. They were still different, but now they were all black and ugly alike. He tried to keep looking at the unburned slope, and sometimes he rode along with his eyes closed.

They came at last to the place where Bart had tied Betty when he had first come to the fire. They dismounted and looked around. Bart saw the horse-droppings, disintegrated now a little by the rain. There was the tiny open space where the disorganized men had sat, after the blow-up had run them out. The grass still showed where they had trampled. Two paper lunch-bags lay there, and a waxed container of K-ration, and a crumpled wad of red and white paper that held twenty neat cigarettes. They were all like relics of long ago.

Bart pointed across the canyon. "There's the first line that Slugger's boys ran up the slope." It was only eighteen inches wide, but he could follow it clearly, red with black on both sides of it. If they had ever tied that line in, the Spitcat Fire would have been written off at one acre.

A little farther up-canyon, to the right, he saw the undercut line angling up the slope, black above it, green below. He pointed that out too.

"That's the only part of the original line that held," he said. "We got that line tied in and burned out, you know. If the wind hadn't got us, we'd have held her at about forty acres."

"Let's take a look," said the Supervisor.

They plunged down to the creek, and clmbed up the other side. They came to where the burned radio-set lay in a blackened snarl of wires and tubes. They scrambled on up the slope, walking on the now cold ashes of the burn.

"Look there!" said the Supervisor.

On the blackened ground lay the stiff and bloated body of a squirrel, the hair of the tail burned away until it looked rat-like.

"Poor little devil!" said Bart, and he felt suddenly sick at the thought of all the little animals.

The Supervisor turned the body over with his boot, and they saw that the tiny feet had almost been burned away as the confused creature had made its final dash across the red-hot forest-floor, trying to reach some place which would probably have been no safer than the place it had just left.

Near-by Bart located the pine which had been struck. They could clearly make out the long spiral weal. The tree itself had suffered little, and had not been caught in the crown-fire. Possibly its top had been blighted; even so, it would live and even grow, perhaps for a century still.

The Supervisor knelt at the base of the weal. "See," he said, "it runs out along the buttress-root. The fire must have caught in the dry needles and smouldered. A man could have spit and put it out, then."

"What we needed was an access road, and a lookout on Howell Mountain."

"I've asked for them, you know, but there never was money. We'll probably get them now."

"After the horse is stolen!"

"Well, we have other horses."

And standing there on the blackened hillside, the Supervisor thought to himself again, "Yes, we have other horses."

More roads, more lookouts, better trained crews, an educated public, cleaner methods of logging—they would come in time. No longer, either, would the fire-fighter be essentially just "a man with a muck-stick." Helicopters, "wet water," baby cats, infra-red cameras for the scout-planes, "man-made rain," chemical bombs with proximity fuses—they were already at hand, or might come.

For, he trusted, the fight would go on, and some time the people would be sure that the forest was not a mine, as the old-fashioned lumberman thought, to be plundered once and for all, and also that it was not, as Bart liked to think, a perpetual primeval park. As man had tamed the apple-tree, so also he would tame the pine-tree, until it grew for his service.

When that time came, he would make sure that it did not burn.

10

She had been hard at it all morning, washing windows like an overworked housemaid. She had got most of the soot off them now, except for those on the east side, which were all cracked from the heat so that she dared not scrub them for fear of knocking chunks of glass out. Everything that she had not washed was still sooty from the smoke, and what had been the shining white paint was all blackened and blistered and curled up on the side next to the fire.

There had been plenty to watch all morning. Men were still patrolling the line. In mid-morning a red tanker had come lumbering up past the lookout, its heavily chained drive-wheels cutting deep ruts in the soft fire-line. The muddied faces and clothes of the crew showed the infinite labor they had taken to get it up the steep road. She saw them work along the trail, pausing now and then to unlimber a hose and drag it into the burn to douse some still smouldering stump.

Now and then also, from far off, she heard a snag go crashing down. Though the crisis was over, there was still plenty of mop-up going on, to make sure.

Nevertheless, things were rapidly getting back to some kind of normality. Her two chipmunks (they had had the good luck to live on the right side of the line) were out foraging this morning. When they disappeared suddenly, she looked around and saw the hawk, dipping and rising gracefully on the up-draft. She wondered where he had gone during the fire. Now probably, she thought, he would have good pickings, for around the fire the forest must be full of confused and homeless little animals, easy prey.

About noon she saw three deer come uncertainly up from

the unburned side, cross the line, and walk down into the burn. There was no underbrush to cover them, and they stood out sharply against the blackness. For a while she caught glimpses of them through the trees, wandering about as if looking for familiar places where they had browsed and slept. Later they came back, their dun flanks streaked with black smears. They walked uncertainly across the line. Though a man was in full sight, they stood a moment, as if not knowing just what to do and making a final decision. They looked back at what had been home so recently, and now was so unaccountably ruined. You could feel the confusion in their minds. After a minute they moved off, still slowly, into the underbrush on the unburned side, and disappeared.

"Poor things!" she thought. "Displaced animals!" Now they were mere trespassers on the range of some other deer, and would be quick victims to the first mountain-lion that happened along. . . .

She ate lunch, and then cleaned herself up as well as she could. She put on some well-pressed gray slacks, and her dark-green man's shirt, open at the throat. She did the best she could with her hair.

The afternoon was sunny, and she kept alert. But she saw nothing big enough to think twice about. The tanker-crew and a couple of other men were in full sight. She wished they would go away.

"The girl observed a tanker-crew and a couple of other men in full sight. [Well, here we are thinking in words again!] She hoped that they would go away. [Why not!—It won't be long now, and a few thoughts won't hurt me.] 'Girls that live in glass houses shouldn't have callers in the day-time.' But she reflected that she might stand beside the fire-finder, as close to the center of the lookout as possible, and probably anyone looking up from the ground would not be able to see what went on there. . . . 'Yes, children, I first met your father at a forest-fire!' "

And then she wondered, though she could not quite find the words for it, whether she could feel the way she did about Dave, if it hadn't been for the fire and her own being part of all those who were fighting it and for her feeling the way she did, even before he came the first time. . . .

When he came that afternoon, she solved the glass-house problem by standing right next to the fire-finder, and it worked very well.

Then they stood close together on the east catwalk, looking for smokes—but there weren't any. She told him many things —of how, for instance, she got her Spanish name because some great-great-grandmother fell in love with a Californian and let him carry her off one night (so the family story went) on a tall black stallion.

"Well," he said, "I've got no black stallion. Would a red jeep do?"

"Considering how times have changed, I'll think it over. . . . Yes, that would be very satisfactory."

11

A day before, the fire had been roaring toward the sky on an unbroken front of a mile. Now at the bottom of the canyon on the eastern face of Cerro Gordo, a single little flame licked upward between two logs. It wavered and flickered in the sunlight, seeming to go out and yet springing up again. Then a small shower of embers fell from one of the logs, and the gap between them widened. The draft which had kept the flame alive was impaired, and the flame flickered still more uncertainly.

The flame leaned over, recovered, flickered again. Then,

as a man blows out a match, a puff of air suddenly extinguished it. From between the logs rose only a faint wisp of smoke, as from a dying cigarette.

12

Though the fires die down and trees grow again, by the names you shall remember, Americans—by Burnt Woods and Burnt River, Arroyo Quemado and Bois Brulé. There the red flower bloomed in the forest; there the red wolf bit and tore.

Even in later years when the gullies lie bare on the rocky mountainsides, or else the pines stand in rows neatly, like peach-trees, and the red wolf is caged—even then, by the names, remember that it was not always so. Burntwood Creek, Bare Mountain, Brush Valley—even when you say them, remember the smell of smoke in the morning, and the copper sun at noon, and the crimson glare at evening, not of sunset. The flame ran through the dry leaves; the bushes roared like the fiery furnace; the high trees were torches to heaven. Snorting and wild-eyed, the tall horses galloped before the rolling smoke; the trembling buck stood in the shallow to cool his charred hooves; the little chipmunks ran about aimlessly, chattering, like shell-shocked soldiers. Remember also Peshtigo and Cloquet, Hinckley and Bandon. There the red wolf broke from the forest; the houses were like brush-wood before the heat; the men and women ran jibbering like chipmunks until flame swept around them and left the charred bodies to grin, hideous, in the morning sun. All this too was part of the price of the taking-over of the land.

13

The words of Agur, son of Jakeh, even the prophecy: *There are three things that are never satisfied, yea, four . . . the grave; and the barren womb; the earth that is not filled with water; and the fire that saith not, It is enough.*

14

Smoke and cloud had vanished. Through the rain-washed air the sun shone brightly, and along the crest of the range the highest peaks were dazzling-white with snow. Moist and clean, the northwest wind from the ocean blew steadily across the long ridges, and from high-swinging cones, opened by the fiery heat, the winged seeds drifted downward to the earth.

"Speech finely framed
delighteth the ears" —
          The Apocrypha